The Pink Pepper Tree

The Pink Pepper Tree

Muriel Bolger

W F HOWES LTD

This large print edition published in 2014 by
W F Howes Ltd
Unit 4, Rearsby Business Park, Gaddesby Lane,
Rearsby, Leicester LE7 4YH

1 3 5 7 9 10 8 6 4 2

First published in the United Kingdom in 2014
by Hachette Books Ireland

A CIP catalogue record for this book is available
from the British Library

ISBN 978 1 47127 506 7

Typeset by Palimpsest Book Production Limited,
Falkirk, Stirlingshire
Printed and bound by
www.printondemand-worldwide.com of Peterborough, England

This book is made entirely of chain-of-custody materials

*This one is for Glenn, Jillian and
Graham – with love*

PROLOGUE

She stared across the bed and out the window at the stark, bare trees that were struggling to show any signs of spring. A lone pink camellia was promising colour at one edge of the lawn. A woman and a little girl walked back to their car. She'd seen them before. As the child opened the door, the wind whipped her scarf from around her neck and it flew across the tarmac, a splash of brightness in an otherwise monotone view. The woman ran to retrieve it. She tied it in a big knot under the upturned chin and scooped the little one up. Before they got back into the vehicle, the little girl raised her arm and they both waved back at the building. Then they drove off. June wondered who they were waving to, a cherished parent, a grandmother or granddad perhaps?

She shifted her gaze back to Lorcan's bed, looking at his creased face with its greyish pallor and lank hair. It had been floppy, thick and blond when she'd met him, just eight years earlier, and he used to constantly run his hands through it to push it off his face. With his eyes closed, he looked much more than his fifty-two years.

The room was pretty for all its functionality, its technology and its alien machinery: the staff couldn't have been nicer. He hadn't had a kind word for any of them however, or for her. They all insisted that they understood – it often happened in these circumstances. It didn't bother them at all. She'd sat patiently on and off over the past few months, bringing in little treats, favourite home-made biscuits, snippets from the papers that might interest him. She knew he was far too young to die, and that he must be resentful and frightened. There was a time he would have been able to admit that to her, but not now, not any more – not even to himself. He had been important in his world. But that world had become clouded with secrets and deception, and he was having difficulty separating the different elements. She was watching him shutting down.

As her mind roamed over their life together, he opened his eyes. 'What are you still doing here? Didn't I tell you to go home?'

'Right. OK. I just thought I'd stay . . . in case . . .' She reached her hand over his to offer comfort. He pushed it away.

'In case what? I might disappear? I'm not likely to escape, am I?' He closed his eyes again.

If June were taken aback, she didn't show it. She had learned to cope with such insensitivity.

2

The door behind her opened. His son Sean came in and kissed her, and she stood up. 'I'll be back in a little while,' she said, making a sign at him to phone her if there was any change in his father.

She went down the corridor to have a coffee.

A day later, she phoned his daughter. 'Ashling, your dad has gone. It was very peaceful in the end – he just fell asleep.'

'Oh, June, how are you? Were you with him? Was Sean there with you?'

'He wasn't. He'd just popped back to the office for a bit. I'm going to phone him now.'

'He wasn't supposed to leave you on your own.'

'It wasn't like that – he'd been there most of the time, but he didn't go to bed last night. He needed to go home and change his clothes and call in to the office on his way back here.'

'I wish I had stayed last weekend.'

'You couldn't have known. No one could.'

'I'll ring you and let you know what flight I can get on and I'll be there as soon as possible.'

The death notice read:

> February 27th, in the care of the staff at Orchard Hospice, Killiney, Lorcan Sean Overend, son of the late Marion and Timothy Overend, predeceased by his first wife,

Carol, deeply regretted by their daughter Ashling, son Sean and his wife June. Missed also by his brother Patrick and sister-in-law, Tanya, and his niece and nephew, colleagues and friends. Humanist service tomorrow 11 a.m. in Blackberry Lane Funeral Home, Killiney, followed by private cremation. No flowers please.

There was a clutch of notices in the newspapers stating that various offices and clubs he'd been associated with would be closed for a few hours 'out of respect' for their former colleague/ member.

'I've got your coat,' Ashling said, holding it up.

'I don't need that. I'm not going to the funeral,' June announced, moving aside.

'What?'

'I'm not going to the funeral.'

'You're not going to the funeral?' Ashling echoed in disbelief. 'You can't not go. What do you mean?'

'Exactly that. I'm not going.'

'You can't do that,' Ashling repeated.

'I can and I am. Now, you go and say your goodbyes to your father. I'll do mine in my own way. Make sure you tell everyone they are invited back here afterwards.'

Ashling turned to her twin, a pleading look in her eyes. 'Sean, you've got to do something.'

'It's June's decision. I'm sure she's given it a lot of thought.'

'You can't stay here on your own. I know it must be really hard for you, but you're just panicking,' Ashling said. 'We'll be there with you.'

'I'm not going to be on my own, Ashling, Danielle's on her way over. And I promise you I'm not panicking. Sean is right – I have given this a lot of thought. Now, go – everyone will be waiting for the family before things can get under way.' She walked them to the hall door.

'What'll we tell people?'

'Nothing, Ash. This is my choice. I don't want to be there. That's all.'

She waited until they were in the car before going back inside. She walked into the drawing room, her lovely blue and yellow room, and went to the picture window that overlooked the sloping lawn. In a few weeks, the fringe of daffodils and narcissi would redefine its wintery profile. It was from this vantage point that she always enjoyed the most glorious views of Dublin Bay. She turned away and thought, *It's over. Isn't life strange? It's not how I would have wanted it to end, but it has. I'm free.*

PART I

EIGHT YEARS EARLIER

CHAPTER 1

It was a frenetic month at the wine importers. New lists were arriving daily and June's bosses – two brothers – were just back from sourcing fresh labels and suppliers, covering wine shows, and doing vineyard visits. It had meant plenty of overtime for the ten staff.

June went to check that everything was set up in the tasting room for a session with the buyers from one of the big supermarket chains. She knew how important this was. Getting an order with these high players meant the difference between just surviving or having a bumper year – multiple orders even more so. There was still a bit of suspicion among some of the public that supermarket wines were not quite up to scratch, that somehow they might be buying something inferior, just to beat the off-licences in price. June knew this was not the case and together they had collaborated on wine-tasting evenings and educationals to get this message across. They were also considering starting a wine club to increase their own customer base.

'That looks great, Kelly. Thank you,' she said, taking in the room.

The glasses sparkled, ten in all at each place setting, arranged diagonally across the table with several polished silver spittoons in between. The red wines were already opened to breathe – plain numbered labels obscuring their branding and origins. The whites were chilling in the coolers. Pens and note sheets sat waiting for comments and observations.

'Come on, Kelly. Time for a coffee before the posse arrives,' June said.

Kelly came in when needed – she was their Jill-of-all-trades and could do the computers, the orders and the dispatches, as well as setting up and clearing away. She never minded what was asked of her and could fill in when anyone was away. She was older than the rest of the staff and was always cheerful.

'Any holiday plans?' June asked as they sat having their break.

'Yes. I have. Instead of the usual painting holiday in the West, I've decided to go to Australia. I have family in Sydney and I've been promising myself for years that I'd go. I'm going to be fifty in November and think it's time I did a bit more living.'

'You're absolutely right. High summer and all,' June agreed. 'You'll love it. You might even end up with a bushwhacker.'

'Chance would be a fine thing,' she said. 'What about you? Are you off somewhere exotic, as usual?'

'I am, but the itinerary is still up for discussion. I'm meeting Danielle after work today to discuss that very thing. She has this harebrained idea that we should visit the places we were in as students – but with money in our pockets this time – staying in nice hotels along the way, none of your slumming it in student hostels.'

'That sounds like a great plan.'

'I've never been one for sitting still on a beach, so it does appeal. We'd be following the route we took ten years ago at college – that was the best summer ever. I didn't need much persuasion to agree to do it again – nice hotels, good food and decent wine.'

'"Decent wine" – someone is talking my language,' one of her bosses said from the doorway. 'If we clinch these guys today, there'll be bonuses all around.'

'I'd prefer to take extra holidays, or leave of absence for a few weeks if that's possible,' Kelly said.

'That shouldn't be a problem. We'll talk about it later,' he said. 'Now, is there any more coffee in that pot?'

Danielle and June had been friends since they first met in Montessori, when they were four years old. Their mothers had parked beside each other and even before they had been ushered into the classroom, the two pig-tailed adventurers were chatting to each other. While other children clung to their

11

parents, some crying, it was their mothers who had misty eyes at relinquishing their daughters to a big new world.

They became inseparable, and even though they went to different secondary schools and made new friends, they never lost touch. Then, when on the first morning of Freshers' Week they agreed to meet up on the university campus, the old rapport came flooding back. Even though they had opted for different courses – Danielle for languages and June for international business studies – they had plenty of opportunities to meet up. Danielle was now rangy and blonde, and her flint-blue eyes gave her a Nordic look. She wore prints and layers, velvet and beads, and pinned her hair up or twisted it to one side, often spearing it with a pencil to keep it out of her eyes at lectures. Beside her, June felt ordinary. She didn't see herself as others did, a pretty, vivacious, funny, curious woman, full of zest and mischief – in fact, she was the ultimate denim girl – the one who looked good in painted-on and distressed jeans, who could turn casual into chic with a scarf. She was almost as tall as Danielle, but with velvety brown, almond-shaped eyes.

That first week, they joined every society going, induced and seduced by the promise of getting-to-know-you parties, the free beer and the degree of potential talent displayed by men who were trying to get them to join up. By the second month, they had dropped out of most of them, content instead to hang out with the group of friends they had formed – a group that fluctuated over the years, but who in the main stayed in touch.

Danielle fell in and out of lust and love quite frequently and June lost count of how often she'd sat and listened to the litany of 'never again', 'what's wrong with me', 'I've no taste in men' confessions.

She didn't change after they'd left college and moved out into the world. 'You've just turned thirty and you're still bending my ears with your tales of woe,' June teased as they chatted on the phone, deciding where to go for dinner.

Happily, June also knew the recovery periods were short – nowadays a bout of retail therapy or a weekend away and out Danielle would be, interviewing for a replacement in jig time. Again. And it usually didn't take her too long to find one either. The last one had been a classical musician who was 'resting', but it turned out he really wanted to rest in a nice apartment where he could practise and where someone else paid all the bills and supplied the meals and other benefits.

That evening, Danielle and June were meeting in a little Italian restaurant near the canal. Even though it was a Monday night, it was always popular for after-work rendezvous.

'How did this morning go?' Danielle asked.

'Couldn't have been better. We got our biggest order to date from that chain and everyone is delighted. I've even managed to get two extra weeks off, so what are the plans?'

'Two weeks? On top of your annual leave?'

'Yep, the guys both agreed because I had to man the place when they were away. They said I deserved it.'

'I wish my board of management appreciated me like that.'

'What are you talking about – with your long teachers' holidays?'

'Why do you think I opted for that career path?' she laughed. 'They never give me free wine samples though. Now, what are we going to do and where are we going to go?'

After they had ordered the speciality of the evening – carbonara – with Pinot Grigio, Danielle spread some brochures out on the little table. 'We could start in Switzerland, and go back to the little inn we worked in near Lauterbrunnen and get our revenge by leaving our room in the state some of the guests left theirs – do you remember? Or we could head straight in to northern Italy and into the south of France – or do it in reverse.'

'This is a bit like being a child at the sweet counter. Where do we begin?'

'So much choice . . . it's great, isn't it? What does Peter think of you heading off for so long?' Danielle asked.

'We haven't exactly discussed the time frame – I mean, he knows we've been thinking about it. I didn't get a chance to tell him about the extra leave as he's been at meetings all day. You know how easy-going he is, though, he'll just say, "Off you go and enjoy yourself." There's no way he could get away this summer with the renovations at the restaurant. He has to be there to oversee it all. He might fly over and join us somewhere along the way if he can, and I'll keep a week free to do things with him later on.'

'That sounds great.'

'Let's have a think about the places we most want to visit, make a list and meet up at the weekend to put some shape on this adventure. It's such a broad canvas, we can't do it all, and while we should have a vague idea of where we're headed, we can change our minds as we go along.'

'I can't wait,' said June. 'I want to go next week!'

'I'm afraid I can't get the department to change the school holidays to facilitate you, madam, so you'll just have to be patient.'

Peter came around to June's the following evening. They'd been together more or less for four years, having met when June had gone to his restaurant, The Pink Pepper Tree, one night with Danielle and two now long-forgotten boyfriends. He'd been on front-of-house duty and had looked after them very well. A few times during the evening, she had caught his eye and he'd smiled. He had a boyish look and jet-black curly hair. She thought he might have Italian blood in him, but she later learned that his grandfather and father were Portuguese and that he owned the restaurant.

The next time they met, it was just her and Danielle eating at his restaurant, and he asked her out. It was a very comfortable relationship. When she had asked him how he chose the name for the restaurant, he said, 'It's after The Pink Pepper Trees that grow on our farm in Portugal, in Alentejo. I think they came from Peru originally. Maybe some day I'll take you there and you'll see for yourself.' She had laughed at him. She never thought he would, but he did. That was the beginning.

She loved him to bits, but she often wondered if it was enough. 'What's the difference between being in love and loving someone?' she'd asked Danielle early in their relationship.

'You're asking me?' Danielle had replied. 'How should I know? I'd give anything to have what you have with Peter.'

Now June knew. She had grown to love him unconditionally and she knew it was special. It was being in love – and that was so much more than loving someone. She missed him when he wasn't around and just thinking about him brought a smile to her face. They were very good together. He was thoughtful and caring, and they had a great sex life. At the start of their relationship, they had both been sure that they didn't want too much commitment, and yet they had fallen into an easy and eventually exclusive relationship.

They laughed a lot, shared the same interests, had the same friends. They liked murder novels and movies, and they both enjoyed cooking. They each had clothes and possessions in the other's place. That hadn't been a conscious decision, more an evolution over the years as things were left behind after their nights together. Peter had proposed a few times, but they had always been light-hearted, and June had never accepted – though he'd never felt rejected either. Both were very happy and easy with the arrangements they had and they both knew they'd end up together, when the time was right.

Peter stayed over the night before the girls' depart-ure and after a passionate love-making session, while they were still wrapped around each other in a steamy afterglow, he asked, 'How am I going to manage without you? I'll miss you like crazy.'

'Me too, but it's only four and a half weeks.'

'Five and a half. I'm going to Portugal to visit my folks once the work on the restaurant finishes. So I thought I'll hold off on the grand reopening until after then. Knowing the builders, they'll probably overrun anyway. I might even be able to persuade the folks to come back for it too.'

'It would be nice to have them both there.'

'Is there any point in proposing to you again before you desert me?' he said, lifting himself up on one elbow, and running his hand over her smooth shoulder and down to her breast. She stroked his inky chest hair.

'Now that's what I call a romantic proposition. No down on one knee, no string quartet, no champagne. Have you even got a ring?' she teased.

'Woman, what more do you want? I've just given you my life force – and I'm sensible enough to know that naked-boy-on-bended-knee might not be my best look. So what about it? Is it the right time for us?'

'Maybe . . . probably . . . yes, definitely . . . ask me when I get back from the trip!' She sat up and kissed him and they made love again, slower this time, before falling into a deep sleep, curled up together.

June was sitting in the kitchen of the home where she had grown up. The home where music had always been a feature, where, every night, her father would play the piano after dinner to relax. He had taught her too and she often found it a great way to escape. Her mother could also play but June hadn't heard her for a while. Sometimes, she still expected to hear the tinkling of the notes drift around the house when she visited. Tonight, though, it was the aroma of roasting vegetables, warm garlic and pork filet that were concentrating her mind, as her mother poured some of the wine that June had brought over.

'Whoa – if I drink all that I'll have to stay. You're very heavy handed.'

'You know where your room is. Relax and enjoy

it. To us,' her mother clinked. 'Mmm – that's delicious. Thanks, love.'

'Perks of the job.'

June made a point of going back once a week, usually on Tuesdays, for dinner and a chat to hear what her mum and her cronies had been up to. This usually took some time. Branch had lots of people around her – between her bridge friends, her book club friends, which they now referred to as the prosecco club, her supper society friends, friends of the National Gallery, those in her local history classes and at the charity shop where she worked one morning a week, she was rarely left at a loose end. Lately, she'd joined an active retirement group. Any time she mentioned this, she prefaced it with, 'You only have to be over fifty-five to join; it's not for fossils, you know.' She was sixty-one.

Everyone called her Branch now, though it was her husband who had started it. Her name was Olive, and she was the peacemaker, always trying to smooth things over for everyone. When June was at secondary school, Branch, with time on her hands, had filled in for her husband's secretary when she'd gone on maternity leave. Branch had loved it and the patients had loved her. When the secretary went on to have two more babies in the following two years and had decided to become a stay-at-home mum, Branch had stayed on. She'd now been widowed for several years and, it had taken her a long time to accept losing her husband. They had been good together and although she still missed him terribly, she enjoyed her own company and had made a life without him. It was never dull, and she always had some tale to tell about someone June knew – or who she though June should know.

'You must remember Mary McCambridge – her sister was that tall woman who used to dye her hair that awful mahogany-red colour; it used to look like a helmet, and she had that dreadful pea-green raincoat. She lived down the road from Maura Governy and they all used to go on holidays together. Do you remember they went to the same place in Greece every year? Can you imagine anything as boring – with the whole world to explore – to keep going back to the same place all the time.'

At this point, June had usually forgotten why the story had been started in the first place, but she let her mother prattle on happily.

'Now, tell me, where are you pair going to go? It's a pity Danielle couldn't come over this evening as well.'

'I know, but she was asked to give some kid a grind for his exams for the next two weeks and the money is great. Apparently he's a spoiled little brat who mitches half the time. I told her to come over later if she feels like it. Anyway, we're still deciding, and every time we think we have a plan, we end up changing it again. We want to revisit some of our old summer-job haunts. Danielle wants to go to do the French Riviera and go to some of the places she went to when doing her Erasmus year. We have to see which end we'll start from and join the dots up in between.'

'You must go on the canals at Midi.'

'Why? That isn't even on our list.'

'Henry Slevin – he's in the local history group – did that last year and still raves about it, so much so I've added it to my bucket list. I'd love to steer a barge through those locks. That, and do a bit of inter-railing. Billy and Margaret Murphy, in the active retirement group, were talking about organising a cruise next year, but I think I might try and get them to go inter-railing instead.'

June laughed out loud.

'What's so funny?'

'I'm just visualising Billy and Margaret Murphy on their walkers with their fluorescent backpacks.'

'I told you, we're not all fossils. Besides, that pair could well afford to go on the Orient Express if they wanted to, but they'd probably show their free travel passes first, just in case they could get a discount.' She took the bottle and topped up their glasses.

'Now, what does Peter think of it all?' Branch continued. 'Doesn't he mind you going off like this?'

'No. He's great – and he thinks it's a great idea too. He'd love to be coming along.'

'What's happening there? Or should I not ask questions like that of my only daughter?'

'Funny, he asked me that last night too, and I told him to ask me again when I come back from the holidays.' She grinned. 'I'm not saying any more and I don't want you to either! Promise.'

'Oh, darling, nothing would make me happier. He's a really decent, open guy. I loved him the minute I met him.'

'That was mutual. If you weren't my mother, I'd have been jealous. Not a word to anyone though till I get back.'

'I promise. Not a word. But it would be lovely to be a grandmother. If only so that I could bore all the others who have been boring me about their little darlings for years.'

'Thanks, Mum, that sounds like a real good reason for me to reproduce.'

She smiled indulgently at her daughter.

June and Danielle's plans continued to change every time they met. After a while, they became more realistic and decided to concentrate on the French Riviera, instead of trying to visit everywhere they had been in the past. There was only a week to go when June got a call from Peter.

'I have to go to Portugal. Dad's had a bit of an accident, though it's not too bad, fortunately. Someone drove out of a side road right into his car and he's a few broken bones. But he'll be out of commission for a bit.'

'That's dreadful. I hope he'll be all right.'

'He will, but I feel I should go over for moral support. See that he has enough help with the stables and around the place to stop him worrying – and to stop Mum fussing about him overdoing things.'

'Of course, you have to go. Be sure and give him – give them – my love.'

'You'll be gone by the time I get back, so make sure you two have a great trip – and don't you worry about me at all,' he laughed.

'I'll try not to. And good luck with the builders. I'll be dying to see the new place when I get back. Be good. I love you, Mr Braga.'

'You're not so bad yourself, Miss Cusack! Take care of each other.'

'We will.'

CHAPTER 2

'Monte Carlo here we come,' Danielle said to June as they sat in the back of the taxi on the way to the airport. 'We'll be sipping champagne by lunchtime.'

But they weren't. The French air-traffic controllers were at it again, and neither of them had thought to check before leaving for the airport that the threatened two-hour stoppage mid-morning was actually going ahead. Consequently, as the flight from Nice hadn't even left for Dublin, they had to spend most of the day hanging around the overcrowded departure lounge. The planned pre-lunch arrival in Nice became an early evening one. By the time they'd negotiated their transport it was well past eight o'clock when they arrived at their boutique hotel in Monaco.

Tired from a frustrating day, they were really looking forward to a shower, a relaxing meal and a glass of wine. They had planned to stay in superior luxury on a handful of nights during the trip, and had chosen some very up-market establishments, with full spa facilities and all the trimmings of decadence and indulgence. They had carefully picked this five-star hotel in Monte Carlo for the first few nights to put them in the mood for their 'grand tour', as Danielle kept referring to it. In between, they'd booked some *auberges* and family-run places, and, for the rest of the time, they'd stay wherever their fancy took them.

At the Hotel Metropole Monte-Carlo, the uniformed doorman led the way for them and another carried their bags in to a palatial foyer. The warm air outside contrasted with the air-conditioned calm inside.

'Nice, very nice,' Danielle muttered. 'This smells of wealth and opulence. I like it!'

'We have a reservation,' June said, handing over her passport to the *soignée* receptionist, who typed something on her keypad. She excused herself and disappeared behind a mirrored door. She re-appeared minutes later with a manager in tow.

'*Mes dames*, I regret to tell you that we have given your room away. We were expecting you before lunch and as we had no communication from you, we assumed you were not arriving. We have just given your room to another couple, less than an hour ago. *Je regrette mais* we are completely booked out.'

They looked at each other in disbelief.

'Haven't you anything at all? Or can you find us an alternative place? We got caught up in the flight delays because of the strike. We left our homes at seven this morning. We're tired and hungry and in need of a shower,' June pleaded.

'*Je regrette*. That is not going to be easy. There is Pharma Week here in Monaco. There are three international medical conferences on and the music festival – and it's high season – everything has been booked for months. There isn't a room anywhere. We've already been looking for others and every phone call we get is from our fellow hoteliers looking for rooms. Can we offer you something to eat, or drink perhaps, while you decide what to do?'

June was trying to hold it together. She nodded, buying time. 'We don't really have much choice, do we?'

The man came out from behind the desk. 'Come with me,' he said, and led them to a quiet corner in an anteroom off the lounge.

'I know it's not as you planned, and it is highly irregular, but if you cannot find anywhere you could stay here on these armchairs. They are quite comfortable and you would not be noticed back here, and we could find you a room in the morning.'

Danielle was absolutely furious. 'Nothing like this ever happened when we slummed it,' she said as he left them to talk.

'It's not really his fault. We never thought to ring ahead either.'

'Well, I have no intention of sitting here for the ten or twelve hours until someone checks out. We're in Monaco, for God's sake. Let's go out and enjoy it.'

26

'That's a great idea.'

'Could we leave our bags with you? We're going to go out to eat something,' June asked when the manager returned with menus.

'Of course. Let me make a reservation. I have a friend who has a lovely bistro not far from the Casino. She will fit you in. Again, I am so sorry this has happened. I can assure you it doesn't happen very often.'

They freshened up as best they could in the rather plush powder room and took the hotel shuttle to the bistro.

'We have grown up in ten years. At twenty, we'd have ranted and raved and you'd have thrown a yuri-yari,' said June.

'Me? You're the short-fused one. You'd have crowned that poor man for inefficiency, and it would have got us nowhere. Peter's mellowed you.'

'Back then, though, we wouldn't even have walked through the door of that hotel in the first place. Instead here we are, paying punters, and we look more like two scruff bags than we ever did then. So much for sophistication, eh?'

The restaurant was noisy, smoky and full of atmosphere and they were ushered out on to a terrace with a panoramic view over the waterfront. Spread out like baubles on a dark cloth, yellowish lights twinkled and reflected on the water. The balmy air was filled with the scents of flowers, perfume and food.

'Now this is more like it. And if we can't get any sleep tonight on those chairs, we'll commandeer some of the comfy loungers by the pool tomorrow, before the Germans are awake,' Danielle said.

They ordered lobster bisque, broke their crusty bread and dipped it in their bowls to mop up every last tasty drop. Then they had *coquilles Saint Jacques*, topped with aromatic herby breadcrumbs.

'I often dream about these,' laughed June. 'Aren't they fantastic?'

'Deffo. Forget your snails, scallops are my all-time favourite and I'm going to have a sinfully delicious brûlée lemon torte and top it all off with a glass of dessert wine. Often when I'm teaching my French class, I find myself fantasising about such things. That's sad, isn't it?'

'Not a bit. But you need to get a life. You've been single now for how long – a whole month?'

'Actually it's almost two. Since just after the big three zero – the oboe player, remember?' God, I never want to hear Bach's 'Solo in G Minor' ever again. What are you going to do to celebrate your birthday?'

'That's one of the reasons I kept a week's holidays. I thought Peter and I might get away for a few days together. I don't want a party, although I have a feeling he'll want to do one in The Pink Pepper Tree to show off the new place. It would be good for publicity too. Spread the word and all that. If he does, then I'll go along with that. It's a huge investment for him.'

'That sounds like a good plan.'

'He's proposed again.'

'And?'

'Well – I didn't want to appear too eager – so I told him to ask me when I get back. I'm going to say yes.'

'That's so heartless, but I'm telling you here and now that I'll not wear lavender, mauve or any sweet-pea colour!'

'I'll remember that. Now come on, let's eat up. I want to walk along by the marina and pretend that one of those yachts is mine.'

When they asked for the bill, they were told it had been taken care of by the hotel.

'We should have ordered champagne,' Danielle laughed.

They headed off down the path, towards Quai Antoine, jostling with parties of revellers, hand-locked lovers and other gawkers who, like them, were marvelling at the size and variety of boats moored along the quay. Some were in darkness. Others were festooned with coloured lights. Some of the larger ones had uniformed staff dancing attendance on their occupants.

'Do you think they own those or do people just rent them to show off?' Danielle asked.

'I'm sure some are owned, but you'd need serious dosh to keep one of those. I'm sure the mooring fees would be as bad as a mortgage, here more so than anywhere else.'

'June, trust you to be practical. I was only thinking of the luxury of it all.'

'So was I. But you can't have luxury without money. Just look back. Could you imagine living in a fabulous apartment up there, looking out on this every day? Do you think you'd ever get tired of it?'

'I'd like the opportunity to find out.'

They turned to retrace their steps and make their way back to the hotel and their waiting armchairs, feeling much happier about the situation than they had earlier. A little farther along, a large party of beautifully dressed men and women were boarding one of the really big yachts. It had a red carpet leading to the gangway and waiters standing about with trays of cocktails. As they passed by, they heard someone call out from above them, 'Danielle. Is that you, Danielle Roche?' They looked up and saw a man waving at them frantically, but because of the lights behind his head, they couldn't see his face.

'Don't go anywhere. I'm coming down,' he shouted.

'Who's that?' asked June.

'I haven't a clue, but what are the chances?'

A tall, good-looking, outdoor type, with naturally sun-bleached hair and a deep tan, pushed his way past those still boarding and shouted, 'Danielle. Danielle. Is that you?'

'David? I don't believe it. What are you doing here?'

'What does it look like?' he laughed. 'I'm working! It's Pharma Week in Monte Carlo and the company's hosting a few of the seminars, so I've been roped in to help with hospitality. What about you? What are you doing here – and who is this?'

'You two must have met before. This is June. You know The Pink Pepper Tree? She's going with Peter who owns it.'

'That's right, I do remember you, June. You've cut your hair. You both look terrific. It's been a while but, as the song says, I only had eyes for you, Danielle.'

'God, Froggie, you haven't changed,' she joked.

'Froggie, I haven't been called that for a long time. We have to get together. Where are you staying?'

They told him about their hotel dilemma.

'Come on here with us. We've had a no-show – a consultant from Korea – you'll have to double up and it's quite a small cabin. It's not one of the luxury ones, but it should be better than a sofa, and you'll have a bathroom. We'll be here for a few more days, and we could do with some extra female company. Why is it that so many neurologists are men? And quite boring?'

'We couldn't do that – look at them – the

beautiful people. We've hardly combed our hair since we left Dublin.'

'Let's get your bags sorted and get you on board. I won't be missed – this shindig will go on for hours. These guys know how to party.'

He took a pager out of his shirt pocket and went to talk to a colleague. A car arrived minutes later. Within an hour, they were back on the sumptuous yacht, showered and dressed and feeling more human. If it had all looked gorgeous before, it was even better close-up. David introduced them to medics and their partners, and though most were surprised by what had happened over their reservation, the Americans weren't at all.

'Why let a good room go to waste? It's all about the mighty dollar – or the euro – isn't it?' said one corpulent guest.

'But the hotel wouldn't have lost out,' Danielle said, trying to explain the situation.

'No, but they weren't going to take that chance,' he argued.

'Fancy meeting someone you knew in Europe,' said another.

'Yes, that was a bit serendipitous,' June agreed. 'My friend and Froggie went out together briefly in a former life.'

Colourful and elaborately enhanced cocktails and glasses of champagne flowed and flowed as the two friends got as merrily inebriated as everyone else over the next few hours.

June texted Peter at some point.

Slumming it at a party on a ginormous yacht in Monte Carlo. Really do wish you were here with me.

'You Irish, you have Guinness in your veins. I read that nursing mothers drink it all the time. Is that true?' asked a tall Norwegian with mesmeric blue eyes. He'd been chatting June up since they arrived and she was flattered by his attention. He wasn't her type at all, but she could just imagine the stir he'd cause doing his rounds in any hospital.

'That may be a bit of an exaggeration. But I believe it used to be prescribed for some, because it's rich in iron, I think. I'm not sure if they still do that, though. I didn't think nursing mothers were supposed to drink.'

His colleagues, who up until then had been more interested in discussing the papers they had delivered and heard that afternoon, suddenly joined in and someone ordered a round of B52s. Froggie was being very professional. The multinational pharmaceutical company he worked for was at the cutting edge of several life-changing drug therapies, which meant its presence at such global conferences was vital. Although he normally headed up marketing, his familiarity with their client base was invaluable at such gatherings – not that he'd needed much cajoling. He was a natural in the role, remembering names and introducing everyone to new people, making sure the guests were being kept happy and entertained.

Inside, a small casino had been set up and had attracted a fair section of the invitees. A jazz pianist and saxophonist played smouldering tunes in the lounge, where a few people were dancing.

'Come on, Froggie. For old times' sake.' Danielle led him on to the tiny dance floor.

The Norwegian invited June to dance. 'Your friend . . .'

'Danielle,' June prompted, sashaying ahead of him.

'Yes, Danielle. Why does she call him Froggie?'

'She has a theory that all her boyfriends all start out being knights in shining armour, or potential princes, but she's convinced that once she's kissed them they all turn into frogs.'

The Norwegian laughed. 'And – do you agree with her?'

'No. Not always,' she smiled, waving her arms about trying to match the improvised rhythm of the piano player. She wasn't doing very well, and then she stumbled. 'And now I've had way too much to drink and I am no longer in a position to agree or disagree with anything. If you'll excuse me, I'm going to bed. It's been a very long day and most interesting night – it was lovely to meet you.'

'I will see you safely to your cabin,' the Norwegian said, putting his arm protectively around her waist.

'There's no need, thank you.'

'In those heels and after those drinks, I think there is. We don't want a casualty on our hands.

Maybe you should take them off.' He held her steady as she stepped out of her shoes. She waved them at Froggie and Danielle and, with some unintelligible miming, managed to let them know she was retiring. She negotiated the steep stairwell, giggling. 'I'm really tipsy.'

'Yes. You are. I can see that,' he agreed.

She dropped her key. 'Damn,' she said loudly and laughed, dropping one of her shoes.

He picked them up and opened the door for her. 'Shush, it's late,' he said, and he leaned forward to kiss her.

'Stop!' She pushed him away. 'You can't do that – I can't do that – I'm spoken for.'

'So am I. My wife's asleep farther along the deck.'

'Well, don't keep her waiting.' She stubbed her toe on the little step on the doorframe and let out some colourful expletives.

He laughed at her and gave her a hug. 'You really have had a good time, haven't you?'

'Abso – so – lutley. A great time alto . . . together.' She giggled and he guided her into the room. She threw her shoes down and, as she propelled herself thankfully in the direction of the lower bunk, she walloped the side of her head on the edge of the top bunk and passed out.

When she woke late the next morning, it was to the gentle purring of the ship's engine and the pounding of several hammers inside her brain. She put her hand to her forehead and discovered a large bump. How had that happened? She had no recollection of hitting her head.

She realised the yacht was moving and, when she could focus properly, she looked out the port-hole. They were out on the open seas, a clear blue sky above them. The mirrored waters stretched to the horizon and were dotted with sails and bubbling wakes from other boats, all doing the Med as it should be done.

There was no sign of Danielle, so June showered and felt a bit better. She arranged her hair to cover the swelling, which had taken on a purplish hue. She also had a bruise on her arm. *I hope I didn't pass out and make a fool of myself in front of everyone*, she thought. *I need to find Danni and find out.*

A mobile phone on the locker startled her, as it announced a text. She didn't recognise the ring tone. She picked it up, but it wasn't hers. It wasn't Danielle's either. It beeped a second time. Puzzled, she put it back down and tried to remember what had happened the previous evening. Her final recollections were of waving her shoes at Danielle and Froggie on the dance floor, and someone helping her down the stairs. She had a vague notion of someone trying to kiss her and of her pushing him away. Now her head hurt like crazy and she couldn't remember what Froggie's real name was.

'I didn't do anything stupid, did I? Please tell

me I didn't,' she said to Danielle, when she finally made her way to the buffet breakfast and found her sitting with Froggie.

'Relax. I don't think you were capable of doing anything, so I wouldn't worry a whit. I came back to the cabin shortly after to check on you and you had crashed. You were snoring, by the way. If you keep that up, you'll be paying for single rooms for us both. I met your blond admirer and he said he'd seen you safely to your room and you were comatose.'

'My blond admirer? What are you talking about? You'll have to point him out so I can thank him when I see him. Is he around anywhere?'

'No, they're all off at the seminar today,' Froggie said.

'I think this admirer may have lost this. It might be his. Can you check when you see him?' She handed him the phone.

'Sure, I'll see him later.'

'Danielle, how do you look so bright and fresh?' June said, fiddling with her hair, but Danni didn't seem to notice anything.

'*I* wasn't trying to prove that the Irish and the Scandinavians couldn't out-drink each other,' Danielle replied.

'I swear that is the last time I'll ever drink like that. I'd forgotten how awful a thudding hangover can be, and I ache – it must have been all that dancing. Talk about not mixing the grape and the grain – I don't know what I mixed last night, but it was lethal, especially after such a fragmented day. Where are we going, by the way?'

'To Nice. This trip is for the amusement of corporate spouses and partners. It's a mishmash of activities – a bit of shopping and sightseeing, a visit to a gallery and an al fresco lunch day. You two can join us or stay here on board, it's up to you. You don't have to tag along, but I'd love your company and you might enjoy it. Before we get there, though, I have a few things to sort out, so please excuse me for a bit.'

Danielle spotted June's bruise. 'How did that happen?'

'I'm not certain, but I vaguely recollect a collision with the bunk bed or with something else while I tried to find the bathroom during the night.'

'What are you like? And I never even heard you swearing.'

The yacht swung around, exposing the long sweep of the Bay of Angels with its perfect curve and backdrop of the rugged mountains peeping through a blue heat haze.

'Now that's what I call a view. It looks totally different from out here.'

'This is what I came away for,' said June. 'There's something romantic about the whole Riviera. I'd love to have been around during the glory days before this was all so developed, when people came to do their European tour and paraded up and down the promenades under their parasols.'

'Me too.'

'It *is* pretty perfect,' said Froggie, arriving back, clipboard in hand.

June noticed them exchange a glance and wondered if anything had happened the previous evening. She was recalling that they had gone out for about six months a few years earlier. It was probably one of Danielle's longer liaisons. She couldn't remember why it had ended, but then she seldom could with Danielle's relationships. They had a habit of blazing a trail like a comet and then fizzling out just as quickly, leaving no trace behind them. But he seemed to be a really nice and thoughtful guy, one she wouldn't have put in the usual Froggie class at all. She'd tell her that when she got her on her own later on.

'You've no idea how grateful we are that you came to our rescue,' June hesitated. 'Eh, I can't keep calling you "Froggie".'

'Why not? I don't mind, and it's kind of grown on me. So, ladies, are you going to come ashore with us?'

They both nodded. 'We'd love to.'

'That's great.'

'It's fantastic for us, but honestly, you don't have to include us. You've been so generous already,' said June. 'We don't want to be hangers-on.'

'You're not. It was great bumping in to you both. I can let my guard down. Sometimes, you can get too much of small talk, especially if the people you're talking to don't have the lingo. And, as you may have noticed, some of those here are not exactly a bundle of laughs. Right, I think we're ready to get going.'

The day passed very quickly. They looked at unpriced items in designer boutiques around Place Magenta, admired the variety and colour of the produce on the street market stalls, and stopped to look at curiosities in the antique shops. 'Isn't this the best start to the holiday we could ever have had?'

'Truly amazing. Can it get any better?'

That evening, Froggie told them to glam up for a gala event. 'It's been five star so far – what can we expect to top it?' June asked.

'You'll have to wait and see, but I promise it will be memorable. Posh frocks all the way. We have the bigwigs flying in from Geneva and Washington too.'

With that kind of build-up, they took extra care getting ready. June's long red crepe dress hugged all the right places and she wore her hair in an upsweep to one side. After several changes, Danielle opted for a coffee-coloured chiffon number, with godets adding a flamenco touch to the hemline.

'Well, we certainly look the part,' June said as they gave themselves a final look in the mirror. 'I actually think we got a touch of sun today.'

'Come on, let's go and see what the rest of the style is like.'

They joined the others walking back along the quay towards the famous Casino which had been the hub of social intrigue, passionate liaisons and much more over the decades. June saw the Norwegian she had been talking to the previous night and he waved his phone at her and smiled a thank you. A very glamorous-looking woman with a flawless complexion and a geometric-style hairdo accompanied him and promptly took his arm in a proprietorial way. She shot a scathing look in their direction when she saw her husband looking over.

'Well, that says "hands off" louder than if she shouted it,' said Danielle.

'She needn't worry about me. I'm spoken for and I'd have no interest in him anyway. He isn't my type at all.'

They walked along towards Casino Plaza, where the fountains splashed merrily, mingling with the many tourists taking photos of the famous land-marks. The men, looking great in white dinner jackets, admired and envied the array of sports cars that were parked along outside, while the women sparkled in designer dresses and lots of bling. As their large party filed in, several paparazzi bent and crouched, looking for good angles as their cameras whirred on the off chance that there might be some celebrities or minor royals among them.

Just inside the pillared entrance, they were shown into Le Train Bleu restaurant, which had been reserved completely by Froggie's company. Farther along were the gaming rooms where fortunes and dreams had been wagered, won and lost.

'Is it true that Coco Chanel designed the costumes for the theatre here? And is it still there?' one woman asked Froggie.

'I'm afraid I'm not very well up on such matters, but I'll find out for you,' he said, smiling graciously.

'I believe she did,' June intervened. 'I read somewhere that both Picasso and Matisse actually painted sets for the Ballets Russes here too.'

'Golly. So much history to take in,' the woman said, and moved on.

The restaurant was a feast of rich reds, yellows and gold, replicating exactly the décor of the *wagon-lits* on the iconic Blue Train that brought the royals, the rich, the curious and the intrepid travellers to this little-known rocky resort, tucked away between France and Italy.

'This is exactly what I meant earlier today when I said I'd love to have been around at the turn of the twentieth century, that glorious Belle Époque era. They knew how to do things then, such style. Just look at the décor. I think I was born in the wrong time,' June sighed.

'I'm with you there. Then, you didn't have to worry about luggage or excess baggage charges either – the porters just whisked your trunks away and reunited you with them at journey's end – no worries about anything but the pursuit of happiness,' Froggie said.

'From where I'm looking at it, we're doing exactly that twenty-first-century style,' Danielle laughed.

'You're right,' June said, 'but I love a dollop of nostalgia – there's something so romantic about that era. I wonder when they stopped using those trains?'

'I think it was only whenever the TGVs came along. It used to take twenty hours or something outrageous – now you can do it in five,' Froggie replied.

'I don't think I'd have minded that. I'd have revelled in this – I *am* revelling in this – keeping the golden age alive in this little corner of the world. It's fabulous.'

'She doesn't get out much,' Danielle said to Froggie.

When they were seated, he was off again, this time to say a few introductory words, welcoming everyone and introducing the company president, who was Chad something or other the Fourth. June often wondered what it was about some Americans that they needed to create and promote their own dynasties, however minor, to make them feel important.

Coming back into focus, she heard President Chad the Fourth say, 'We've had some very exciting news today. News that we'd like to share with you all tonight, and for sure you'll remember where you were when you heard it. It's so appropriate that we're all here in this wonderful setting

43

for Pharmaceutical Week, because this company is celebrating. Our new drug therapy for Alzheimer's disease has just got the go-ahead from the US Food and Drug Administration to go into human clinical trials.'

The audience broke into cheers and sustained clapping. When it subsided, the president continued. 'As most of you know, we've been working towards this for the past six years, collaborating with some of the world's top specialists in pharmacology, in science and in medicine. It's one of the most heavily invested drugs in our history to date – in fact in medical science to date – and we have every faith in it. We are prepared to continue with it to the end, no matter what it takes in manpower, finance and expertise. This is no gamble – it's a sure thing – and it will change the lives of generations to come. The timing is perfect, coming as it does this week, and we have much cause to celebrate, so let's begin.'

There was more sustained applause.

'As a small token of recognition for your loyalty you'll all find an envelope under your plates with a voucher for some gambling chips. Some are for 500 and a few of you will find 1,000 – and there's one envelope with a 10,000 jackpot somewhere too, so you can try your hand at gambling Monte Carlo style. We hope you'll have luck, maybe even break the bank. If you do, remember we'll be looking for sponsorship in the future.'

Everyone cheered. 'Now let's raise our glasses – to us and the clinical human trials.'

The night was indeed memorable and it was almost four o'clock when they made their way back to the yacht, having watched some action at the tables. June was more interested in observing the people who were playing, some sticking rigidly to the same format at the roulette tables, others covering different options at each turn of the wheel. The croupiers were all tall, young, devilishly handsome and sexy. Among the gamers, there were many older men with young, svelte, beautiful women by their side – and all with jewellery that competed with the amazing chandeliers. Surely they couldn't all be escorts. She also noticed several older women with good-looking young bucks by their side. The older women had seemed to be more attracted to the slot machines and were piling in money with a dedication that appeared to border on obsession.

Danielle stuck to her favourite colour and won for a while. Then she got reckless, doubling her bets and, in no time at all, she had used all her credit. June's stash lasted only slightly longer, but they didn't mind at all. After a stuttering winning streak on black, their chips soon evaporated within what seemed like only minutes.

'We're bust,' said June. 'Yet I feel like we just won the lotto being here at all, so I don't mind one little bit. I like being caught up in all this. It's heady stuff, this keeping up with the Joneses, but it's very easy to get used to it, isn't it?' Most of the delegates were due to head back home the following day and June and Danielle started talking about where they'd go next.

'There's no need for you to rush off,' Froggie said, visibly relaxing as his duties finished for another day. 'We have the vessel chartered for tomorrow night as well, so you can use it as a base. I'll be busy during the day making sure everyone gets away, but I could be free for dinner tomorrow night, if you're not sick of my company.'

'We'll have dinner with you only if you let us treat you,' June said.

'Done deal, so. I'll see you here around 7.30.'

When they got up the following morning, June and Danielle headed for the old town with its palace and cathedral and climbed the steep hill that overlooked the bay of Monte Carlo. When they arrived back at Palace Square, it was just before midday and the bells began to toll, announcing the changing of the guard outside the Grimaldi Palace.

'This is like something from a fairy tale,' June said, as they jostled for a position in the crowd that had suddenly surged over to one side of the sun-bathed square. White-clad sentries left the shade of their toy-town boxes and marched along by the cannons as the changeover took place. It was all over in ten minutes.

'Definitely a Kodak moment,' teased Danielle, as June fished her camera out of her bag.

'I promised Peter I'd take a picture a day – one that sums up what we were doing – just to make him jealous,' she laughed.

She snapped a few more images and they headed off through the labyrinth of cobbled streets, stopping in a leafy little square to drink coffee and enjoy some warm croissants. They bought postcards in a tobacconist's across the street and spent ages writing them, dying to share their unexpected adventures. June sent one to Peter, saying she was missing him and she wished he'd been able to come along. She also wrote one to his parents, to the guys in the office and another to Branch. They were tourists with no time constraints and no money worries, carefree and ready to enjoy and absorb every little detail.

Over the years, June would often recall these halcyon days, wondering if she had made enough of them. If she had realised what life was really going to deal her, would she have done anything differently?

'As you seem to be getting on so well, Danielle, would you like to have Froggie to yourself this evening? I could always have a headache.'

'Don't be daft. Although I have to say, I am a bit surprised by him. He's so much more mature than when we used to date. Then, he was like an eager little puppy dog, always baying at my heels and talking about himself. He's grown on me.'

She grinned sheepishly. 'He also looks a lot better than I remember. He used to be really scrawny and gangly, like a marathon runner.'

'Angular is the word I would have used. And I agree, he looks much better now that he's grown into himself. He's actually very easy on the eyes.'

'Back off, June – you have your own fella!'

'I know. And in case you haven't noticed, *we've* both matured too. Maybe our body clocks have started ticking – trying to give us a nudge in the nest-making direction. What do you think?'

'I don't know, but the thought of settling down doesn't freak me out the way it used to, so there's probably something in that theory. You and Peter seem ready for commitment and all that.'

'I think we actually are. I can't believe I'm saying that. I never thought we'd be having a conversation like this. Did you?'

'No. And, for the record, Froggie hasn't said anything about keeping in touch when we get back, so say nothing. He spends a lot of his time in Geneva these days and I'm not sure about long-distance relationships.' She paused for a bit before asking, 'Do you think he's a little too uptight for me?'

'No, I think he's had a very busy and demanding week, with a lot of responsibility. It can't be easy shepherding such a large group, with all those nationalities and different languages. Just imagine it. I think it would give me nightmares.'

'Well, we'll see how he is tonight, when they've all gone home. Where will we take him?'

'Let's do a recce and find somewhere up here. We can make a reservation before we do the palace.'

They were a little disappointed that the tour was so short, taking them through the state apartments and the lavish throne room. Their guide explained that the palace served as the administrative centre for the principality, and that work goes on irrespective of the tourists.

After the tour, they made their way back to the yacht to prepare for their final night in Monte Carlo.

They took their time getting ready, packing somewhat in between drying their hair and deciding what to wear. Danielle picked a short black dress cinched in with a tiny gold belt, which showed off her legs, while June opted for palazzo pants in soft cream with a cream and black geometric top.

Froggie looked more like a French man than an Irish one with his dark eyes and deep tan. He looked very relaxed in a pale-yellow, short-sleeved shirt and navy slacks.

'Ladies, you look terrific,' he said approvingly when they met up. 'I'll be the envy of everyone in the restaurant.' He had organised a car to take them back up to the old town. When they arrived, he said, 'That's it. The phone and pager are off for the night, so I can enjoy your company.'

49

They ambled around for a bit, taking in the views and the different faces of the tiny principality, whose fate had been saved by gambling but whose citizens were not allowed to bet.

June thought that Froggie was certainly much more at ease now that his work had finished, and could sense that Danielle could feel it too. The place they had booked was a family-run bistro that was quintessentially French and it turned out to be a great choice. They discussed the menu, and lingered over the food when it arrived. They savoured the wines and enjoyed the accordion and piano music that accompanied a husky-voiced singer, who rounded the evening off by giving her all to a selection of Edith Piaf's songs. Her finale and encore was, of course, '*Non, je ne regrette rien*', and she encouraged the diners to join in, which they did with gusto.

'That's my anthem,' said Danielle. 'Never regret anything.'

'You could do a lot worse,' Froggie said.

'Well, there is absolutely nothing to regret about the past few days, Froggie,' June told him. 'They were perfect. Thank you so much again for rescuing us, and for spoiling us. You've been fantastic.'

'Like I said, it was great for me too, and I very much look forward to catching up with you, Danielle, when I'm back in Dublin next month – and you too June.'

'You'll have to come to The Pink Pepper Tree – in all its new splendour. I know Peter is planning some media events, so we'll get you along to one that fits in with your busy schedule.'

'I'll look forward to it. Now, what are your plans for the next part of your trip?'

'We're picking up a car tomorrow and we're going to try to avoid the *autoroutes* and just go exploring. We've earmarked several things to do, like visit the Picasso Museum at Juan-les-Pins, the lavender fields at Grasse, the markets, everything, but knowing us we'll probably not get to half of them.'

'I wish I could tag along. I've quite enjoyed the freedom from my usual role. The rewards of working with a pharmaceutical giant are great, but these multinationals do take their pound of flesh in every possible way. It's not like at home where you can take time off here and there, or get a few extra days if you talk nicely to the boss. They pay well, but in the process, they think they have actually bought you too.'

'But you seem to enjoy it,' June said.

'I do, I love it. I wouldn't do it otherwise and this week was a bit of a break from the usual routine. Now it's back to the more serious side of things. These new human drug trials will create quite a stir, even though public consumption could still be years away from being a reality.'

They realised most of the diners had drifted away, and he said, 'Let's get back to the yacht. I almost feel she's mine, having spent the past week on her.'

'Always the dreamer, Froggie,' Danielle laughed.

'I know what he means, though,' June said. 'It's so easy to be seduced into that sort of lifestyle and I'm delighted I had the chance to see and enjoy it all first hand.'

'At last, a kindred spirit who can see where I'm coming from,' he said. 'Before we go back, you have to see the palace by night. The buildings are all floodlit and the square looks quite magical. It's only a few minutes away.'

It was every bit as beautiful as he said.

'Live the dream, Danielle, while it's there,' June heard him say to her friend. 'Things like this don't last forever.'

'When did you turn into such a romantic?'

'Somewhere along the way. When you weren't looking.'

June excused herself as soon as they were back on board to give them some space – and she wanted to phone Peter to give him an update. He was in the restaurant and up to his eyes, so their call was frustratingly short.

'I'm missing you like crazy,' she told him.

'And that's a ditto from this end,' he laughed.

She knew she'd caught him at a bad time, so she just said, 'I'll call you tomorrow and we can talk then.'

She was almost asleep when Danielle eventually came back to the cabin, but not too sleepy to enquire, 'Well?'

'Well . . . what?' Danielle laughed.

'Well – you know – the pair of you . . .'

'No. I decided to wait until he's in Dublin. With a bit of distance, I'll have a better idea of how I feel.'

'God, Danielle, that's very restrained – you *have* grown up.'

'Go to sleep,' Danielle laughed, kicking off her high heels. 'Just go to sleep, will you?'

CHAPTER 3

They left Froggie the following morning with fond farewells and promises to meet whenever they were all back home. They picked up their hired car and spent the four weeks filling their days with memories. They shopped, walked, lazed, joined tours, visited galleries and exhibitions, ate picnics on beaches, on park benches and in market squares, and they lingered happily over copious bottles of wine and delicious meals.

Paris had been their ultimate goal, but they soon realised they'd never make it that far, and cancelled their hotel. There was too much to do and see along the Riviera and in Provence. They meandered from the coast inland and back to the sea again, making it as far as Arles, where they visited the haunts of Van Gogh.

They shopped at flea markets, unable to resist the bargains and the bargaining. Danielle sought out vintage clothing while June kept an eye out for unusual pieces for the restaurant. Eventually she found exactly what she wanted – some distinctive oversized platters. One was oblong and featured an embossed lobster; the other had mussels all over it and came with eight matching finger bowls.

'And how do you propose getting those home?' Danielle asked, lifting one up. 'They weigh a ton. You might get away with the bowls among your clothes but the big ones are sure to get broken if you pack them.'

'I'll have them shipped from somewhere – that way they'll be insured if anything happens to them. Besides, they don't cost a fortune and Peter will love them.'

They swam and walked, took forest trails and even went horse riding one day. They conversed almost always in French. June sketched and painted when they took some down time from their busy schedule.

One weekend they joined an art class in an *atelier* run by a totally eccentric artist with a drooping nicotine-stained moustache. He insisted the leaves on the olive trees were blue and that tomatoes and nasturtiums were the same colour orange.

'That man's a fraud,' Danielle declared after ten minutes, which sparked off the nearest they came to an out-and-out fight between them during their whole trip. Danielle wanted to walk out and get her money back, convinced the tutor was colour-blind.

'I refuse to paint either of those subjects,' she announced. A Dutch couple agreed with her, while a Charles-Atlas-sized American said, 'French painters have always done their own experimental type of art. Maybe this guy is a genius.'

'You think?' Danielle replied witheringly, wondering what his interpretation of the subject matter might be like. And with great restraint she refrained from uttering the expletives that were hovering on her tongue. 'I'll show him experimental,' she said, and did sunflowers instead and stuck a few purple ones in the middle – 'just to be subversive'.

The tutor's reaction was to keep telling her, '*Cherie,* you are not good enough to be *magnifique.* Your friend, on the other hand, has real talent. You are a lost cause – there is nothing I can teach you. You are *une cause perdue!*' Then he stalked off, muttering under his breath, 'It's always the true amateurs that come here thinking they are going to go away with the skills of Cezanne, Matisse or Renoir. Then they won't take instruction from the maestro.'

June physically restrained her friend from going after him, while the other students laughed at the comedy being played out in the courtyard.

'Don't rise to his bait. He's enjoying his sense of power. He probably sees himself as the next Van Gogh.'

'Deffo, but if he keeps this up I'll cheerfully lop his ear off and we'll see how much he feels like him then. In fact I might relieve him of both at the same time! That would get him a few lines of publicity and his fifteen minutes of fame for sure.' He ignored her for the rest of the day.

However, by the first evening when they set off for the village *en masse* for dinner, Danielle was actually really enjoying herself, and they all had too much wine over a very pleasant repast. The maestro tried to pinch her bottom as the whole group walked back up the cobbled street from one of the little restaurants in the village where the *atelier* was located. She gave him a whack and told him she'd report him to the police first thing in the morning. Of course she didn't, but far from discouraging him, he thought that was great fun and spent the Sunday leering at her over his easel, walking by and standing too close behind her as he reached over her shoulder, cupping his hand around hers and guiding her brush, making suggestions as to how she could improve her work and asking, 'Is it better for you today?'

'Dirty old man,' she muttered. 'Haven't you heard of personal space? Well, you're invading mine right now,' she said, pushing him away.

'I find feisty women *irrésistible*, totally *irrésistible*.' He was so close she could feel his garlicky breath on her ear. He squeezed her hand before he stepped away, muttering *'irrésistible!'* When he was back behind his own work she tore up her painting of the countryside, glowered back at him and began painting an olive grove with turquoise nasturtiums, aquamarine onions and purple tomatoes growing on the trees.

'You'll have to have that framed,' laughed June.

'I think I will. And another word from you and I might just give it to Peter to hang up in the restaurant.'

'I'd better warn him.'

Along the way they met people from all over, sometimes dining with them, and arranging to meet for a day or two or visit a gallery together before heading off on their own again. There was no shortage of things for them to do and the days passed in a haze of enjoyment as they attended open-air concerts and recitals, watched floral parades and firework displays and joined in village festivals and celebrations – and the sun always seemed to shine and Danielle worked on her tan with dedication.

'If only we had fine weather like this at home,' Danielle said one afternoon when they were nearly halfway through their trip. 'We'd have a totally different lifestyle and wouldn't have to hibernate in winter.'

'It must be much easier to grow old somewhere like this,' June said as she watched a group of old men all sporting berets, some smoking pipes and all playing *pétanque* under the shade of a knot of gnarled trees.

'I always think we're mad celebrating our national day in March,' Danielle said. 'We ought to change that to June or September and that way we might actually have some sunshine to enjoy and those poor little baton twirlers wouldn't turn blue with cold.'

'Maybe we should have a referendum. We've had them on all sorts of less important things. You know, before we set off, I thought I'd enjoy the pampering in the opulent hotels much more than I actually do, but I've now decided that the smaller hotels have much more character and people talk to you.'

'I think you're right,' Danielle agreed. 'I can't remember any of the concierges or managers, apart from the one the first night and he really did go out of his way to help us.'

June was really missing Peter and kept in touch by phone every few days. He had been forced to put off closing the restaurant for a few weeks.

'There's a problem with the new windows we ordered for the conservatory,' he'd told her. 'They're coming from Sweden and there's been a production breakdown. If I go with another supplier, I'll be at the end of the queue, starting all over again, so I'll have to stick with the original ones.'

'That's a shame. I thought everything would be on schedule once it started.'

'So did I, but did you ever know of a building project going according to plan? That's why I thought it better to stay open until we're ready to lace into it.'

'You'll not be able to hop over and join us for a few days, then?'

'No, tempting as that sounds, I'd better hang around. I've already messed up everyone's leave and they've all been really good about it. Besides, I have already booked to go back out and see the old man the week you come home, and I don't want to let him down. I'll make it up to you, I promise.'

'I know you will.'

'Keep sending the postcards. I'm mad with envy when they arrive, but I love getting them.'

The weeks passed far too quickly. Danielle and Froggie kept in touch – she by postcards, he by phone.

They finished their grand tour with a few days in a charming higgledy-piggledy farmhouse where they were allowed into the kitchen to be taught how to make *tarte tatin* by the rotund proprietor.

'I don't share my recipes with everyone, but as you ladies seem to appreciate the finer things in life, like my *cuisine*, I'll let you in on some of my secrets.' He also shared his family recipe for *crème patisserie*, insisting a tiny rasp of nutmeg with the vanilla gave it its secret *je ne sais quoi*.

Outside, his garden was as disorganised as his home. Night-flowering white tuber roses glowed happily beside his courgettes; nasturtiums invaded the untidy rows of herbs and onions while the chickens had the run of the yard. All this was supervised by a lazy calico cat that never seemed to move from her vantage point beside the clumps of parsley, and by a majestic-looking cockerel that woke them each day at an ungodly hour, nudging them not to waste a minute of this time.

'Good God, it's only half past four,' Danielle said. 'We'll never settle down to normality after this.'

'Unfortunately, we will. A few mornings in the office with queries from suppliers will soon put this all out of my mind – but I'll never forget it.'

'If I could find a way to package what we've just done and sell it to my classes, they'd all want it so much, they'd be fluent in no time. It's been wonderful, every bit of it, and I bet when we're old women we'll still be talking about it.'

'You're probably right there. It has been the trip of a lifetime. I'm so glad we did it. I have to remember to send those platters I bought. Are you going to send anything back?'

'No. Most of what I bought is squashy, but I do need to buy an extra bag.'

After doing what packing they could, they made their last foray into Nice and managed to sort out everything they needed remarkably quickly. This left them enough time for a final road trip so, having bought cheese, pâté, olives and some crusty bread, they headed for a beach on the Bay of Angels to have a last picnic.

They had their caricatures drawn on the promenade by a frighteningly thin woman hidden beneath a black straw hat and a flowing, poppy-printed kaftan. They couldn't wait to see the finished products as passers-by stopped, smiled and commented.

'They're brilliant,' they agreed. 'We'll have to have them photocopied.' The artist had captured them perfectly, despite their exaggerated eyes, oversized teeth and mouths, and diminutive necks and shoulders.

'We have to keep them to remind us of this trip,' Danielle said, unwrapping their last picnic as they sat on the beach soaking up the sunshine.

'I'm going to remember this, all of it, and I'm going to miss it,' June said.

'Me too. But right now, I'm going back to that cheese merchant to buy some more of this to bring home and, tonight, for our last supper, I'm going to indulge myself with all my favourite food.'

'That sounds like a plan.' June agreed. '*Foie gras* with Sauternes, *moules marinieres*, scallops, *tarte citron*, champagne, the works.'

And they did. After finishing their packing, they taxied to a restaurant in a village close to the farm. There, they feasted in a little courtyard lit almost entirely by tiny lights and candles. They reminisced and laughed, plotted and planned. Then they headed back, knowing the cockerel would have them awake at an unmerciful hour, ready to leave for the airport in good time.

As though in sympathy with them, it was raining on that last morning as they made their way to

Nice airport, excited at the prospect of going home but sorry their trip had ended. As they checked in, they were told that there was another air traffic controllers' strike and they would be delayed. The official was so surprised when they turned to each other and laughed that he then offered to check-in their other bags at no extra charge.

'You are the first people not to complain since I came on duty this morning,' he told them. 'You'd think I had started the strike myself, deliberately, just to frustrate everyone's travel arrangements.'

'Our holiday began in exactly the same way and it just got better all along. Hopefully, the same thing will happen going the other way,' Danielle told him.

'I hope so too.' He handed them vouchers for lunch in one of the restaurants. Then he added another two for wine and winked at them. 'Thank you, ladies. I hope you won't be delayed too long.'

'*Non, merci à vous, monsieur*,' Danielle said.

'See, things are looking up already,' June said, 'and I know I'm ready to go home, and to Peter.'

'Another week would have been nice.'

'Don't be greedy. You've got Froggie's visits to look forward to as well. Because of this delay, I'll probably miss seeing Peter before he flies out to his dad, so we'll both just have to practise a bit of patience. And do you know what the worst thing is? He's made me swear that I won't go anywhere near the restaurant until we can see it together.'

'I could always go a-snooping and report back.'

'I couldn't let you do that. He'd never forgive me – or you.'

'He'd never know . . .'

'Don't you dare!'

CHAPTER 4

The delay did mean that Peter and June missed each other at Dublin airport – frustratingly, June and Danielle's plane arrived only an hour after his had left. Instead, their jet streams possibly merged somewhere along the way as they flew by each other in opposite directions.

Fortunately, Peter's father was on the mend and due to have the cast removed from his broken leg, but Peter wanted to keep his promise to visit. The delays in starting the building work had meant they were way behind schedule and he was happy he'd put off closing up. The only problem now was that Matt, his architect, had gone on holiday the week before, and left the project in the hands of a female colleague whom Peter hadn't met.

'She knows the restaurant,' Matt assured him. 'She's very ambitious and anxious to make her mark. I've briefed her fully and she can reach me by text, although don't let my wife know that or she'll divorce me. I've been forbidden to make any contact with the office while we're away.'

There was no good time to do such major work.

Business was booming, and buying the adjoining premises had been a stroke of luck and good fortune. His grandfather would have been proud of how he was using his legacy as he had been the one to encourage him in the first place.

They had always been very close when he was growing up on the family's sprawling estate in Alentejo. As the only grandson, he was the one who would carry on the Braga name, and that gave him a special place in his grandfather's heart. The estate now produced world-class olives and olive oil. They had a vineyard but it had been neglected for years and was only now starting to produce wines again. It had been brought into the twenty-first century very quickly and efficiently by Peter's sister, Rosa, who'd studied viticulture and oenology before taking a year out to work in the vineyards in Stellenbosch in South Africa. At first, her grandfather and her parents had thought her interest was just a passing fancy, but Rosa was slowly making a name for herself and when one of her wines got a commendation at a Brussels trade fair, they suddenly began looking at her in a new light.

Their grandfather's passion had been his stables, his Lusitano horses and his carriage driving. It was this passion that had brought him to Dublin for the Horse Show one year, and where his son had met his future wife, Peter's mother. She came from a horsey family in County Kildare. After a whirlwind courtship, they married and she moved to Portugal, happily swapping her life on the stud farm in Kildare for one in the ranch in Alentejo.

When her parents were alive, Peter and Rosa had spent many happy summers and Christmases in Ireland with their maternal grandparents and it was there that Peter's love of cooking was nurtured. Granny H always had bread proving near the range. Soda bread, rustic soups, tea bracks and apple tarts – the house always smelled of welcome and warmth. They could never understand the Irish kids who couldn't wait to get away for their two weeks in the sun every year. They were happy messing about in the stables and riding out with grooms, and they never cared about the weather.

The changes to the restaurant were four weeks behind schedule and it was looking like September before Peter would be able to open again and there was nothing he could do to speed things up. He'd met Zoe, the new architect, several times and she'd made an impression. She was almost proprietorial in her dedication and attention to detail. She never seemed to leave the site. No matter when he turned up, she was there. She'd made it obvious that she liked him, but he'd quickly put her straight, telling her about June.

He put Zoe and the restaurant out of his mind as he boarded the plane for Portugal. He was looking forward to seeing his family, but couldn't wait to see June. It was only another week until they would be together again. It seemed as though she had been gone forever.

'Look at you, all sun-kissed and glowing.'

'We hate you!'

'Five weeks away. Don't you know tans are so last year?'

June's colleagues welcomed her back with the usual mix of humour and interest when she arrived back in the office.

'If my tan offends you so much, I think I'll just have to eat all the goodies I brought back by myself,' she laughed, putting a carrier bag on her desk.

'Are there pralines . . . or cheese?' one asked.

'Or dark chocolate with almonds?' another asked.

'Maybe.'

'Then maybe we can forgive you, this time. I'll put the kettle on!'

'You better wait until ten o'clock, or you'll have me fired before I'm back in the door.'

'This arrived for you yesterday,' Kelly said, handing over the large box containing the platters.

'Already? I wonder if they're all still in one piece.' She lifted the box and shook it gently. 'They seem to be intact. They're a surprise for Peter. I want to give them to him on the opening night.'

June was right about slotting back into the work routine easily. She'd been home a week already and Peter was flying back that afternoon. She was cooking for him and ran about her house putting away laundry and tidying up while a casserole cooked in the oven.

She had brought the platters and bowls home from work and hid them in a suitcase in the back of a wardrobe in the spare bedroom.

The sun was shining through the long sash windows and she thought, as she often did, how lucky she had been to have this house on Raglan Road. It pre-dated the modern apartments and pokey flats that most of her friends occupied and was a real oasis not two miles from the heart of Dublin, with its beautiful garden at the front. In the back she had apple trees, and though she liked to look after the tubs and flowerbeds herself, she let her parents' gardener, Young Joe, do the heavy-duty jobs. He was the one who'd made sure everything was watered and tended while she was away.

Young Joe was all of sixty if he was a day. His father, Old Joe, had worked for her grandparents and parents. He'd always been around her parents' house when June was growing up and he'd always looked old, but he could lop branches bigger than himself and clip hedges with great accuracy and speed. He was partial to the odd drop of whiskey too 'to keep the chill out of me bones'.

Her father had run his very successful obstetric practice from his consulting rooms in the house and June had never given much thought to the house, just assuming it was his workplace when he wasn't at one of the hospitals he was associated with. She used to love looking at the ever-expanding photo gallery that lined the stairwell – pictures of the countless babies her father had delivered over the years, some sets of twins and one of triplets too. Others kept in touch on birthdays and at Christmas and there were images of candle-blowing, Santa hats and first communions galore.

After her father's funeral, June had been astonished when Branch had announced, 'Your dad and I decided a long time ago that the place on Raglan Road should be yours.'

'How do you mean "mine"? I could never afford those rental prices.'

'You don't have to – your father wasn't just good at medical matters, he was a shrewd businessman. He bought that house in the eighties, along with a few other properties. He always had you in mind for that one.'

'But he never whispered a word about it. I had no inkling.'

'That was his way of doing things. As you know, he was never one for shouting anything from the rooftops. All the charity work he did and he never let his name be associated with any of it. There is one thing, though – he left me any rental income from the sitting tenants in the basement, but that's not a problem. He has more than adequately provided for me, so if you ever want to have the space back or want to sell up I won't stand in your way. Consider it yours too.'

'I can't believe it. I always loved that house and it must be worth a fortune now.'

'Well, let's just say it should set you up.'

'That's an understatement if ever I heard one, Mum. I'll have to stave off the fortune hunters now that I'm such a good catch.'

The house had everything – Dublin's most exclusive postal code, even Herbert Park virtually down the road, with its walks and roses, its pond and ducks, and there were loads of places to eat dotted around the neighbourhood.

June had welcomed Branch's help in furnishing the house. She knew that her mother wanted her to get on with her life and not be held back while she herself got used to widowhood.

'I don't want you to feel that you're responsible for my well-being. I've seen too many friends become totally dependent after being bereaved, especially the men. In the end, they just drive their children away. I've no intentions of letting that happen.'

'Mum, you'd never be one of those mothers. You're far too independent,' June had told her.

They'd gone to the house several times before deciding what to change and they'd both shared a tear or two as they removed the picture gallery and other personal effects that her father had treasured. 'I never realised you had such a flair for this sort of thing,' her mother had said when they were looking at swatches of material for the curtains. 'I'm impressed.'

'That's because I never had to compete with you – I always loved anything you did in our house, apart from that Cabbage Patch Doll wallpaper and duvet cover you imposed on me when I was growing up.'

'I thought they were sweet.'

'No, they weren't. Those dolls were scary with their floppy, oversized heads. I used to imagine that they'd come alive and eat me during the night.'

'Wait until you have your own and we'll see what you inflict on them,' she'd laughed.

It had been at her mum's suggestion that she'd taken Danielle in as a flatmate while she was studying for her master's. June used to hold her breath every time Danielle arrived back with an excited, 'Wait until you see what I got today, June. You'll love it,' before producing her latest newspaper-wrapped *objet trouvé* from a crumpled polythene bag.

Without any encouragement at all, Danielle managed to turn her room into a haven of reclaimed, previously loved and often discarded shabby-chic jots and tittles. Many of these were of dubious origin, often things she'd found in skips, scrounged, or bought in charity shops and at car-boot sales.

'Gold spray paint is the answer to everything,' she'd say as she transformed old picture frames, a wicker washstand and a wobbly bedside locker. By the time she left and went out into her own place, the bedroom she had occupied looked like a fortune-teller's booth, with colourful drapes, tie-died curtains on the four-poster bed, rag rolled walls, garlands of fairy lights along the mantelpiece, and dusty dream-catchers dangling from the window casing.

In complete contrast, June and her mother had tried to keep the period feel of the house everywhere else – with all the modern conveniences that had come along since it had been built one hundred and fifty years earlier. The result was a very sophisticated space, but with June's personality stamped all over it. Her artwork was modern, and so too were the rugs, with big brave slashes of colour on them. She had accessorised with quirky lighting, masses of bold cushions and throws.

Her mother had suggested June take her dad's piano, but she'd been adamant. 'No, Mum, but you must start playing that again. I haven't heard you play since Dad died and that's not healthy. I notice you haven't had any of your musical evenings either. Why not?'

'I'm too busy to organise them.'

'But why don't you play any more?'

'Sitting there where your dad used to makes me too sad. It's that room, I still feel him in there.'

'Then it's about time we changed it. As soon as we've finished here, let's give your sitting room a revamp, move things around and give a new feel to it.'

'Yes. Maybe. But you still should have a piano of your own. I promise I'll start playing again if you take your dad's one – I'll get a smaller one. The baby grand will look fabulous in the drawing room and it'll be out of direct sunlight too.'

'OK, but be warned my mission is to get you back playing and back with your musical group as soon as possible. It'll be good for you.'

June also inherited the grandfather clock that stood in the hallway. It had come from her grand-mother's house. When she'd been younger, she'd been lifted up to it to reach for the key that was kept on the top. It was inclined to lose a minute or two each day, but she had got used to it and it never bothered her any more. She always felt safe when she heard it strike, no matter what the hour, and she always found herself counting the chimes. That clock kept her company, speeding along with her moods and creeping slowly at other times when she willed it to go faster – and going faster is what she wanted right now. She hadn't seen Peter for almost seven weeks but it seemed much longer.

Peter wouldn't be with her until about eight, so June had shopped on her way home from work. She spent time setting the table and changing the bed linen. She showered and put on some of the sexy new underwear she'd bought in France. Then she slipped into a low-cut black dress. She looked at herself in the mirror and was very happy with what she saw.

She kept remembering that she'd told Peter to propose again when she got back. She wasn't sure if he'd take that suggestion literally and ask her tonight, or wait until The Pink Pepper Tree was ready for its grand reopening. Then again, as that was now going to be delayed maybe he'd do it on her thirtieth birthday, in a few weeks' time. She was ready for the next step and very excited to become Mrs June Braga.

CHAPTER 5

He arrived with an armful of flowers, his cheerful smile causing a wave of desire to bubble inside her.

'Lilies, I love them. Thank you. God, I've missed you,' she said, reaching for him. He smelled familiar, with just a hint of the zesty after-shave she'd given him lingering on the collar of his linen jacket. Peter was a natty dresser, doing casual with a continental flair that many Irish men never quite managed to achieve. He was a good deal taller than her and he made her feel safe beside him.

'Me too. You look sensational. That suntan and the hair, it's different,' he said, nuzzling her. 'I like it, it really suits you.'

She thought he looked tired, although she knew travelling could do that to people. They kissed and hugged and it felt so good that, for a minute, she thought about turning off the cooker and taking him straight up to her bedroom, but he put paid to that idea when he said, 'I'm starving, and something smells really inviting.'

She put the lilies in a vase, arranging them loosely, and checked her handiwork. She started to find their perfume overbearing and cloying. White flowers energised a room, she'd read somewhere, but tonight they wouldn't need flowers to do that and they certainly added a touch of elegance to the sideboard.

They had so much to tell each other. Over the meal, which had followed a French theme, they caught up on how his parents were doing and the progress at the restaurant, on her trip, meeting Froggie and living the high life in Monte Carlo.

'I'm not sure if I remember him exactly, I think I do. But is Danielle seriously interested in him?'

'She won't admit it, but I think she is. She's different around him, in a good way I mean. Does that make sense?'

He nodded. 'And do you approve?'

'Definitely. He's such a regular guy, unlike some of her freaks. I sometimes thought she went out with some of them just to shock me. Do you remember that fellow who lived in the caravan – the new-age traveller who had five kids? You asked him if they were all his and he told you they weren't, that he worked for a condom company and they were the customers' complaints.'

'How could I forget? He was a real weirdo and he stank of garlic, if I remember rightly.'

'And wacky baccy too. He had a tattoo on each hand saying left and right.' They laughed as they remembered.

'I'll have to remind her of him one of these days,' she said.

'I must seem very dull and one-dimensional compared to all that.'

'No one could ever say that about you. You have it all – charm, personality, looks, sex appeal and, of course, a half-demolished restaurant,' she said with a cheeky grin. 'What more could any gal want?' She reached over and kissed him. 'And I love you, Mr Braga so much. Now, let's have dessert.'

He helped her as he told her about the delays and about his architect going on holiday right in the middle of everything.

'What's his replacement like?'

'She's called Zoe. She's tall, with short spiky hair and . . .'

'I meant as an architect. Does she like the concept?'

'She certainly gives the impression she does. She's very hands-on and is always around to oversee everything.'

'Do the workers mind?'

'Not at all, she seems to be quite a hit with them. Two days before we closed, the new kitchen equipment arrived on schedule – the original schedule – right before lunchtime, but we were still up and running and had nowhere for it, so I had to send it back for them to store. The delivery guys were getting stroppy about the waste of time and money but she appeared by chance and, within minutes, they were loading it all back again on their truck, all talk of extra charges forgotten.'

June made coffee and as they waited for it to percolate, he said, 'She had a great suggestion – she saw the paintings you did for me of The Pink Pepper Trees at home and she thinks that we should put a stained glass window of them at the return of the stairs.'

'I like the sound of that. It would look fabulous with sun shining through and you could backlight it from outside at night time. It would give the place a real sense of identity.'

'I knew you'd agree. I copied your originals and gave them to her to get some drawings done up for it.'

'I can't wait to see it.'

'Patience, missy, all in good time. I promise it will be worthwhile.'

They took their wine and sat on the squashy sofa, which was the setting for most of their fore-play and the scene of a lot of their amorous activity. After a while, they made their way up to the bedroom, but June couldn't shake the feeling that Peter was preoccupied. Usually, black lacy underwear and an almost non-existent wispy thong would set his pulse racing, let alone after an absence of six weeks. Her body was fit, toned and tanned and she was feeling very sexy too. He climaxed quickly – too quickly – and unusually, made no effort to satisfy her.

'I'm sorry, love, I didn't realise I was so tired, after the flight and everything. I probably shouldn't have waited until tomorrow to go to the restaurant, because my head is spinning with questions about what was going on while I was away and with things I need to do. I'm sorry – it's not fair on you.'

'That's understandable. You've a lot on, but you can relax now that you know your dad is back in charge at home,' she heard herself say, trying to hide her disappointment.

And she wasn't at all surprised when he said, 'I think I'll head back to my place tonight, unpack and get some things straightened out for tomorrow. Do you mind?'

She knew that she could say she did and that he'd change his mind, but she also knew him well enough to know that that wasn't fair when he'd rather be elsewhere.

'Of course not. We'll catch up during the week.'

'Thanks for cooking that lovely meal,' he said as she opened the door and he leaned over to kiss her.

'And for the flowers. Love you, Mr Braga.'

'You're not so bad yourself, Miss Cusack.'

She watched him go down the granite steps and disappear into the night. She couldn't believe it was only eleven when the clock chimed. He never went home that early. She toyed with the idea of ringing Danielle and then decided against it. She'd have to listen to her trying to decide how to play things with Froggie, who was coming to Dublin that weekend, and she just wasn't in the mood. That was a major difference between the friends. June never discussed the intimacies of her relationships with anyone.

June could still smell the cloying scent from the lilies and relegated them to the porch. She felt sapped and, deciding to leave the dishes until the morning, went to bed.

When she looked back over the next few weeks, that was when she first realised things were beginning to unravel, but she had no idea how badly or how quickly that would happen.

CHAPTER 6

June and Danielle went to Branch's for dinner the next night so she could tell them all about a trip she was planning.

'I got so envious of you pair off on your travels that I booked an escorted tour of Lake Garda and Verona and I'm off next week for ten days. I don't know anyone else on it, so that should be interesting. Who knows what sort of people I'll meet.'

She served them a delicious meal, but June wasn't hungry. She'd felt off-colour all day, in fact since the previous evening. But she needed to be with Peter, because her intuition kept telling her something wasn't quite right. She didn't know what exactly, but she also knew that they could sort it out when they were together. Or perhaps she was being stupid – maybe it was the shellfish she served the night before. She played around with the food on her plate and made her excuses to go and crash in her old room. She had no appetite for staying up late enjoying the wine and a good gossip and just wanted to sleep.

★ ★ ★

She was still feeling a bit off-colour the next morning and turned down the offer of any breakfast, but she felt much better after the walk to work. She was looking forward to the day, as they would hold the first of their wine club evenings. It was going to be great to finally get them going after all the effort everyone had put in to organising them.

The wine club, which had been the result of a brainstorming session one wet wintry day months earlier, was now getting a lot of publicity. A little piece had appeared in a weekend magazine and suddenly they found they had to turn people away. When she heard the receptionist telling someone on the phone that they were booked out and didn't keep a waiting list, she decided to talk to her bosses.

'It seems a shame to lose all those potential customers. Why don't we take the names of anyone who rings up and plan some other sort of themed event. Maybe a food and wine dinner at The Pink Pepper Tree' – she grinned – 'or we could pick a different place for each one, with a little spiel before each course on both the menu and what wines are a good match.'

'That sounds genius to me,' one of her bosses said. 'And we could ask some of our clients to give the talks, that way they'd feel they were important and they'd also get publicity and potential customers into their shops.'

The others agreed. 'We might even be able to

work together on special offers, wines of the month, seasonal food pairing and that sort of thing.'

'It'll take a bit of planning, but I think it could fly. Make a note of every enquiry and tell them we'll get back to them.'

The first wine club event was due to start at 6.30. Kelly arrived in mid-afternoon, bringing her good humour with her as she set up the tasting room.

'I'm going to make us a few sandwiches before the guests arrive. That way, if any of you want, you can enjoy a drink with something inside you.'

When June smelled the egg and onion, her stomach heaved again and, like a bolt of lightning, she realised it might not be something she had eaten that was making her feel sick. It could be much worse. She rapidly started thinking back, calculating dates. Could she be pregnant? No, she couldn't be. She hadn't slept with Peter for nearly two months.

As if some judgemental god was watching this turmoil play out, the little radio in the kitchen droned on in the background, a familiar jingle heralding the ad breaks and one they had all heard over and over: 'An unwanted pregnancy need not adversely affect your life.'

'Did you ever hear such nonsense? That ad should be banned. It must have been a man who wrote it. It probably even contravenes the trade descriptions act,' Kelly said with uncustomary vehemence. 'Of course an unwanted pregnancy affects your life. It not only affects your life, but your relationships, friendships and much more. Sometimes, it puts an end to them forever!'

'Well, I'm never going to have kids,' one of the assistants said. 'What about you, June?'

'It's definitely not on my immediate to-do list.' She forced a laugh, trying to focus.

'That ad is probably paid for by some right-wing radical group,' said JP, one of the bosses, who had three children. 'And I've done my bit. Now all I have to do is be nice to them for decades to come so they'll put me in a good nursing home when I'm gaga.'

'Charming prospect,' muttered one of the sales team.

'Every pregnancy affects your life and those around you, whether adversely or otherwise. Kids are great, but they are trouble too and they are expensive. Very, very expensive,' JP added.

'And you have a wife, JP,' said Maisie, one of the waitresses for the evening. It can't be easy for anyone doing it on her own. I wouldn't have the guts – even for a free stroller, rent allowance, a washing machine, soap powder and the children's allowance. Never.'

Her boss laughed. 'What innocence! Don't ever change, Maisie.'

June wanted to escape, to go anywhere to think – and to get a pregnancy testing kit and be alone until she knew for certain. But she couldn't. She had to put on a smiley face and greet the guests, making them feel tonight was all about them and their enjoyment.

She got through it somehow. It was deemed to be a huge success. She got a taxi home, stopping at a late-night pharmacy on the way. She took the test and cried herself to sleep when the result was a very definite positive. She phoned in sick the next morning and her boss joked, 'You weren't supposed to drink everything, you know. Only sip and spit.'

She forced a laugh. 'JP, it must have been the cheap plonk you slipped in when I wasn't looking.'

'Around here such accusations are a sacking offence. We'll see you when you feel better. There's no rush, and thanks again for last night. It seems to have been a great hit altogether. We've already had a few calls enquiring when we're having the next one.'

No matter how she tried, though, the dates didn't tally. And Peter always used protection. But she hadn't been with anyone else. Unless, unless, unless . . . the yacht. Now she dredged up every fragment, playing and replaying the evening over in her mind, but she couldn't remember clearly. She had a vague recollection of someone trying to kiss her, of pushing someone away, then nothing. If it hadn't been for the phone that she'd found in the cabin, she probably wouldn't have any recollection of it at all. It seemed so long ago.

Then she remembered the bump on the side of

her head and the bruise on her arm. Now she had an awful feeling that something had happened – and that he'd left more than a mobile phone behind. Had he forced himself on her? Had she co-operated? Had she been too drunk to resist? She felt such a fool. A hopeless, helpless fool. And she felt violated and defiled.

How could she tell Peter? Would she tell him? He'd never suspect it wasn't his. A few weeks here or there would make no difference. Babies came early and late. He was about to propose again. She was about to accept. They were going to be married. But she didn't know if she could do that to him – if she could live with such a deception. She wanted so badly to talk to Danielle, yet something stopped her. It had to stay her secret if she was to carry it off and get away with it. She could never tell anyone. Ever.

She felt she was going mad, with hundreds of unanswered – and unanswerable – questions spinning around her head.

She went for a walk and found herself making her way towards the tree-lined road that divided Herbert Park. She turned away from the squeals of the children in the playground, instead walking into the park proper. This had always been a haven, somewhere she used to go with her parents to feed the ducks when she was little; somewhere to picnic on a sunny Saturday when the office workers abandoned the neighbourhood; somewhere she'd been so often with various boyfriends.

She and Peter even had a favourite bench. She sat down there to clear her head, but couldn't think. *I need to see a doctor,* she told herself and, relieved at having made some kind of decision, walked towards a nearby clinic in the hope of getting a walk-in appointment.

Half an hour later, the young medic confirmed what she already thought – that she was about six or seven weeks gone. She needed more time to let this information ferment. She called Peter a while later and told him she had a tummy bug.

'I'll come over and mind you.'

'No, don't. I'm going to go home and try and sleep it off. I've had it for a few days and I'm feeling totally whacked. Besides, there's no point in you coming down with it too. I'll be fine by tomorrow and we can meet after work.'

'Great, but take care of yourself. If you need anything just shout and I'll be over.'

'Thanks, I will.' His thoughtfulness made her feel even more wretched.

She went to work the next day, looking pale beneath her already-fading tan, but she got through the day somehow. She was still no clearer in her mind about what to say to Peter – pretend it was his, or tell him everything. Saying nothing wasn't an option, nor could anything be gained by postponing it. Had that guy really raped her?

The wine importer where she worked in Mount Street was tucked underneath a functional office block, its shop front on ground level between a hair salon and a coffee shop. Its offices, tasting room and kitchen were on the floor above. The rest of the building was home to a publishing house, an advertising agency, two legal firms, and a small graphic design company. Those working in the various offices were a social bunch, meeting on the stairs and in the lifts, buying cappuccinos, lunching and often drinking together in the local haunts.

Peter knew some of them by now too and, as always, he waited for June outside the building where, since the smoking ban had come in, people congregated for their last nicotine bonding session of the day. He was standing by the kerbside, tanned and looking good in jeans and a checked, short-sleeved shirt. The weather was hot and sunny and everyone was making the most of it.

He spotted her and then gave her a hug.

'I've brought the stained-glass window drawings to show you,' he said, taking her hand as they walked across the bridge over the canal and into the Old Schoolhouse Bar. They stopped to admire two swans that looked at the world with an hauteur and distain that suggested they owned it, or at the very least that they knew they were the superior beings.

'I wonder how long they've been together. Don't they say swans mate for life?' June said, regretting the comment as soon as she'd said it.

'So I believe. Romantic, isn't it, that notion, especially when they all look identical. I wonder how they tell the difference. Maybe they just think they are still with the same one while they're really as lecherous an any other species.'

'Oh you cynic,' she laughed. 'You just destroyed my illusion. There was I thinking he'd die of a broken heart if anything happened to her. Let's try and find a seat outside and enjoy the nice evening.'

'The usual for you, I presume.'

'Great,' she said. Then she remembered. 'Actually no. I think I'll just have a juice – apple, please.'

'Still detoxing after spending all that time with Danielle?' he asked.

'Not quite. The tummy's still a bit off. Although we did do our best to help the French economy in our own little way.'

He turned to go inside, then hesitated for a minute. 'June, there's something I need to tell you.'

'And there's something I need to tell you too.'

'Revelations? OK. Hold the thought. I'll get the drinks first.'

She wondered what he needed to tell her – probably that the restaurant was running over budget, or over time again. She knew it was a hugely costly undertaking, never mind the losses he was incurring by being closed for a month, but he was shrewd. He'd done his homework and he knew what to expect – from that quarter at any rate.

He came back outside and put the glasses on the table. 'Right, now, ladies first, what did you want to tell me?'

'No, you said it first, so you go first,' she insisted, buying time, not sure if she could actually lie now that she was face to face with him.

'Well . . . OK. This is very difficult, June, but I've, eh, I think I've met someone . . . and, eh, I really like her. Nothing's happened, but I wanted to be honest with you and tell you before anything does. I owe you that.'

Her focus shifted. *He's met someone. Who? When?* She felt disconnected, dizzy as a new layer of confusion descended on her. She felt like she was going to faint.

Peter didn't notice her reaction, intent on getting out what he needed to say. 'I never intended this to happen and I'm a bit shocked by the intensity of it all. It's Zoe, the architect who is working on the project with me.'

June felt the blood drain from her face and a pounding in her head and chest, before she slumped back in her chair. Peter jumped up and caught her, preventing her sliding off it.

When she came to, Peter was on his hunkers by her knees. 'June, you fainted. Are you all right?' People moved away, back to their tables. 'Should we get you to a doctor?'

'No, I'm fine, Peter. Really, I'm fine. I'm just pregnant.' She looked at him.

It was his turn to blanch. 'Pregnant – is it

ours . . . mine, I mean? Of course it is. Forget I said that.'

'Yes, it's yours . . . ours.' She searched his face for . . . she didn't know what.

Although the stream of rush-hour traffic droned by and the buzz of chatty drinkers surrounded them, they were locked in a bubble of incredulous silence. He had a strained look on his face.

This was not going at all as she'd hoped. She'd wanted to talk to him. Read the reaction in his eyes. See how he really felt about the news – even tell him about her fears. Maybe he would be willing to rear someone else's child. Out of love and loyalty. Or would he see it as the ultimate betrayal? He would make a great father. But what had he said about Zoe? Was it too late? Had she lost him anyway?

But it was out now and June didn't know how to take it back.

'Well – I wasn't expecting that.'

'What were you saying about Zoe?'

'That's not important now. Let's get you home. We can talk there.'

He flagged a taxi. June nodded and sank grate-fully into the back seat, still feeling a little weak. He took her hand but they said nothing on the short journey back to Raglan Road.

'Forget what I said about Zoe. It didn't mean anything at all.' He made tea and sat down beside her. 'A baby. That wasn't what I expected to hear, but heck, we'll be great parents – what with your good looks and charm and with our business acumen, this little one will have to be a winner.'

She smiled at him.

He hesitated before suggesting, 'Perhaps we should get married now.'

'No. Definitely not now. Not because of this.'

'But it's what we planned . . . You promised you'd put me out of my misery and say yes next time.'

'Ah, but have you the ring with you this time?' she teased.

He laughed. 'I knew I'd forgotten something, but I'm telling you now, when I turn up with it, there'll be no excuses.'

'I'll keep you to that. I wasn't expecting this to happen either, and I'm still in shock, if I'm being truthful. And I'm feeling wretched. What was I like, making an eejit of myself, swooning like a helpless female in a Jane Austen novel? What did they call it back then – having a touch of the vapours?'

'Something like that. Are you sure you're feeling better?'

'Yes. But what did you mean about Zoe?

'It was nothing. Call it a moment's madness. A flirtation brought on by working long hours and very closely with someone – and the fact that you were so far away. Nothing happened between us. I promise you. Nothing at all. Not even a kiss,' he assured her, stroking her arm.

'I'm glad to hear it. Now, I'd just like to lie

down and be on my own for a bit. Please, let's talk tomorrow.'

'If you're sure.'

'I am. I haven't told anyone yet, and I'd like to keep it that way for the moment.'

'Of course. And I am truly delighted. Me a dad! Can you just imagine it?'

'Yes, I can. It's me being a mother that I'm finding harder to get my head around, and how a tiny speck of humanity can make a grown woman feel so goddamn awful. I now know why those lilies got to me when you brought them the other night. Their scent nearly overpowered me.'

'Are you sure you don't want me to stay with you?'

She shook her head. 'No, I'll be fine. I just need to lie down.'

A while later, she noticed he had forgotten to take his drawings with him from the hall table. Curiosity made her bring them into the dining room where she unfurled the scroll and spread the pages out. She had been surprised and flattered that he'd shown Zoe the sketches and watercolours she had done when she was in Portugal with him. But she was more astounded by the perfection of the details they hoped to achieve in glass. There was elegance in the long multi-pronged leaves as they tumbled from the branches. The contrast between these and their tightly packed bunches of peppers that ranged from the palest baby pink to rosy red was so dramatic. The leaded lines breaking up the sections on the pen and ink drawings even further enhanced their depiction. She could almost smell their woodiness and could see Peter and herself sitting under the largest one on his family's estate, where his grandfather used to go every evening to look out over the ranch and to have an illicit smoke away from his wife's judgemental eyes.

She still remembered the first time she saw these sprawling evergreens in Alentejo, some with little white flowers all over them, others laden down with berries. They weren't the most spectacular trees, but they had a majesty about them that enchanted her, as Peter had promised her they would. She had filled a whole sketchpad with them, and with the vagaries of the patterns in the fantastic bark on the cork trees, taking time to paint them while everyone took siestas. Peter's family had even had a large one framed and it hung in the hallway of their home. Would she ever go back there again? she wondered. Would she have long, girly chats with his sister and try Rosa's new wines? Or go riding out together on their Lusitano horses? To do that, she'd have to deceive the whole Braga family, convince them that her child was their flesh and blood. Could she do that and get away with it? She didn't know if she could, but what was the alternative? This was getting more and more complicated by the minute.

She had got on with his mother from the very first moment. She had never lost her Kildare lilt and was thrilled that her son had found himself a nice Irish girl. 'One who understands our ways,' she used to laugh. 'Who knows why I can't eat dry bread with olive oil, but why I have to have butter on it – always – and preferably Kerrygold.'

Yet who would ever know or even suspect that Peter had nothing to do with her child? He or she would grow up in an idyllic world, with doting grandparents, the first grandchild on either side, at home in both Portugal and Ireland, and he or she would be surrounded by genuine love.

If she told him the truth and tried to raise it on her own would that be fair to the child knowing what he or she could have had if she said nothing? She knew she'd never tell the real father – she didn't even know his name or where he was. But she'd know. She'd always know.

And what was this Zoe woman to Peter? Where did she fit into the equation? He said nothing had happened – it was only a flirtation, but could it be more? Maybe her heightened hormones were reading signs that weren't there. Should she ask Peter about it again or not mention it? She wouldn't give him up that easily – she loved him so much and he was worth fighting for. But before she could do anything, she had to sort her head out. Who would have thought her dream holiday could have turned into such a nightmare?

She needed so badly to talk to someone. Who could you trust with such a secret?

★　　★　　★

Peter was back in his apartment before he realised he'd left the window drawings in June's place. Normally a man who was in control of life, everything seemed to have shifted and very quickly, and he felt that he was treading on quicksand.

The news that June was pregnant was great, now that it had sunk in, and he'd be a good dad, like his own father and grandfather. Family was important to him. What wasn't good was the timing, or the fact that he had developed feelings for Zoe, very strong visceral feelings, and he knew they were reciprocated, even though they hadn't acted on them, yet. When they were in a room together the sexual tension was palpable and he didn't know how to turn it off. Was there a default setting that would re-programme him to where he had been just a few weeks earlier? Something to delete these new feelings and wants, as though they had never existed? She'd only come into his life by chance, but she had blasted her way into his consciousness and senses in a way that had never happened him before. Before he could even see her, he could feel her presence when she walked on to the site. He'd wanted to ask her out almost as soon as he'd met her, to take her home and make love to her, again and again, but loyalty and love – because he did love June – made him hold back. He knew absolutely nothing about who Zoe was, while everything he knew about June he loved. Was lust stronger? They'd had numerous coffees amid the building debris and he had told her he was in a long-term relationship and wouldn't make any move until he'd spoken to June in person about his feelings. Zoe said she'd wait forever if it meant they could be together.

She tried to kiss him, but he stepped back. 'No, I have to do this properly and honestly, and it's not going to be easy. I have to tell June first. She deserves that.'

As he tried to calm his feelings, he thought again about how quickly everything had changed. Only three weeks before Zoe came along, he'd told June he'd ask her to marry him when she returned – and he'd meant it. 'With all my heart,' he said to himself softly. Then he'd decided to wait until her thirtieth and do it properly. And the ring – a diamond cluster with a pink diamond in the centre – was still in the jeweller's in Grafton Street, waiting for his decision. 'I would never have thought of myself as being a fickle type.'

Although nothing had happened with Zoe, things were definitely different the other night when he'd been with June. He'd kept thinking what it would be like to be lying there with Zoe instead, wondering what she'd be like to make love to. *Would it be more exciting or the same? Does familiarity with a lover's body mean that hot sex becomes a little less hot – maybe even a little pedestrian?* He'd never thought like this before. June had always been enough for him – he loved her curves and what she did for him – what they did together – so why this? Why now? *Why do Zoe's gamine face, her boyish figure, her blue eyes, her laugh and her spiky hair keep coming in to my mind, all the time?*

He knew he'd left June unsatisfied the night he'd got home and it didn't make him feel good. He used tiredness as an excuse, but who was he making excuses to – June or himself? He'd needed to get home to think. He wanted to call Zoe now, explain, hear her voice, but he stopped himself. She knew he had been going to tell June and she was waiting for him to call. He'd wait and see her the following day and tell her what had happened. He had decisions to make, one way or another, and whatever he decided, he knew that someone was going to get hurt.

In the shower, he resolved to put Zoe out of his mind, forget he'd ever met her. When the work was finished, he wouldn't have to see her again and life could get back to normal. In fact, as soon as Matt got back from holiday the following Monday, she'd be off the job. Then it would be just him and June, as it had been – but with a baby of their own on the way. Zoe would have to stay as his guilty fantasy.

A dad. He couldn't really believe it. He couldn't wait to tell the folks, and Rosa. Aunt Rosa. She'd be thrilled, but a promise was a promise. He knew a lot of women were superstitious about telling anyone until the first twelve weeks had passed, so he'd hold his peace for a bit and spoil June in the meantime. She looked wrecked.

*   *   *

June had a bath to try to relax. If she'd told Peter what had really happened, she could hardly expect that he'd want anything more to do with her, and she couldn't blame him for that. She was the one who had slept with someone else; even she knew she would never have done that willingly. Had that Scandinavian spiked her drink or forced himself on her? Had he raped her or had she complied? Had she been capable of that? She tossed and turned in bed all night, trying to imagine life on her own with a baby. That had never been on her agenda and certainly was not now, not at this stage. She saw the chances of furthering her career disappearing fast. The wine world and babies were not exactly mutually inclusive, at least not for a single mum.

She saw herself having to call on her mother when the child was sick and when she couldn't take time off work to mind it. But her mother had her own very busy life and that wouldn't always suit. It wouldn't be fair either. If she decided to do it on her own, the child would be her responsibility and hers alone. She could always get an au pair, even though that would be abdicating part of her role. She wanted any child of hers to have what she had – two loving parents, security and happiness. She saw early-morning crèche runs and irate bosses when she had to leave in the middle of meetings.

She worried that she'd end up resenting the child. That must happen to some people surely, she reasoned, and that wouldn't be fair either. She was gripped with a very real fear of the unknown and her heart thumped with anxiety. She only slept for a few hours that night and dragged herself up the next morning, feeling even more wretched.

She went to work late and, as luck would have it, her bosses had asked Kelly in to cover for a few days. Most of the staff had gone outside to eat lunch by the canal, taking advantage of another balmy day. Kelly was working through and leaving early, so she heated a bowl of soup in the microwave to tide her over. As soon as June smelled it cooking, she had to run to the bathroom.

When she returned, Kelly looked at her and said, 'Forget the tummy bug – my money's on you being pregnant.'

June knew sometimes it was prudent to keep your mouth tightly zipped and she just sat staring back at her colleague, saying nothing, but her tears let her down.

'I'm sorry, June. I shouldn't have said that. Me and my big gob. I won't say anything to anyone. You have my word on that.'

'Kelly, I have never known anyone with a smaller gob. Your middle name is discretion, but thank you. I've only found out and it's very complicated, not to say the last thing in the world I expected or even wanted to happen. I'm so mixed up.'

'It often happens that way. I became pregnant at sixteen,' she announced.

'I had no idea.' June didn't even know Kelly was a mother.

'No one in here has. I lived in Cork then. In fact, I don't talk about it. I have a daughter. She has two children of her own now, which is why I've decided to make the trip to Australia this year, to meet my grandkids. That's where she is. I'm hoping she'll understand me a bit better, now that she's a mum herself.'

'Oh . . .'

'I'm telling this back ways.'

'Is that why you were so angry at that radio ad the other day? I had just – literally just – put two and two together, and worked out why I felt sick.'

'That ad always makes me see red. My pregnancy not only changed my life, adversely and otherwise, but it changed the lives of those around me.'

June wanted to ask how and why, and a hundred other questions, but she knew Kelly well enough not to push her. If she said nothing, she might learn more. Already this information was more than Kelly usually volunteered.

'But you managed?'

'Yeah, with great difficulty, and with loads of guilt. My parents stood by me, partly because they knew the father's family and hoped we might eventually get married and make it all all right in their, and in everyone else's, eyes. Obviously that never happened and he eventually disappeared into the sunset.'

'Were you together for long before . . .?'

'Not at all. I only did it with him for bravado. It was after a school disco and only because the others in my class were always boasting and talking about how great it was to lose their virginity. I felt they were laughing at me because they knew I still hadn't. I was terrified – and it was a disaster. I didn't even like the guy. He had braces on his teeth and spots and he smelled of sweat and beer. I still hate the smell of beer. I also believed that it was impossible to conceive the first time you did it.'

'I remember hearing that old wives' tale too. You must have been devastated when you realised.'

'I was, because the school wanted me to leave – "a wanton, wayward child, flaunting bad example in front of the other pupils" was how they put it to my parents. They had a school board and council meeting and a vote. I only managed to get back in by a majority of two, but did they let me know that I was there under sufferance. It was dreadful. There was one teacher who was brilliant. She used to tell me to hold my head high, get my exams and thumb my nose at them all when I did better than everyone else. So that's what I did.'

'How did your parents take it?'

'They had married late so they were getting on – I had been a change-of-life surprise for them. So when I broke the news, it was just too much. After the shock and their disappointment in me

103

had settled, and when Cara was born, they were really brilliant. They were besotted with her when she was tiny, and they were relieved about me finishing school too. I should have moved out, but I had no money. I couldn't even drive back then so I was totally dependent on them for everything. I felt smothered and resentful and angry, all the time, even though I loved her to bits. Then Mam had a bad stroke when Cara was about eighteen months old. I had just started at Crawford Art College in Cork, but I had to give that up to look after them both.'

'That must have been very rough,' June said.

'It was. My father really resented me, what I had put them through. He blamed me for Mam's condition. She was never the same again. Every single day, he told me things like, "This is not how I visualised my retirement. Your mother and I should be enjoying ourselves, without these worries and extra responsibilities," and "I saw us being free: free to travel and do all the things we had looked forward to. God knows I worked hard all my life – and for what – this? We deserve better. Now look at her, not able to do anything for herself." I can still hear him.'

'But that wasn't your fault. That was a bit unfair.'

'Rationally I knew it was unfair, but I always felt it was partly true too. If someone says something often enough to you, you begin to believe it. I was trapped. So was he. So was Mam. I couldn't leave. Cara hated the fighting, the snide remarks and the bitterness. She often told me I should have aborted her. That hurt. We didn't get on at all as she grew up, especially in her teen years when my father got tetchy with her all the time too. After Mam died, he constantly badgered her not to end up like me. She got out as soon as she could, and I couldn't blame her. I did my best to give her a happy childhood, but it seemed as though everything conspired against us along the way.'

'Are you closer now?'

'It's hard to say. She got a visa and did nursing in Sydney. Then she married without telling me, and that hurt. She's only been home once, but she does email more often now than she used to, and she says she can't wait to see me. Luckily, I'm staying with some cousins, so if it doesn't work out I have a safety valve. Isn't that a dreadful thing to say about my own daughter?'

'No, Kelly, in the circumstances, I think it's totally understandable. But you know she'll have matured a lot in the years she's been abroad, and with her own children, your grandchildren, you'll have much more to bond over. I'm sure it will be just fine.'

'I really hope you're right. I still feel I let her down and think that I could have done things differently, how I'm not too sure. So you can see why I get mad every time I hear that commercial about unwanted pregnancies and I wonder how many young girls who were like me are listening to it thinking, it won't necessarily change anything. It makes me want to shout at the radio. It should say an unwanted pregnancy is just that – unwanted – and it changes your life forever, and do you know what, it changes other people's attitudes to you too. So be prepared for anything.'

'Surely not in this day and age . . .' said June.

'Oh, I don't mean they are judgemental or anything like that, although some probably still are, but I was never free to go out with my friends, so they kind of melted away then. People get tired of including you when you have excluded yourself, and having a child at the wrong time can do that. Especially when you're young. In the beginning, the baby was a novelty among my mates and everyone loved passing her around, cuddling her and buying presents for her. But when she started getting wilful and more demanding, even meeting the girls for coffee became difficult. They didn't have the patience for tantrums and terrible twos. One of my friends said having Cara was the best contraception any of them had, and she was right too.'

They laughed at that. June wanted to tell her about her predicament, and how she had told Peter the baby was his, but some of the others arrived back from lunch and the moment was lost.

'As Shakespeare said, quite inappropriately in this case, "Mum's the word", but your secret's safe with me,' Kelly whispered, taking her soup bowl to the sink. Later, before she left, she passed by June's desk and slipped her a piece of paper with her number on it. 'Ring me if you want to. If not, we never had that conservation earlier on, OK?'

'OK.' She smiled and felt like hugging Kelly, realising her support had come from the most unexpected source. 'Thank you, Kelly. You'll never realise how much that means to me.'

CHAPTER 7

Zoe was at the restaurant early the next day. 'Well, what did you think? Did you like the outlines for the window? Aren't they fantastic?'

'Zoe, I haven't seen them yet. I'm sorry. I had other things on my mind. I left them in June's last night, but I'll look at them later and give you a ring about them tomorrow.'

'We need to make a quick decision because some of those coloured glasses may have to be ordered in from Hungary or Italy and that can sometimes slow things down a bit, and it is a big window,' she said, looking at him intently. He felt she could see the turmoil in his soul. He turned away and busied himself with some inconsequential work. This was going to be harder than he had thought. He went back into his office and phoned June.

'Hi, how are you feeling today?'

'So long as I don't have to see or smell food I'm fine. How are you? Still shell-shocked?'

'Yes, a bit, but in a good way. I can't get my mind around us being parents yet, and it's hectic

108

here, but in a good way too. I left those sketches behind me.'

'I know. I looked at them. They're really beautiful. I love them – you can almost smell the woody aroma. They are very lifelike.'

'Can I pop over and collect them later?' He was suddenly aware that Zoe had followed him and he cut the conversation short. 'We can have a chat then, love. I can't really talk now. I'll come and meet you after work.' He hung up.

'I thought that maybe we could have a talk too,' Zoe said.

'I told you, I'll let you know tomorrow, but they get the thumbs-up from June, by the way. She loves them.'

'I didn't mean about work. I meant about us. I know you feel the chemistry too. I know we have a real connection. Did you tell June about us?'

'In a way, yes, but there is no "us", and there never will be. June is pregnant, as I'm sure you deduced from the phone call you just overheard.'

She pretended she hadn't. 'What? How do you know it's yours?'

'Because I know June.'

'Did she tell you that before you told her about me or afterwards?'

He paused for a minute before answering. 'After.'

'Don't be such a fool then. Tell her to go to hell. She's trying to hold on to you.'

'Be realistic, Zoe. She's not like that. You have

to understand there can be no "us". You must realise that. I'm sorry—'

'Sorry. You're sorry. So am I. I thought there was something much more between us than a professional entanglement. I was prepared to wait until you told your girlfriend, no matter how long that took. You know, I'm not sure which is worse – the lying, cheating bastards I've attracted in the past, or someone with principles! Lots of women trap men by getting – or pretending to be – pregnant. It doesn't work. Have it your way and I hope you won't live to regret it.' She walked out and slammed the door behind her.

So do I, he thought, before pushing that notion away as best he could. This was his June they were talking about and he knew that she wasn't pretending. June didn't do subterfuge.

Peter had wanted to own a restaurant ever since he was little, though his friends had thought he was weird. When they were outside throwing shapes and practising their cartwheels for when they'd score goals for Portugal and earn millions in fees and transfers, he'd be found in the big farmhouse kitchen in Alentejo pestering Isabel their housekeeper to show him how to skin rabbits or stuff birds, make pastry and identify the subtleties of the olive oil that they produced. When he came to his Irish family, he did the same, following his grandmother around asking questions about food and recipes, and watching her cook. She even bought him a giant-sized chef's hat when he was twelve and photographed him in front of the Aga with a tray of cakes. He still had the photograph in his apartment. They had all dismissed his interest as a fad, until he started protesting about having to stay at school. He argued it was a waste of time when he could be learning his craft. It was his Portuguese grandfather who got around him eventually. They were sitting in his spot, under the shade of the oldest and biggest pink pepper tree, looking out over the olive groves, and Peter was denuding one of the drooping branches of its berries, avoiding eye contact in his defiance as he listened to the old man he adored.

'Stay at school and do a business studies course, then follow your dreams. You'll have my blessing and a much greater chance of success if you know how to run your operation, all of it, not just the kitchen. If you rush things, you'll end up working for someone else all your life. Do you hear me, son?' Peter had reluctantly agreed that he had a point. 'Now get back inside and do your homework and make me proud of you. I want to smoke my pipe and I can't let your grandmother see me.'

Peter was used to this charade played by both his grandparents. She knew his grandfather smoked but pretended she didn't – he knew he couldn't fool her but still he pretended to. Lately, his father had taken to doing the same because his mother hated the smell of his pipe around the house.

As he waited for June, he wished his grandfather

were still around to see how he was growing the business he'd helped him start. He'd been so proud when he opened up first in a much smaller place in a not so fashionable part of town. Of course he had been right in his advice. He always was, but the older man never rubbed that in. Peter hoped he'd garner as much wisdom as he had along the way.

'What would you like to do, go somewhere for a bite to eat?' he asked June when they met.

'I really couldn't face eating right now and you're going to end up looking like a greyhound hanging around with me if I continue to be off my food. But do you know what I'd love to do – see the work in progress. I know you wanted it to be a surprise, but I'd really rather see it as it goes along.'

'As you wish, missy. Let's head. You know me, any excuse to go back there and keep an eye on my baby – my other baby!' He laughed. 'Up to now, it's been the most important – well, after you, that is – the most important thing in my life and now, well, now it's slipped down another notch. I still can't believe it, you know.' He enveloped her in a huge hug and kept his arm around her as they walked.

June revelled in the closeness of him. It felt so right being there, close enough to feel the heat of his body through his jacket, smell his warmth and feel cosseted and comforted by the familiarity of his nearness.

It has to get easier as it goes along, this deception business, June told herself, trying to visualise what life would be like without Peter in it. Surely she couldn't be the first woman to have done this.

They arrived at the scaffolded site. The door in the temporary screening was unlocked.

'That's odd,' he said. 'I'm sure I snapped that shut when I left.' He pushed the door tentatively and shouted, 'Anyone there? Hello?'

A female voice came from the top of the stairs.

'Hi, there, it's only me.'

'You left the door open – I could have been anyone walking in and helping myself to tools and equipment.' June could see he was annoyed. 'Stay there till I get some light, June. The floor has holes all over it and there's stuff everywhere.'

'Some of the tile samples were delivered to the office today and I thought I'd drop them off. There's another lot outside in the car,' Zoe said, coming down the stairs. She walked past them with barely a nod in June's direction.

June was delighted to have a chance to see the woman who had become her competition. Peter made no attempt to introduce them. He threw a switch and random bare bulbs created eerie pools of hostile light, throwing shadows around the premises. 'It's not the grand illumination I was envisaging, so you'll have to use your imagination.'

Zoe came back, struggling under the weight of

her load. Peter went towards her. 'Give that to me. I'll bring it up,' he said, taking the box.

'You know, that's the easiest part of our job,' Zoe said, standing beside June, looking her over. 'I'm Zoe by the way. You must be June. As I was saying, the easiest part of our job is being able to visualise what our clients never can. Then it's just a matter of making sure they know we can carry it off for them. Most of them haven't a clue, although Peter seems to be the exception. He shows great vision. He knows what he wants and why he wants it. He's so easy to work with.'

June said nothing. *Don't rise to the bait,* she told herself, as she sensed there was a subliminal thread. Zoe was not just talking about the building work, and subtle she certainly wasn't. June eyed the now vast dusty space with its trailing wires, exposed supports, half-recessed power points and boarded up window spaces. She knew every nook and cranny in the original part, and it was here, in the wee small hours after everyone had gone home, that she had listened to Peter tell her of his dreams of enlarging; where together they had plotted and planned the new premises right down to the last detail. They had often made love in here too, but Zoe didn't need to know that. Peter knew and that was enough.

June picked up a hard hat and stuck it on her head and started to walk about. The patio furniture was stacked drunkenly in the conservatory, its cushions covered with heavy-duty polythene sheets. Peter had offered it to a local retirement home and they were delighted to accept. Now it was awaiting collection. Otherwise there were few traces of the old interior.

Zoe went back up to the office and June fumed at her proprietorial attitude to both Peter and the job. She played it cool and pottered about a bit before deciding to follow them. In the cavernous space, the voices echoed from above and she heard Peter say, 'No, Zoe, don't do that. I told you, no. There can't be an "us". Not now. Never. You have to understand that. Will you please leave?'

'What about the window?'

'I'll discuss it with Matt when he gets back on Monday.'

'I already emailed him and asked him if I could take this job over from him,' Zoe said. 'As I am already so involved—'

'I think that was taking quite a liberty. That decision is mine to make, not yours. Now, will you please go?'

'OK. But the tiles?' she pushed.

'We'll have a look at them later. I'm leaving these decisions to June. She's the one who selected these samples and this place is as much hers as mine, or soon will be.'

'Has she any experience in these things? These decisions should not be left to wannabe decorators. Surely even you can see this sort of thing will be completely outside her comfort zone.'

Pretending she hadn't heard a word, June called, 'Can I come up?'

'Of course. Zoe is just leaving. And be careful on those stairs. They're very gritty.'

Zoe muttered goodbye and Peter never mentioned her again as he spent the next hour showing June all the changes. June was watching for any nuance that might betray what she'd overheard or what Peter was feeling. But she couldn't find any. They eventually went back to her place and studied the stained glass window plans together.

After a take-away, from which she only managed the prawn crackers, he said, 'I'm out of my depth here. I don't know how to behave around a pregnant woman. Can we make love? Do you feel like it or what?' He laughed.

She laughed back at him. 'If I said it's total abstinence for the next seven or eight months, do you think I'd be able to keep my hands off you and stick to that?'

'I should certainly hope not.' He reached over and kissed her, deeply, before leading her to the bedroom, where they made tender love, without the usual passion and zest. She put it down to her condition and to the turmoil she felt. She tried, unsuccessfully, to keep Zoe out of her mind for any length of time. She felt she was being stalked by this creature she had hardly even heard of and who was now in the bed between them, as real as if she was physically there. Did Peter wish she was, instead of her? Would he have been

116

with her now if she hadn't told him about the baby?

Her mother was going off on her Italian adventure, and June insisted she'd take her to the airport. It was an early start and she left Peter sleeping. She wished she could have told her everything and asked for her advice. Her mother was wise and had the ability to see around problems and ahead of them, to what might be farther down the line, rather than taking fire brigade action any time anything went wrong. She would have loved a big family but had lost several babies in the first term of pregnancy. This was a cruel irony as there were dozens of young women and men walking around Dublin who had been called Brendan and Brenda after her late husband, by grateful mothers whom he had helped bring to full term and safe delivery.

If she knew what her daughter was struggling with, she would examine and analyse all the avenues open to her and their consequences, and advise her. But how would she advise her? What would she want June to do?

When she got back Peter had gone. He'd left a note. *Pick you up later, around 7. P X*

Froggie was in Dublin that weekend and they had all arranged to meet up. Danielle was unusually subdued about the prospects. 'I'm actually nervous about seeing him. It feels different, here on home turf, than being away in the glitzy glam of Monte

117

Carlo. And it feels like a date, which I'm sure is not how he's visualising it.'

'Is that how you want it to be?'

'Deffo . . . well, I think so.'

'It's bound to be different. Real people don't live like that all the time. It's easier to see someone's true colours out of the sort of spotlight we were all caught up in. And now that you've had some distance you can see him with a bit of perspective. And you don't know how he's looking at it either, so chill and play it all cool. Let's just concentrate on having a good night.'

'How's the tum? You still look a bit peaky,' Danielle said.

'This bug kind of knocked the stuffing out of me, but I'm getting there,' she lied.

When they met, the guys did remember each other, and chatted as though they were old mates.

'I hear you're doing a big renovation on The Pink Pepper Tree,' Froggie said as they took their seats for dinner.

Delighted with a new audience, Peter expanded on his plans and June added, 'It's going to be fantastic – I was actually allowed in to see the progress yesterday and although it's early days, you can already see its potential. It's so exciting.'

'I hear you showed these ladies how the millionaires live. I hope you haven't spoiled them for ordinary mortals like me.'

'I doubt that very much. Those events are all a

bit OTT for my personal taste, but I'd be lying if I said I didn't enjoy most of it, in spite of the hard work. There's something about some of our species, that once they are given anything for nothing, they expect more and more. It doesn't matter that we'd flown them from all over the world, business and first class in many cases, put them up in the five-star hotels and on the yacht – once the goodie bags were put out on their seats, they all wanted to see what the others had got, in case they had missed out on something, or someone was getting a bigger gee-gaw than they did. I wouldn't mind, but the same greedy feckers are probably making enough in one afternoon's consultations to wing it away first class anywhere they'd like to go.'

'That's incredible,' said June.

'But true. And some of the spouses and partners are even worse. One of them who was billeted on the yacht demanded a spa treatment because those staying in the hotels had them included.'

'Are you serious?' Peter asked.

'Well, you didn't hear us complaining,' June said, excusing herself to go to the ladies' room. The plates of food being delivered to the next table had triggered her over-sensitive sense of smell and she needed to escape urgently.

'Are you in town in two weeks' time?' Peter asked Froggie while she was gone. 'June has a significant birthday and I'm gathering a few friends to help us celebrate, but she knows nothing about it. She thinks it's just the two of us, so say nothing.'

'I'll make a point of being around.'

The evening went really well and the couples parted company after the meal. June hit a wall of fatigue, which she managed to hide from Danielle, although, by this stage, Danielle would probably not have noticed if she'd fallen asleep at the table – she was as completely preoccupied with Froggie as he was with her.

As the women hugged goodnight, June whispered, 'Go for it, girl – you have my wholehearted approval!'

'As if I ever needed that!' said Danielle.

CHAPTER 8

The Macy brothers, JP and Neil, were good at what they did. They knew their wines and their business inside out. That Monday, they had started ordering the Christmas stock during their weekly strategy meeting and they took their time working through the agenda, looking at delivery dates, going over orders, scheduling vineyard visits while the harvesting was in progress. They encouraged all the staff to get involved and not to be afraid to give their opinions, whether they agreed or disagreed with anything. JP was inclined to go on a little, but Neil was well able to rein him in. The future of their wine club now seemed a certainty, but its direction was the point of a prolonged post-mortem.

As the meeting concluded, Neil asked June to stay back a few minutes. JP then surprised her by saying, 'You know it has always been our intention to expand this operation, maybe even open another outlet down the line – well, the time seems right and we'd like you to be involved.'

June hesitated, wondering what else they had to say, but they sat waiting for her reaction.

'Involved – in what way?'

'In management, maybe even a partnership later on,' Neil replied. It's obvious you have a feel for the trade. You know your wines and you know us. You're great with the suppliers and clients and you have language skills. You're a perfect fit for us.'

'I'm very flattered that you think of me like that,' she answered, 'but how do you see the role?'

'Ideally, and initially of course, we'd love to see you do more of the wine fairs and that end of things, gradually moving into buying.'

'Buying?' She was surprised. 'I'm not sure if I am ready for that just yet.'

'You're probably not,' said JP, 'but you never will be if we don't let you have your head and let you develop that nose too.'

'Is it something you'd be interested in?' asked Neil, sensing her hesitation. 'We wouldn't be throwing you in at the deep end, you know. We'd be there beside you.'

Last week she'd already have said yes without any hesitation. 'Such an opportunity was beyond her dreams. How things had changed in such a short space. What would they think of her if they knew the truth? She mustered her enthusiasm, sat up straighter and said, 'It sounds like a terrific opportunity and I'd love to give it my best shot.'

'It will mean a lot more travel, so we need to look at your salary and to set up an expense account for you.'

'It sounds better and better,' she smiled.

'And if you wanted to, down the line again, of course, we'd be willing to sponsor further studies – you might even end up as a Master of Wine.'

'That'll certainly give me something to aim towards.'

'Righto so,' said Neil. 'Have we a deal?'

'Definitely. Yes,' she answered. 'And thank you.'

'Let's shake on that,' JP said, and they did.

She couldn't wait to tell Peter, but she didn't want to do it over the phone. That afternoon, he called to say he'd been delayed at an important meeting and that he'd catch up with her later, at her place.

Danielle called her too; having spent the rest of the weekend with Froggie, she was 'bursting to tell everything'. To date, Danielle's taste in men had been ill-judged, to put it mildly. June had been an onlooker over the years, watching her being seduced by a succession of long-haired, angst-ridden, navel gazing poets and would-be artists, computer nerds, wellness and sports junkies. By comparison, Froggie was looking good – very good. He was handsome, intelligent, well mannered, witty and kind. June approved whole-heartedly. And even though she wanted to tell Danielle her own news about her promotion, she wanted to tell Peter about it first.

On impulse, she decided to take a detour on her way home and go to see him at the restaurant. If he was still tied up, she'd leave him to it and go on ahead and prepare some dinner for them. One of the workmen pointed upstairs, shouting above the din, and when she pushed the door open she was surprised to see Zoe there, in a pair of figure-hugging jeans, a tight sweater and a hard hat. She was leaning provocatively by Peter's desk, drinking coffee and laughing with him. Wasn't she supposed to be off this job since this morning now that Matt was back? But Peter didn't seem to be having any problems with her being there. It all looked very cosy, too cosy in fact. Was Zoe the important meeting that had detained him? He looked up guiltily as she came in. Or was that in her imagination? She had a distinct feeling that she was interrupting something.

'Is everything OK?' Peter asked.

'Absolutely. I just had some news for you, but it can wait till later.'

Before he could say anything, Zoe remarked, 'What an exciting life you seem to lead, June, always full of news. It makes the rest of us seem rather dull, don't you think, Peter?'

Peter must have told her about the baby. She had asked him not to tell anyone. And now, instead of defending her against Zoe's barbed comments, he just shrugged and grinned before his gaze went back to Zoe.

June wanted to tell her to get out of their lives and leave them alone, regretting her decision to come by. She was about to leave but then she thought better of it. *That supercilious little bitch – I have a right to be here – she's the one being paid to do so. I'd like to wipe that smug smile off her face.*

'That's the way it goes. The stars must be aligned in my favour these days,' June said, smiling directly at Zoe. 'I find that some people attract good vibes, others don't. Others are like leeches – they just suck the life force out of you, like vacuum cleaners. Have you ever noticed?' She was surprised at how catty she sounded and was immediately mad that she had let herself down like that. 'I'll see you in a bit, love,' she said to Peter.

'I'll walk you down those stairs,' he said. She turned back to say something, but he was already looking at Zoe with a shrug and look that said more than a casual glance should.

'I thought she was off the job,' June whispered when there was a lull in the hammering.

He steered her out on to the path. 'It's not that simple – she'd already worked on Matt to allow her stay on.'

'Who's paying for it? Haven't you ever heard the saying "he who pays the piper calls the tune", Peter? Or were you afraid he might find out why you wanted her off the project?' Before he could answer, she turned to go and he made no attempt to stop her, or give her a hug or a kiss. She was furious with him. How dare he treat her like that. She felt as though she had been dismissed and she knew he wasn't too pleased with her turning up unannounced.

She worked herself into a frenzy as she walked home from the restaurant. Peter had told her he'd get rid of her and he hadn't. She told herself one minute that she was overreacting – they were only laughing and drinking coffee. She hadn't caught them in flagrante. The next minute she put it down to hormones. But if she were being really truthful, she knew the greatest threat was coming from within herself and had nothing to do with Zoe. Her guilt – the guilt of the deception she was entering into. But even acknowledging this didn't make her feel any better.

She prepared the meal – a medley of seafood with salad that wouldn't require cooking later on. She'd only manage to eat the crusty bread anyway.

When Peter arrived, he was quieter than usual. She was still mad at him but tried to hide it. She wanted so badly to ask him why he had told Zoe about the baby. She refrained from mentioning her, but she seemed to be there in the room between them, hovering like an unpleasant odour. He didn't ask what her news was and she didn't tell him.

They rowed later that night. They were sitting together on the sofa. She snuggled up against him and he put his arm around her.

'You poor pet. It's a shame you can't enjoy eating anything, but your morning sickness will pass in a few weeks,' he said, stroking her shoulder in a comforting gesture.

'It can't happen soon enough,' she said, before

blurting out, 'So Zoe managed to get around you then?'

'I wouldn't put it like that and I fail to see why that should be a problem for you. She's right in the middle of something, and it makes sense to let her finish it.'

'What's that exactly – that she's right in the middle of – that Matt couldn't finish?'

He hesitated for a fraction too long before answering. 'Oh, it's just to do with the tiles and the wet areas. She ordered them all today. As soon as the plumbing is finished, they can begin work on those.

'Did you get the blue mirror-flecked ones that I love?'

'Actually she decided against those,' he said. 'She went for the other ones.'

June could sense a feeling of loss creep over her. He took his hand away and sat up straighter. They'd decided on those tiles before she'd gone away. She'd spent hours choosing the colour schemes and he'd told her he loved them.

'But, Peter, I don't understand. We decided on the blue mirror-flecked tiles to make the wash-rooms rooms bigger. They were to reflect the stainless steel and chrome as well as the blue through the skylights.'

He said nothing. She took his hand again, but it felt detached, there was no warmth in its response. 'The buff ones will look dreadful with those swanky black sinks. They need a contrast, otherwise the whole scheme will look dated and dull, not modern and fresh, the way we envisaged it.'

He didn't look at her as he spoke. 'Well, I'm sure Zoe knows what she's at – maybe she knows a little more about those things. I probably shouldn't have asked you to get involved in them. They're not really your area of expertise and obviously it's all a little outside your comfort zone.'

That was almost word for word the conversation she'd overheard between them the other night, although she recalled there had been the reference to a wannabe interior decorator thrown in somewhere for good measure.

She took a deep breath and said in a measured tone, 'Obviously. But, right now, Peter, so are you. W-a-y outside my comfort zone! I'm going to have an early night, so that I can be at my best within mine.'

He stood up. 'Look, I'm sorry. That came out all wrong, June. I didn't mean to hurt you. I know you put a lot of thought into it all.' She said nothing. 'Do you want me to stay?' he asked hesitantly.

'Not particularly, but that's your call.'

He stood there for a few seconds before he spoke. 'Right so, I'll head. I've an early start tomorrow.'

She didn't get up to see him out and regretted it a few minutes later. She felt empty, lonely and mean-spirited. She wished her mother wasn't away. She missed talking to Danielle, but she was still avoiding doing that, apart from several truncated, light-hearted and always-rushed phone calls. Danielle knew her too well, and she knew that she would sense straight away that something was not right. And June still hadn't made her mind up what she would tell her, if anything. It was fortunate for her that Danielle had Froggie to occupy her mind at the moment and that she hadn't seemed to notice anything amiss at all. But that wouldn't last forever.

Up to now, she'd only been able to think of one thing – being pregnant. As if that wasn't enough, now Zoe has wormed her way into her consciousness and into Peter's too. She was lodged there, like a nerve pain. Now there's the new job offer – a really good promotion, the very thing she had always envisioned in her successful imaginary future. Would she, June Cusack, really end up as a resentful single parent – the result of an assault by someone whose name she couldn't even remember, if indeed she'd ever known it. Was she destined to be an embittered jilted lover with unrealised career ambitions?

It suggested a very bleak future for her and her child, one that was as far removed from her own childhood as anyone could imagine. What a bloody mess. She got into bed and tossed and turned, but couldn't get comfortable. Why was she letting that little upstart get under her skin? What if Peter still wanted to go off with her? Where would that leave her, and the baby? She loved him with all her heart and she knew she didn't want to lose him. She couldn't bear the thoughts of that. He was worth fighting for and she'd let Zoe know what she was up against.

Remembering her dad's advice never to let the sun set on an argument, she decided to call Peter and ask him to come back. She dialled his number. But it was busy. It was also busy the five times she tried over the next half an hour. And with a woman's intuition, she knew where he'd gone for consolation. With a slow realisation, June began to come around to the fact that perhaps it was she who had the fight on her hands.

Danielle was also avoiding June, because Peter had confided in her the night they had all gone out together that he'd chosen the engagement ring and that he intended to propose properly on her birthday. Danielle knew how bad she was at keeping secrets and was afraid she'd let something slip and spoil the surprise, so she was pretending to be busy too.

'Meetings about the curriculum, training days, you wouldn't believe all the preparation, and we're not back at school for another week.'

'Let's grab a sandwich at lunchtime then. I've been offered promotion.'

'Fantastic – I hope it means lots more money,' Danielle said.

'Of course, and more travel.'

'Can't wait to hear everything.'

The lunch hour passed quickly. June realised she had never seen her friend like this about anyone before. Danielle had a glow of contentment. 'Froggie has obviously won you over,' June said.

'Maybe long-distance relationships are the answer. What does Peter think of your new job?'

'We didn't go into it in too much detail because he's up to his eyes at the moment, but you know Peter, easy-going as always. He knows that I've had to put up with the unsocial hours that come with owning a restaurant. If I do decide to go for the Master of Wine qualification, there'll be lots of study involved. Of course it'll mean compromise, but isn't that what life is all about?'

'God, I can't believe that's you talking like that – are we all growing up?'

'We sound like our mothers.' They laughed. 'And it doesn't feel so bad, does it? Now, I'd better get back to work,' June said. 'Before they rethink giving me the promotion.'

Peter didn't phone her that day and she didn't call him. She was dismayed and confused by his behaviour – she had at least tried to apologise the previous night. He hadn't.

But when he arrived that evening with her favourite chocolates and ice-cream, she was surprised and delighted, and more than a little

131

relieved. Whatever problems they were having, she was determined they'd be able to work through them.

'What can I say? I'm sorry, June, forgive me. I was a total prick and I don't deserve you. I've fired Zoe. Matt's back on the job and I want to make it up to you. I've cancelled the tiles too, by the way. I don't know what I was thinking. We're going with the ones you chose. I think I probably panicked a bit at learning I was going to be a dad and there's so much going on keeping on top of the contractors. Can you ever forgive me?'

'Is that all, Peter?' she laughed. 'That's some speech!'

'I'm really sorry. I don't know what I was thinking. We made all those plans together, not just for our restaurant, but for our future together, and nothing's going to jeopardise that now. Can you forgive me?'

He hugged her tightly, kissing her hair, and it all felt so right again. They *would* get through this. 'I can completely understand. I'm still panicking myself a little, trying to get my head around it all. It's huge, isn't it? One minute I'm thrilled, the next I'm scared witless.' They clung to each other with a kind of desperation and relief.

'Do you suppose everyone reacts like this when they find out?'

'I'm sure a lot do, if they're honest.'

'I love you, Mr Braga, so very much.'

'You're not so bad yourself, Miss Cusack,' he

said. Then he kissed her, deeply and hungrily, and she responded just as passionately.

'You know I love you too? Are you sure you're in the mood?'

'Positive, but you better put that ice-cream in the freezer first,' she said, running up the stairs, relieved and happy. After they made love, she told him about the promotion.

He was delighted for her. 'Just think, I could have my own personal wine master on the staff in the future.'

'I'll not be on your staff – you won't be able to afford me. I'll be an equal partner, maybe even your boss. Besides, there may be other Bragas by then, needing to share their mother's love and attention.'

'Let's have this one first,' he said. 'When is it due?'

She felt herself redden and was glad that he was lying beside her and couldn't see her face. 'I don't know the exact date,' she told him. 'I think they work that out when you have the first scan – which is at about twelve weeks. That's why I don't want to say anything to anyone until I know everything is OK. Mum lost a few babies in the early stages, so I'm just being cautious. I haven't even told her yet, or Danielle either.'

'I didn't know that, about your mum. OK, let's just keep everything crossed meantime.'

For a while, she actually let herself believe it was their baby. But then the truth took over and she felt a sense of panic rise within her. She moved uneasily beside him.

'Nausea again?'

'Afraid so.'

'Can they give you anything for that?'

'There has to be something. I'll go and have a chat with the GP tomorrow.'

He made no attempt to leave her that night and they snuggled up under the duvet and fell asleep, his arm protectively across her stomach.

When she arrived at work the next day JP met her with the greeting, 'Well, we're about to throw you in at the deep end. How do you fancy going over to London for a few days to meet some new suppliers? It'll mean a visit to Vinopolis too.'

'I've been dying to do that. When are you thinking?'

'Next week. I know it's short notice, but there's a new-world wine conference on next Thursday and Friday, and a few sessions and tastings are happening there, so it would be the ideal opportunity for you to make the most of the experience and meet a few new people. It's nothing too heavy. I actually think they are introducing some wines from China and Thailand, which should be interesting, if not exactly what our customers might be ordering yet. What do you think?' he said, handing her a schedule. 'I know I've sprung this on you, so if you can't do it I understand. Have a look at that and let me know.'

'That's no problem. I can go, and I'm really excited about getting to see Vinopolis.'

'It's great – it would never work here though, we don't have the numbers to sustain that sort of attraction. But we loved the concept – all those regions and labels under one roof. It's definitely a layman's tour, but it's fun to see,' said JP.

'Listen to him – being all nonchalant – he was in his element, sitting up there on his Vespa in the Italian section. They projected the rolling views of Tuscany on to the windshields so you felt you were driving through the countryside, while they told you all about the grapes and the soil,' Neil said.

JP grinned sheepishly. 'It was very realistic and I always wanted a Vespa. Now let's get your flights and accommodation organised.'

'I can do that,' said June. 'Do you want me to check if Kelly's free to fill in while I'm gone?'

'Please. I'm sure she'd be delighted with the extra few bob towards her trip Down Under.'

Back at her desk, she dialled Kelly, who acted as though they hadn't had their conversation the previous week. However, June felt she had to say something and before she knew it, she had asked Kelly if she would meet her one evening after work. They arranged to catch up in town the following Tuesday. Usually Tuesday nights were spent at her mother's and Peter met his mates for a game of poker and a few drinks, so meeting Kelly wouldn't disrupt any plans.

★   ★   ★

135

'I haven't been here before – it's really nice,' Kelly said as they took their seats at a table by the window in a little place looking out on Wicklow Street.

'The food's good too. Peter and I come here occasionally on a Saturday for brunch or a late lunch – there's always a good atmosphere.'

'I can see that,' Kelly said.

They took a few minutes to order. While they waited for their food, they talked about her promotion. 'I probably should have told the guys about the baby when they broached the promotion, but I couldn't,' June said. 'They just sprung it on me and I had no chance to think of the right way to put it. It changes everything, though, especially as they said they specifically want me to undertake a lot more of the travelling for them. How can I do that with a baby on the way, never mind when it's actually here? I'm torn in every direction.'

'Poor you. You're not having a good run of it, are you?'

'There's more.' She paused as their plates of steaming pasta were placed before them. When the waiter left, she said, 'It's not Peter's.' June couldn't look at Kelly as she let that bombshell sink. Then she told Kelly about the night on the yacht.

'I was more drunk than I've ever been, and I let someone bring me back to my cabin and that's when it happened. I remember pushing him away,

136

but then nothing. I did have a few bruises on my head and arms the next day, but I thought I had just fallen or bumped into the bunks.

'You mean you were raped?' Kelly said, suddenly in a fury.

'I haven't actually said those words out loud. They sound so awful. But, yes, I think I was. I keep asking myself can you be raped if you're too drunk to resist? And I did let him walk me to my cabin.'

'No wonder you're so upset. Being drunk doesn't give any guy the right to force himself on you.'

'I know that. I do remember telling him I was spoken for and he told me his wife was asleep down the corridor. And I remember telling him to stop, to go back to her. After that it's a total blackout.'

'The bastard. Well, that certainly does complicate things for you. Can you contact him? He has to take responsibility. In fact, he should be prosecuted for what he did.'

'I don't want to do that.'

'Does Peter know all this?'

'No. And I'm not sure what to do. It's all such a mess.' She told her about Zoe and what Peter had said. 'What would you do if you were me?'

'I can't tell you that, but when I had a problem, my mother used to make me write things down on a sheet of paper – the pros and the cons – then she'd tell me to read them over three times – then fold it in half and decide what decision I could live with. It usually worked.'

'I should do that, if only to try and sort out the muddle in my head. I'm so confused, I can't even decide what the priority is any more.' She took a diary from her bag, ripped a page out and started scribbling.

'It's got to be worth a try.'

Pros	Cons
The baby is Peter's	The baby is not P's
I'll tell him it is	It'd have a good home and family
I have to be honest with him	It would mean deceiving him forever
I could have it	No, I couldn't
I might learn to love it	I might not
I have to get Zoe out of my mind	I can't tell P that either
I'll fight for him	Does he love Z?
The guys will understand if I put off taking the promotion for a while	Will they hold it open?

She chewed the end of her pen, wondering if there was anything else to add. Then she said, 'I could always have an abortion.'

'Are you really considering that?' Kelly said. 'It's so . . . so final and you might have awful guilt afterwards.'

'And I might have more if I have a child who looks like his father – a constant reminder of how he or she was conceived. Could I live with that? I wasn't really considering going down the abortion route – I was just trying to balance my arguments,' she said, before adding, 'and they are not very good when you see them written down. Wouldn't you agree?'

'You do have options, you know. You could keep it, or you could always try and be honest with Peter. If he's half the guy you think he is, he may just surprise you and still want to stay with you, even marry you, when you explain what happened. You owe him that much. If he doesn't, then maybe he's not the man you deserve. Besides, pretending the child is his is a huge deception to keep up for a lifetime and that's what you'd be signing up for. It's not something you can change your mind about halfway through, because that way you'd be confessing that your relationship with Peter – married or not – was built on a lie and he'd be justified in thinking you had conned him.'

'That's what makes it all so difficult,' June said. 'We'd end up hating each other.'

'And if he is serious about his feelings for this other woman, wouldn't you be forcing him to live a lie too, pretending he'd rather be with you? You've also got to factor in that it wouldn't just be the two of you any more, it would be the three of you. You have to think where that would leave your child, if he or she ever discovered that their father wasn't really their father at all.'

'God, the more I think about it, the more complicated it gets.'

Kelly waited for a moment before adding a new option. 'You could always contact the real father.'

'Most certainly not. I don't even know his name, although I could find that out easily enough if I wanted to – which I don't. I don't ever want anything to do with him. I wouldn't want any child of mine growing up knowing his father was capable of that.'

'I can understand that. So from where I'm seeing things, coming clean with Peter is your best option and the sooner the better.'

'Kelly, how did you get to be so wise?'

'I don't know if I am, but it probably came from being on the outside looking at others making mistakes. I vowed I wouldn't do any of the silly things I saw others doing. When I looked after my parents, I had a lot of time to do that.'

'And did it stop you from doing silly things?'

'Did it ever! What do you think?' she laughed. 'Look at me and my daughter, hardly able to communicate for years, so don't canonise me. I'm just as fallible as anyone else. I now firmly believe that we all make slip-ups, intentional or otherwise. They are part of life. It's how you deal with them that makes the difference.'

'I'm with you there.'

'Just remember you have so much going for you if, in the worst-case scenario, Peter walks away. You have a good job already, you own your own house, so it's not as though childcare will leave you broke, and I'm quite sure the Macys will hold that offer open for you – they won't want to lose you, and you can still do a lot of the extra work for many more months, even if the travel goes on hold further down the line. Pregnancy is not an illness, you know, once the blasted sickness abates.'

'Thanks, Kelly, you make it all sound so logical. It's been great to have you to talk to. I really appreciate it. I better go and tell Peter while I still have the courage.'

'Any time. I wish I had had someone to confide in when I was in your condition.'

'Would it have made a difference?'

'In hindsight, yes. At the time – who knows? I was far too young to deal with it all. Count your blessings. You have maturity and security on your side.'

June folded the page from her diary and tucked it into her bag. She'd read it again at home, although she knew what she had to do. She insisted

141

on paying the bill. 'You're much cheaper than a therapist,' she said to Kelly as they made their way to catch their buses.

'I know. Best of luck with it all,' she called, running to catch hers.

'Thanks again,' June said.

She'd normally walk back home from town, but she felt drained, emotionally and physically, although now she was feeling more confident. She had already reached some conclusions. It was time to come clean and stop hiding from what was the right thing to do. It was time to tell Peter the truth, face to face, and if she stalled now she knew she might lose her nerve. She figured if she told him before she went to London, he'd have the time to mull over it and give her an answer when she got back. As she waited at her stop, she rang Peter's number. She'd ask him to come over before he met his friends. They usually didn't meet till after nine. He didn't pick up and she didn't leave a message – this was too important for that. He'd see her missed call anyway. She started rehearsing what she'd say to him. How could she break it to him? What was the best approach – to start with an apology, a confession, the whole story?

She sat downstairs on the bus and stared out the window. It had started to drizzle, the sort of rain that sneakily drenches you in minutes, and she didn't have an umbrella with her. The bus slowed as it rounded the top of Kildare Street at St

Stephen's Green, and was held up outside the Shelbourne Hotel while a convoy of several limos with tinted windows offloaded their passengers. They seemed to be outnumbered by minders. Enormous logoed umbrellas were magically produced by the liveried doorman and were solicitously positioned to shelter the VIPs, whoever they were. She didn't recognise any of them, but some onlookers obviously did and a knot of them had gathered in anticipation of their arrival, ignoring the change in the weather. They cheered and one of the celebs acknowledged their presence with a wave before disappearing through the revolving doors.

June looked with envy at the crowd inside, realising the last time she had been in there, she'd been as carefree as they all appeared to be. Laughing, chatting, flirting, flattering, posers making highfalutin promises they'd never keep: they were all there, amid the town's minor and nine-day-wonder celebrities – and they were all enjoying their brief reign as the beautiful people about town. She sighed.

The limos moved off and, just as the bus started to inch forward, something caught her eye in the brightly lit foyer – the back of a tall woman with a spiky hairdo. She couldn't have said with any degree of conviction that it was Zoe, because she never saw her face – it was hidden by the man she was kissing. But she knew she could identify him anywhere. It was Peter.

⋆   ⋆   ⋆

Peter had taken a call from Zoe earlier that day, as he was about to leave the site.

'Will you meet me for a drink? There's something I need to say to you.'

'I don't think it's a good idea, besides which I'm very busy.'

'Please, just one drink. I know you meet your buddies tonight, but we could grab one before that,' she said. 'Just one, Peter, you owe me that.'

He didn't think he owed her anything, but he did feel bad about the way he had treated her. Before June told him she was pregnant, he'd given Zoe the impression – no, that wasn't fair, he'd *told* her that he was going to tell June he wanted a break, and that they would be together then. She had been guilty of nothing apart from an over-enthusiasm for his project and a strong physical attraction for him. She made no secret of her feelings, so he'd told her about June.

For the last two weeks of June's holiday, Zoe had used every ploy she could think of to get Peter to take her out on a date, but he had refused. He'd wanted to take her out – he'd actually wanted so much more. When she had brushed against him accidentally or had touched his hand, he'd felt his breath quicken and a wave of desire envelop him. He'd told himself over and over again that when June was back, he'd forget these feelings. But they hadn't disappeared. Now he had to do the honourable thing. He'd spell it out in no uncertain terms and he'd do it in a public place where they couldn't argue.

'OK, I'll meet you for one drink in the Shelbourne Bar, at half eight. I have to be in Dawson Street at nine.'

CHAPTER 9

Although she hadn't closed her eyes the previous night, June went into the office on time the next day. *That bastard. That bitch. Damn the two of them.* June hated them, wanted to hurt them. She had wanted to jump off the bus and run into the hotel and tell them what she thought. And she might have, if the bus hadn't driven off, leaving her dreams and hopes behind. Peter hadn't responded to her missed calls and she'd gone to bed eventually, but had kept her mobile beside her, just in case he called.

She'd heard the clock strike every hour, and her mood swung between being angry, offended, furious, let down, jealous and really upset. She knew her emotions could not be blamed on her hormones. She'd got up, made tea, gone back to bed but still couldn't sleep.

As she lay there, she'd gone over what she'd seen. She couldn't believe it. So much for making a confession and throwing herself at Peter's mercy and his good nature. Did she really want a man like that in her life? She was so confused, she couldn't decide which worry was the most urgent – coming clean or trying to hold on to Peter.

She found it hard to concentrate on the work she had to get finished before she went to London the following day. Fortunately, the guys gave her the afternoon off to prepare, and she left the office at lunchtime, with their good wishes ringing in her ears.

She had made up her mind to stay in London until Monday, her thirtieth birthday. She couldn't yet think about how she'd handle Peter and the plans he'd made to celebrate. Her mother was due back from her Italian trip on Saturday so she left a message telling her of her change of plans.

'I'll have a lot of networking to do over the next few days, and won't have my phone on half the time. We'll catch up when I get back, OK? I'll let you know then if this promotion is all it's supposed to be,' she laughed, to lighten the tone. 'Hope you had a great time.'

She phoned Danielle. 'I suppose I'll have to get used to this – you ringing me up telling me you're off on your all-expenses-paid fact-finding missions to the Napa Valley or Stellenbosch or some such exotic place.'

'Well, London's hardly that exotic,' June said.

'It is to me. I've just come from a get-to-know-the-new-staff meeting and some of them look about eighteen. It'll be like throwing them to the lions when the teenagers meet them. I can't believe I looked like that when I started. When we were at school, I thought all my teachers were in their nineties!'

June deliberately didn't mention her birthday – she knew Peter and Danielle had been whispering about it, but she also knew that she didn't want to be part of whatever plans he'd made. She had already ignored several calls from him. She didn't know how to handle the situation. She wanted space in every sense, but she knew if she kept doing that, he'd turn up on her doorstep and she definitely wasn't ready to face him, so the next time his number appeared on her screen, she answered.

'Hiya,' he said, 'I've been trying to reach you all day.'

'I've been busy getting ready for this trip to London.'

She waited to see what he'd say next, but there was just an awkward silence, which she was determined not to break. Besides which, she didn't know what to say to him.

'What time are you off?'

'The first flight in the morning.'

'You'll need an early one so. How are you feeling?'

'Not great really. Did you have a good night last night – with the lads?'

'Yeah – the usual – just a few drinks and a catch-up.'

'Is that what they're calling it now?'

'Pardon?'

'I said, is that what they're calling it now? I saw you and Zoe in the Shelbourne, looking very cosy, kissing in fact, so you needn't lie to me.'

There was another awkward pause before he spoke. 'That wasn't what it seemed. I can explain.'

'Don't bother. I don't want to know. Now I have things to do, so let's leave it at that.'

'We have to talk. It wasn't like that. Believe me.'

'I have nothing to say to you right now, Peter, except goodbye. I don't want to hear your excuses.' She rang off, a physical pain in her chest.

She sat at the table in the kitchen looking out at her garden but not seeing anything at all. Instead, it was at that precise moment she knew what she had to do. She opened her laptop, made a few more phone calls, and scribbled a few notes in her diary. She ignored more of Peter's calls and changed her message saying she was already away. She didn't want to talk to him, or anyone else. She repacked her bag, went to bed early and slept from pure exhaustion.

Next week will be better, she told herself. *I just have to get through these few days professionally and show Neil and JP they were right to put their trust in me. I'll show them I'm up to the job and I'll bloody well shine at all those exams. I'm in control of my own destiny, no one else is.*

She was ready and waiting for the taxi when it pulled up outside her house the following morning. On the way to the airport, she heard that cheerful voice again in the middle of the ads telling listeners, 'An unwanted pregnancy need not adversely affect your life.'

Really, she thought, clenching her fists. *And what the hell would you know about that?* She wanted to shout at the radio, but her rage soon passed as the driver kept up a running commentary on the snippets of news that filtered through from the early-morning programme and she had no choice but to answer him. She was relieved when he eventually dropped her off.

The journey went smoothly and she took the Heathrow Express into London. She had time to check in to her hotel. Fortunately, they already had some rooms ready, so she was able to unpack before the first seminar. As soon as she was in work mode, June put everything else aside. She had to get this right and prove herself and she was surprised to discover that she could actually concentrate on the business in hand. She was delighted to recognise a few faces too, exporters who had visited Macy Brothers in the past.

Vinopolis was an interesting experience, and it was a novel way of exposing punters and tasters to lots of new brands, but she wasn't convinced it would work for Macy's. She texted her bosses:

I agree with you – it's not for the cognoscenti (like us!!), but a great attraction for the enthusiast and the bluffer.

She was ambivalent about the new wines on offer from Thailand, but when a number of the producers invited her to visit some of the hundred or so vineyards in Yantai-Penglai in China, she came back down to earth with a bang. She had things to do and visiting China was not one of them, not yet at any rate. She cried off the dinner on Friday night, knowing she'd not be missed, ordered room service and went over and over her dilemma time and again. She checked out the next day and took a taxi to the address she'd written in to her diary. Then she turned her phone off.

Her room in the period townhouse was airy and bright, decorated in warm tones with matching bed linen, a comfortable armchair and a television set. There was a menu on her bed. It was obvious from the frontage on the quiet square that, over time, several of these desirable dwellings had been knocked into one. The plumbing made its ancient presence felt as it clanked and clunked behind the walls and under the floorboards. Before she was settled, there was a discreet knock on her door and a young woman came in.

'Hello, June. I'm Josetta. We talked on the phone. Can I come in?'

'Of course.'

'How are you feeling about things now? I assume you haven't changed your mind?'

'No, I haven't. In fact I'm more certain than ever.'

'Well, that's very understandable in the circumstances. Let's go through things again.'

As soon as June had finally made up her mind, she found it was easier to focus. She knew she couldn't keep the baby. If she hadn't been raped it would have been a very different scenario. But to spend her life looking at a child and thinking its father was a monster was unthinkable. She couldn't go along with the deception that it was Peter's either, even if they did have any chance of a future together. Not now, now that he seemed to have forgotten all about her.

Her life was changing, with new job horizons, and a baby conceived in such horrible circumstances was the last thing she could deal with. When she'd dreamed of becoming pregnant, of becoming a mother, she'd never thought she could feel animosity like this. She knew that she couldn't keep the baby knowing how she felt in her heart. The counsellor was very understanding about her predicament.

'It is a very difficult time for you, but you do appear to have looked at all the angles. We have some staff who have had terminations themselves, if you'd like to talk to them about anything.'

'Believe me, Josetta, I have done nothing but consider the options since I found out. My mind is so addled and no matter how much I try to find reasons for not going through with it, they don't seem nearly as important as those for going ahead. I am absolutely certain this is the right decision.'

'Well, just remember you can still change your mind if you want to. There are no problems about that. We have you booked in for 12.30 tomorrow, so let's have one of the team examine you.'

A young doctor went through the procedure with her, confirming she was suitable for a termination. 'It's quite straightforward and we don't expect any complications. I see you're not going home until Monday, so you're very wise to take the extra night with us to recover before your flight.'

'When will the morning sickness go away?'

'As soon as the pregnancy hormones stop being active, and that'll start happening when the procedure is over. It varies, but hopefully in a week or two, you'll have forgotten all about the worst of it. Now feel free to come and go as you like today, but we'd like you back by 6.30 this evening.'

When they left her room, June burst into tears. It was such a relief to have it all out in the open. She felt she could breathe again. There was a huge sense of liberation: of being in control after the rudderless anxiety she had been feeling for the past several weeks. When this weekend was over, she could get on with her life, with or without Peter in it. Had she really lost him to Zoe? Before her trip with Danielle, it was unthinkable to imagine a future with them not being together. He was the love of her life. She knew that with every fibre of her being, yet after what she saw from the bus, that seemed impossible. She'd still have to meet him and tell him the truth though.

153

She owed him that much, and it was no consolation to think that he'd probably be relieved.

Telling her mum and Danielle would be a different matter entirely, but that could wait. She wondered, not for the first time, if her father would have understood. He must have had patients over the years in similar or worse dilemmas. What would he have advised her to do?

She decided against sitting in her room all day and took herself off to Knightsbridge where she moseyed around the shops. She made a dent in her credit card buying some new business suits and two pairs of shoes. *Investments in my new future*, she thought. She'd have to look the part. She also bought Kelly a top in soft pistachio for her holiday in Oz, as a way of saying thank you.

She meandered in to the Food Hall in Harrods and marvelled at the array of goods on offer. It was heaving with people from all over the world, seeking gourmet delights or perhaps foods that reminded them of home. But when the waft of garlic, smoked meat and salamis reached her nostrils, she knew she had to escape as quickly as possible.

There seemed to be babies everywhere, in buggies and in designer clothes, in the shops and in their window displays. She felt panic rising in her and she hoped she wouldn't live to regret the decision she'd made. She hailed a taxi outside and went back to her refuge. It was only then she realised she hadn't eaten a thing all day. She filled the kettle in her room to make tea and hung her new clothes in the wardrobe.

Josetta came by later on and June was glad to see a familiar, friendly face. Josetta insisted June have a light supper, and went through everything again, leaving June more relaxed than she'd been for weeks.

CHAPTER 10

They couldn't have been nicer at the clinic. There was no sense of anyone being judgemental. People respected her privacy and she was surprised at how calm she felt. There seemed to be a hush everywhere, even outside in the refined streets. The world hadn't gone into shock at what she was about to do. A nurse came and collected her and they walked to the operating room. The nurse told her there was no need to be nervous, and she wasn't. She was terrified – terrified she might regret her decision – but at the same time certain that she had no alternative. She was more terrified that she could never love this foetus that had arrived uninvited and unwanted into her body.

The procedure was textbook and she experienced very little discomfort. A few hours later, she almost regretted not going straight to the airport afterwards instead of staying over. She longed for the familiarity of her own home, the comfort of her own bed, but they had advised the extra night because she was flying, just to be sure, and she conceded they probably knew best. She dozed and read some of the wine notes she'd picked up and dozed again, wakening up to the unfamiliar early-morning traffic sounds of a city starting a new week.

She was thirty today. The plan had been for Peter to take her out for dinner to celebrate. She knew he had made more plans than that from the way Danielle changed the subject every time June had mentioned her birthday. She wasn't sure she was ready to tell him what she had done just yet. He'd probably spent the weekend with Zoe after the way she had left things between them. She didn't feel like seeing him, not today of all days. Josetta had told her to stay there until about eleven, so that she'd be well rested before her journey.

She decided to start getting back into the real world and turned her phone back on. She skipped through the missed calls, and then she played her messages. His call was the first one. She listened to his voice, the voice she loved so well: *'Happy birthday, Miss Cusack. Would you like me to collect you at the airport?'*

Definitely not, she wanted to reply. Then she found the same message in her texts. Instead of phoning him, she cut and pasted the same message that she'd sent to other well-wishers.

Thank you for remembering and for reminding me! Thirty – it sounds so much older than twenty-nine! I'm in transit. Talk later. Luv J.x.

She did phone her mother though and almost broke down when she heard her cheerful voice. 'Happy birthday, darling. You're making me feel very old having a thirty-year-old daughter.'

'You'll never be old. I can hardly keep up with you and I'm dying to hear all about your trip.'

'Well, I'll see you later. Have a safe journey, love.'

She promised to catch up the minute she got back. As she packed her case, it began to rain, then hail, outside, with violent gusts hurtling it against the window, startling her with their sudden severity. She checked out and waited for the taxi that had been called. It made its way slowly through the gridlocked traffic, the pathways suddenly deserted as the cloudbursts drenched everything and everyone within their range. June was glad of the train journey that took her right from Paddington into the airport. She had a mid-afternoon flight and had given herself plenty of time.

Heathrow was always busy but it seemed worse than ever, and as she checked in, the overhead noticeboards were lit up with the details of delayed flights. The ground staff explained that the un-expected weather front that had caused the hail storm was continuing to sweep across the UK, forcing them to cancel all flights. They were predicting that it could take anything up to seven hours to clear the backlog.

The terminal building was teeming with people.

There were families whose children were already high on sugar fixes and anything else that would placate them for another while. Irate passengers and frazzled business travellers stood about checking and rechecking the signs, whose messages stubbornly refused to change.

June suddenly felt the need to move about. She was relieved her ordeal was over and wanted to be on her way and face the consequences, so they could all get on with their lives. She wandered about the shops. This was as far removed from how she had envisaged spending her thirtieth as she could go. As she looked in a jewellery shop, she realised that she could have been sporting an engagement ring before the day was over if she hadn't got herself into such a mess.

She didn't want perfume or a new watch, or a handbag, travel accoutrements or a digital camera or anything else the shops had. She wasn't tempted to buy a ticket for the red Ferrari on display, although it seemed many other travellers were. There was a queue of hopefuls handing over twenty pounds a pop. *They must be making a fortune on that promotion*, she thought. She couldn't concentrate. She should have been enjoying cards, flowers, presents, probably even champagne and cake in the office. She should have been thinking about dinner with Peter. She had fantasised about Peter's proposal so many times since she'd promised to say yes the next

159

time he asked. She wondered if he had actually bought a ring.

Then she came back to reality – even if he had, she wouldn't be the one wearing it. He had betrayed her and she couldn't ever accept that. He had broken their trust. What they had together was gone and they would both have to live with that. She also had to live with the fact that she had been prepared to keep secret what had happened to her and deceive him and everyone else – and she'd decided that before she even knew of Zoe's part in their lives.

She stopped by a huge display of teddy bears. On one side of the door, Paddington Bears in all sizes smiled at her from under their sou'westers. Some were suitably attired in bright yellow rain-coats and boots. Competing on the other side of the entrance was a mountain of the Harrods bears, kitted out in a variety of themes from tartan and hand-made sweaters to waistcoats and dickie-bows. Their signature branding was not so discreetly embroidered on their left paws. On impulse, June stopped and picked up a large one and looked into its friendly face. She had never been a dolly type of girl and this teddy brought back a comforting childhood memory. It was soft and warm and she hugged it tight for a moment. Was life going to be like this now – peppered with unvoiced regrets? She noticed an assistant watching her and grinned as she put it back. She grabbed a seriously overpriced box of champagne chocolate truffles and went to the counter to buy them for the girls in the office.

'May I see your boarding card, please?'

'Sorry, I was miles away,' she said, fishing in her handbag.

'Yes, but you'd be surprised at how many people have moments by the teddy bears. They seem to have that universal effect.' She smiled. 'I'm a bit of a fan myself.'

She took the truffles and as she left she heard someone call, 'Madam, Madam, please wait.'

She wasn't going to turn around but, when she did, another assistant came from behind the counter with a distinctive green bag.

'That gentleman asked me to give this to you.'

She looked up but she didn't recognise the tall man, dressed to perfection in a tailored navy suit, white shirt and yellow-and-blue tie. His blond hair flopped boyishly onto his forehead. She couldn't help but notice that he had vivid blue eyes, and a winning smile.

'I don't think so.'

'I do,' he said, coming towards her. She was surprised to hear his Irish accent – for some reason she'd assumed he was a foreigner. 'You looked a bit lost and forlorn there, so I thought this little chap would cheer you up.'

She felt her lip tremble. *Don't let me cry. Please don't let me cry. Not here. Not now.* 'I was, but that's too kind, and not necessary at all,' she managed to say.

'I know. Have you been stranded too?' he asked.

'Yes, but I'm hoping to get home later on.'

'Me too. Where's home?'

'Dublin.'

'Ditto.'

June felt a little faint and was finding it hard to concentrate on his face. 'I think I need to sit down.' She looked around but there wasn't a seat to be had anywhere.

'Come with me, I have a lounge pass. I'm Lorcan Overend, by the way.'

'June Cusack. Are you sure you don't mind?'

'My pleasure.'

There were only a few seats left and he commandeered two of them, before going to fetch her some water. He strode across the lounge as though he owned it, yet he didn't appear to be cocky or conceited. He nodded to someone he recognised as he went. He had an air of authority about him, and June admired that in a man. He was a good bit older than her too, she noticed. Probably married with a designer wife and a house full of designer kids, but he seemed nice, and she needed someone to be nice to her after what she had just been through. And it'd help pass the time.

'Would you like to have something to eat? As lounge food goes, the sandwiches don't look too bad at all.'

'No, thank you. I've had a bit of a bug the past

few days and I'm still not very hungry. That's probably why I felt faint back there.'

He sat beside her and she looked into the bag he'd given – there amid the gold tissue paper was a bear in his own logoed carrier bag.

'He's really sweet, but you shouldn't have.'

'Enjoy him. You'll have to give him a name.'

She felt the blood drain from her face. It was as if he knew what she had done. What would she have called her baby if— She hadn't even thought about that and the realisation shocked her. Subconsciously, she knew that by not letting the baby become a person in her own mind, she would be able to forget it more easily. She felt her lip quiver again and thought she was going to throw up.

'You look awful. Do you want to go to the ladies' room?'

'No, I'll be all right in a few minutes. I just feel very weak.'

'You've got to eat something. God knows how long we'll be here.'

He brought back a selection of lounge food – cheese and crackers, an egg and lettuce sandwich, shortbread biscuits in a packet of two, a chocolate muffin, some tea with lots of sugar cubes, and a miniature bottle of brandy.

'This is purely for medicinal purposes,' he said, splashing half of it into the hot drink. She felt herself relaxing again.

'Are you sure you're up to the flight?'

'The running of the bulls wouldn't keep me off it. I can't wait to sleep in my own bed again.'

They talked on and off for the next few hours. She dozed a little and he checked his laptop. She texted a group message:

Still at Heathrow – stranded by freak storms! Don't know if I'll get back tonight.

Eventually the flight was called.

'I'd love to take you to dinner sometime, if you'd let me – that is if you're not . . . attached.'

June was flattered. She didn't feel very good about herself – perhaps this was exactly what she needed to give her a lift. Peter was unlikely to ever want to have anything to do with her again and, right now, she wasn't sure how much she wanted to do with him either. She still ached for him, though; maybe going out to dinner with a stranger would help.

'I'd like that,' she said, deliberately not answering his question. She gave him her number. She could always find an excuse if he ever did ring.

They were seated apart on the plane. The pilot apologised for the delay and warned them they'd find Dublin was now getting the brunt of the storm, so they should be prepared for a few bumps en route. The idea of sitting on the Aircoach for half an hour didn't appeal at all, so June decided she'd take a taxi, before remembering that she now had her own expense account and such things needn't bother her any more. It was a nice feeling.

She did manage to doze, and forty minutes later, the plane touched down in Dublin airport. She was sure her new acquaintance would have rushed straight through passport control and out into Arrivals, but he hadn't. He was waiting for her in the tunnel. As she claimed her bag, he offered her a lift home. He was passing right by the end of her road and it would have been madness to refuse. She felt she could trust him and she was grateful. He'd never know what an ordeal she'd just gone through, or how she had messed up the lives of others that she loved most in the world.

'I'll be away quite a bit on business over the next few weeks, but I will call you, June,' he said as she took her case from him. 'I promise.'

She thanked him and she wondered if he ever would.

She dropped her bags in the hallway and checked her phone. There was a rake of messages and missed calls. It was 11.25. She knew her mother would still be up, so would Danielle. She texted them to say she had just arrived home, was exhausted and would contact them first thing in the morning.

She gave Peter's message more consideration.

I know you've been delayed. Can we meet tomorrow after work? I know you're mad

165

with me, but we have to talk and sort things out properly. Love, Peter x

She punched in her reply.

Yes, you're right, we do. Meet me after work, usual place. June x.

She didn't even bother to unpack before she sank in to her own bed.

She decided not to go in to work until the afternoon, but she phoned Kelly that morning to let her know. Then she tried to concentrate on writing up her notes from the wine trip conference, but her mind kept wandering. She missed Peter more than she had ever thought possible, and whenever she thought about him kissing Zoe, she experienced actual darts of pain in her chest. Had she taken him for granted? She didn't think so. Could she have missed any warning signs that he was tiring of their relationship? She didn't think so. Was there any possible way to fix things? The answer was also a negative to that.

That afternoon after work, her heart did a little flip when she saw him standing on the path outside her office. She knew this wasn't going to be easy. He kissed her on her cheek and with a hand under her elbow, he led her away from the office exodus. She noticed the piles of leaves and debris in the gutters, the aftermath of the storm that had finally ended summer. There was a definite hint of autumn in the air, that leafy smell that heralded the beginning of the darker days ahead. *Is that a metaphor for our friendship,* she wondered.

'Will we head to the Schoolhouse? Or would you rather go somewhere else?'

'No, that's fine with me,' she answered.

He didn't comment when she ordered a white wine.

'Right, now I have to say sorry for—'

'No, wait, Peter. Let me go first this time. I have to say I'm sorry. I have a confession to make, one that's overdue. The last time we were here, I panicked. I didn't mean to lie to you, but you telling me you had met someone was all too much. Everything was happening too fast. I had just discovered that I was pregnant and I told you it was yours. Well it wasn't. It happened in France. It was the result of a drunken night. Someone took advantage of my state and I have no recollection of it happening at all.'

'What? You mean—'

'Just let me finish, Peter. I have to get it off my chest – all of it. I'm not making excuses, but I want you to know that I was never unfaithful to you before or since then, and it's not something I'm very proud of. I wasn't even aware I'd had sex until the morning sickness started when I got back home. It happened the first night when we had no hotel room and we stayed on the yacht in Monte Carlo.'

'Who was he? Have you been in touch with him since?'

'No. I don't even know his name – and I don't want to know it. He was someone I had just met on the yacht. The drink was flowing and we were together in a crowd the whole time. He saw me back to my cabin and he tried to kiss me. I remember pushing him away. I must have blacked out, that's all I remember.'

'Did he force you to— Did he rape you?'

'I think so, but I honestly don't know. I never spoke to him afterwards although I did see him with his wife once or twice over the following couple of days. He could have spiked my drink.'

'The bastard. He should be locked up for that, June. What are you going to do?'

'Nothing. I can't deal with confronting him or even making the effort to find him. I don't want to think about him or what he did – I want to forget it ever happened. I've only told you because I need to explain everything. Peter, I could have gone on pretending the baby was yours and you'd probably never have found out. In fact, you've no idea how tempting that was – and as I'm being totally honest, you may as well know that I did give it serious considera- tion. You'd be a wonderful father, no child could ask for better, but seeing you and Zoe kissing the other night made me realise that I couldn't go through with it. I was livid seeing you together and incredibly sad, but I knew I couldn't force you into a situation over which you had no control. You'd only end up hating me for taking you away from her and I'd end up hating myself for what I'd become. There'd be no winners.'

He tried to talk but she stopped him again.

'I had to make some drastic decisions. I didn't want to be a mother to a child I'd resent every time anyone mentioned a father. What would I tell him or her when they'd be old enough to ask questions? I'd have to lie again.'

'So, what are you going to do?'

'I've already done it. I've had a termination – that's why I stayed on in London and why I avoided your calls. I needed to tell you face to face. No one knows about it, not even Danielle. I'll tell her when I'm ready, but not yet. I have to tell Mum too. But no one else. Will you please respect that? Tell Zoe I miscarried while I was away if she asks. I just want to put the whole sordid thing behind me.'

'Why didn't you tell me everything before now? I could have come over and been there to offer you some support.' He reached over and put his hand on hers.

'I tried, but it seemed the moment was never right.'

'Poor you.' He left his hand on top of hers. She

took comfort from the heat and the familiar feel of him, but she knew it was just a gesture, albeit a nice one, but a gesture between friends. Nothing more.

'I felt so ashamed, afraid and . . . smothered, especially smothered.'

'So that's why you decided to miss your birthday. I thought that was odd. Then I thought you were just trying to get back at me. Look, this whole Zoe thing, I never planned it to happen. I never set out to hurt you. You must believe that.'

'Believe me, I had more pressing things on my mind. I was going to tell you before I went away and then I saw the pair of you together. It was only then I decided what I had to do. I hadn't considered an abortion until then, but weighing up everything, I just knew it was the right decision for me, right now. Now you have your freedom and I have mine to pursue my new career.'

'What happened between us, June? I thought we were a sure thing. Then suddenly it all went out of kilter.'

'Maybe we began to take each other for granted, assuming we'd always be there – together.'

'Do you really think so?'

'No, but I can't think of a better excuse.'

'I hadn't factored Zoe into the equation. I never meant to hurt you.'

'I do actually believe you when you tell me that,

and I never meant to hurt you either. That was the last thing on my mind,' she said. 'Do you love her?'

'I'm not sure – I think I might. I didn't see it coming, though, I promise. But if I don't try to find out and pretend she's not there, then I'd be living a lie too and I couldn't do that to you. You'll always be a very special part of my life, Miss Cusack, no matter what happens – one of the most important in fact.'

'And you a part of mine, Mr Braga.'

'I'm sorry.'

'So am I.'

He leaned over and kissed her tenderly on her damp cheek.

'My folks will never forgive me for letting you get away. Rosa already looks on you as a sister.'

'I'd like to keep in touch with her. Would you mind?'

'Of course not.'

'My mother will be disappointed that I let you get away too. She'll miss you.'

'I'll miss her too.'

'It just goes to show how much we'd become a couple, doesn't it?'

He nodded. They finished their wine in silence and then left.

As he walked her to the corner, she asked, 'What about your stuff?'

'If you don't mind, I'll come by some day and collect it when you're at work.'

Sensing a chasm already widening between them, June flagged down a taxi and he wrapped her in a comfortable hug before she climbed in.

'Don't be a stranger. If you ever need me for anything please feel you can call me,' he told her. 'I really mean that, June.'

She nodded. 'I know.'

'And thank you for your honesty,' he continued. 'That can't have been easy.'

'It wasn't. It was the hardest thing I've ever had to do. Just be happy, won't you?' she said. She wiped her tears away before she rang Danielle en route.

'Can you come to Mum's? I need to tell you something, both of you.'

'I'm on my way. Righty-ho. See you in about fifteen.'

June sensed from her friend's enthusiastic reaction that she was assuming her news bulletin involved an engagement ring, and so, as she wasn't prepared to discuss what had happened in front of the taxi driver, she just said, 'See you in a bit.'

Her mother was fussing at the Aga when June let herself into her childhood home.

'I wasn't sure if I'd see you tonight after the fiasco of the storms and missing your birthday and everything, so I thought I'd make a casserole that would keep if you couldn't make it. I wondered if you'd have Peter in tow.'

June steeled herself before answering. She wanted to tell them both together – she couldn't face going over it all twice. 'No, he had plans. You shouldn't have gone to so much trouble.'

'It's your favourite, *coq au vin*, with a large accent on the *au vin* bit. And I brought home a bottle of *Aperol*, it's an aperitif that we had a few times. I'm still not sure if I like it, but as with so many of these things, they're something of an acquired taste. What do you think?'

Danielle's arrival delayed the sampling. 'Something smells divine,' she said as she liberated a chilled bottle of champagne in its own cooler bag from her enormous satchel and put it straight into Branch's fridge.

'Belated Happy Birthday, darling,' Branch said when she'd poured their drinks.

'Wait, are we celebrating anything else? Did I miss something?'

'Nothing at all, Danni, just my arrival into a new decade,' June said. 'God, that is tart. It would certainly waken up your taste buds. What's in it?'

'I believe it's made with rhubarb and bitter orange, blended with what they said was "the subtleties" of herbs. The Italians raved about it.'

'That sounds disgusting and I can tell you there's nothing subtle about that. It's like rocket fuel,' Danielle laughed, putting down her glass. 'That's enough to make me teetotal.' They laughed as she tried to swallow a mouthful. 'Let's have some of my fizz.'

'How's Froggie?' June asked, trying to be as normal as possible.

'Fantastic,' Danielle replied, a wide grin spreading across her face at the mention of his name. 'He's in town all this week, so we'll have to get together.'

'Yes, I'd love to see him.'

Knowing her daughter well, Branch picked up on some nuance in that reply and kept the conversation going about her break until they were well through their dinner. She regaled them with the oddities and eccentricities of her travelling companions and the quirks of those who went on escorted holidays.

'There was one old couple who refused to sit beside each other, on the coach or at meals, but they shared a bedroom. No one ever saw them exchange a word yet they went off on great trips all the time. They went to India last year and they were quite fascinating when you got talking to either of them on their own. Put them at the same table, though, and they might as well never have been introduced to each other before. It was all very strange.'

'Weird,' agreed Danielle. 'Now, June, you've kept us waiting long enough. What's the big news?'

'Well, I wanted to tell you both that Peter and I have split up.' She watched as they exchanged a look. 'And I know you both thought I was going to tell you we'd got engaged.' She laughed uneasily. 'You can't deny it – the first thing you both did when you saw me was look at my left hand. And you with the bubbles chilled and all.'

'I . . . I had hoped . . . and there I thought I was being discreet by holding my tongue and saying nothing,' Branch said.

'But you can't have split up – what happened? Peter had arranged a surprise party for last night and only cancelled it because you were stuck in Heathrow, and while he didn't actually say he'd bought a ring, he certainly implied he had. I've had that bottle in the fridge all week in anticipation.'

'I didn't realise that,' June said, a dart of sadness engulfing her. 'It's complicated.' Her voice broke. 'It just wouldn't have worked. Besides, he has met someone else and—'

'What? When? While we were away? Isn't that typical? He didn't waste much time, did he? How fickle – the cheating sod.'

'Danielle, hold the head, will you? He wasn't out playing the field, looking for anyone else. It's someone he met through the work on the restaurant – the architect, in fact. He assures me that they haven't actually got together yet.'

'My poor darling, you must be gutted. I thought you were so solid together, but you haven't been yourself since you got back from your trip. I didn't want to pry.'

'No, Mum, I haven't. There's more to tell – and

you must promise not to hate me.' June hesitated, not knowing how to start.

'We won't hate you, whatever you've done,' her mother said. 'But what can be so bad that you felt you had to make an appointment to tell us – together?'

'I had an abortion.'

That was greeted with an incredulous and stunned silence, broken by Danielle.

'When?'

'At the weekend – in London.'

'But Peter was here. Did he know?'

'He does now. I told him this afternoon.'

'And he walked away from you?'

'No, it's not like that at all. And it wasn't his.' June started to cry – and there was no holding back the tears when they started. 'I couldn't tell you until after I'd spoken to him because I'd allowed him think it *was* his and he suggested we should marry straight away. He would have stood by me. I was raped.'

'You were what?' Danielle almost screamed.

'How? . . . When?' Branch tried to formulate questions, but she couldn't breathe. 'How did this happen?'

June carried on as if she didn't hear them. She had to say everything she'd rehearsed, so that they understood how hard the decision had been to have the abortion, how much she'd thought it through. 'Mum, I know how much this will hurt you. I fully respect that Dad spent his life trying to give people the babies they wanted so desperately, and I know you still mourn the ones you miscarried, but I have to live with myself. I have to be able to look in the mirror and know I'm not living a lie, every single day. If I'd managed to con him, that's what I'd be doing.'

'June, you're a big girl,' her mother said. 'My approval doesn't really matter, but how did this happen? When did this happen?'

'I don't want you worrying – either of you. I've had all the tests done and I'm fine, there's nothing physically left over from it.'

'June, why didn't you tell me?' Danielle asked. 'I knew there was something – you've been acting really bizarrely since we got back, rushing off the phone, not wanting to meet up. I wondered if you didn't approve of Froggie or something like that. I never suspected a pregnancy, never mind . . . rape. I could at least have come to London with you.'

'That's what Peter said too. I honestly didn't mean to cut you out, but I had to think everything through – there was a lot of soul searching to do. I just wasn't ready.'

Danielle got up from the table and hugged her. 'I can't believe it.'

June took Danielle's arm. 'I had to be sure about what I had to do before I could talk to anyone, then my priority was to tell Peter he was off the hook. But you have to swear you won't tell anyone, especially Froggie.'

'Of course, but what's Froggie got to do with this?'

'Nothing, but he might feel he has something to do with it. I was raped on that first night on the yacht in Monte Carlo. He might want to go after that medic, feel he should make him pay in some way – and I don't want that.'

They both had tears in their eyes. 'But everything was perfect that first night in Monte Carlo.'

June nodded. 'It was, so you see why I don't want you to tell Froggie.'

'You have my word.'

Branch brought a lemon tart from the counter and put it on the table. 'When you've blown out your candles, you make sure you wish for a new beginning, or something like that.' She gave her daughter a hug. 'My poor child. You've been through such an ordeal – and all by yourself. Are you sure you're feeling OK? Do you want to tell us about it?'

'Physically fine, but mentally, I feel like I've been to hell and back.' She told them what she could remember. 'But it's so much better now that you both know. You've no idea how I was dreading telling you. Now I just have to get used to life without Peter in it, and that's going to be hard. I really love him, you know.' June wiped her eyes and tried to lighten the mood. 'And now it looks as though I'm going to have to watch this one and Froggie in the first flush of love.'

'We'll try and not be in your face about it.'

'No, be happy – it took you long enough to find each other. I'm lucky to have the new challenges of the job to concentrate the mind for a bit.'

'And we'll have to find you someone else,' her mother said.

'I'm not ready for anything or anyone else. Peter's a one-off and I don't think anyone will ever take his place.'

'How often have you heard me say that?' said Danielle. 'And look, when I least expected it, along came Froggie.'

June was forced to tell her bosses about breaking up with Peter on the Monday morning, after their weekly meeting. They had taken on board her suggestion that the wine club should try organising some supper club evenings, matching food and wine at different restaurants, and they had suggested going to The Pink Pepper Tree as soon as it reopened.

Neil Macy said to her afterwards, 'I'm sorry to hear about the pair of you, but from a very selfish point of view, it will probably mean you can get away more and I won't need to feel guilty asking you.'

'That's my little brother for you, sensitive to the last,' JP said.

'He's right, though, isn't he? I'm footloose now and ready to develop my new role, with no distractions. I can focus all my energies on getting to know what's expected of me, ease myself into it.'

'Ah, now, that's where you're wrong . . . about the easing bit, that is. I may just have something interesting for you to cut your teeth on. We got a mail over the weekend from Hennie Goosen in Stellenbosch. You might remember him? He was here two years ago with the South African traders. He's heavily involved in some wine development educational programmes and he has a group of students that he's working with, trying to broaden their horizons. Many of them have probably never heard of Ireland, but he wants someone from here to give a few talks over there on the markets and on our customers' general attitudes to South African wines. He actually asked me if I'd do it, but the more I think about it, you'd be perfect. And you're a woman.'

'That's very sexist of you.'

'I didn't mean that offensively. My thinking was that many of these kids generally don't expect to get other than the most menial jobs, and seeing that women have the same opportunities as men might inspire some of them to push themselves a little harder.'

'Isn't that throwing me in way above my depth?'

'Probably, but that's the best way to learn. Anyway, we have all the info you need on file and we can go over your presentations together

180

before you go. It'll just be like talking to our buyers here, but without the hard sell, and we've seen you do that very efficiently. Hennie's organisation is taking the tab for all the expenses and it should be an experience. He's a generous host.'

JP muttered, 'He can afford to be. As if he wasn't rich enough, he married into serious dosh, vineyards, the whole shebang – but he's not averse to splashing the cash and making the most of it.'

June laughed. 'And I thought you guys were swamped with work every time you were off on your trade missions, with no time for pleasure. Seems like I was wrong about that. I can't wait. When is this going to happen and how long will I be away?'

'In about a fortnight and we're talking about being there for almost three weeks, if you agree,' said Neil. 'Hennie has offered accommodation in his home, but if you'd prefer you can stay in a hotel or in one of the wineries, or try a bit of both, although I'd advise staying with his family for the main part. He lives in a gorgeous old manor amid the vineyards. South Africa is beautiful, but some of its social codes are different from ours, if you know what I mean. I know we'd be happier if you had someone looking out for you, wouldn't we, JP, and you mightn't feel so confined.'

'I think I would be too,' June agreed.

'Right, then you just need to make sure your passport is valid and we'll do the rest.'

For the first time since she'd talked to Peter the previous week, June felt herself smile a proper smile. She was going to South Africa, it would be coming in to summer there and she'd certainly not have time to mope and feel sorry for herself. Yet none of this did anything to stop her wanting to pick up the phone and tell him. He was the first person she wanted to share her news with.

Branch was delighted with this new turn of events, convinced that it would help her daughter move on from her ordeal.

'Don't go falling for someone over there. I like having you close by.'

'There's little fear of that,' June replied.

'Typical of you, June, when one door closes, double ones open.' Danielle tried to keep her reaction light-hearted. 'What I wouldn't give for that trip.'

'You wouldn't give Froggie up for it!'

'You're right. I wouldn't.'

This latest career development gave June the perfect excuse to ring Rosa – she'd worked in Stellenbosch when she'd been a student – and tell her that she and her brother had split up. No explanations, no blame: they had just grown apart.

'I've met Hennie a few times,' Rosa told her. 'He's sound. You'll love it and hate it over there. Well, I know I did, and my perceptions didn't change over a year. I know apartheid is supposed to be finished, but it's still there, bubbling away in lots of places. It's not only a matter of colour, but it's tribal too, so my advice is to say nothing, avoid getting dragged into discussing it at all.'

'That'll be difficult for me! You know how I shoot first and then regret it, so I'll have to learn to hold back.'

'You had better start practising then!'

'I had, hadn't I?'

'I'm sorry you'll be away for Peter's opening. We could have had a proper catch-up then. It's the worst possible timing for me. I'll be up to my eyes here but I couldn't miss it, so I am literally flying in to Dublin on the Friday and back to Portugal on the Sunday.'

'We'll make up for it another time.'

'I hope we do.' She paused. 'June, you do know you are always welcome here, as my friend.'

'Thanks for that. It means a lot.' They promised to keep in touch, and although June felt happier after talking to Rosa, their chat was tinged with sadness as she knew they would probably lose touch in time. She also knew she'd miss Rosa. Each had come so close to being the sister they never had.

Two days later, June arrived home and immediately sensed that Peter had been to collect his

183

things. She walked around the house, opening drawers and looking in cupboards. Empty spaces and naked hangers stared back at her. He hadn't touched their DVDs and there were only a few gaps on the bookshelves.

She found her pink pepper tree drawings and paintings on the hall table, a bouquet of white roses beside them with a little card in his bold handwriting. 'Good luck in the future, wherever it takes you.' It was simply signed 'Peter'. No 'Mr Braga'. No kisses. Had she been moved aside so quickly?

PART II

CHAPTER 11

Considered as something of a whizz-kid in his profession, Lorcan Overend's luck in business started when he was still at college and he set up a dot com company, which he sold on a few years later for an obscene amount of money. Not long after that, his fortunes flourished dramatically, again in his favour, when he wrote an innovative software program aimed at future-proofing banks from the dire consequences predicted if the millennium bug struck at midnight on 31 December 1999. The bug didn't strike, but it had made him a millionaire over again. With updates and licensing agreements, the royalties kept flowing after that.

These achievements were only two among many. The games he had written initially as a hobby were consistently in the top ten in worldwide sales and popularity, and now contributed hugely to his income. From the proceeds, he had bought a beautiful Victorian mansion just outside the desirable village of Dalkey and a 35-foot yacht that he kept in Dún Laoghaire. It was named *SEAS*, from the first two letters of each of his children's names,

Sean and Ashling. He and his wife Carol enjoyed the fruits of his inventiveness wholeheartedly. They had a busy social life, numerous holidays each year. Shopping trips to Dubai and New York were occasional perks too. Carol travelled with him all over the world when she could, their twins accompanying them when it was feasible. Otherwise, they were well looked after by a live-in nanny and an au pair.

Seven weeks after his return from London, Lorcan still found himself thinking about the woman he'd met at Heathrow. He didn't know what it was about her that had captivated him and made him buy the teddy bear for her – he wasn't usually given to such gestures. Yet he couldn't forget her face, the wistfulness that showed through when she thought no one was noticing her. Had he recognised some hurt in her big brown eyes as she stood there looking lost? She had looked so vulnerable and alone and something about that had struck a chord with him.

He was out of practice. He hadn't asked anyone out to dinner in a long time; he knew he wanted to follow up on that offer, yet he had held back. He had been in the States twice since their encounter and found himself thinking of her at all sorts of odd times. This is ridiculous, he told himself, all she can do is say no.

A reminder beeped on his phone. The kids! He had a deal going with them – on Wednesdays, he collected them after sport or homework club or whatever activity they had on that day and they could choose somewhere to eat. Carol had never approved of fast-food joints, but he felt they all needed a bit of nonsense in their lives – him as much as them – and, bit by bit, they were becoming more discerning, looking for better options than burgers and fries.

He was happy that Ashling and Sean seemed to be settling back well into the school routine. They had had enough upheaval over the past eighteen months to unsettle anyone, and he'd had to stand by helplessly, not knowing how to guide them through it. He often wondered how he had survived himself. At times, he felt as though he were outside a window looking in at his life, within touching but not fixing distance.

No one could have foreseen the events that had changed everything so dramatically and finally. They had been sailing all day that Easter Monday and had just come back home, ravenous and elated after one of those unseasonably hot April days that take everyone by surprise. The kids had gone to take showers. Sandrine, their au pair, had set the timer on the oven before going out for the evening. Strictly speaking, they could probably have dispensed with an au pair now that the kids were older, but it was good to know they could take off together when Lorcan needed to answer some emergency or other. Delicious smells filled the kitchen. Carol's parents, who had retired to France, would be back later. They were home for Easter and were out catching up with their friends.

He poured gin and tonics for Carol and himself and she sliced a lime. He could still see her make a funny face as she licked her fingers and tasted its bitter zestiness. They raised their glasses to toast each other and without any warning hers just slipped out of her hand. It splintered on the porcelain tiles.

'Don't move, I'll get the mop,' he'd said, going into the utility room. In the seconds it took to come back, she had slumped on the floor. He called her name and her eyelids fluttered a few times. He reached for the phone on the wall and dialled 999. The kids reappeared just as the ambulance pulled into the driveway of Bayvue, but she had already left them. The haze that descended then never really lifted from his recollections of the sequence of events of that evening. All he recalled was that the paramedics assured them she would have felt nothing as they placed her gently on the gurney and took her away in the ambulance.

They had to wait a few days for the post mortem and later the inquest results, which showed a ruptured brain aneurysm. Her parents were distraught, although they did their best to hide how much from the children. He didn't believe his young, fit, active, healthy wife was dead. She was only thirty-six. In a blink, he had lost his partner, his kids their mother, and the heart went out of the life and the beautiful home they had so lovingly made together.

Friends and family rallied around, muttering platitudes that rang hollow. He wanted to tell them all to go away, but he was afraid of the silence and the emptiness that would replace them. He had no words to console his children. He had no words to console himself. There were none. He was a shell. Nothing made sense any more.

He'd find himself looking at Ashling and Sean, two teenage kids, wanting to grow up but not ready to leave the past behind them. They had been forced to face the serious problems of adulthood before their time. He knew that they were lost too, and that they were trying to be brave for him. He couldn't tell them how bereft he was – that wouldn't be fair on them. He needed to be the strong one to get them through this, yet he had never felt so adrift and rudderless. He envied their closeness – they had each other to talk to and turn to, and they were on the same wavelength, probably even more than other siblings because they were twins. He'd often found Sean asleep on top of Ashling's bed, having gone in to her room when he'd heard her sobbing, and he used to want to climb in beside them, to take comfort from their warmth.

His abiding sense of how he felt in the immediate aftermath was one of coldness and emptiness, a chill that no open fire or bright sunshine could penetrate. He felt useless and was convinced that if he'd been the one who'd gone, that Carol would have made a better job of coping with the kids than he did.

He took them to bereavement counselling, and it seemed to help them. He went to two sessions but found they made him feel worse.

He switched his office arrangements and worked from home as much as he could. He hired a housekeeper, Mrs Fitz – or Misfit as Sean called her when she wasn't listening. She was a haphazard cleaner and hated ironing; her cooking skills were limited too. If it was Monday, it was roast chicken, Tuesday beef casserole, Wednesday leftover beef casserole. That was when they made the Wednesday eat-out pact. But Mrs Fitz made great cakes and chocolate chip biscuits, but more importantly the kids liked her and she liked them. She encouraged them to have friends back to the house, although he had resented it when she told him she thought 'it might put a bit of life back into the place'. He knew nothing would ever do that, but he had to concede that she'd had a point when he heard laughter coming from the family room or saw her playing a computer game with them or saw a gaggle of them running around on the tennis court outside.

Jolting out of his daydream, he realised he was now running late. He saved his work, went out to his car and headed for the school. He joined the line of four-wheel drives waiting for their kids to emerge, girls with names like Saskia and Sequoia and boys called Olan and Etain. His two spotted him and made for the car.

'Hiya, Dad. We're starving!'

'Good. So am I. So what is it to be this week?'

'Italian,' they replied in unison.

'Perfect,' he said, and he put the car into gear. He always felt happier when they were together.

After losing Carol, he'd stepped back from the social scene they'd enjoyed as a couple, finding it too painful to see their friends together, acting normally and getting on with their lives as though nothing had happened. There were too many reminders there of the things they used to enjoy and he found it easier to avoid such situations.

'Do you think we should sell the yacht?' he asked the twins one evening.

'Dad, you can't do that,' Sean protested.

'Mum loved it and so did – do – we, and we'll have good fun again next year, when we can laugh again. I'll make the picnics for us,' his daughter said innocently. He wished he could put a time frame like that on his grief. Would it magically lift on a certain date and would everything seem right again? He knew it wouldn't, that it couldn't.

When friends suggested dinner parties, he knew they were hinting at him meeting new people – and for 'people' he read 'women'. He eventually was persuaded to turn up to one, given by Penny (he'd always thought of her as Pushy Penny) and Des. Their daughter, Amanda, was in school with the twins. Lorcan wasn't going to go, but Des was a life-long friend and he'd run out of excuses not to accept. They'd been at school together, shared their love of the water and were both members of the same yacht club. It had been Des's father who'd taught him how to sail. Initially Penny had tried to come between the friends, wanting to monopolise Des completely, and she had almost succeeded. When Lorcan had first met her at college, she was the golden girl – Miss UCD, Miss Popularity, a leading light on the debating team. Her goal was not only to get a good degree in architecture, but to come out with a 'suitable' husband. And she had done both.

Lorcan always thought of her as having snared Des – that's how he put it, although he knew that it hadn't been quite like that. Along with several others, Des had fallen for her the first time he'd met her, and it had proved to be a good and solid match. She irritated Lorcan beyond belief, but he put up with her for his friend's sake. They now lived in a house she had designed, one that had featured in a few interior design magazines, including America's *Architectural Digest*. Penny had been photographed in that photoshoot reclining provocatively on one of the overstuffed settees. Now she only worked for friends and spent a lot of her time playing and talking about golf. Her ambitions of late had turned to the pitifully limited one of becoming lady captain at some stage. But for all that, and her inability to engage in any conversation without bringing up that four-letter word, she was likeable and fun.

Des had tipped him off that tonight's dinner was to reveal the latest revamp, and Lorcan was delighted there were already some friends of his there when he arrived. The doorbell rang again and, welcoming in a heavily made-up woman, Penny mouthed to Des, 'She's his date.' Lorcan happened to see this exchange and cringed. Introductions were made. His 'date' was a ditsy woman called Toni, from the golf club, of course. She giggled a lot.

'Oh, I love what you've done in here. The pale walls are fantastic. I always thought the red ones were a bit bordello-ish.' She turned to talk to Lorcan. 'Colour is my thing.'

'Really?' he replied. It only ever bothered him when he came to change his car, but he was going to be told anyway.

'Yes, I go into people's homes and go through their wardrobes with them advising them on what colours they should wear if they are winters or summers, that sort of thing. I advise them on their decor too. Colour can be mood altering.'

He was saved from replying when Penny announced it was time to sit down. He wasn't a bit surprised when he found himself next to Toni, or that she hadn't finished talking about colour yet.

'What colour is that on the walls? It's Farrow & Ball, isn't it? Is it Elephant's Breath or Eskimo

Boot? Whichever, those amber amaryllis look dramatic against it.'

Penny was delighted the new look was getting so much attention, but that hadn't been her sole intention that evening. Over mussels in white wine, she asked Lorcan how the twins were coping.

'Remarkably well. I think they found the summer holidays a bit difficult, but being back at school and all the routine that entails is good for them.'

'And what about you?' she asked. 'Loneliness can be an awful state, although you'll have no worries there, a new widower like you is like catnip to some desperate females out there. Oh, I didn't mean you, Toni,' she said, but Toni didn't seem to have registered the comment anyway.

There was an awkward moment at the table, his friends squirming for him. One of the guys stepped in. 'Can you not say the same about widows or the divorced? Or have they more sense?'

'It doesn't seem to work that way,' Penny answered, looking towards Lorcan. 'But where there's a widower, there's always a wife apparent, or two, in waiting. Trust me, widowers never stay that way for long.'

Lorcan was furious. He turned to Toni, desperately trying to think of something to talk about. Carol used to say that whenever she was stuck for conversation, she'd always ask the other person what they were reading. He tried this. Toni giggled and tossed her hair back before replying, 'You mean a book? I don't really read books. Do you?'

'A lot,' he said, and he turned his attention to the food in front of him. With one exception, everyone at the table had been Carol's friend too. Was she that easy to forget? Not for him she wasn't.

'I'm not actually looking for a new wife. I'd just like my own one back again. And I can't have her. She's irreplaceable.'

'You never know what life has in store for you. You shouldn't slam doors shut before they open properly,' Toni said. 'That's my motto anyway.'

He stopped himself from telling her that he wouldn't bring someone in on the kids, not yet. Not for a long time yet, if ever.

Toni carried on talking almost as if he wasn't there. 'You'll change your mind, believe me. I've seen it happen time and again. You'll be snapped up once you're back on the circuit. Wait and see.'

Penny chimed in, 'The girls at golf were just saying—'

He held his hand up. He didn't want to know what the girls at golf or bridge were saying.

'Subtle as ever, Penny,' he said. 'I'm glad my private life is such a source of curiosity and speculation. Perhaps you'd like to tell them there is nothing to report. When and if there ever is, I'll give you the exclusive on it and you can notify the media. Now, if you'll excuse me I think I'll get back to the kids. It was nice meeting you, Toni, and I'm sorry to have wasted your evening.'

Some of the others tried to persuade him to stay

till the end of the meal, but he declined, saying he had lost his appetite. Des walked him out to the hall.

'Look, mate, I'm sorry about that. She didn't mean any harm. You know her, tact has never been her strong point.'

'I know that. Don't worry about it. I'm probably being oversensitive.'

'Will I call a taxi?'

'No, thanks. I think I'll walk.'

He left and headed along the coast road to clear his head.

After he had closed the door on his friend, Des spoke quietly to his wife, who had gone into the kitchen to check on dessert. 'That was a bit heavy, even for you, Penny. Don't you think?'

'Oh don't be a moan. He'll be delighted when we've set him up with someone suitable – just wait and see. Toni obviously wasn't right for him.'

'I think he'd much prefer it if we stayed out of his business.'

But Penny was determined to manage Lorcan's love life, and his rebuff wasn't going to stop her from trying to set him up with some of her other friends. Over the next few months, there were more pathetically embarrassing encounters in friends' houses and at the yacht club, so he decided to just be busy on whatever date she proposed.

Gradually, though, he found himself getting back on track, and taking an interest in his work again.

To him, buying the teddy bear had been a positive indication that he was coming out of the catatonic state into which he had retreated. Now it was time to act on it.

He found renewed interest in writing a programme designed for hospital administration. He used to develop games as a form of relaxation and now Sean and he were working on a new one together. He was happy they shared this interest and wished he had a common one with his daughter. Perhaps they should go back to sailing. She'd always enjoyed that.

CHAPTER 12

Two weeks later, as June waited in the lounge in Heathrow for her connecting flight to Cape Town, she remembered meeting Lorcan. He hadn't phoned and she wasn't that surprised really. She had half hoped he might, but she dismissed the encounter as just a fleeting event. He had been kind, and she had needed kindness then. For that, she'd always be grateful. She couldn't pretend being without Peter was easy, but she had to be positive and was determined to throw herself into her career from here on in.

She settled back to enjoy the luxury of her flight, which took her down over the continent of Africa. Clear skies allowed her to witness the most amazing sunset she had ever seen. An enormous orange ball hovered for a short time in a greenish/blue sky. Ribbons of cloud languidly trailed in front of it, changing from pink to yellow before the sphere dropped and disappeared in front of her eyes, leaving the sky behind in inky blackness.

'Glorious or what?' the man in the next pod to her said.

'I never saw anything as beautiful.'

'So I take it this must be your first time to South Africa. It's something we do really well – our sunsets – and that one was a beauty. Where are you headed?'

She told him she was heading to Stellenbosch on a business trip.

'I'm based in Cape Town, although I live out that direction. I shunned the family business – they're in wine production too – in favour of IT. It's difficult to become disentangled though when all the relatives are involved, so I get roped in every now and again. It's a pity we're flying in the dark because you'll miss seeing Table Mountain as we come in to land. You should try and go to the top while you're there.'

'I'll not really be in control of my own programme, I'll have to do what I'm told and go where I'm taken, but I'm very excited about it all.'

'I hope you'll not be disappointed,' he said. He gave her his card. 'If you find yourself at a loose end or need rescuing from the tedium of the same company for three weeks, give me a call. I'd be delighted to show you around.'

'I certainly hope that won't be the case,' she said, 'but thank you.' She handed over her card, telling him where she would be staying.

'I know Hennie – well just about everybody in

Stellenbosch knows Hennie – he's a very genuine guy.'

They landed in Cape Town an hour later and, as expected, Hennie Goosen was waiting for her as she walked out into Arrivals with her luggage. Luckily, he recognised her, because she would not have picked him out in the waiting crowd as someone she had met before in Dublin. He was a slight wiry man with a neatly trimmed beard and a very strong Afrikaans accent. He spoke rapidly and she found she had to consciously tune in to follow everything he said.

'Welcome to South Africa. We're delighted you've come to join us. You must be exhausted, but we'll have you home in about forty minutes and you can relax then.'

'I'm not too bad. The flight was very pleasant and it's a real bonus not having to deal with jet lag.'

'So everyone tells us. It's never been a problem for me, but I know some people who take days to recover after flights, especially to Oz or from the States.' He lifted her suitcase into the jeep as though it weighed nothing and drove out of the airport. They passed what seemed like miles and miles of shanty housing. June was astonished by the extent of them, but said nothing. Sensing her reaction, he said, 'There's no way to avoid seeing those. Not our biggest triumph and still lots more to be done, but there'll be plenty of time over the next few weeks for social and history lessons.'

Hennie asked after the Macy brothers and kept the conversation general. By way of complete contrast some kilometres away, they drove through the cultivated countryside, turning off at one of the many grandiose entrances. The gates swung open to admit them to a curving driveway that stopped in front of a perfect manor house.

'Well, June, this is where I hang my hat. It's much more than just a home, though. It's our hub. Out the back, there's the staff accommodation, and all the other bits to do with winery are up that driveway over there, in what we pretentiously call the west wing. I'll give you the guided tour in the morning.'

The front door opened and a petite blonde woman who could have stepped out of a photoshoot in Italian *Vogue* emerged. 'That's Kima, my better half.'

Kima walked towards the car as June got out. 'We are delighted to welcome you to our home. You must be exhausted. Come in.'

She explained that June would be joined by some Australians and an American for their project. They had flown in that morning, but had all crashed out earlier on. June turned to get her bag and quickly realised that there was someone else delegated to do that. By the time she'd been given something to eat and drink, she twigged that there was also someone assigned to serve them, to clear away and to take her effects to her room. When she finally got there, she had passed her tiredness threshold. She took in the big room with its chunky furniture and lacy bed coverings. It had a period feel about it, but with a distinctly Dutch influence – solid, functional and homely.

She opened the screens and walked out on to the balcony, breathing in the unfamiliar warm earthy smells and listening to the strange night sounds of Africa, before remembering she had no insect repellent on. Memories of bites inflicted on holidays and lumps that stubbornly took months to disappear forced her into a hasty retreat inside.

Then she noticed that her bags had been unpacked and everything had been put on hangers in the wardrobes. Her toiletries were missing so she figured they had already made their way to her en suite. She wandered in to take a look and was astonished at the opulence of this room. The centrepiece was an enormous old-fashioned cast-iron bath, its gilded clawed feet perched on a plinth. The tub was already filled with hot water and there were flower petals floating in it. Someone had placed a small table at a perfect distance, complete with a stack of fluffy towels. Her wash bag was sitting on top of these. She undressed and luxuriated in the lavishness of it all, but she couldn't get the glimpses of the shanties out of her mind. Her first impressions were those of total contrasts, black and white in every sense.

Pampered and relaxed, she wrapped herself in a generous bathrobe and wanted to share the day with someone. If she was truthful, she wanted to share it with Peter but that was no longer an option. She was slowly getting used to that idea. She was ready to focus on this new chapter, this new beginning, and embrace it fully.

She realised her phone was still powered off because of her flight. But it was too late to send texts to her mother and Danielle anyway, they'd have to wait until the morning. She climbed into the oversized bed with its starched bed linen. It smelled faintly of jasmine. No doubt the Goosens had laundry staff to look after that too.

Already she was decidedly uncomfortable with the idea of servants doing for her what she could do for herself, but she remembered JP telling her, more than once, 'They do things differently over there. Don't try to change their world in three weeks! It can't be done.'

She remembered Rosa telling her much the same thing. She smiled in the darkness and thought, *They're probably right too*!

The following morning after breakfast, June got a good look at the manor house, which Kima, who was fully made up and dressed in tennis whites, told them had been in her family for six generations. It was furnished in a mixture of antique and modern pieces. Even the scalloped roofline reminded June of those she'd seen when she'd visited Amsterdam. The dining room opened onto a large wrap-around terrace with views towards the gentle vine-lined slopes, which appeared to have been precision planted in rows that disappeared over the hills as far as the eye could see. Beyond, the Great Drakenstein Mountains were still just out of focus in the early-morning mists, their peaks jutting through in places. June could smell the heat in the air and was captivated by the strange birdsong. It was in this setting that she was introduced to the two Australians and the American, whom Hennie had invited to work with him on his project. Kima seemed to detach, taking on a glazed look as her husband enthused about his plans.

'Don't let him bore you. He's inclined to get carried away,' she said.

He just laughed at her and continued, 'We try to give some of the more promising ghetto kids a chance to get involved. They've been making wine in these parts for over 200 years, so it's part of all our heritage, even though it's only in the past fifty or so that it's made its mark internationally. If the French had had their way, we'd never have started.' He laughed. 'There endeth the history lesson.'

'For the moment,' Kima said. She then asked the girl who was serving the fresh orange juice to have the car brought out front for her. 'If you'll excuse me, I have an appointment at the club. I'll see you all this evening.'

When they heard the car pull away, Hennie spoke again. 'Everything you see around you here owes itself to Kima's family. As she says, they've had this estate for six generations, but she hasn't a clue about the business, nor does she want to. She takes great pride in the end result though.'

'Does she mind you taking strangers like us in to your home?' asked one of the Australians.

'Not at all. My wife is what could be termed a social butterfly. She was never brought up to work and revels in her role as wife and hostess – and, dare I say it as she can't hear me, as the lady of the manor. And she does them all really well. She'll kill you with kindness and, by the time you leave, you'll know every one of our neighbours from miles around. Now let's do the tour and introduce you to the team.'

They piled into a jeep and were driven around the vineyards and the estate, to the tasting rooms and the cellars. June was very impressed. It was a considerable operation – much larger than she expected. They stopped occasionally to inspect the vines, which Hennie explained wouldn't be ready for harvesting until February. Their fresh green leaves contrasted sharply against the red earth. June was once again struck by the beauty of her surroundings and by her luck in being there at all. Their tour took them back to some long buildings, which concealed a sea of stainless steel vats and all the trappings of a modern-day wine-producing enterprise.

'The youngsters you're going to meet will spend a year with us, partly in residence on the estate, and this is where you all come in. This is our fifth year doing this and we've taken on a few of them on a permanent basis at the end of each one. However, the biggest disadvantage is that they have never had much opportunity to travel outside their shanty towns. The way I see it, they need one-to-one exposure to the wider world and to people from different cultures. So my thinking on this is that maybe the best way to give them that boost of confidence is by letting them meet and befriend people like you who are working in the same industry and talk the same language. I admit you're my guinea pigs on this as this is the first time I've added anything like this to the programme, so if you have any bright ideas please let me know. I'm open to suggestions. I may be off on a wild goose chase on this one, but I want to try it anyway.'

'I think this could be a mutual learning curve for us all,' June said, and one of the Aussies agreed.

Once the initial shyness between the students and the mentors was overcome, which in some cases took a few days, there was a lot of discussion and a lot of laughter.

June found the easiest way to keep in touch with Danielle and Branch was via email – as it enabled her to explain everything in a way she couldn't in a text.

'This place is amazing,' she'd written to Danielle after she'd been there a couple of days. 'It's beautiful and intriguing and the people are lovely.

I just can't get my head around having them do everything for me. It makes me very uneasy, even uncomfortable. I'm afraid that if I'm friendly with them, they might think I'm being patronising and if I'm not then I'll come across as being superior or uppity. So I stand there grinning like a fool and saying thank you too many times for everything.'

She read Danielle's reply as she relaxed over a glass of wine a few evenings later. 'Stop worrying and just be yourself. You'd never come across as being uppity or superior. I'd swap places with you in a heartbeat, except I'm going to Geneva next weekend to stay with Froggie and nothing's going to get in the way of that!'

June smiled at the thought of how well Danielle and Froggie's relationship was going.

'Today we visited a township or *lokasie* where some of the students grew up. One of them – a young woman called Lerato (I have to keep thinking of Loreto before I can remember that) – was so proud to show us her home, but I had to concentrate on keeping a smile on my face so she couldn't see my real feelings. The poverty defies description – I'll never complain about anything again, I promise. But what amazed me most of all was that despite the only water being available from communal taps or water spigots on street corners, there were lines of washing every-where and the whites really were whiter than white!'

It was the first opportunity June had had to email Branch, and she wanted to tell her everything so her mother could share in it all. She explained about the programme, which she felt had been well-thought-out. Most of the day was spent on tastings and teaching Hennie's protégées what to look for, how to identify the subtleties and nuances of flavour, developing their noses, forging new friendships and opening their horizons. The rest of the time, Hennie wanted them all to experience his South Africa.

They took the cable car up Table Mountain and marvelled at views that stretched across the sea to Robben Island. All around them, furry dassies dashed around and sat on hind legs like meerkats begging for titbits.

'They look like squirrels,' the American remarked.

'Improbable as it may seem, their nearest relative is the elephant,' Hennie told them.

'You're joking,' one of the students said. 'They're poles apart in size.'

'That may be, but genetically the elephant is their nearest kin. Don't ask me how that happens but it's a fact, according to their DNA. A bit like us and apes, I suppose. I like to think we don't look too like them, but then I avoid mirrors as much as I can!'

Kima lived up to her reputation, hosting barbecues and dinner parties for all and sundry, and June was pleasantly surprised to find her companion from the flight at one of them. Over thick steaks and salad, she made the mistake of getting embroiled in a discussion on apartheid with him and let her tongue run away with her.

'We had a "them" and "us" in Ireland for too long – the big house syndrome and the peasants. Although it was a long time ago now, it's still in the psyche. That's probably why I feel so uneasy here.'

'Is that how you feel here, June? Uneasy?' Hennie asked, appearing at her side. 'I'm sorry to hear that.' He moved on to his other guests, but she could tell from his tone and body language that he was hurt. She went to follow him, but her companion caught her elbow and steered her away towards the other end of the patio. Realising she may have said too much, she tried to soften her comments, but only made matters worse. 'The Irish tend not to like being waited on hand and foot. We don't like the idea of servants.'

'Then perhaps you'll let me tell you a few home truths about life here in South Africa. If it weren't for people like your hosts, Kima and Hennie, a lot of the people they employ as servants' – he emphasised the word as though it was ugly and unsavoury – 'would have no work, no opportunities and no future. Because of your hosts, and others like them, most of them manage to support families and educate their children.' He didn't stop to allow her react. 'Don't let Kima's nonchalance fool you. She's a very capable, educated woman, and she doesn't have to do all the entertaining she does, nor get her hair and nails done so often, nor does she need the army of staff she employs here at the manor. Hennie doesn't have to get involved in the wine development programme, he has more than enough to do running the winery, but he sees it as a way of giving something back. There are lots of people like them. We don't all agree with what happened in this country in the past, you know.'

She felt mortified and embarrassed. When this reality had been explained to her, she realised she'd brought her own prejudices with her and let them skew her reality. But before she could think of anything plausible to say in her defence he continued, 'Work gives people dignity and pride. They don't want hand-outs – they want to feel valued and respected, just as we do. People like the Goosens do that. It's not slave labour, you know. They pay all their workers the same wages, irrespective of colour or creed.'

'I'm so sorry. I didn't look at it like that. I didn't think.'

'Obviously.'

'I need to find Hennie and apologise.'

'I wouldn't do that tonight if I were you. Let him cool down. Do it in the morning. Now, I'm going to head off.' He said goodnight, but didn't renew his offer to show her around Cape Town.

Feeling chastised and ashamed, June slipped quietly back to her room. How had she been so blinkered? As she got ready for bed, she heard the cars gradually take the last guests home and she thought back over what had happened and what had been said. If they were to put her life under a microscope, she would come across as being spoiled, privileged and protected. What right did she have to judge anyone else, or to be so sanctimonious?

She just wanted to get on a plane and go home, but that wasn't an option. She'd have to swallow her pride and try and smooth things over. 'I seem to be doing that a lot lately,' she said to herself.

Before she went to sleep, she checked her phone for messages. She scanned the texts and then noticed she had voicemail. She played the message back first, and was so grateful to hear a friendly voice that she almost wept with relief and a wave of homesickness. It could not have come at a better time.

Hi, it's Lorcan Overend here. Remember me? We met in London, well in Heathrow. I promised to contact you, but I've been doing a lot of work-related travel since then. I'm sorry I missed you – I gather from your phone message that you're away. Hope you're having a nice time wherever you are. I'll give you a call when you return. Take care.

She was tempted to ring him and then thought she might sound desperate – and she wasn't certain if the only reason she wanted to call him was because of the rotten evening she'd just had. But she did play the message twice more, liking the rich timbre and friendliness in his voice. He had decided to contact her after all. She now had an excuse to phone him when she got back.

The next morning, she came down early to breakfast, hoping to catch Hennie before everyone else appeared. All traces of the evening's barbecue had gone and order had been restored. She found Kima and Hennie standing by the railings drinking coffee. She took a deep breath, walked over and asked if she could join them.

'I owe you both an apology,' she began, hoping one or the other would step in and say it wasn't necessary, but they didn't. They let her squirm as she tried to explain what she had said. 'You are wonderful hosts and have made me feel so at home here, I feel like a part of your family. I never meant to upset you, or anyone, but I will understand if you'd prefer me to leave, or move to a hotel for the rest of my stay.'

She could feel Hennie's eyes boring into her. Then he smiled. 'That won't be necessary. We can understand your attitude and how our world might seem to someone who doesn't know it. You're more than welcome to stay, June. We'd all miss you if you bailed now. Especially Lerato, you seem to have become her role model. Anyway, I think you've learned something from last night. Remember the saying "never judge a book by its cover"? We all say it, but few of us ever pay any heed to it.'

'Well I'm afraid I'm guilty on all counts of that,' June admitted.

'I think most of us are at some point,' Kima said. 'It's very easy.'

'I hope I haven't come across as being too judgemental or superior to the students. That's the last thing I would want.'

'You haven't,' said Hennie. 'They admire you and they trust you. I know that, but do you know what I'd really like you to do for them? I'd like you to tell them about your life in Ireland and about your impressions of our way of life here. That's the reason we brought you down here in the first place, to exchange ideas and to expose them to different cultures. That way they can ask questions – and so can you.'

'Hennie, that's one of your best ideas,' Kima said, smiling at her husband. 'Would you be comfortable doing that, June?'

'Absolutely, but it seems as though I may be the one who has the most learning to do.'

'Possibly, and that may be exactly what they need to hear from someone like you.'

Just then, the others came through for breakfast, and Hennie and Kima hugged June before joining them at the table.

June couldn't believe the three weeks were over. She was genuinely sorry to be leaving and they all promised to keep in touch. Apart from her major faux pas, it had been a wonderful experience on so many levels, not least having the opportunity to see at first hand just what was involved in making a major producer a globally successful one.

Her mind was buzzing with ideas for her new role with the Macy brothers and her horizons were broadened much more than she had ever imagined possible. She'd done a lot of soul-searching during her time away – the distance had helped her think – and had accepted that Peter was in the past. There was no point in recriminations – they would change nothing. Now all she had to do was get on with life.

But on the flight home, between dozing and eating, she couldn't help wondering if the restaurant had reopened the previous Friday night. Had it been the glittering occasion that she and Peter had planned together? Had Zoe been by his side?

She remembered the mail she had recieved from Danielle before leaving.

I don't like telling you this but I can't pretend it didn't happen either. Froggie and I were invited to the opening of The Pink Pepper Tree. I have to admit I was sorely tempted to go, but we declined – out of loyalty to you! I did send a card from the two of us, wishing Peter well. And I'll keep all the weekend supplements and papers in case you want to see them at some stage.

Her friend knew her well. June knew she probably would want to read them. She berated herself – she'd have to stop thinking like this. Frustrated, she picked a movie from the menu, and then fell asleep shortly after it started.

CHAPTER 13

In the weeks following the restaurant opening, June couldn't escape Peter and Zoe. The papers were full of pictures and column inches covering the beautiful people who had turned up – gallery owners, politicians, pop stars, promoters, models and some of The Pink Pepper Tree's loyal regulars. The stained-glass window, which had just been finished hours before the guests were due to arrive, had caught everyone's imagination. Most of the newspapers chose it for one of the main photographs.

Critics flocked there to eat and then write their opinions of the menus, the flavours, the ambience and the service. It was heralded as 'top end' and 'excellent', even as 'a possible contender for a Michelin star in the future'. Occasionally, Zoe was in the photographs, beside Peter or with some visiting name or other. The diarists and photographers were delighted to have a new venue where they were sure to find more than a few celebs in the one place at any given time. It made their work much easier.

June was relieved that neither Branch nor

Danielle ever made any mention of the articles and reviews. She didn't either. She did cut out and keep a few of them, telling herself it was for the shots of her window, before giving herself a stern talking to. Then she binned them.

Danielle felt her life was on a high. Froggie was coming back to Dublin with regular frequency, and staying with her.

She'd told June everything when she'd got back. 'After that night out, we spent the rest of the time in his apartment, well in the bedroom actually. Don't let anyone tell you that long-distance relationships aren't torture, but the sex is fantastic.' June had laughed with her friend. 'Well, you know discretion has never been my strong point.'

During their first proper catch-up since June's trip to South Africa, they started to talk about what they would do at Christmas. Danielle had two weeks off school and was determined to make the most of it. 'Froggie is coming home to see his parents first, but he wants me to go skiing for the New Year. 'I can't ski, June. I'll make a fool of myself in front of all his friends.'

'No you won't! And, anyway, that's never stopped you from doing anything before. Just think of the *après ski* and the parties and those ski instructors. I read somewhere that they are hired for their looks before their accomplishments on the slopes.'

'Then maybe you should come along too. Start looking around.'

'No, thanks. I'm not ready to do that yet. I'm still getting my head around being single and I don't want to end up with my leg in plaster, thank you.'

'And it doesn't matter if I do? Some friend you are!'

CHAPTER 14

Lorcan Overend was sitting in his office at home with his phone in his hand. Outside, leaves were falling with each gust of wind, freckling the lawn and the driveway. He'd picked his phone up a few times already and scrolled down to June's number. He dialled before he could change his mind again.

'Well, hello,' she said when he introduced himself. 'How nice to hear from you.' She tried to sound calm but was delighted he'd called. In the week since she'd come back from South Africa, she had nearly called him, but hadn't managed to dial his number, secretly hoping he'd get in touch, as he'd said he would.

'I thought I'd let you settle back down from wherever you were, and I also thought it was time to check up and see if you've given that bear a name yet.'

She laughed. 'Not officially, but I've been toying with Tarquin or Turlough. What do you think?'

'You just made that up! No self-respecting teddy can go through life with a name like Tarquin or Turlough. He'll suffer from feelings of being

221

unloved. Maybe he'll even have problems with his identity if he doesn't get a name soon. We need to sort this out as a matter of urgency. Are you free tomorrow evening?'

'You know, I think I could be.'

It's amazing, I travel extensively and never mind sitting on my own in eateries, bars or diners all over the world, but I suddenly feel like a self-conscious schoolboy, thinking that everyone is looking at me, knowing I'm on a first date. I shouldn't have come in so early. Lorcan looked about the restaurant, trying to look nonchalant.

He had agonised long and hard over making that second call. *She must think I'm nuts – a grown man objecting to what she calls her teddy bear, but, heck, as an ice breaker it seemed to work. Maybe I'm not as much out of practice as I thought I was.* He found himself smiling. He hadn't asked anyone out on a date since his first date with Carol. *God, is it any wonder I'm feeling gauche about this?*

He needn't have been so anxious – as soon as June arrived he relaxed, stood up and kissed her on the cheek.

'You look great,' he told her, admiring the emerald outfit that complemented her colouring. 'Much better than when we met that last time.' She flushed and, a little flustered, he muttered, 'Now that was probably the wrong thing to say. I'm sorry.'

She laughed. 'Don't be. It's the truth. I was

feeling pretty terrible that day. Thank you for rescuing me and for this little fellow.' She produced the teddy and sat him on the table against the window. 'I thought he should have a say in this naming ceremony.'

'OK. Let's get our priorities right,' he said.

'I've been thinking about it and I quite like Bartley.'

'That's certainly an improvement on Tarquin and whatever the other one you wanted was. I like Bruno.'

'Then why don't we call him Bartley Bruno or Bruno Bartley? Both have a certain ring to them.'

'I agree.'

He called the waiter and ordered a bottle of champagne. They toasted their fluffy friend, Bartley Bruno, then each other. Then they ordered their meals, falling in to easy conversation as though they had known each other forever. He was afraid he'd scare her off at this stage and she wouldn't go out with him again if she thought he had too much baggage. And he knew he didn't want that to happen, so he held off telling her about the twins. He didn't go into Carol's death either. He brushed over it, saying he'd been on his own for a few years.

'Tell me about yourself. Where have you been?'

'I'm not that interesting at all. I was away on business of sorts when you left your message, and you came to my rescue with that too. I got it just when I needed to hear a friendly voice.'

He listened as she told him what had happened.

'I got myself into a real mess and was feeling very vulnerable. I just wanted to run away and disappear.'

'I know exactly what you mean. I hated and loved the place too and for those very reasons – I also landed myself in hot water for speaking out.' As they waited for their coffees, he decided he could open up to her about how he was feeling. 'I didn't know whether I should contact you again.'

'And I didn't know if I should reply.' They both laughed. 'I'm glad you did phone,' she said more seriously, looking directly at him.

He topped up their glasses. 'Can we do it again – soon – without the chaperon?'

'Shush, you'll hurt his feelings,' she said, lightening the mood again, as she put the bear back in his bag. 'And yes, I'd love to. I really enjoyed this evening.'

'So did I, very much.'

He walked her up the steps to her front door and he kissed her on both cheeks. When she had gone inside and turned off the alarm, he went back to the waiting taxi, whistling as his feet crunched on the gravel driveway.

Apart from the porch and hall lights, his house was in darkness when he got back. He couldn't believe it was almost one o'clock. The au pair had left a message for him on the kitchen table. Penny had called – she was having a dinner party the following week and would like him to come. Another of her potential wife-in-waiting events no doubt. The note said she'd call back and he decided he'd still be busy. He sat at the table and thought back over the evening. He had a good feeling about June, but he regretted not telling her about the kids. That was a mistake. It was going to be harder to do it the next time.

He called her the following day and made arrangements to meet later in the week. He had been given tickets for a concert – he wasn't sure how she felt about classical music, but she seemed to like the idea. He found himself whistling again, something he hadn't done for a while.

As June was getting ready for the concert, she thought back on their previous date. She had enjoyed herself more than she'd expected, and had found Lorcan very easy to talk to – and attractive. She'd been over the moon when he'd called her again. He'd said he would, but her confidence had been knocked by Peter's sudden change of heart towards her and didn't fully trust that Lorcan would want to go out with her again. She couldn't help comparing Lorcan with Peter – she knew Peter would be the yardstick by which she measured any other man she met, for both good and bad traits. But Lorcan was so much older than Peter, and his maturity appealed to her. He was funny, wise and loveable and she wanted to find out more about him. She knew she wasn't looking for a relationship – but she was looking to get out and meet people and enjoy herself.

They met for a drink before the concert, and Lorcan decided to tell June everything he wished he'd told her before. He couldn't bear the idea of enjoying more of June's company if there was a chance she wouldn't want to know him when she knew everything.

'June, there are a few things I need to tell you.'

'Why do I get the feeling I'm not going to like them?' she asked. 'In my experience, sentences which include the words "something I need to tell you" are usually ominous. Are you going to tell me you're married?'

'No, I was, but as I told you last time, I've been on my own for a while. I'm widowed. Since Easter last year. I haven't dated anyone since Carol, my wife, died and that's one of the reasons I hesitated in contacting you. I also have two children, one of each – they're hardly kids anymore – they're twins, and have just turned fifteen. I'm forty-five. I know that's a lot to take in and if it frightens you off and you'd rather not meet again then that's your decision and I'll understand.'

'I'm sorry to hear that – not that you have children, but that you lost your wife. Were you happy together?'

Encouraged by her reaction, he continued. 'Yes, very, and I'd be lying if I said the last year and a half or so had been easy, but we're getting there – wherever there is. I know that's a lot to throw at you, but I wanted to get it all out in the open. Certain things are sacrosanct and my kids have to come first, no matter who I meet or where my life takes me.'

'I couldn't argue with that.'

'I like you and feel I'd like to keep on seeing you, if—'

'And I'd like that too,' she replied.

He relaxed back into his chair, knowing she meant it.

CHAPTER 15

June was very busy at work and she had immersed herself in it wholeheartedly, mainly because she enjoyed it but also because it stopped her dwelling on the what-ifs of her life, and it stopped her from making comparisons. She'd been out with Lorcan many times, though she hadn't met his family yet. She looked forward to seeing him and felt their friendship was growing, though it had none of the passion she'd shared with Peter.

Christmas was fast approaching and orders that had been taken over the previous months were checked and re-checked before being dispatched to their clients. The wine club, which had gained momentum from the first night, had taken on a life of its own, and Kelly had been given more responsibility for organising the evenings. She was delighted with the extra money, as she counted down the days until she left for Australia.

'I'm quite apprehensive the closer it gets,' she admitted to June. 'Supposing nothing has changed and Cara resents me as much as ever. I know I made mistakes with her, but I didn't have much choice.'

'She won't feel the same as she did, not now that she's a mother. You were very young, hardly more than a child yourself. Tell her how you felt. I'm sure she'll understand.'

June had encouraged Kelly to embrace the new role, telling her it was about more than just extra money. And June had been delighted when Kelly had suggested bringing in a chef for one evening to talk festive food and what wines to serve with the traditional fare. The approach of the Christmas season also gave June lots of ideas. She contacted a hamper company, and gained a lucrative deal supplying some of the more exclusive wines they stocked.

The evening events meant working late, but June didn't mind that. It kept her occupied and gave her a reason to take things slowly with Lorcan, until she had a chance to work out how she really felt. She found herself going to lots of parties and receptions in the few weeks before the holidays.

Two weeks before Christmas, the girls in the office had brought in lots of goodies for elevenses to send Kelly on her big adventure Down Under.

'You can think of us on Christmas Day when you're sizzling away having a barbecue on the beach,' June said as they bid each other farewell. And then she spoke more quietly. 'Don't worry about Cara too much, everything will be fine.'

Kelly gave June a hug and thanked her for listening. 'I promise I'll send you a text to let you know how it all went.'

June met Danielle for a meal in their favourite little Italian restaurant. When Froggie was home, she never saw much of Danielle, and so she was making the most of their evenings before he arrived.

'Do you remember sitting here last spring when we planned our grand tour? So much has happened since then,' June said.

'I know. Then, you were firmly spoken for and I was still interviewing. Isn't it time you started dating again?'

June smiled, but before she could reply Danielle said, 'I hope you're not sitting at home every evening on your own.'

'As if. You needn't fret. I haven't started watching the soaps yet.'

'That's a relief. I was worried about you, in case you were moping.'

'There's no need. I've no time to mope. Work is hectic, but very enjoyable. I still miss Peter – I think I always will – but . . . I have been on a few dates with someone else.'

Danielle squealed with delight. 'You kept that very quiet. Who is he? Where did you meet? Do I know him?'

'Hang on there: one question at a time.' She laughed at her friend before filling her in on the main details. 'He's great company and very kind and I like him. I really like him.'

'*Like* him?'

'Yes, a lot, but I'm not in the headspace for anything more. You know that.'

'Is he?'

'Possibly. Probably.' Then she added, 'He's a lot older than me.'

'You've not gone for an old sugar daddy!'

'How's forty-five?'

'Pushing it a bit – that's fourteen . . . no, fifteen years' difference.'

'There was eleven between Mum and Dad and it didn't seem to matter.'

'So long as he has all his own teeth, some hair left and no hangover tum, he might do.'

'No, he's fit, has loads of floppy hair. Strange as it may seem, I haven't actually asked him if his teeth are all his own, but he looks good when he smiles – and he does that a lot.'

'That's important too, but does he make *you* smile?'

'Actually, yes, he does,' she said, realising that he did.

'This sounds encouraging. When can I meet him?'

'Soon. Maybe over Christmas – before you head off on the *pistes*.'

'We still can't persuade you to join us?'

'No way, although it's going to be a peculiarly quiet Christmas this year; everyone seems to be

231

going away, and there's no restaurant to keep me busy,' she said, thinking back over the past few years when she'd helped Peter in the mad whirlwind of the festive season. 'I'll not be flying off to Portugal this year either,' June said, almost as if she couldn't quite believe it. Do you think he'll have taken Zoe to meet his family yet?'

'Probably. I wasn't going to tell you in case it upset you, but Froggie and I bumped into them in town last weekend. He asked how you were and I told him you were fantastic. Can't you spend Christmas with your new friend?' Danielle asked.

'No, that's not an option.'

'Why? Is he off somewhere too?'

'His children have to come first.'

'His *children*? You didn't mention them before now. How old are they?'

'Twins, who've just turned fifteen.'

'Good God! Has he any other minuses?'

'No, he's an open book.'

'Believe you me – no man of forty-five is an open book.'

'You're such a sceptic, Danielle.'

'I'm not. I'm just being protective. I don't want to see you getting hurt again.'

'I won't be. I'm taking it all very slowly and I'm a lot wiser now.'

'It's not always that easy. Remember that love doesn't have a brain.'

'Who are you telling?'

'Just be careful. Don't rush in to anything.'

'Don't worry. I've no intentions of rushing anywhere.'

Lorcan managed to avoid Penny's invites until she cornered him at a Sunday lunch in the clubhouse. He spotted her family when they came in and managed to steer the kids in the other direction to a table that was partially hidden by the huge Christmas tree. But Ashling, unaware of her father's reasons for keeping a low profile, waved across at Penny and Des's daughter, Amanda. Within seconds, the waiter was over telling them that Penny and Des wanted them to join them. He couldn't refuse, but was relieved that there wasn't a 'spare' set up for him to meet.

As the meal progressed, he found himself sitting back observing the dynamics of a normal family. Amanda seemed to have a really good relationship with Penny and she clearly adored her dad. Des was good with Sean and took an interest in what he was doing. He probably would have loved a son. Did they appreciate how lucky they were?

He only came back from his reverie when Penny said, 'You're miles away, Lorcan. I was just saying I'd take the girls shopping when the sales are on.' He realised that his daughter probably missed the girly-ness of having a mother to shop with.

'That's very good of you, Penny,' he said. 'I'm a bit of a disappointment in that department, I'm afraid.'

'You can come too, Sean, if you'd like.'

'Shopping? Thanks, but no thanks!' They all laughed at his reaction.

'A typical man,' Penny said. 'Leave the shopping to the women, then complain when all you get is socks and jocks for pressies.'

'What are the plans for Christmas?' Des asked.

'Carol's parents are coming back over from France and they'll be with us for a few days before they head off to their place in Connemara.'

'You have to bring them to us one of the days as well. It would be lovely to see them.' He stalled and Penny continued, 'The twins will be staying over with us on New Year's Eve, won't they?'

Lorcan saw his children exchange awkward glances, and he wondered if it was because they didn't want to go or because he was missing something.

'It's the first I heard of it,' he said. 'But then, I'm sure they don't tell me everything, do you?' He smiled at them.

'Amanda's sixteenth is on the first and she wanted a party so we decided to combine that with ringing in the New Year.'

'You've got to be there,' said Amanda. 'You said you would.'

Sean spoke up, looking at his sister. 'Dad, she wouldn't let me tell you in case you were doing nothing on that night. We didn't want to leave you on your own.'

'Isn't that sweet of them?' said Penny. 'We'll

have them and that'll leave you free to enjoy your-self. It's about time your dad started socialising again, isn't it?'

Des shot his wife a murderous look, which she chose to ignore, but she did stop talking. No one answered her. Des asked Sean about the state-of-the-art laptop he was hoping to get for Christmas and the moment passed. It was mid-afternoon when they managed to detach themselves and Lorcan took them to buy their Christmas tree. While they were decorating it, he brought up the matter of the party again.

'You've got to be honest with me, kids. I'm doing my best, but you didn't come with an instruction manual, so I'm going to make mistakes. How do you think I would have felt if you missed Amanda's sixteenth and I discovered later it was because you didn't want to leave me on my own for one evening? Terrible, that's how I'd feel.'

Ashling came over and put her arms around him. 'You rock, Dad.'

'Is that why you don't want to go shopping with the girls too, Sean? In case I might miss you?' he teased his son.

'Unlikely – an afternoon traipsing around town, listening to them talking about what's "so-oo on trend" is enough to drive me around the bend. I can't think of anything I'd hate more.'

They were quiet for a bit as they took various decorations from their boxes, each with their own memories from previous Christmases.

'Dad,' Ashling said, in that voice that always made him take note, 'can I ask you something? If you got married again, would that mean you didn't love Mum any more?'

'Poppet, I'll always love your mum. Even if I got married a dozen times, which I won't, nothing will ever change how I feel about your mum.'

She surprised him by replying, 'That's what Sean said.'

'Sensible lad. Now, let's go and string these bulbs on the trees in the porch.'

When the twins had gone to bed, he sat in the lounge, the only illumination coming from the dying embers in the grate and the fairy lights casting elongated shadows around the room and across the carpet. He figured his kids seemed to have moved ahead of him in thinking about life and the future. And they had been discussing the what-ifs of another relationship with each other. That was progress, wasn't it?

It was too late to ring June. They had yet to sleep together, but he knew it was going to happen. On their past few dates, he had gone back into her house with her and they had kissed, a lot, and become much more intimate. He wasn't quite sure if the reluctance to go further at that stage was mutual or more on his part and he was much relieved when she'd told him it wasn't.

'Don't think I'm playing hard to get or that I don't want to. I do. When I met you in London, I was literally finishing a long-term relationship

236

and I promised myself that I'd take my time before rushing in to anything or get involved with anyone again.'

'I understand,' he told her, his arms wrapped around her. 'And, truthfully, I'm still feeling a little guilty about starting a relationship at all.'

'What are we like? Two consenting adults acting like awkward teenagers. I just want to be sure that I'm not doing anything on the rebound – for both our sakes,' she said, taking his face in her hands.

'Do you think you are?'

'I wasn't sure on the first few dates, but the more I get to know you, the more I get to like you.'

'That sounds promising.'

'It's meant to be. It'll be worth waiting for.' She smiled coquettishly at him. 'What about you?'

'I feel happy for the first time since losing Carol. Thanks to you, I look forward to each day now instead of dreading it. I didn't see that coming – and it feels good and right.'

They kissed again, deeply and passionately, enjoying the sensations and the newness of exploration.

'I'm going home before I get completely carried away. I don't want you to feel I forced you into anything before you were ready and I want it to be special, not something that happens in a rush.'

She agreed. 'So do I, and it will be. I know that.'

Now he smiled to himself, remembering. It seemed that Pushy Penny *was* going to play Cupid after all, without even being aware of it. If the twins were staying at hers, then he'd be free to spend the night with June.

He put the guard up in front of the fire, flicked the switches on the fairy lights and went to bed.

CHAPTER 16

It was the weekend before Christmas and Lorcan took the kids to the airport to greet their grandparents. The place was buzzing with expectant families and friends. Tearful and joyous reunions surrounded them as familiar carols and seasonal tunes mixed with the cacophony in the terminal building. It seemed like everyone was on the move and in a hurry to get wherever they were going. The swing doors opened, disgorging another batch of travellers, laden down with rucksacks and pushing overloaded trolleys. They spotted each other immediately.

'If your dad doesn't mind, we'll dump all this stuff with him and steal you two away to do some shopping for your presents. How does that sound?'

'Fantastic, but what about lunch?' said Lorcan.

'We'll take care of that. We have so little time with this pair, it'll give us a chance to find out what's happening in their lives.'

'I'm sure they'll welcome a break from my company. It'll also give me a chance to do some shopping of my own.'

'Don't spoil them too much,' he shouted from

the car as they disappeared into the throng making its way up and down Grafton Street. He sat back and rang June.

'What are you up to?'

'I'm in town with Danielle.'

'Oh, I was going to ask you if you'd fancy meeting for lunch.'

'What a nice idea, but I thought you were tied up all weekend.'

'I've been given a reprieve for the rest of the day. Ask Danielle to come too. I'm dying to meet her.'

'She's saying yes – she wants to meet you too!'

'Great, let's make it the Westbury. I just have to find parking first.'

'We're on our way,' she said.

Christmas wasn't going be so bad after all, he thought, as he indicted and pulled back out into the crawling traffic. He eventually found a space and, when he got to the hotel, they were waiting for him in the foyer. 'You've been busy,' he said, eyeing the collection of bags they had between them.

'So, you're Danielle. I've heard a lot about you and your adventures with June.'

'And I've heard a bit about you too,' she said, looking at him approvingly. 'I've been looking forward to meeting you.'

'Well, I hope I pass,' he grinned.

'You'll do!' She laughed back.

'Pay no attention to her,' June said. 'Come on,

let's go and see if we can find somewhere to sit. I'm starving.'

Lorcan knew one of the managers, who magicked a table for them. It overlooked Harry Street, which was filled with people spilling onto the footpaths from the hostelries on either side. He had always loved this pre-Christmas buzz. He felt even happier when he saw Danielle give the thumbs up to June when she thought he wasn't looking.

After they had ordered lunch, Danielle excused herself for a few minutes. When she was gone, June said to him, 'This feels funny, meeting in the daytime. It almost feels clandestine.'

'I know exactly what you mean. I hope you don't feel like I'm hiding you away.'

'I'm delighted you caught me – us – in town.'

'I like Danielle – she's exactly as you described her – fiery and fun.'

'I can tell she likes you too. She's a straight shooter. If she didn't, you'd know – she'd give you the silent treatment.'

Over June's shoulder, Lorcan saw Danielle walking back across the room. She stopped to talk to a couple for a few minutes, before coming back to their table. She said nothing, but he was curious because the guy kept looking in their direction. When the couple were leaving, he saw the man say something to the woman, who hesitated and stood back. The man then walked over to their table. He nodded at Danielle and Lorcan, before addressing June. 'Hello, June, I just wanted to say hello and wish you a Happy Christmas.'

'Peter, I never saw you. How are you?' Lorcan saw her scan the room as though searching for someone. Her eyes rested on the woman, and she seemed flustered. 'Oh, this is my . . . friend, Lorcan Overend.'

Lorcan found himself saying, 'Surely more than a friend, June. How do you do? Will you join us for a drink?'

'Eh, no, but thanks. Zoe and I have to get back to the restaurant, what with the week that's in it and all that. But I couldn't just disappear without saying hi,' he said, looking at June. 'Enjoy the festivities, and give my love to Branch.'

Then, with a nod in Danielle's direction, he walked back to the woman who was waiting for him. She took his arm in a possessive way and they disappeared down the wide staircase.

While Lorcan paid the bill, June said, 'Well, I wasn't expecting that.'

'It was bound to happen. Dublin's very small,' Danielle replied.

'I know.'

As Lorcan returned to the table, Danielle gathered her bags and said, 'Now, if you two will forgive me, I still have loads of things to buy, so I'm going to head off. I'm delighted to have met you, Lorcan. No doubt we'll see each other again.'

When she had gone Lorcan asked, 'Who was that guy? Was he the ex?'

'Yes, but that's all history. Now, tell me, what do I give a man who has everything?'

'A bit more time and attention – how does that sound?'

'Perfect, but only if that's on a two-way agreement.'

'I've been given a pass for New Year's Eve. Can we spend it together – in the real sense?'

'There's nothing I'd like more.' She smiled at him and took his hand and he felt a warm surge course through his veins.

June found herself out of sorts that evening. She rang Danielle.

'You have to get over it.'

'I thought I was, but bumping into Peter like that really threw me.'

'It was going to happen sooner or later.'

'Do you think he's taking Zoe to Portugal in my place?'

'Probably.'

'You're not very sympathetic.'

'It's called tough love. Zoe is part of his life now and he may well end up marrying her. What was it you used to quote to me at college? "Sometimes letting things go is an act of far greater power than defending or hanging on." Well, it's time to take your own advice. You've got to let go. What about you and this Lorcan? Is that going anywhere?'

'I'd like to think it might, but it's early days yet. I do really like him though.'

'That's good, because I approve. Put the past behind you and get on with it, will you? For everyone's sake.'

June was a bit annoyed at Danielle. Through the years, she had sat for hours and listened to her friend's sob stories and tales of break-ups and let-downs. She thought she'd made all the right noises in all the right places, even when she sometimes felt unsympathetic or didn't entirely agree with what Danielle had said. But June also knew Danielle had been right. She always spelled things out as they were, not as you'd like them to be.

Despite acknowledging that, she couldn't help wondering how Peter had felt at meeting Lorcan and at his declaration that they were more than just friends. She told herself she didn't care and, by the time she went to bed, she had convinced herself she really didn't.

Lorcan was her priority now and they were finally going to spend the whole night together. Just imagining it gave her a warm glow of desire and she curled up under the duvet. He made her feel safe and desirable and she realised she hadn't felt like that since the abortion.

CHAPTER 17

June went to her mother's for Christmas Day and was delighted to find that she had reverted to her old traditions.

'The place looks fabulous,' she said, dropping her things on a chaise longue in the hall.

'The new décor begged for new decorations, so I went on a mission to get a new festive theme. I thought it could all be part of my de-cluttering strategy, but I think I may have gone a bit overboard. I think I bought more than I cleared out,' she laughed. 'I realised I'd been keeping things exactly as they were when your dad was alive and it was about time that I changed.'

'I think he'd approve. It's very stylish and sophisticated.'

Young Joe had delivered the tree that now stood elegantly festooned in the hallway. As June put the presents she had brought beside the stack already scattered beneath it, she did recognise a few bits and pieces, but now everything on it was silver, white or turquoise. When Branch was selecting them, the heavily perfumed assistant in Brown Thomas had told her it was what they called their 'winter wonderland theme – subtle but understatedly dramatic'. Young Joe had also delivered and set June's tree in place the previous week, but she had been so busy she had only finished dressing it on Christmas Eve.

'I hope you haven't thrown out all the old decorations – they are part of my childhood, my history, Mum, a very special part.'

'I knew you'd say that. Don't worry. I left them in a box in your bedroom. It's up to you to jettison what you don't want.'

June preferred more colour and a less studied approach, so her theme, if you could call it that, was an eclectic one – a mixture of the things she'd acquired on her travels and bought because she liked them.

She had arrived early to be there before the usual stalwart guests who came for dinner every year. It had been her intention to help with the preparations or at least set the table, but everything was done and already deliciously tantalising smells were escaping from the kitchen. Branch poured them both a glass of champagne, which they drank with mince pies.

'I know this is probably not a combination that you wine buffs would recommend, but they are two of my favourite things, and that's what Christmas is all about – enjoying your favourite things with friends and family.'

'I'll drink to that – to champagne and mince pies and to my fabulous effervescent mother.' They hugged each other just as Froggie and Danielle arrived.

'I've brought him over for your inspection,' she said to Branch, after they'd exchanged gifts. 'Then it's off to my folks and then his for proper introductions and dinner with his family. What do you think? He's easy on the eye, isn't he?' she said, kissing him on the cheek.

'And obviously easy-going too to put up with that level of scrutiny,' Branch said. 'It's really lovely to meet you, but don't let this one give you the run-around. She's like a daughter to me and, much as I love her, she can be a menace.'

'I've been finding that out for myself,' he grinned. 'It's nice to know I have an ally when these two gang up on me.'

'Have you started on the mince pies and bubbly without me?' Danielle asked, before explaining to him, 'It's their traditional Christmas morning brunch.'

'And I thought my family was odd,' he said, tucking in with the rest of them.

'Poor Froggie, you don't know what you're letting yourself in for, do you?' June said.

'Less of the one-sidedness – I'll be under the microscope when I get to his house *and* he has two sisters to dissect me when I leave. I'll have to make sure to use all the right knives and forks and not slurp my soup or lick my plate.'

'You'll charm them, I'm sure,' said Branch.

'Now, we have to run off. We daren't be late. We'll catch up when I get back from skiing – if I come back in one piece.' Not long after Froggie and Danielle had left, the bell started ringing as other guests arrived. They were made up of a few neighbours, a distant cousin of June's, two nearer ones, and a much-loved aunt from her mother's side and an uncle from her father's. He always brought some hand-made chocolates and a bottle of sherry. He usually drank a bottle of whiskey.

Branch had also invited some of her old music crowd for drinks. Most had been friends for many years, but since her husband had died, she'd stopped entertaining them. June was delighted as she thought they were great value. They always had yarns about when they were young and she could have listened to them all day.

In the middle of it all, Kelly texted from Australia.

Happy Xmas. Spent day on beach with Cara and family! Things going really really well. Much better than expected. I may never come back! I love it here. Hope you are enjoying the holidays. Love K.

After drinks the music friends left, but not before making arrangements to meet again soon and resume their soirees, to which they invited June.

'Bring your young man with you,' one said, and June saw her mother shake her head as if to warn him that there was no young man.

June answered, 'I think he'd enjoy that very much.' She smiled at Branch's startled expression. It was only later that she told her all about Lorcan.

June's uncle had already taken over the role of host and bar tender, as he usually did, helping himself to top-ups of the single malt every time he filled anyone's glass.

By the time dinner was served, he was always in flying form and regaled them with funny stories from the law firm he owned, which specialised in marriage breaks-up and divorce settlements. Then he'd fall asleep after dinner and snore gently until it was time to go home, declaring every year that it was the best Christmas ever.

The Christmas break in Ireland seemed to get longer every year as everyone took it as an excuse to catch up with friends and relations who had come back for the holidays, some of whom would only be home once a year. It also usually involved a bit of bargain hunting at the sales and a day at the races. Lorcan and June decided to go to the Punchestown New Year's Eve meet.

It was a beautiful crisp day. There had been an early frost but a course inspection had seen the ground being declared fit for racing. The mood was festive, helped by mulled wine and mince pies on arrival. June backed a rank outsider and won a hundred euro on the second race, while Lorcan's choices let him down badly. They had a good day and drove home in anticipation of spending their first night together.

June had prepared a dinner for them and set about putting various dishes in the oven to heat. The fire was still burning and Lorcan was topping it up with some logs when she came into the room.

'I hope you're hungry,' she said, putting a tray of nibbles down.

'I am, but not for food, for you,' he said, taking her in his arms and kissing her passionately. She felt herself yielding to his touch, kissing, tongues exploring each other. They ended up making love on the rug in front of the fire, where she and Peter had often done the same thing.

June couldn't help comparing how different his body was. Peter was taller and leaner, his torso covered in a furring of dark hair. Lorcan was smooth and fair, Nordic almost. She gave a shudder. Nordic. If she'd been worried that the sight of his blondness would trigger a memory of that night on the yacht, she needn't have been. She had never been able to remember a single thing about that night; it was her mind playing tricks. She consciously concentrated on Lorcan and on satisfying him, which she did, and he certainly satisfied her. They eventually got around to eating dinner and as the clock chimed midnight, they were on their way upstairs with a bottle of bubbly, to start making love all over again.

'A new year – who knows what it might bring?'

'Let's just make sure it's all good,' she said, kissing him.

CHAPTER 18

'Mum always used real napkins, then if it was a wet day, they didn't go all soggy on us.'

'Sensible lady. I'd never have thought of that,' Mrs Fitz said.

Ashling had made the picnic, or rather supervised while Mrs Fitz assembled it.

'And those plastic cups,' Sean said, pointing to ones that had weighted bottoms. 'The polystyrene ones can blow away too easily if it's windy and cause pollution.' Lorcan grinned above his son's head and Mrs Fitz got on with the job.

'Forgive the instructions. They're excited. It's been a while since we did this together.' The three of them had worked on their boat, *SEAS*, over the winter and were ready to take full advantage of spring and get back into sailing.

En route to the yacht club, his daughter asked, 'Dad, is it true you have a girlfriend?'

'Whatever gave you that idea?' he asked, buying time, but tightening his grip on the steering wheel. He knew this was going to happen sooner or later, but he had put off telling them about June, in the belief that the more time that passed, the easier it would be for them to accept that he might have a life outside theirs.

'Amanda told me. She said her mum and dad met her with you the other night.'

He glanced in the rear-view mirror at his kids. 'What else did she tell you?' he asked, furious with Penny for involving them in her meddling. It wasn't her place to tell them anything. He knew when they bumped in to each other coming out of the cinema that she'd jump to conclusions. Fortunately, there had been no time to talk as he and June were leaving, and Penny and her girl-friends were just arriving.

'She said she was very nice, not at all like Mum, though. Penny thinks it's time you found Mrs Overend the Second. She said it's not healthy for widowers to be on their own for too long.'

'She actually said that to you?'

'No, she didn't,' said Sean.

'Not exactly,' Ashling continued. 'I mean she didn't say it straight to me – I heard her telling one of her friends on the phone.'

'Poppet, sometimes it's better not to eavesdrop on other people's conversations.'

'She does it all the time. She's always earwig-ging,' her brother said.

'I am not. But Dad, do you have a girlfriend?'

'Actually, I do.'

'Are you going to marry her?'

'I haven't thought about it. Would you mind if I did?'

'I would. I like it just being the three of us, and Misfit too. I don't want a step-mother,' she said.

'I'd hardly cast June in that category. June's her name, by the way.'

'But we'd still have a step-mother if you married anyone.'

'You're right there.'

'Does she have children?'

'No, she doesn't – she's never been married.'

'You don't have to be married to have children,' Ashling replied caustically.

'I do know that,' he laughed.

'Hello – do I get to have a say in any of this?' his son asked.

'I think we're all jumping ahead of ourselves here. I am seeing someone, but that doesn't mean I'll want to marry her.'

'Can we meet her and see whether we like her?' Sean asked.

'Or scare her off?' Lorcan laughed.

'I'm being serious. It's not just your decision, you know, Dad. It would affect us all, if we hated her, or if she hated us.'

Lorcan didn't totally agree with his son on that, but decided to let it go for the moment. 'Let's just bide our time and see what happens, but of course you can meet her if you want to.'

'I don't want to,' said Ashling. 'The last thing I want is someone trying to take Mum's place.'

This was never going to be easy, he thought, as he reversed into a parking space. 'Let's talk about this later, among ourselves, not in front of Amanda and Des. OK?'

They busied themselves getting their wet gear and the hamper out of the car. The other two were already waiting at the clubhouse for them, with another sailing friend, and, not for the first time, was he glad that Penny's penchant for golf had won that day.

'Great to have you back, mate,' Des said, slapping him on the back.

When they got on board, the adults concentrated on navigating their way through the outstretched arms of the piers with their lighthouses glistening in the sun. They headed for the open sea into the face of the wind. Dalkey Island shimmered above the water with Sugar Loaf Mountain behind it. They hadn't sailed together since Carol's death, and Lorcan now realised how much he'd missed it and how he'd dreaded getting back to it at the same time. It had been one of her great passions. Looking at his kids and the concentration on their faces, he knew they'd missed it too.

'I think we'll book you lot in for a sailing course this summer. Do you like the sound of that?'

'Can I go on it too, Dad?' Amanda asked.

'I was including you as well. You and your mum and dad have really helped Ashling and Sean over the past while, so let it be my treat,' he said. Des accepted and the kids were delighted.

During the day, there were long silences, as each became preoccupied with their own world, disturbed only by the sound of the waves lapping as they sliced through them, the wind in the sails, and the shrieks of gulls wheeling around overhead. Lorcan sat back. He hadn't expected to be faced with all that this morning, but it set him thinking. He considered asking Des to tell Penny to back off. That wouldn't be fair on his friend, though. He wasn't responsible for his pushy wife's interfering behaviour.

Although he and June had only met briefly in October, and gone out not even a dozen times before the New Year, the few months since then had been dominated by thoughts of her. And with more frequent and intimate liaisons. They were compatible in so many ways and their sex life was wonderful.

He did see her as being a part of their life – his and his children's – long term. He was falling in love with her, but he had to make sure he didn't blow it by handling it the wrong way. Was he crazy to want to marry someone after such a short time? And someone so much younger than he was?

Yet he had felt the same way when he'd met Carol and he'd been right.

He'd been living with a serious girlfriend for two years, but within weeks of being introduced he moved out of her arms and into Carol's, five years his junior. And since June had come into his life, he felt he was being given a second chance. But marriage? Why not? It would certainly mean they could stop pussyfooting around, always going back to her place, choosing moments that didn't interfere with his home life. They could be a family together. Much as his kids meant to him, it was demanding being a single parent, and it could be bloody lonely at times. But it wasn't just them he had to consider. Would June really want to be saddled with someone else's children? He'd have to broach that cautiously.

And what about if she wanted her own family? Was he ready to do it all again? What would the twins say to that? He could honestly say she had made him happy again, very happy, but there were a lot of things they hadn't got around to discussing yet.

CHAPTER 19

It was a beautiful sunny Friday morning and June decided to walk in to work. She was looking forward to the weekend. Lorcan was coming around that evening and staying over. It didn't happen too often, and they intended making the most of the occasion when it did. They'd been together now, in the biblical sense, for just over six months and she was happy, happier than she thought possible when things finished with Peter.

In work, she checked her email. There was one from Hennie Goosen. They had been in regular contact since her South African trip and he kept her up to date on the progress of the students. They were about to complete their year with him and he had selected two for permanent employment at the vineyard – one being Lerato. He'd attached a photo of the 'graduation'. She smiled at the memories, brushing aside the cringe-making night when she'd let her mouth run away with her. She was typing a reply to Hennie when her mobile rang.

'Is this a bad time? Can you talk?' Danielle shouted into the phone. She always did that, but she sounded even more animated than usual. As soon as the school holidays had begun, she'd gone to spend the summer with Froggie in Geneva.

'I know you're at work, but I didn't want to put it in a text message. I had to tell you myself.'

'Is everything OK?'

'Deffo! Guess what? I'm getting married. Froggie proposed last night.'

'Wowee, congratulations. That's terrific news. I'm really happy for you,' June said. 'I wasn't expecting to hear that this morning.'

'I wasn't expecting it at all, but he has been asked to go to New Jersey for a year and we didn't want be apart for that long, so he decided to ask.'

'New Jersey? When? And what about your job?'

'Soon – he's due to start there in October. I'll apply for leave of absence for a year and hope they'll give it to me. They'll have no problem getting a replacement for me – there are loads of qualified teachers out there looking for work.'

June couldn't get a word in edgeways.

'So we thought we'd get married before then. Probably at the beginning of September, if we're to have a honeymoon first.'

'That doesn't give you much time to prepare.'

'I know, but in his corporate world, spouses are considered a necessity. Apparently they still frown on co-habiting couples. Can you believe it – in this day and age?'

'Are you serious?'

'It's the double standards I don't get. America

has the highest divorce rate in the world. You can be a home-wrecker or a philanderer with three or four failed marriages behind you and kids by several different people, but as soon as rings are exchanged, the slates are wiped clean and it's all deemed to be very respectable again.'

'I'd love to know how they afford the alimony and the child support,' June joked.

'Well I can assure you I only intend to do it once,' Danielle said. 'I think I've met my soul mate in Froggie.'

'So do I. Where will you marry, in Dublin or over there?'

'We have to work all that out. I'd love to do it here beside the lake, with just special friends and family.'

'That sounds perfect.'

'You know I'm not a meringue sort of girl. Give me a vamp-ish vintage frock and a flirtatious fascinator and I'll be happy. I don't want a huge affair. You will be my bridesmaid, though, won't you?'

'Just try and stop me. Can I get to wear a seductive hat too?'

'Deffo. It could be you next.'

'Being all loved up is obviously affecting your brain,' she laughed.

'You will bring Branch and Lorcan, won't you? She's my second mum and she has to be there. And it looks like he could be a keeper—'

'Like I said, being all loved up is obviously

affecting your brain. Actually, I am going to meet his kids tomorrow for the first time, and I'm really nervous. Suppose they hate me.'

'They might at first but once they get to know you they'll love you.'

'Is that supposed to reassure me?'

'Stop worrying – they'll probably be as nervous as you.'

'I hope you're right.'

She put the phone back on her desk and sat there mulling over Danielle's news. She was thrilled for her, but she knew she'd miss having her around. She'd only been gone to Switzerland a few weeks and already it seemed there was an unfillable void. There were no weekend drinks, cups of coffee, long lunches, walks along Sandymount Strand or girly nights at Branch's.

This time last year, they had been getting ready for their trip – so much had happened in the interim. Kelly passed her desk and she told her Danielle's news.

'Bridesmaid? You know what they say – goin' to a weddin' is the makin's of another.'

'Oh go away,' she laughed, but she proceeded to tell her about meeting Lorcan's kids the next day. 'One would be bad enough, but twins. If they hate me on sight I'll be a double target.'

'Cheer up – you might hate them back and it could be open warfare.'

'God, I hadn't thought of that.'

'I'm joking, June. Of course no one is going to

hate anyone. It'll be fine, I promise you. If you love him you'll love his kids too, for his sake.'

She didn't doubt that she loved him at all. But was she in love with him? She loved the way he handled himself, self-assured and confident. She loved the way he moved about his world as though it had been made with him in mind – comfortable and contented. She loved the way he got on with everyone, affable and interested, and she loved the way he cared for the twins. He always put them first, but he never made her feel second best.

They shared passion, lust, uninhibited sex and real comradeship – surely that was more than most couples had. Occasionally, though, she wondered if it was enough to plan a lifetime around. Would she have had more with Peter?

Lorcan had never said outright that he'd consider marrying again, or whether he'd like more children. Neither had he ever asked her if she wanted any. She had never told him about the abortion and knew she never could, or would. She still didn't know if she'd want to get pregnant again. But she liked him being in her life – she liked it a lot. She felt protected and secure when he was around and he supported her in her career and ambitions.

When she'd met him first, she had been at a very low ebb, riddled with insecurity and a sense of loss and hopelessness. And he had appeared, her knight in a bespoke business suit, and a teddy bear to break down barriers. Bartley Bruno now sat permanently on a wooden travelling trunk in her bedroom as a reminder. Occasionally she picked him up and gave him a cuddle, remembering that darkest of days in London and Lorcan's reassuring smile.

As she shopped that lunchtime, she felt contented – steaks, salads, cherry tomatoes, crusty bread, assorted cheeses, strawberries and cream. She had lots of wine at home. If this weather kept up, they'd eat in the garden. Young Joe had been in the previous day to cut the lawns and trim the edges. The containers and hanging baskets she had planted earlier in the year were thriving and were full of haphazard colour. She loved her garden and was determined to take full advantage of having such a lovely space to call her own.

Lorcan collected her from work and they went home together. She cooked the steaks and they took them onto the patio. They sat in the garden for hours. It was still bright when they went upstairs to bed.

They undressed each other slowly, hands exploring, exciting. Since they'd started sleeping together, they had got used to each other's bodies and needs. He nuzzled her neck and behind her ears, before moving on to her breasts. Their breathing quickened in unison. She felt his arousal matching her own. Then he lifted her gently and laid her on the bed, where they brought each other to noisy and very satisfactory climaxes. The grandfather clock chimed in the hall just as they uncoupled and he laughed out loud. 'Was that a fanfare for us?' he asked. 'If so, it was perfectly timed.'

They lay back, sated and spent, and fell asleep in each other's arms.

When she woke, his side of the bed was empty and she could hear sounds coming from the kitchen below. She ducked into the shower and was just coming out, pulling on her bathrobe, when he appeared, wearing his.

'Would Madam like pancakes with bacon, maple syrup and a little cream on the side?'

She laughed. 'Madam certainly would.'

'And would Madam prefer to eat in the garden or indoors? It's a gorgeous morning.'

'Then it has to be the garden.'

'I'll just go and iron your newspaper, to dry the ink so you don't get it all over your hands, Madam.'

'That won't be necessary, Jeeves. Just leave it on the garden seat. I'll be down in a minute.'

'Very well, but would Madam like a kiss before the bacon burns to a frazzle?'

'Yes, I do believe she would.'

He ran his hands under her bathrobe and she responded instantly, pulling him closer and kissing him. He had nothing on underneath his robe either. She pushed him away.

'You don't really have the bacon on yet, do you?'

'No, I don't. I have to confess I had other delights in mind for Madam first.'

'Great, Jeeves, then let's try them together.'

It was a good hour later before they came downstairs and Lorcan began to prepare the promised breakfast. June collected the paper from the hallway and carried it out to the garden with a glass of orange juice. She looked at the headlines – nothing earth-shattering there. There was a photo of President Mary McAleese with some Irish fashion designers, a report of another well-known property dealer filing for bankruptcy, as well as speculation on some sports star who was being questioned after random drug testing showed up irregularities in his samples. Boring, boring, boring. She folded it and took up the weekend supplement instead.

She wasn't prepared for what she saw on the cover though – a picture of Peter and Zoe in front of the stained-glass window in The Pink Pepper Tree. The headline read: 'Workplace Romances – can they have happy endings?' She flicked through the pages and found a smaller version of the same image inside, alongside pictures of some other couples. The caption read: 'Recently engaged workmates Zoe Synnott and Peter Braga.' The spread ran over six pages of the magazine.

Do workplace romances invariably result in embarrassment or do they ever have a future? Although most of them do fail, it seems they don't all end in disaster and awkwardness. Sometimes they do work out, as in the case of the four couples we feature here. Three of them are already married, the fourth announced their intentions to tie the knot only last weekend.

June felt a wave of something wash over her. Peter and Zoe engaged? Was it anger, disappointment, jealousy? She wasn't quite sure. She was annoyed by her reaction – why did he still have such a hold on her emotions? They were all living their own lives. She read on.

The newly engaged couple met while architect Zoe Synnott was asked to stand in on holiday cover for a colleague while Peter Braga's award-winning restaurant was being enlarged and redesigned.

'It was love at first sight, for both of us. Cement dust and bare light bulbs may not be the most romantic of settings, but we never noticed them. And now we're getting married. We were both in other relationships but once we met we knew. Call it destiny or whatever. I didn't believe in workplace romances before this. In my experience they usually ended in catastrophe, with people avoiding each other, even changing jobs, but I'm delighted to say I was wrong about them,' Zoe told us.

'Sorry to interrupt you, Madam, but breakfast is served,' Lorcan said, crossing the patio with a laden tray. She put the magazine aside to make space for it and he kissed her on the head.

'Thank you, you spoil me,' she said. The magic of the previous night and that morning was fractured, but that wasn't his fault. She went through the motions of pretending to enjoy her breakfast, and she could have been eating sawdust for all she tasted. If he noticed a change in her mood, he said nothing about it.

'Why don't we head over to Herbert Park for a walk before meeting the kids?' he suggested as they finished up. She hesitated. Herbert Park had been special to Peter and her, but he didn't know that. She'd never told him.

'Let's just enjoy the garden for another little while, then I'll go and get ready.'

When she went back to her bedroom she retrieved her phone. She'd put it on silent the night before. There were numerous missed calls and texts – from her friends, her mother, there was even one from Danielle, who must have seen the feature about Zoe and Peter online. She actually did smile when she read hers. It simply said:

The smug wagon – she hasn't got the legs for that skirt!

Good old Danielle, trying to cheer her up. Kelly had sent one wishing her luck for that afternoon. It was followed by a second.

Just saw the paper. I'm here if you want
to ring me.
K xx.

She didn't return any of them. She couldn't deal
with how she felt about Zoe and Peter getting
married. It was too much to take in – and she had
enough to deal with meeting Lorcan's kids. She
turned the phone back to silent and put it into
her handbag.

The entire journey to the yacht club, she went
over the article in her mind. Peter engaged.

Sensing her agitation, Lorcan tried to put her at
ease. 'There's no need to be apprehensive, love,
it will be all right. I promise. I warned them to
be on their best behaviour.'

The fine weather had resulted in a big turnout
for the end-of-regatta festivities. Apart from the
activities on the water, and there were a lot of
them, the veranda was filling up and smoke rose
from the row of barbecues, which were manned
by a few club members all wearing striped aprons
and matching hats.

Lorcan spotted his children and, as he took her
elbow, June tried to put the thoughts of Peter from
her mind. This day was important to Lorcan and
she owed him to make an effort.

'Don't let them intimidate you,' he whispered
in her ear. 'They may think they are grown-
ups, but they are only kids, and you're the first

girlfriend I've introduced them to, so they're probably a bit edgy too.'

'Don't worry. I'm sure I'll love them if they are anything like their dad,' she said.

He took her hand and squeezed it. 'They're more like their mother actually.'

Well, this day can't get any worse, June thought to herself.

Two gangly kids approached her, and Lorcan did the introductions. 'Hi, kids, this is June. June, this is Ashling and Sean.'

'It's lovely to meet you both. Did you have a good party last night?' June asked them, feeling like she needed to start a conversation brightly.

'It wasn't a party. It was just a sleepover at a friend's house,' Ashling said. There was an awkward silence for a second or two, before she spoke again. 'Is the food ready yet? I'm going over to Amanda – she's kept a place for me.'

'Not so fast, young lady. We've only just got here.'

June noticed her shoot her father the kind of look that said, *I've done my bit, I've met her, so now can I go?* He ignored her.

Sean made more of an effort. 'Dad didn't tell us if you sail or not.'

'I've done a little, but I wouldn't be in your class at all. I hear you're both very good.'

'Mum was a brilliant sailor,' Ashling said.

'So your dad told me.'

'She won gazillions of trophies for it, didn't she?' she said to Sean.

'She did. But we could show you . . . if you'd like that . . . couldn't we, Dad? You could come out in *SEAS* with us.'

Lorcan nodded at his son, who was almost as tall as he was. 'That sounds like a plan.'

'I'd like that very much, thank you,' said June. 'Now why don't you go and join your friends, I think they are waiting for you.'

They didn't need to be told twice, and Lorcan and June watched them as Ashling gave Sean an earful on the way. Before she could say anything to Lorcan, he leaned in and whispered, 'Here comes trouble. Brace yourself for the third degree from Penny.'

'Pushy Penny?'

'The one and only – you've been warned.'

'Look at you two, canoodling in public. The twins told me you were coming this afternoon. June, it's nice to meet you again, properly this time. That film was crap, by the way. I wouldn't recommend it. You made the right choice going to the other one. Come and join us. We've kept places at our table.'

Lorcan steered June along behind Penny. Thankfully, there were some other friends there too and after the introductions were made, June relaxed. She wasn't in the mood for an inquisition, but she knew she must be the topic of curiosity and speculation. This had been Carol's territory and, by all accounts, she'd been very popular. That knowledge made June feel like a bit of an interloper. She'd have cheerfully addressed a seminar rather than face this lot.

The food was delicious – lamb and vegetable kebabs, steaks, sausages, salmon darnes, ribs, chicken – with salads of every description. The conversation was lively and she was glad that Lorcan wasn't trying too hard to make the kids engage with her. She was grateful to Sean, who offered to get her something to drink. He was definitely trying, she felt, while Ashling was giving her the silent treatment. She and Amanda seemed to have joined forces in an effort to veto the idea of Lorcan having any sort of girlfriend at all, and they showed this in their monosyllabic, dismissive answers.

I am the adult here. I can wait and see how this pans out.

'How did you two meet?' Penny enquired, directing the question at her.

'At Heathrow airport, over a teddy bear,' she replied.

'A teddy bear?'

'Yes, a teddy bear, not just any old bear, though. He's called Bartley Bruno Bear actually.'

'A teddy bear?' she repeated.

'Yes, and we had our first date a few months later, at his naming ceremony.'

Everyone around the table was intrigued and wanted to know more.

Penny looked at her as though she were mad or drunk, or both. Lorcan sat back in his seat, enjoying this exchange. Ashling pretended not to be interested at all, but she was.

Des laughed, winking at Lorcan, and said, 'Now, Penny, why didn't you think of that? You could have had a teddy bears' picnic and paired him off then, instead of all those blind date machinations and dinner parties.'

'What's a machination?' asked Amanda.

'You had blind date dinner parties for my dad?' Ashling said incredulously.

'That's just a turn of phrase, Ash. It was just a way of distracting him, of helping him to forget.'

'Forget what? My mum? He doesn't want to forget her. He told us that.'

'Of course he doesn't. That's not what I meant.' Penny looked at Des for support, but as Des was about to offer Ashling some comforting words, the bell rang to announce that desserts were being served from the bar. So, instead, he stood up and said, 'Come on, kids, let's beat the queue and see what's on offer.' He herded the three of them away.

'Now, tell us more,' one of the other women said to June. 'Do you play golf?'

Later that evening, they all left the club to go their separate ways. Lorcan and the twins dropped June home and the conversation in the car was neutral – mostly about the day and the barbecue. June decided against inviting them in – she didn't want to appear too eager to please or to be trying too hard to ingratiate herself with them.

'I'll call you tomorrow,' Lorcan said, leaning over and kissing her on the cheek.

'Bye, guys,' she said, as she waved them off and went back inside. She'd worry about them and their reactions later, but first she had a date with that newspaper feature. She poured a gin and tonic and sat down to read through the whole article.

Zoe hadn't held back.

'An autumn wedding, no point in hanging around now that we know we're right for each other.'

I'm sure that's not what Kelly meant when she said 'goin' to a weddin' is the makin's of another thought June.

'We'll probably honeymoon in Portugal. Although I've travelled, I don't know Peter's country at all.'

'I'm able to say thank you – obrigada, and vinho tinto – red wine. Do I need to learn anything else?' she joked with her fiancé.

June speed read through to the end before reading through it all again.

'No, it wasn't a surprise. She chose the ring herself.'

'I always wanted a modern setting.'

'I'll leave all that to Zoe. I'd really prefer a quiet wedding, but Zoe likes to make a splash. She's at her happiest when she has a project – the bigger the better, one involving lists, schedules and things to arrange.'

'Of course we'd like a few children, but not for a while. We're both from small families. He has only one sister and I just the one brother.'

Her landline rang. It was Branch.

'How are you? I tried your mobile lots of times and left messages. Did you see the paper? Did you know they were engaged?'

'No, Mum. Danielle and Froggie's announcement was a surprise. This one was a shock. I've only just had a chance to read it all.'

'Are you OK about it?'

'What do you think? Of course I want Peter to be happy. He deserves that, but I don't like Zoe. I never have and I never will. If it was anyone else, I hope I'd be pleased for him. I just don't think they are suited at all.'

'Would you like me to come over?'

'No, thanks. I've had one hell of a day.' She proceeded to tell her of her encounters with

Ashling and Sean and with the family's circle of friends.

'That sounds like a real ordeal.'

'It was.'

'You'll be all right, June. We're strong women.'

'I hope you're right.'

'I am, you'll see. Get a good night's sleep and it won't seem so bad in the morning.'

'If only life was that simple, Mum. If only.'

CHAPTER 20

Over the summer, when she wasn't travelling for work, she met Lorcan's children more frequently. Sean continued to make things easier for her than his sister and she was grateful to him for that. He talked to her about a programme he was trying to write and she was flattered when she learned that he hadn't told Lorcan about it because he wanted it to be a surprise.

Ashling still took every opportunity she could to tell her how great her mother had been, especially when her dad was present. It was as though she felt that by drawing comparisons between Carol and June, she'd make him realise that Carol was better and that June was certainly not a worthy replacement. June never contradicted her or responded to her comments, sensitive to Ashling's feelings and how hard it must be for her to see someone else in her father's life.

June kept up the habit of dining with Branch on Tuesday evenings when she was in Dublin and she told her, 'Sometimes I feel I'm competing with a ghost. It might be easier if I had met the woman. That way I'd know what I was up against.'

'It's only natural that she'd behave like that. Carol will always be the mother she lost, the mother she had no chance to say goodbye to. No one will ever replace her and the best thing you can do is never try to. She's probably feeling possessive about her dad and doesn't want to share him with anyone. In time, she'll come around to you, but it will be on her terms. You're doing the right thing, keep remembering she's a teenager now with hopping hormones. Think back to what you were like when you were at that stage – rebellious, troublesome and argumentative. Everything your dad and I did or said was wrong. You thought we'd been put here to destroy your life.'

'I wasn't that bad!'

'Yes, you were, but you turned out all right in the end.' She smiled. 'More than all right. Just be patient. She'll come around eventually, especially when she sees her dad is happy with you.'

'She heard us talking about going away together and I don't think she's very pleased about the idea.'

'She'll get used to it, when she realises you are part of his life now, or am I presuming too much at this stage? I don't mean to pry, but you've seemed much happier recently.'

'Oh, I am, Mum, and you're not prying. I'd love to see my future with Lorcan, and his kids too, but look at how things went wrong for Peter and me. If all that taught me anything, it's not to take anything for granted.'

'There are no certainties in life so just enjoy each other and live in the moment. Go off and have a great holiday – you deserve it.'

'So, what do you think – a couple of weeks in France or would you prefer to go somewhere else?' Lorcan asked June the following weekend over coffee.

'France sounds perfect.'

They'd taken to spending Saturday mornings together while the twins had their various extra-curricular classes, a practice that continued now that the school holidays were here. They were seated at their usual window table in a local café.

'The twins go to stay with their grandparents in France for the first two weeks in July every summer. Then they come back together and head off to Connemara. They have a little holiday home there. We could fly over with them and see them safely ensconced – then we can go off on our own.'

'Don't you think Carol's parents might feel that's a little presumptuous on my part, just turning up like that?' asked June.

'No, I don't. We can't avoid it forever. I want you in my life. We've known each other now for the best part of a year and it's over two since they lost their daughter. The sooner everyone knows about us, the easier it will be for them to accept us as a couple.'

'I know that, but I don't want to presume that they'll accept me.'

'They'll love you, like I do,' he reassured her.

They had booked in to a local pension just a few minutes down the road, but Carol's parents offered them beds for the night. As they had never stayed together yet in front of the kids, they declined. It just didn't seem right, somehow, in his former in-laws' house.

'We'll pick the car up here in the morning and leave you to enjoy your holidays without us getting in the way,' Lorcan said, kissing everyone, before they set off down the road, arm in arm.

'That wasn't too bad, was it?' he asked.

'No, it all went surprisingly well. They're lovely.'

Carol's parents had been warm and welcoming and had prepared a feast for them all. They'd eaten in the garden. The twins had behaved and their grandfather had told her of his love of wine. That had proved to be a common bond. When he'd heard about June's work, they'd gone off in a world of their own. He'd showed her his 'cellar' – a selection of special wines for special occasions that he had collected, and had insisted on breaking open a vintage one for them to enjoy. After dinner, he'd told her that he was delighted to see that the twins were coping so well.

'I'm not so sure Ashling approves of me,' she'd confided.

'Don't worry. I'll work on her for you,' he'd said. 'By the time we bring them back to Ireland, she'll be your biggest fan. Nothing will give our daughter back to us. The nearest thing we'll ever have are her children, and if they are happy, then so are we. Lorcan is a good man and it's good to see him looking so happy too.'

'You've no idea how much that means to me. I have to admit I'm a bit lost around them. I'm afraid if I try too hard, they'll think it's an act – and if I pretend indifference, they'll think I don't care. I don't think I've found the right balance yet.'

'From where I'm standing you seem to be doing a pretty good job of it so far,' he'd said, putting his hand over hers and squeezing it.

June relayed her conversation with Carol's father to Lorcan as they walked back to their pension.

'They are lovely, and that's another hurdle out of the way. And now we've two teen-free weeks to enjoy ourselves in *la belle France*.' He pulled her closer and kissed her on the lips.

They drove into the Pyrenees and Spain, making the fishing village of Collioure their base. They climbed mountains and walked along beaches, dined on fresh fish and delicious lamb, as well as on local Catalan dishes. They made love with heightened passion and ardour because they knew their time together like this was so limited. In no time, the two weeks were over and they thought about returning to reality.

'It's been perfect, hasn't it?' she remarked, when they were sitting in a little bar by the waterfront.

'The time has gone by so quickly, I wish we could do it all again.'

'Would you consider marrying me?'

'Marrying you?' She laughed, taken aback by the suddenness of this proposal. 'You can't be serious. Where did that come from? We hardly know each other. I've never even given it a thought—'

'I wasn't expecting you to say yes right away, but I wasn't expecting such a vehement rejection either. I thought we were sound.'

'We are. I didn't mean it to come out like that, Lorcan. I just wasn't expecting it.'

'Forget it. Just forget I asked.'

'No, let's talk about it.'

'I'd rather not. Just drop it.'

And they did, but it hung there between them and, in bed that night, they didn't make love. She lay there, wondering why she had reacted so negatively. She loved him and could see herself as his wife. But there was so much more involved – she'd be taking on someone else's role as a mother to two teenagers who were as close to her in age as her husband would be, give or take a few months. And if Ashling objected to her as her father's girlfriend how would she feel about her as a step-mother?

They were civil to each other the following morning as they finished their packing, and when she tried to soften the atmosphere, he had only thawed a little.

On the plane, she took his hand. 'Lorcan, just

give me a little time to think things over. Marriage is a very big step and we've not been together a year yet. What about Ashling and Sean?'

'I wasn't asking you to marry me tomorrow, just to say you would at some stage.'

'I will, at some stage. I'd love to, but just give me time, OK?'

'OK.'

CHAPTER 21

Although talk of weddings was in the air with Danielle and Froggie's looming, Lorcan didn't mention his proposal again. June was flying to Geneva a few days ahead of the big day to be on hand with bridesmaid-ly duties. She had finished work early to get her hair trimmed and was charging down Grafton Street when she ran smack into Peter and Zoe coming out of a jewellery shop.

'Hello there,' Peter said. 'How are you doing? Work going well?'

'Yes, thanks, good . . . and the restaurant?' she said, avoiding eye contact with Zoe.

Unfortunately, Zoe wasn't to be ignored. Taking his arm, she said, 'I suppose you know we're getting married next week. We've just been getting our wedding bands engraved. Haven't we, darling?'

June could see Peter was uncomfortable. 'It must be the season for it. Froggie and Danielle are tying the knot next week too, in Switzerland,' June said. 'I'm sorry but I must fly, I'm late for a hair appointment. I'm flying out in the morning. Have a nice wedding.'

'*Have a nice wedding!*' *Who says that?* she thought as she pushed her way through the crowds on the busy street. '*Have a nice wedding.*' *What a lame thing to say.*

Of course she had known they were due to get married. How could she not? It was hard to avoid it since he, his restaurant and his fiancée had become the darlings of the society pages. She knew Peter had never sought nor liked such publicity, but Zoe seemed to lap it up, so this had to be her doing. Ever since the piece had appeared about workplace romances, she courted publicity and featured regularly in *Social and Personal*, *VIP*, *The Gloss*, *Image* and *Irish Tatler*, and on the social pages of the weekend magazines. Occasionally, he did too. Despite herself, June read these when she came across them.

'I can't believe you've pulled it all together so quickly,' June told her friend the next day as she ran through the arrangements.

'It's got to be perfect,' Danielle said. By the time the twenty-five or so guests arrived from Ireland that second week in September, everything was ready. Her parents, Branch and Lorcan had travelled together and, by all accounts, had had a great journey over.

The night before the service, Danielle, Froggie and their other guests headed to an *auberge* in the mountains and all sat down in its beer garden to sample traditional *raclette*. They scraped the melted cheese off special implements and dripped it over little potatoes, an assortment of cured meats, gherkins and pickled onions. Then they all cooked their own favourites on the fondue sets that were placed along the centre of the enormous table.

'This mightn't be the epitome of elegant dining, but it's fun,' Froggie said.

'It's delicious and perfect for the occasion,' Branch said as they all sat, their large napkins tied around their necks, the mood happy and infectious.

The only dark cloud for June was Danielle's impending departure for the States.

'You can come and visit,' Danielle said, when June told her again how much she'd miss her. 'You can *all* come and visit because I'll be lonely over there too. And I won't be allowed to teach until I get a work visa, if they'll give me one at all.'

'It's truly beautiful here,' Branch said to Froggie's mother. 'I would never tire of that scenery and those Alps playing hide and seek in the mists and clouds. It's quite spectacular the way it changes on a whim.'

She agreed. 'I loved Vevey, with its swanky boutiques. You can almost smell the opulence there. I was afraid to go in and ask the price of anything though after seeing a sparkly belt in a window for 1,000.'

'It's the cars that get me,' her husband said. 'I've never seen so many Lamborghinis, Ferraris and

Porsches in my life. It's all very Bond-ish altogether.'

'Did you come across that *confiserie* or *chocolaterie* or whatever they call it, Poyet's, just off the market square? It makes replicas of Charlie Chaplin's shoes in chocolate; they sell them in miniature shoeboxes. I'm going to bring them back as pressies to the office!' June said.

'Charlie Chaplin's shoes – not Louboutins?' Lorcan remarked, 'that seemed to be a very odd choice, surely?'

'Not really. He spent the last twenty-five years of his life here,' Froggie said. 'The shoes are replicas of the ones he always wore when he played the tramp. You know someone stole his coffin shortly after he died and held it for ransom?'

'Who paid that?' someone asked. 'His family or the government?'

'No one. It turned up intact. He's buried in the grounds of his home now. You'd be amazed at the numbers who come here wanting to visit it and to see his statue. But enough of that,' Froggie said, standing up. 'Everyone, I'm under instructions from my soon-to-be-bride that it's time you all went home and got your beauty sleep. We have a big day tomorrow, and I know you'll all want to look your best for the photographs.'

That got a laugh and they all, eventually, disbanded and went back to their various hostelries.

Branch had sat across from Lorcan during the

evening and used the time as an opportunity to observe him from a distance. She had met him numerous times and liked him, but she had reservations, which she kept to herself until the wine and the atmosphere got to her at the end of the evening. Back at the hotel, she and Danielle's mother went out on to Branch's balcony for a final nightcap. During their chat Branch couldn't help but confide her doubts.

'I know he ticks all the boxes and he's already talked marriage, but she stalled him and that's what worries me. June usually knows her own mind and doesn't prevaricate. I know he's generous and kind, he's a charmer too and looks good, but he's fifteen years older than her and he already has his family. How would you feel if it were Danielle in the same situation?'

'I can't really answer that. No one can. Although I'd have to agree with you – I'd have reservations too and would wonder if he was looking for a substitute mother for his children. Do you think she's still carrying a torch for Peter?'

'I think she may well be – but he's definitely off the radar now that he's getting married. Besides, Lorcan's kids will be gone in a few years.'

'Marriage is always a lottery and if they love each other, they'll make it work. You have to trust June. She's not stupid and she's not a starry-eyed teenager either. She's a career woman and she knows what she wants from life. We can't protect them forever.'

'That's the hard part, isn't it? Anyway, she hasn't said yes, yet. Now, enough of that, let's drink to your daughter and her future happiness.'

'And to her second mother – the one she could always run to when she's had a row with me! You've always been there for her, Branch.'

They clinked glasses. 'And you for June.'

'We'll have to make plans to go out and visit her in New Jersey. You know how her dad hates long flights.'

'I'll consult my diary as soon as we get back home,' Branch laughed.

Danielle had predicted that she would be happy wearing a vampish vintage dress and a flirtatious fascinator, and she had gone in search of both on a visit to Évian in France, on the other side of the lake. She had given June permission to wear what she liked – so long as it was vintage too – and she'd chosen a sea-green chiffon number that she'd found in a boutique in Dalkey. It scooped low from her shoulders at the back, in an elegant drape, which emphasised her small waist. She teamed it with some green and white strappy shoes and a feathery concoction that matched them.

As she made her entrance into the registry office, Danielle was stunning. She looked as though she had stepped through time from the pages of vintage *Vogue*. Her genuine Givenchy dress, which could have been made for Audrey Hepburn, screamed chic. It was a navy sleeveless number in silk chiffon, with a bateau neckline, a fitted bodice, full skirt covered a structured underskirt. Only a narrow belt with cream trim and a diamanté clip broke its line. She wore a simple choker of pearls and peep-toe shoes. Instead of the fabulous fascinator she had originally wanted, she had opted for a shallow pillbox hat. This was perched at a gravity-defying tilt on one side of her head. They both carried posies of off-white roses.

Danielle and Froggie had to have their civil ceremony indoors in the registry office. They had originally wanted to make their vows on a pleasure boat on Lake Geneva, but that wasn't permitted by the canton law. But after the legalities had been dispensed with, they had a blessing on the water followed by a meal on board while they cruised along the Montreux Riviera, with its esplanades and tropical trees, marinas and stylish Belle Époque hotels, all remnants of a more leisurely time.

When June looked at the photos of that day years later, she could still conjure up the feelings of friendship and happiness that cocooned them all. It was as perfect a day as one could ever wish for.

It was also the day she agreed to marry Lorcan.

PART III

CHAPTER 22

June wanted a spring wedding and a date in May was agreed upon, but even this caused friction with Ashling, who insisted that as the first of February was the beginning of spring in Ireland then May was actually summer time.

'Don't be so petty,' her brother told her.

'I'm not. It's a fact.'

'So that makes August autumn, does it?' he asked.

'That's enough, you two,' said Lorcan. 'The date's set and it's May, whatever season it falls in. It suits June's work and it suits me and that's final.'

Ashling had reluctantly agreed to be the bridesmaid, while Sean was delighted to be their best man.

'I thought asking her would make her feel more involved,' June told Branch, 'but she seems determined to make it hard for me.'

'Well, you can tell her that I'm very honoured you asked me to give you away. What a shame your dad isn't around to see this day.'

'Carol's parents are being really supportive too, they said they wouldn't miss it for the world.'

Even after their engagement, June never stayed overnight at Lorcan's house.

'I think we should let the kids get used to the idea of us as a pair first,' she'd told Lorcan. 'When we're married, they'll accept it. I'll be your wife then, not an imposter. At least I hope that's how they'll see it – especially Ashling.'

Talking about life after the wedding opened up lots more questions for June – the main one being where they would live.

'I know Bayvue is your home, but I honestly would feel happier starting fresh in a different house,' she told Lorcan one evening over dinner. 'Do you feel it would be too much to expect of the kids to move? Do you think they might see it as me persuading you to erase more memories of Carol?'

'They might. I know they love the house and it's handy for school and their friends, but they also have to realise that I have my own life and that I'm entitled to make choices too – choices with you. They are adaptable; they've proved that. They're also growing up. I don't want you to feel you're living in Carol's shadow all the time.'

'I think that's exactly how I would feel in her home.'

'That's no way to start our lives together. In a few years, they'll do their own thing, whatever that will be, so I'm planning ahead for us, for the rest of our lives.'

'What about you all moving in to Raglan Road? Or would that be more traumatic for them – not only having to leave all their memories behind, but having to move in to my space?'

'I'm really not sure.'

'Why don't we ask them?' she suggested. 'That way we don't need to second-guess what they are thinking. Bring them over on Saturday, I'll cook for us and we can have a proper discussion.'

As always, Sean was more amenable than his sister, but she had definitely thawed towards June now that the wedding was going ahead. June thought that maybe her grandfather had finally got through to her. Then she completely surprised them all by saying she'd love to move to a totally new house – new beginnings for them all together. Lorcan and June knew this was a big leap, and decided to ignore her emphasis on '*if*' they all had to live together.

'Can we have a say in where we go? And pick our rooms?' she asked.

'Absolutely. We'll all go house-hunting together. This has to be a group decision,' Lorcan assured them.

June told Branch about the plan to move, and she advised her not to sell the house on Raglan Road. June had been reluctant to sell her father's house anyway and Lorcan had no problem with her renting it out rather than selling.

June was upset when Danielle told her she wouldn't make the wedding. Even though June knew Danielle would have been there if she could – Danielle was happily pregnant with a honeymoon baby and had been advised not to travel long haul for the six weeks before her due date – she still felt sad that her best friend wouldn't be there to share her day.

'Of course I'll be there in spirit but I know it won't be the same. Please, please come and visit.'

'I'll miss you so much. But I promise I'll come over as soon as the baby is born and we're back from honeymoon. If I'm going to be the child's godmother, I'm not going to do it by proxy.'

Bayvue, as its name suggested, had a great view of the bay from the edge of the gardens. It was rambling and old and full of character. It was also full of Carol. Every nook and cranny was imbued with her style and her taste. Her face beamed from picture frames dotted about the rooms. June was looking forward to having a new house that would enable her to put her stamp on things. But as they perused the property pages and websites, they couldn't find anything that suited. The rooms were too small or there weren't enough of them. Some had virtually no gardens to talk about. Others needed so much work that they'd be co-habiting with builders and tradesmen for months.

Lorcan contacted an old school friend who was in the business and was told about a new house on the market, which hadn't yet been advertised.

The house ticked so many boxes even before they viewed it. The owners were going abroad and wanted a quick sale and it was only five minutes away from Bayvue, so it would still be easy for the kids going to school and seeing their friends. They all fell in love with it straight away. It was a modern, bright and airy house, built on period lines, a little further along the coast in Killiney, with bigger mature gardens, a pond with koi carp swimming around in it, a den and an unimpeded sea view from the back. It had a tennis court too.

They put in an offer and it was accepted immediately. Now they found that as well as planning a wedding, they had a move to orchestrate, and the sale of Bayvue.

Work was busier than ever at Macy Brothers, and June's schedule included attending a wine fair in London in March. The timing wasn't great with all the preparations June had to make, but she was determined to make it all work.

Fortunately, Kelly was still on hand to help. Her life had taken a turn for the better since she'd returned from Sydney. She now Skyped Cara regularly. Her son-in-law's mother had died just after Christmas and his father had moved in with them. Kelly often had a chat with him too and read bedtime stories to the grandchildren they shared.

'They're saving to come over for a visit,' she told June. 'Dave's father has never been back since they emigrated thirty years ago and Dave was only in Ireland once. They've loads of cousins in Wicklow who they've never even met. I'm so glad that Cara has got an extended family. I always felt she missed out by not having brothers or sisters growing up.'

'She probably didn't, I never missed it. I honestly believe that whatever you are brought up to is what you accept as the norm.'

'You're probably right. It was just another thing that I tagged to my list of guilt.'

'It's time you forgot that list, Kelly. Why not invite them over this summer? They can stay in my house – that way they wouldn't have to pay anything for accommodation while they're here.'

'I couldn't ask you to do that.'

'You haven't asked, I offered. My house will be free from the end of May and it would save me having to look for tenants straight away. It would mean I wouldn't need to get a house sitter and, with so much going on, that would be one thing less for me to worry about. One big thing! I hardly get to see Lorcan at all these days.'

'They could pay you.'

'I wouldn't let them. They'd be doing me a huge favour. I have so much to organise before the wedding and when we come back from our honeymoon.'

They had planned a three-week honeymoon in the Seychelles, and the twins were flying out to join them for the final week. 'Then I'll be heading over to the States as soon as Danielle pops to meet little Froggie.'

'I hope to God she doesn't start calling the child Tadpole!'

'Even she wouldn't do that!' They laughed. 'Now get on to Cara and give her the news. Tell them they can stay as long as they like.'

'I can't wait; she'll never believe it. Thanks, June.'

'Don't thank me. I'm the lucky one.'

CHAPTER 23

It was a manic five months. The move to Hill Crest was scheduled to coincide with their return from their honeymoon – a new beginning for a new family. He said that often, and she knew it meant a lot to him.

Mrs Fitz was put in charge of overseeing the physical move – making sure all the boxes were packed and labelled and put in the correct rooms for unpacking in the new house.

With six weeks to go, June was feeling under increased pressure organising the various strands of her life. She was determined not to let any one part slip, and after putting long hours in at the office, she came home to handle the wedding, honeymoon and house move.

Lorcan was frantically busy too, ironing out a glitch in some piece of software that a foreign investment bank had introduced. He hadn't been one of the developers on it, but had been called as a trouble-shooter when serious problems began to arise. This meant long hours and added stress. June was doing a great job of not letting anyone see how much it was taking to keep on top of everything. Only Branch noticed how tired and increasingly stressed June was during their weekly Tuesday dinners. Branch decided to take matters into her own hands and arranged a 'chance' meeting with Lorcan to put him straight.

'It's her big day, and I know you want it all to go perfectly too, but she can't do everything. She's not superwoman. Have you seen how exhausted she is? She needs your support and some actual help. She'd kill me for saying anything, so don't let her know I did.'

'I hadn't realised. She's so capable. Look, I'll sort things out and, thank you, Branch. I want her to be happy; after all, she's taking on my family too. I promise I'll give the upcoming nuptials full priority.'

June was delighted to get his call. 'I just want to tell you I've passed on the banking problems to a colleague and I'm all yours. What do you need me to do?'

She laughed. 'Loads!'

The wedding day was beautiful and as perfect as June had hoped. But when they boarded the plane for their honeymoon, the franticness of previous weeks took its toll and June and Lorcan were both asleep before the attendants came around with the drinks.

Though June had never relished the idea of a beach holiday before, she now embraced it fully. They spent the next two weeks relaxing by the pool, eating good food and taking long walks on the white sandy beaches. By the time the twins joined them, the tropical islands had worked their magic. They were married, bronzed, relaxed, happy and, together, they were ready to face whatever the world would throw at them. June had chosen to keep her own name – it was something she'd always planned to do, but she also sensed the kids preferred it too.

The move went smoothly and within a few weeks Hill Crest began to feel like home, even though she was still inclined to head for Raglan Road when she left the office. *Old habits die hard,* she thought.

The rooms at Hill Crest had their windows perfectly placed to catch the morning and evening sun. Those at the back overlooked the long patio and lawns with the sweep of Killiney Bay below. The pond was set to one side, where some stately old trees shaded it for part of the day. To the front, the gardens sloped gently upwards and wide herbaceous borders provided endless colour and variety all year round. The tennis court was tucked away behind a beech hedge.

June had a great time decorating and allocating what went where. She had taken her piano from Raglan Road and it now sat, centre stage, in the lounge. They called it the lounge, but when Penny visited, she insisted on calling it the drawing room. Penny had also tried to muscle in on the decoration of the house, but June was having none of it. She knew she had enough to do to make the house her own and not a replica of what Carol had done, given that she inherited much of the furniture from Bayvue. She was determined that the lounge would be her doing and of her taste and it was – a pale retreat in soft periwinkle and cream, large squashy chairs in an understated pattern and lots of modern art on the walls. She put all the photographs of Carol together on a feature wall in the den, and that pleased everybody.

June found it strange having people around her all the time, having lived so long on her own, but she soon got used to it all – the constant comings and goings of teenagers and their army of friends. Hill Crest became their meeting point, partly because of the tennis court and partly because of its proximity to the beach.

She hadn't realised just how highly regarded Lorcan was until she was privy to conversations between him, Sean and his friends.

'Did your really meet Bill Gates and Steve Jobs?' one of them wanted to know.

'I did, more than once,' Lorcan told them. 'And I hope to meet Bill Gates again this autumn at a conference in Silicon Valley.'

'Is he really the richest man in the world?'

'He's certainly up there among the top few. I do know that.'

'Do you think computers will still be important when we leave school? I mean, will they have reached saturation point by then or is it worth looking at them as a career?' another boy asked.

'Definitely – program development is the way forward. Everything, even the simplest app, needs someone to write it in the first place, so the more skills you acquire in that, the bigger the opportunities.'

'That's what I want to do,' said Sean. 'And then I'll buy the old man out if he won't hand the company over to me.' He grinned.

'Less of the "old man" stuff, young man,' Lorcan said.

'Could I do some work experience in your company, if that's not too cheeky of me to ask?' the young lad said.

'He'll have to take me on as well,' said Sean.

'That's not going to happen. You'll have to find your own placement, like John here just did. That's all part of the process of growing up and taking responsibility,' Lorcan said firmly.

'See what a bully he is. The sooner I can buy him out the better.' They all laughed. 'Then you can all work for me.'

'I want to do art or fashion design,' Ashling announced.

'When did you decide on that?' her father asked.

'When we were unpacking. I saw some of the sketches June did when she was thinking of going to NCAD. She didn't go in the end,' she told her friends, 'she went to UCD instead. She said she'd help me start getting a portfolio together because they take forever. She's very good.'

June was in the kitchen when she overheard this exchange and smiled to herself, flattered by Ashling's praise but also relieved that the abrasive barrier Ashling had erected was finally coming down.

'Did you hear that?' she whispered to Lorcan when he came out to the kitchen.

'I did. Praise indeed. That's a first. Progress at last,' he said as he gave her a hug.

A few days later Froggie rang. She could hear mewling noises in the background,

'It's a boy. Seven pounds, two ounces. Ben, after Danielle's dad, and Mark after mine. They're here beside me. I'll put you on to D.'

Before she could say congratulations to him, Danielle was talking.

'He's gorgeous, adorable and I'm NEVER, EVER, EVER having another one.'

'That's what everyone says,' June laughed. 'Does he look like you?'

'No, he's got loads of blond hair like his dad.' She giggled. 'That's the first time I've said that. It sounds funny. Now he's taking pics of us to send to everyone. You can imagine how I look after thirteen hours in labour! I'm going to kill him! I have to go – the nurses want to do some technical things, I think. Love you. Book your ticket!'

June rushed to check her email and, minutes later, the pics arrived. All she could see of Ben was the still-damp, slicked-down blond hair and a ruddy little face wrapped tightly in a blanket, but his mum's proud smile said it all. It radiated love and happiness.

Three weeks later, laden down with presents from Danielle's former colleagues and from Branch, June set off for the States.

Branch had a glint in her eye and confessed over coffee at the airport that she'd been to dinner twice with Cara's father-in-law while they'd been visiting.

'This is an interesting development,' June said, teasing her mother. 'It's a pity they've to go back to Oz, though. You could do with someone special in your life.'

'I don't want anyone special in my life, thank you,' Branch replied firmly. 'I've done all that and now I want to enjoy my freedom. Besides, I'm too busy to devote my attentions to any one person. I must confess, though, I did enjoy the company, and a little flirtation is always good for the ego.'

Branch had met Kelly's family when the burglar alarm went off and they had used the wrong button to deactivate it. The security company phoned her as a key holder and she went over straightaway. She ended up inviting them to her home for a meal one evening and kept an eye on them during their stay. She babysat one afternoon too so that they could all go shopping together.

From the moment Danielle knew June's plane had landed, she hovered about the front window of their house looking out for the car Froggie had sent to collect her friend. As soon as she saw it pull up, Danielle threw open the front door and rushed out to hug her. After their tearful reunion, and leaving June's bags for Froggie to collect, they went inside and became gooey-eyed over the baby.

June couldn't take her eyes off his perfect little face, his tiny fingers and perfectly shaped fingernails. Her breath skipped as he stretched his arms, and felt a real longing for a baby of her own – something she'd never felt before.

'He's so gorgeous and tiny. I want to take him home with me,' she said to a still-beaming Danielle.

'Well, you can't have him, June, he's mine. You'll have to go home and make one of your own,' Danielle teased, hugging Froggie, who was obviously such a proud father.

'You're right,' she answered. 'I will. You know, I feel as though I've stepped into an American sitcom. The perfect family scene – Mom nursing baby, Dad outside manicuring the lawn, the picket fencing, the oversized fridge-freezer and jumbo-sized washer-drier. Look at you, you're so happy and settled.'

'It's great, isn't it? I never imagined I'd be living in a place like this, but look what I have in here to remind me of our grand tour.'

She took her into the open-plan lounge and pointed to the caricatures they'd had drawn on the Riviera. June had the copy in her new home, just waiting to be placed when she finished the decorating. Hanging beside it was the painting Danielle had done of the olive grove with the turquoise nasturtiums, aquamarine onions and the purple tomatoes growing on the trees.

'God, Danielle, I miss you so much – I've no one to talk to anymore, and the laughs we used to have. When you told me you were staying on for another year, I cried when I came off the phone.'

'I know it's hard – the bad news is it could be longer.'

'Don't tell me that. I don't want to hear.'

'But you'll be so busy between work, your new home and your new husband and family. Can you believe we're both married?' Danielle then paused before saying quietly to June, 'Tell me you're happy, June. Really happy.'

'Give her a break, Danielle – she's only been married a wet weekend. They've scarcely had time to have their first row yet,' Froggie said.

'He's right, but as a bride of several weeks, I can honestly say that, yes, I am happy, very happy.'

'Good. So am I,' Danielle said, cuddling her son. 'Let's make sure we stay that way.'

Despite being so close to the city, June hardly left her friend's side for the four days she was there, and they never stopped talking.

On the Saturday of June's visit, they had a naming ceremony in their garden and invited a few of Froggie's workmates along with a handful of friends they had made since arriving in the neighbourhood. Danielle had joined some literacy volunteers in the local library and one of her pupils came too.

'I love the way everyone warms to a theme over here,' Danielle said as they were preparing the house before everyone arrived. 'It's so kitsch. Talk about niche marketing. They have speciality shops with miles of aisles just for naming ceremonies, showers, sweet sixteen, divorce parties and the like. Wait and see – they'll arrive with balloons and napkins with Ben's name on them, probably cupcakes too – with Virgin Mary blue icing – and all sorts of other banners and party fare. They'll probably bring monogrammed loo roll as well.'

And they did.

June hated leaving. The trip had brought home to her just how much she missed Danielle.

'Just let me have one last cuddle,' she said, taking Ben in her arms. 'I'm going to miss this little fellow. And I'm going to miss you too.'

Life settled into a pattern of sorts. The twins went to France for their usual few weeks with Carol's parents and the newlyweds got used to being a couple in every sense.

As they relaxed into the summer, they spent the evenings June wasn't working playing tennis or walking along Killiney Beach, or they just sat in the gardens at Hill Crest, enjoying the laziness of the long evenings or inviting friends to join them. At weekends, they sailed and sometimes dined in the club. Around all this, they both managed to keep their careers moving forward. Lorcan had found larger premises along the quays for his still-expanding business and had to recruit additional staff.

For June, the wedding, honeymoon and trip to America had left her with a lot of catching up to do to get ready for the autumn conference season, which was fast approaching. She loved the buzz of the conferences, though, and was building up quite a few contacts, which would all be very useful for Macy Brothers – or maybe herself at a later stage.

CHAPTER 24

When she discovered she was pregnant, that autumn, June's initial feelings were mixed. For a moment, it dredged up memories of the last time – the panic, the realisation that she had been raped and the fear of being on her own. She'd thought a few times that if she hadn't been pregnant, she would have fought much harder for Peter, and that she might have won. Now, when such thoughts popped into her mind, she dismissed them.

This time, the timing was right. This time, she could enjoy the whole experience. Even though it was a huge surprise, she firmly believed that this had happened for a reason.

Holding little Ben and the tide of photos that kept arriving of his every move and smile had made her feel broody. Her morning sickness did not. Nor did Lorcan's initial reaction.

'I didn't think we had planned to start a family,' he'd said, as though it was the equivalent of making a budgetary decision to buy or not to buy a new desk or chairs for the office.

'I didn't think we hadn't. Isn't it what married couples usually do?'

'I suppose it is. I didn't give it too much thought, though. You never said you wanted more children.'

'I didn't, and you never asked. And it's not a case of "more" children for me, is it?'

'We probably should have discussed this.'

'We probably should have,' she said, putting her arms around him. 'Instead, it looks like nature stepped in and made the decision for us.'

'How do you think the kids will feel about this?'

'This is their half brother or sister we're talking about,' she said, stepping back from him, 'and they'll probably be mortified telling their friends, who probably all think that their parents only did "it" to conceive them. They can't imagine old people like us having sex for fun and pleasure.'

'When will we tell them?'

'That we had sex for fun and pleasure or merely for procreation?' she said.

'It's not something to joke about.'

'They're not babies and they watch the soaps – if they haven't cottoned on by my dashes to the bathroom and my sudden loss of appetite, then let's leave it until the second trimester. We'll do it together then. There's no point in doing it any sooner – just in case anything goes wrong.'

He agreed. She wished he'd been a bit more enthusiastic, and though he did become more solicitous, she couldn't quite forget his initial reaction and it niggled away at her. Was this baby going to upset the balance of his already perfect family unit?

Branch's reaction was much more animated and genuine. 'I'm thrilled. That's the best news ever. I'm so happy for you, for you both. I'm sure Lorcan is delighted.'

June's hesitation wasn't lost on her mother. 'Of course, but we're not telling his kids just yet.' Even as she said this, she was aware that the twins were suddenly 'his' kids.

'That's wise. Are you keeping well?'

'No, I'm dog sick in the mornings, but I know that it will pass and it'll be worth it all in the end.'

'Of course it will.'

She told Kelly. Mainly because June had seen her looking at her earlier that morning with that 'look', so June knew she'd already guessed. Kelly seemed to have a sixth sense about such matters.

'This time it's for keeps and it feels so right now. I can't wait,' June whispered to her in the ladies' room. They hugged each other before going back to their desks.

Surprisingly, by the end of the seventh week, the nausea vanished. June felt fine again – more than fine – and excited that she had this life growing inside her.

They told the twins at breakfast one Saturday morning, as she tucked into a hearty fry. Sean slapped his dad on the back and said,

'Congratulations, old man. We'll have to draw up a baby-sitting contract, with terms and conditions. I won't be cheap, but I'll be dependable.'

'Mercenary pup,' he laughed back at his son. Ashling was quiet.

'Aren't you happy for us, poppet?' he asked her.

'Well, it's a bit embarrassing, you know, at your age, but yeah. When is this going to happen?'

'Around the end of May.'

'I'm going to ring Amanda and tell her,' she said, and left the table.

Of course Penny was on the phone minutes later to June, to offer her congratulations and to get the details so she could pass them on to the girls at bridge and golf and God knows what other clutch she belonged to.

'She's so transparent you have to laugh at her,' June said, when the call ended.

Lorcan agreed. 'I just wish she'd let me wriggle off her hook, but I suppose that won't happen until she has another widower to fix up.'

Their first Christmas as a new family was wonderful, and apart from the overwhelming tiredness, which everyone assured her was perfectly normal, she was blooming. A discreet bump was beginning to curve June's naturally flat stomach, her breasts were fuller and her skin glowing.

Then, when she was nearly halfway through her pregnancy, in the middle of a meeting with a new supplier who she'd been courting for quite a while, she felt a small leak. She tried to carry on with the meeting but then felt a bigger leak – one that she couldn't ignore. There was too much blood. She knew something was wrong and that she needed to get to the hospital. Kelly called an ambulance.

'I don't need an ambulance – all that fuss for what's probably a false alarm.'

'And if it's not, the paramedics will know exactly what to do.'

They did, but by the time the ambulance pulled up outside the National Maternity Hospital, she knew she had miscarried.

Everyone was kind and considerate. The twins couldn't have been more supportive. Lorcan tried to console her and Danielle phoned constantly, but June was heartbroken.

'You've plenty of time.'

'Early thirties is considered young nowadays to start a family.'

'People miscarry for all sorts of reasons and it certainly doesn't mean it will happen again.'

But it did happen again. A little over a year and a half later. Everything was normal until, at twenty weeks, June felt a leak. It started at home this time and Lorcan took June straight to hospital.

This time, the reason was given a name – cervical incompetence – and they said it was most probably caused by a birth defect that had affected the shape of the uterus or cervix.

'Why wasn't this detected before?' Lorcan wanted to know.

'Usually women have no history to indicate this condition,' the gynaecologist told them, 'and, as there are so many reasons why a miscarriage can happen, it's not always picked up after the first one. There can be a hereditary element to it too.'

'My mother lost several babies and only managed to hold on to me,' June told them. 'Could that be the same reason?'

'It certainly could be a contributory factor.'

'Does this mean I won't ever carry to full term?'

'Absolutely not. There is a procedure we can perform called a cervical cerclage, where sutures are used to stop the dilation,' the doctor explained. 'It gives additional support to the womb as the baby grows. We don't do this until a pregnancy is past twelve weeks but it's extremely successful. Many women who've gone through what you have go on to have several babies.'

The twins were distraught by the news. Ashling tried to hide her tears as she hugged June. They'd often discussed names and they both decided they didn't want to know if it was going to be a boy or a girl until it was born.

June was very down when she came home. Mrs Fitz fussed over her and Lorcan insisted she took some time off work. She didn't want to, so they compromised, and she agreed to handle anything urgent from home, but only things that couldn't be sorted by anyone else in the office.

Kelly was now working full time, doing courses and studying wine in her spare time. She'd surprised her bosses with her interest and enthusiasm and with her ability to remember things about even the most obscure label, and they'd been more than happy to give her extra responsibility.

Two weeks after June came home, Branch met Lorcan. 'I'm worried about June. She's not bouncing back like the last time. Do you think a trip for the two of you might help?'

'Have you suggested it to her?'

'Yes, but she said she didn't want to go anywhere.'

'It's very hard. Losing a baby. I've been through it and there's no saying how long she will take to accept it. Two misses in less than two years is a lot to contend with. She's grieving, and I know she misses Danielle terribly.'

'I know that, and it breaks my heart to see her so despondent.'

'Leave it with me,' Branch said. 'I'll suggest a few days away somewhere and I'll let you know what she says.'

And Branch did – a few days in New York and a few with Danielle.

But June was adamant. 'Mum, can you understand what seeing Danielle with Ben, and Froggie with Ben and Ben on his own does to me? And knowing there's a brother or sister on the way – I just couldn't deal with that right now.'

'Of course, love. I understand. The offer stands, if you change your mind.'

'Thanks, Mum, but I honestly can't face airports and all the hassle just at the moment, with Christmas around the corner.'

After her first miscarriage and now again following the second one, June often wondered if the abortion had been the cause of her problems. She kept those dark thoughts to herself, where they festered. Then during a visit from Kelly, she found herself talking about her secret fear.

'You shouldn't think like this, June. Remember the doctor said there are all kinds of reasons for it – and your mother lost babies too. Don't burden yourself with guilt when there's no need. I've been there and done that, and it doesn't help at all.'

June felt a sense of relief, and when Mrs Fitz brought them some coffee and some of her lemon drizzle cake, June brightened and suggested they take it through to the family room.

'Sit down and join us. You've been working all day, making me feel guilty,' June said.

'There's no need to feel like that – you're convalescing. Enjoy it while you can,' Mrs Fitz said. 'Though I am due a bit of a break.'

'You'll be back at work soon enough, June,' Kelly agreed. 'You should enjoy all this while you can.'

Realising the time, June switched on the television. Since her unscheduled leave, she'd found she enjoyed watching one particular cookery programme where celebrity chefs and their guests pitted their skills against each other. She forgot her angst as she became absorbed in their recipes, their witty and sometimes caustic rivalry. Today's chefs were the darlings of the culinary circuit, appearing on every foodie programme and chat show going. One was French, the other Italian. Both were temperamental. Their guests were a couple who played husband and wife café owners on a popular soap. Both admitted they couldn't cook, and they couldn't. Garlic went flying off the table while one tried to chop it; the other one didn't know how to separate eggs and used about five before mastering the art.

During their exchanges, the Italian chef announced he was coming to Dublin to open a restaurant. June wondered fleetingly how Peter was doing, but Mrs Fitz distracted that line of thought.

'He's a looker that Adamo, isn't he?' she said to Kelly. 'And I believe he's a bit of a boyo. He's always in those gossip magazines that I read in the hairdresser's, with his latest bit of arm candy. Just watch the way he looks at himself in any reflective surface when he thinks no one is watching him. I'd say he has a huge ego and a huge—'

'Mrs Fitz – you're great,' Kelly said, laughing. 'And I'm inclined to agree with you. Anyone who calls themselves by one name only usually has an inflated idea of their own importance. He certainly loves himself, but he can cook.'

Lorcan came in during this exchange and commented, 'I'm delighted to hear you laughing again, June. I've missed that.' He came over and kissed her on the forehead.

'So have I,' she replied, reaching for his hand.

That afternoon was the turning point for her. She set about involving the kids in doing the necessary pre-Christmassy things – mainly shopping, getting the tree and putting up decorations. She knew Sean was probably not even going to pretend to be interested, but she always included them both in everything. If they decided they didn't want to know, at least she had asked him.

June got so caught up in the festive preparations that she didn't notice that the dark cloud that had been shadowing her was lifting. She pushed aside thoughts of all the traditions they were still following, Carol's traditions. She needed to make her own now. She had been willing to forgo any changes to their first Christmas as a family, but now she decided to take command.

They had Carol's parents to stay for a few nights, as always, and they visited Lorcan's friends, but she made sure they entertained hers too.

'But we always go to Penny and Des on New Year's Eve,' Lorcan protested.

'I know, but this year *we're* having a party.'

She invited Branch and her music friends, the

Macy brothers and their wives, Kelly and some of the reps she was friendly with, and, along with Danielle's parents as well as Lorcan's friends from the yacht club, there was quite a gathering. By the time the New Year came, she realised that she was her optimistic self again and ready to go back to work.

CHAPTER 25

Danielle's daughter came into the world in January and a delighted Froggie made all the excited phone calls home.

'She's going to be Alison Ruby,' he announced, before passing the phone over to Danielle.

'I know I said it the last time, but this time I *really* mean it! NEVER, EVER, AGAIN!'

'I heard it all before,' laughed June.

'Well, listen to it carefully because you won't hear it from me again. But she's gorgeous, and adorable and very small. That's it now.'

One tiny curled-up fist peeped out from under the pink blanket in the photos Froggie mailed to everyone, while a bewildered older brother looked on as if to say, 'so this is what all the fuss was about?' June felt a pang of envy, jealous of her friend's happiness, something she had never felt before. She also felt sad beyond belief as she studied the four of them in the next shot.

She couldn't wait for Danielle to come home on leave and she intended spending every minute she could with her. Her family was complete, one of each. So was Lorcan's. June had to remind herself of all the other good things she had in her life.

Though delighted to be home, Danielle soon discovered that trying to have a conversation with her best friend, any sort of conversation, with a toddler and a baby programmed for demand feeding was an impossibility, but they worked around it. Doting grandparents stepped in so the two could have some time together.

'My life's not perfect, June. I know you think it is, but there are times when I hardly see Froggie and even though I've made friends, it's not the same over here. We don't have enough shared history and everyone is always on the go, moving here or there. These multinational corporations own you, body and soul, and there's no way you can say no to them. It's a bit like being in kindergarten, but instead of giving you gold stars and Smarties for good behaviour, you get citations and more and more responsibility. And instead of making everyone happy, that just makes them more and more competitive. Everyone is under so much stress.'

'That sounds awful. How does he cope?'

'He makes the most of it. And he knows it won't be forever. He's been head-hunted a few times, but he's determined to stay put until the new drug goes on general release. That's his baby and when it goes global, he'll be in even more demand and more marketable. He'll be able to choose what he wants to do next.'

'Do you ever see yourself coming back here? I ask that from a purely selfish point of view. There isn't a day goes by when I don't miss having you around.'

'Me too. Can you imagine what it's like over here in picket-fence suburbia? The yummy mummies are so focused on looking good that all they talk about is their latest diets, their kettle bell regimes, their personal trainers and their nail bars. Don't get me wrong, some of them are really nice, but they never tuck into a good feed or a helping of apple crumble with cream and they never drink more than one glass of wine. I think they thought I was an alcoholic when they met me first and I asked for a second one! But anyway, tell me about your life. Are you still happy?'

'I suppose I am really. It's been a rough time but I've come to accept what's happened. I love my work and I'm delighted to be back at it. JP and Neil have given me my head and it's exciting and stimulating. No two days are the same.'

'And Lorcan?'

'Lorcan is kind and loving and the twins have got to like me. As you can see, I have a fabulous home, a great social life and more than enough money to enjoy all these things.'

'Why do I sense a "but" coming next? How do you *feel*, June? And how does he feel about losing the babies?'

June was surprised to find tears welling up, but she said nothing. Danielle came over and put her arms around her friend.

'Oh, June, that was stupid of me. I shouldn't have asked.'

'Of course you should. I've never said this to anyone – and I know he was sorry for me when I miscarried – but he never wanted more children. He's never told me that in so many words, but I know him. He was happy with his lot – the perfect family, one of each. They were Carol's and I can't compete with such perfection.'

'I'm sure you're wrong.'

'I'm not. Can you believe that was one thing we never discussed before we got married? It was probably stupidity on my part, but I felt – and still feel – so guilty about the abortion that I always avoided the subject. He would never have wished the losses on me, I know that. He even suggested a vasectomy to save me having to go through the ordeal again. But I know he didn't grieve for them, the way I did, and still do. They were my babies, all three of them.' She let the tears fall.

'Oh, love, I don't know what to say. I had no idea.'

'Nor has he and it has to stay that way, but I feel he's drifting away from me. He's so self-sufficient, his world runs like clockwork. I'm here when he's away, so his family is OK, and he's here when I'm not. He didn't need a baby, but I do.'

Danielle let her cry, then went off to make some tea. Later June said, 'I suppose we should mention the other elephant in the room while we're still catching up. I know you want to ask about Peter.'

'Do you ever see him?'

'Never. They both pop up in the papers from time to time, usually with visiting film or rock stars dining in the restaurant. I read somewhere that Zoe's gone out on her own and he's taken on a new manager. They have placed orders with us, but I don't handle that end of things.'

The economic boom that had swept through Ireland had seen Macy Brothers' expanding their business. The rash of new restaurants that had opened up everywhere in the capital, and in its satellite towns and villages, meant that demand for their products had increased significantly year on year. Book clubs became Prosecco nights, dinner parties were in vogue again. Everyone pretended to be a wine expert, but such newfound interest meant their wine club and education programme grew legs and they had to hire a bigger venue to accommodate these events.

June immersed herself happily in work. She was delighted to meet up with Hennie and some of his team at the South African Wine Fair in London. He had brought Lerato with his group. She told June that she was going to work with one of the few successful black African wine producers in the region when she returned.

'That's fantastic news, I'm so happy for you. I told you you could do it. Girl power and all that.'

'I knew she had it in her when she told me she wouldn't work for nothing the first day I met her in the settlement,' laughed Hennie. 'She had trouble written all over her, but she had spunk and that's what I admired. Now, when I've taught her everything she knows she's leaving me and I couldn't be more proud. She'll be a great ambassador for my project.'

'You know, June, if you hadn't come to Hennie's that time I probably would have left it all behind when the year was over,' Lerato told her. 'I'd be back doing what most of the women from the township are doing – washing and cleaning for others. Not everyone is like the Goosens, you know. But when I saw you and got to know you, I envied you your self-confidence, your knowledge and the way you just took everything in your stride, all that and the way you kept telling us women it was time we took over the world.'

'I can't take any credit for that. We're all products of our circumstances. Take some credit, Lerato, you did it for yourself by hard work and determination. And I have to tell you I'm a fraud really because I haven't figured out how to take over anything just yet either.'

'Praise the Lord, humility from June,' Hennie teased.

'Please don't remind me.'

'I'm a firm believer that you make a lot of your own luck in this life,' he said.

'Some of it, yes, but other bits are foisted on you.'

'Then it's how you deal with them that counts,' he argued, and she agreed.

He invited her to join his team that evening and they had a great dinner in a well-known, multi-award-winning bistro.

'I was going to try and get a booking for Le Gavroche, but when I read that it's in the Guinness Book of Records for having served the most expensive meal per head, I changed my mind.'

One of his compatriots said, 'I think it was for a group of bankers who spent in or around £44,000 on their night out in London.'

'Now you lot, don't go getting any ideas or we'll be enjoying the good old British fish and chip experience for the rest of our stay here and you'll all be paying for yourselves!' Hennie told his guests.

Her hotel was only minutes away from the restaurant and he walked her back. 'Married life appears to be agreeing with you – you look very well,' he said.

Suddenly, she felt quite emotional. They had a drink in the bar and June found herself telling him about her miscarriages.

'That's hard going, but remember, there's always a refuge for you with us if you need a break. Bring that husband of yours along. I'd like to meet him and I'm sure Kima would too. You know how she loves having house guests.'

She promised she would. 'You're a good friend, Hennie, thank you.

Later that night, remembering what he said – it's how you deal with things that counts, not what you have or wish you had – she decided that perhaps it really was unrealistic to keep hoping for a child of her own. She should be grateful for what she had – and she had a lot to be grateful for.

CHAPTER 26

A public relations consultant greeted them. She had been flown specifically from Rome and teetered at the entrance on impossibly tall, transparent heels. A classy little black dress revealed much more than it covered. Her breasts were doing a wonderful balancing act by staying in their uplifted cups. An equally glamorous assistant checked them off the guest list and handed them name badges. Kelly and June had arrived for the much-vaunted grand opening of Adamo's restaurant. They were representing Macy Brothers, who were one of the main wine and spirit suppliers to this new eatery.

Adamo had finally come to Dublin. He had been a guest on all the major chat shows and his arrival had been in all the papers during the previous week. He was snapped at nightclubs and restaurants, including The Pink Pepper Tree, and no matter how important you thought you were, it was impossible to get on the guest list, or indeed get a booking to dine at his new venue for the first month.

Now the night had finally arrived, a glitzy opening,

attracting glitzy attention. Exotic flower arrangements added to the opulence of the gold and turquoise theme. Champagne flowed. Style was of the essence, and there was a waft of expensive perfumes in the air. Up-dos and curls, figure-hugging dresses and minis topped off long legs on skyscraper heels. There, mingling among the beautiful people, TV crews, and newspaper and glossy magazine photographers June spotted Peter, a head above many of the others.

'I never expected to see you here,' she said when they came face to face and had got over the initial awkwardness of not knowing how to greet each other. Should they kiss, or shake hands? They did both. 'How is The Pink Pepper Tree going? I mean I know it is going very well – I read about your awards and your famous guests. I'm delighted for you,' she babbled on. 'You remember Kelly, who works with me?'

'Of course I remember Kelly. How are you?'

'I'm great. Very busy. Lorcan's off in Silicon Valley hammering out some licensing agreements.' *Shut up*, she told herself, *just shut up!*

'I read about him all the time too,' Peter said. 'Quite the IT whizz man. Winning that EU bank programming system was quite a coup. I see his latest game is set to be the new chartbuster.'

'You're full of surprises. I never knew you were so au fait with technology trends.'

'In my business you have to be like a magpie, it helps to make all your customers feel they are

331

important. Just don't ask me about HGVs or quantum physics, though. I haven't got around to them yet. So how's the world of wine?' Before she could answer, he said, 'Oh, will you excuse me? Zoe's calling me over. I'd better go, she's talking to Adamo – he's her first commercial client since she went out on her own.'

'I didn't know that.'

'It was all very hush hush, embargoes on everything to do with the place and everything having to be passed by his "team" in Rome for approval before they could decide on anything or give anything away. I'm sure Clinton's visit didn't require as much stage managing,' he laughed. She had forgotten how his eyes creased when he did.

'It looks stunning. Give her my congratulations.'

'And mine too,' said Kelly. 'You must be very proud of her.'

'I am, very. I'll pass them on. Now I'd better go over there. It was nice seeing you both,' he said, and he vanished through the crowd, jostling to pay homage to Adamo across the restaurant floor.

'You handled that very well,' Kelly said to her.

'I didn't. I jabbered away like a fool. She's doing well for herself, isn't she?'

'So are you. Life's not a competition,' Kelly said. 'Now, I want to meet this Adonis or Adamo or whatever he's called, in person. Come on, let's do it together.'

Their glasses were refilled as they sampled canapés and amuse-bouches that tantalised their taste buds. Afterwards, they agreed that if he appeared to be a peacock on television he was an even bigger one in person. He smiled a toothpaste-advert smile each time a camera was produced. Between introductions, he made shapes in his perfectly tailored suit. Gold glistened under his open-necked shirt and on his wrist. He puffed out his chest and tugged at his pristine cuffs, showing off oversized, bejewelled cufflinks.

Skipping the queue, Zoe appeared by his side introducing her friends to him. He kept referring to her as his *tesoro mio,* which he pronounced as though singing an aria to her – *tess–ooor–rroo mee-ooh*. In his speech, he praised her vision and her impeccable taste.

'My clever little angel Zoe is so good at design, she could almost be Italian.' He paused to savour the reaction. 'Now, it's up to me to make sure our food matches the sumptuous surroundings she has created for it.'

She glowed in a knee-length gold-lamé, halter-neck creation with ankle strap shoes to match. She had darkened her hair to a chestnut and let it grow longer. It made her look less angular than before and somehow more feminine. June managed to avoid facing her as she circulated and just gave her and Peter a smile and a wave as she left.

'I have to say the place does look very good,' said Kelly, as they walked away.

'And so does she,' June replied, wondering if she hadn't had a little bodily enhancement done in the meantime too. Her recollection was that she had been completely flat-chested when they first met. That certainly would not have been at Peter's urging, he always said he didn't like plastic women – unless he *had* changed that much.

Peter went back to The Pink Pepper Tree, leaving Zoe to impress her client and his entourage. The party would go on until the small hours and he had had enough of the kow-towing. Despite owning one of the most prestigious establishments in town, his interaction with his patrons was always genuine. He relied on personal recommendations and on his quality menus to attract customers. Not on publicity. He never tipped off the gossip columnists when a VIP had booked a table and had been disgusted when he discovered that Zoe was doing so. He'd only twigged when she'd appeared three Fridays in a row, decked out in seriously sexy numbers. She had started commandeering a table in the corner for her fair-weather media friends and plying them with his finest wines so that they'd insist that she was included in the pics for the weekend supplements. When he'd stopped telling her who was coming in, she soon grew tired of hanging around in anticipation.

He was surprised at how little affinity she had for his business. He knew now that she'd only wanted him for the prestige it would give her.

Far from being the caring, interested woman he'd thought she was when they'd first met, he now knew where her priorities were. The reality appeared very quickly after they'd married. He should have spotted the signs when he took her to Portugal that first Christmas. She was bored by the estate, showed no interest in his father's stables and horses, or in Rosa's fledgling wine label. His mother had told him at the time, 'She's no June. You shouldn't have let her get away.'

Peter laughed. 'June told me you'd say that when we broke up.'

'And she was right! Zoe'll run you a merry dance. Are you sure about her – marriage and everything? You're not going to rush in to things, are you?'

He wasn't, but Zoe was very persuasive, and after they had got engaged, she gave that ridiculous interview about work romances to the biggest rag in the country. After that, there was no going back. He wished not for the first time that he'd taken more time to get to know her or had been stronger and called the whole thing off anyway. But he also instinctively felt that she'd soon get tired of him and move on – and he realised that he wouldn't mind that one bit.

He had his suspicions about that Italian chef. Zoe had been flitting back and forth to his headquarters in London a little too often to be credible, and her reasons were becoming more and more fanciful.

It all could have been so different. If he and June – if only he and June . . .

Most architects would have taken the winning of such a prestigious assignment as a pinnacle of their career, but not Zoe. She had set her hopes on higher things, professionally and otherwise. Seduced by his come-to-bed eyes, his sexy accent, the way he pronounced her name, the celebrity competition from his latest much-publicised squeeze and by his fame, she flirted with danger, massaging Adamo's needy ego. And he responded, as she knew he would. She had used every opportunity to fly over to London to discuss the smallest detail with him. Such discussions spilled over into after hours and then to her hotel room and eventually to his penthouse apartment in Canary Wharf. That was when she realised she had him hooked.

She was careful not to let news of her dalliances reach Dublin. She didn't want Peter to find out. She had outgrown him, realising soon after they married that the fun of the chase had been the best part of her conquest. She had hated June on sight, and the fact that she might be beaten by her had made Zoe redouble her efforts to lure him away. Now she had to be clever enough not to spoil things until it suited her. Peter was a popular man and a good man, and, as his wife, she had position and a certain social standing in Dublin. She also got to meet the stars and VIPs that came to town, until she messed things up by being 'too obvious', according to him. After this coup, however, her career was bound to skyrocket and she was happy to bide her time until something better came along. She figured Adamo would disappear back to London and she might see him on his visits over. She didn't expect any more than that.

But then she didn't expect to fall in love with him either. It had crept up on her. It finally dawned on her when she orchestrated yet another visit to London to be with him, only to be told by his latest PA when she arrived that he was out of town for a few days. She tried his phone, his office, his personal mobile, but heard nothing back. That was when jealousy and rage told her that she was in this much deeper than she thought.

CHAPTER 27

Lorcan and June continued to travel a good deal, with each accompanying the other on their business trips. She had successfully taken several of her wine grade exams and was becoming quite an expert. She'd found that the more she learned, the more she wanted to learn. She began forming plans for a wine outlet of her own in the future, perhaps one that would provide advice and consultancy services to restaurateurs.

Lorcan's company was still growing and, following a graduate fair, he'd added two more to his team.

She had put the house in Raglan Road in the hands of an agency that did short-term corporate lets.

Watching Sean interact with his father, it was obvious to June that he was destined to follow in his footsteps. Half the time she and Ashling didn't have a clue what they were talking about and they used this as a cue to escape to the den. There Ashling used her spare time sketching fashion designs and doing preparation work on her portfolio. She was determined to go to art college when she finished school and was trying to amass

338

an eclectic collection to reflect her interests and talents. She'd welcomed June's advice and input and that had proved to be the final bond that brought them together. June would often paint while Ashling drew, neither saying much, and the silences that at one time had been awkward now felt natural and normal.

June had always understood how important it was to let Lorcan's kids have their space. Although she enjoyed sailing, she kept away from it most of the time. Sailing on *SEAS* was something more than just being out on the water for the three Overends. It held something indefinable, yet essential to them all. It was where they could each cherish their own memories of a much loved and missed wife and mother.

When they were all sailing, June spent her time with Branch, who was as busy as ever with her charities and clubs and her social calendar. She now held a musical soiree once a month in her house, and June took Lorcan along occasionally.

June often puzzled over Branch's attitude towards Lorcan. She'd never said she didn't like him, but then she never said she did either. She was perfectly pleasant to him, as she was with everyone in her home, but there was definitely something there. When she tried to press her mother on this she didn't get very far.

'You're dreaming!' her mother said. 'Have I ever been rude to him or made him feel he wasn't welcome? No. Never. I don't know what's got in to you lately.'

June took that as a cue to drop the topic, but Branch's response didn't settle the nagging feeling she had and she continued to watch their interaction more closely than ever.

'If I'd known that you planned to come home for Christmas I'd never have gone away,' June told Danielle on the phone.

'It was a spur of the moment decision. As you know, Dad hates flying and the kids have got so big, we just decided on a quick flit. How are things? Are you still trying for a baby?'

'Chance would be a fine thing!' she said. 'Since the last miscarriage Lorcan just doesn't seem to be bothered with that side of our relationship any more.'

'I hadn't realised . . . have you talked to him about it?'

'I've tried but he won't . . .' she paused. 'He's coming in . . . have to change the subject.'

That Christmas they took the twins to South Africa, so they missed seeing their grandparents. They went first to the Eastern Cape, to Shamwari Game Reserve. Wrapped in blankets sitting in the open jeeps, going in search of the 'big five', they listened to the sounds of this world wakening up. They experienced dawn safaris, eyeballed elephants, gave the ant hills a wide berth, and watched the giraffes negotiate the long thorns of the acacia trees, using their leathery tongues to find the most succulent leaves between them. They were intrigued by a rare glimpse of a secretary bird with its crest of long black feathers sticking up from its head like a container full of quills.

'These birds of prey may look pretty, but that's where the niceness stops. They use their feet to pound their prey to death,' their ranger told them.

'I'd love to see how they do that,' said Sean.

'We have a video back at the information centre which shows one hitting a rubber snake – you can see it all there – right down to the kill and his enjoyment as he eats.'

'Ugh. I don't know how you'd watch that,' Ashling told her brother. 'You're cruel.'

He just laughed at her. 'You're soft.'

'Nature is cruel, but it's beautiful too,' the ranger told them.

'They look like they're wearing cut-off trousers or shorts the way their feathers stop at their knees, if you call them knees.'

'You do. They have scales on the lower part and on their feet to stop them being bitten by their prey.'

Back at the preservation area, Ashling fell in love with some caracals that were being tended by one of the keepers. The kittens' mother had been killed and they were being rehabilitated for release into the wild.

Reluctantly they left their grass-roofed lodges and the new friends they had made around the jeep trips and open-air barbecues to fly to Cape Town. They headed off to stay with the Goosens for a few days. Kima loved having them there and brought them to the country club, introducing the kids to other youngsters. While they played tennis, Hennie took June and Lorcan on a whistle-stop tour of the Stellenbosch wine route. June introduced him to Lerato and she insisted they all go to her township to meet her family. It surprised June that they were now running organised tours to the shanties.

'What an invasion of privacy that is,' she said to Lorcan. 'I wonder how the locals feel about coach-loads of gawkers filing past their homes.'

'Maybe they get a cut from the tour operators.'

'I doubt that very much.'

Ever since she had first been there, she was struck by the maze of television aerials and satellite dishes that now canopied the shacks and galvanised roofs of this and the other endless sprawls of dwellings they had passed on the way from the airport. Inside, the odd plasma screen could be seen casting its flickering images over the otherwise meagre possessions of the occupants.

Lerato, successful in her new job and now earning a very good salary, had moved her family to a purpose-built house on a cleared site close to where she had spent most of her youth. A proper construction with four rooms, she showed this off proudly while her widowed mother fussed about making rooibos tea and producing a home-made cake. Ashling told the little boys about the safari; about the animals they had never seen. Sean had them giggling when he told them how they had learned to track the different ones by recognising the size of their poo and how old it was.

'If it's fresh, then the animals are close by. If it's dried up, it means they had been that way some time ago.' They stared at him wide-eyed, not quite knowing whether to believe him or not.

'I owe all this to June,' Lerato told Lorcan. 'She's my inspiration.'

'She's ours too,' Lorcan said, putting his arm around her shoulder, and June felt a glow. This trip had been a good idea. She felt close to Lorcan again. Being here in this totally opposite world to her own, she knew she had made a difference to someone's life and no matter how tiny that was, it made her feel good. She put her arm around her husband, smiled up at him and said 'thank you' and gave him a squeeze. Maybe they'd get back on track again soon. Perhaps they had just needed to get away for a bit from the pressures of work.

In bed that evening, under the wooden ceiling fan, she inched towards her husband, running her hand down his back. She waited a second or two for a response and when there was none, she moved her hand towards his toned stomach. He let out an exasperated sigh and said, 'Not tonight.

Can you move over a bit to your side? It's too hot in here.'

If he had slapped her she couldn't have been more hurt. She lay there for a while feeling totally alone and rejected. She went into the bathroom and squirted some insect repellent on her arms, then she wrapped her cotton robe around her and went to the main living room and let herself out onto the veranda, where they had all eaten earlier that evening. Lorcan was already snoring quietly before she even left their bedroom. She wanted to get as far away as possible from him. It was there that Hennie found her, sobbing quietly.

'What are you doing out here at this hour?' he asked.

She blew her nose and said, 'I could ask you the same thing.'

'There's a faulty thermostat in one of the cellars and it's triggered the alarm – again. There's a replacement coming in the morning, but meanwhile I can't seem to override it and it keeps going off. Do you want to talk or would you rather I left you alone?' he asked gently.

She just nodded and he led her to a bench at the far end.

'What's upset you?' he asked, taking her hand.

'Hennie, don't be nice to me or I'll dissolve,' she said.

'I've broad shoulders and a large handkerchief, but let me get us a glass of something as I think we'll be out here for a while.'

He was easy to talk to and she found herself opening up as she had never done before. She told him she had married Lorcan because she loved him, but not with the sort of love she'd had for Peter. She realised then that she hadn't given Peter and Zoe a thought for quite a while. Over the past few years, she had managed to convince herself that she hadn't accepted Lorcan's proposal as a kneejerk reaction to their marriage, but now, feeling utterly rejected and raw, she admitted to herself, and to Hennie, that there had definitely been a bit of that in her reasoning. He had offered her stability and kindness at a time when she was at her most vulnerable, and she had accepted it willingly.

'Do you think he was just looking for a mother for his kids?' Hennie asked.

'I didn't think so at the time, but now I'm not so sure. Do you know, in a twisted kind of way I think that being a substitute mother to Ashling and Sean assuaged some of the guilt I still felt at having the abortion.'

'You're very hard on yourself, June. I'm sure you had good reasons.'

She explained and said, 'I can't believe I told you that – I've never told anyone since it happened.'

'It's safe with me.'

'I know that, Hennie. I feel I could trust you with anything.'

'What are you going to do about the situation?'

'I just want to run and get as far away as possible

345

from him, but I won't. There is more than just me to consider. I'll work it out somehow. I have my career to think of too.'

'You could always come and work down here in Stellenbosch for a season or two.'

'It's certainly something to think about.' Some lights started flashing on one of the buildings.

'There's that blasted alarm tripping again. I'll have to sort it out before it triggers the siren and wakens the whole place up.'

'I'm sorry for annoying you,' she said, standing up.

'You didn't. Just promise me that you'll look after yourself, June,' he said, kissing her tenderly on the cheek. 'You're a very special lady.'

'Who's very lucky to have a special friend like you!'

CHAPTER 28

O ne Sunday morning, three weeks after they returned from South Africa, the kids decided to go to Penny's to study, so June and Lorcan went to Branch's for lunch.

They bought the Sunday papers en route, and when June saw a headline that Peter and Zoe had split up, she grabbed the tabloids too.

'The tabloids are having a field day,' she said to Lorcan in the car. 'They're full of this celebrity story, as well as speculative comments from "reliable sources".'

'*A new dish for Italian chef/restaurant owner, Adamo,*' said one.

Another speculated:

> Has Irish architect Zoe Synnott managed to bag the Italian Lothario Adamo? She recently designed his first restaurant in Ireland and since then the pair has been seen out tête-à-tête and clubbing in his favourite venue in London on more than one occasion in recent months. He had nothing to say when asked for a comment.

Zoe is married to Peter Braga, the Portuguese-Irish owner of the award-winning Pink Pepper Tree in Dublin. She met him while working on its renovation.

'Did you see this one?' asked Branch. The heading on one of the redtops shouted, *Adamo Adamant 'She's the one for me!'* It included a photo of Zoe with Peter and one with Adamo, at both of their openings. 'There's very little to substantiate that headline as you read on down.'

'This one is vitriolic: listen to this.'

Grand designs on the boss(es)!

In an interview in this paper when Peter Braga, owner of the award-winning Pink Pepper Tree in Dublin, and architect Zoe Synnott got engaged, she said she was all for workplace romances – now it seems she's making a habit of them.

Was her marriage to Braga a recipe for disaster? Did they let it go off the boil? It looks like it. It also looks like she had her eye on a bigger catch in the form of Adamo, the Italian playboy and TV chef, who now has restaurants in London, Milan, Rome and Dublin. His name has previously been linked with glamour models and film stars.

Branch told them, 'I feel sad for Peter, having his private life splashed all over the media.'

'That's the price of being well known, but it'll be old news in a few days. He's a popular guy. He'll get over her,' Lorcan said. 'That Adamo chap probably will too.'

'That's where men and women differ. I think the sense of betrayal would be very hard to get over. I'm not sure I would ever trust anyone again if they did that to me,' Branch said.

'I doubt if I would or could either, if I opened the papers and read about you having an affair – and a very public affair at that,' June said.

'Maybe she was just a gold-digger to begin with,' Lorcan argued. 'Peter might know that too and be glad to be shut of her.'

June speculated, 'What if he thought he was in a viable marriage and didn't know anything about this until today? If he loves her, even if he did know, he'd still be devastated.'

'I don't think so. I know I wouldn't be, if I thought she was taking me for a ride all along.'

'Life is never that black and white, though – is it, Lorcan?' Branch said, putting down the papers and busying herself with final preparations for their meal.

'Unfortunately not, Branch,' he replied. 'Unfortunately not.'

June resisted the urge to contact Peter. She had resolved to try harder to put the sparkle back in her marriage and didn't need to be distracted by what was happening in Peter's. Still, she couldn't help but remember how proud he had been of

Zoe the last time she'd seen him and wonder if he'd had any inkling about what was really going on – if it had been going on then.

She didn't have too much time to dwell on it, though, because exam panic had set in at Hill Crest. The mocks were only weeks away and the twins decided they knew nothing and so wouldn't get college places when the real thing came along. One minute, they were convinced their friends were all going to fly through and leave them behind, the next they were convinced that they had made the wrong course choices. June promised to drive Ashling in to deliver her portfolio to the College of Art.

Lorcan had to go to the States for a week, so June cleared her diary and provided the steadying and encouraging hand, making sure there was plenty of good food around and that they took breaks and ate when they should. Sometimes she felt her marriage had catapulted her in to Lorcan's generation, forcing her to bypass her thirties, and she couldn't help but resent it when she got so little back from him.

Lorcan did add his own words of encouragement before he left, but he was preoccupied with a new project that was exercising his mind and his time. He had never been one for working late or over the weekends but this project was eating into his free time and he seemed unusually tetchy at times. June wondered if there was more than just the project bothering him, but when she tackled him at breakfast he cut her off, telling her he was a bit stressed at some glitch that they hadn't been able to isolate as yet.

Ashling looked at him and said, 'Dad, don't talk to June like that. She only asked a question.'

'Sorry, sorry.'

'Yeah, Dad, you're a right old grump these days,' said Sean.

'I said I was sorry. I'm just a little stressed out, but we'll get to the bottom of it. I have those new graduates on it.'

'How are they working out? I thought having them on board would free up some more time for yourself, and for us,' June said.

'So did I. Noelle is extremely competent.'

'Is she the busty one? She's hot,' said Sean, who had been at the office the previous week.

'She is, but she's also quick and good at solving problems. I still have reservations about Lisa,' he answered. 'She's definitely not a team player – to be honest, she's a bit of a stirrer. All I can hope is that she's head-hunted at some stage, because I have no legitimate reason to give her notice.'

'What's she doing wrong?'

'Nothing definable, but I feel like she's watching everybody, what they are doing and saying, telling tales and generally causing bad feeling among the others. There's an atmosphere that was never there before. Noelle came to me about it the other day. Lisa told her she felt I was favouring Noelle over her. She actually used the word victimised, saying

351

I was singling her out for mundane tasks and not giving her the challenging ones. She claimed it was obvious I didn't like her and that I was determined to hamper her chances of advancement.'

'And was that true? Were you?' Sean asked.

'Absolutely not – that's why I put the two of them on this latest problem. Let them sort it out together.'

'Was that a good idea?'

'From now on, she's going to be given the impossible and we'll see how she likes that. She'll be sorry she ever moaned,' he laughed.

'That's nasty. I hope you're nicer to your son when he's working for you,' said June.

'He's well able for me,' he replied. 'He thinks he'll be able to buy me in half a dozen years' time.'

'And I wouldn't put it past him. He's a smart cookie,' Ashling said, and she high-fived her brother.

'It's funny how you two only ever agree on anything when you're ganging up on your old man,' Lorcan said.

Despite his protestations, June wasn't quite convinced that there wasn't more worrying Lorcan than he'd admit to. When he left the table, she asked Mrs Fitz to make one of her killer chocolate cakes – they usually restored the humour and equilibrium in the house.

CHAPTER 29

Lorcan knew he was playing with fire as he sat in the plane, Noelle asleep beside him. 'I was so excited last night I never closed my eyes,' she told him when they met at the airport. 'All the times I've been to the States I never made it to New York.'

Within twenty minutes of taking off, she was gone. He studied her face for a few minutes and wondered again why he hadn't mentioned to June that she was going with him this time. He normally travelled alone, unless June was with him, and she seemed to be doing less of that lately. That had been his doing too.

He had been attracted to Noelle since she'd joined his company. At first, her cool efficiency had impressed him. She had an analytical mind that equalled his and they would discuss the vagaries and quirks of some piece of software or of some programming solution for hours on end. They often found themselves still in the office when everyone else had left. On a few occasions, they had had a drink together to continue their debate.

She was small and vivacious and busty, Sean had been right about that – it hadn't escaped Lorcan's notice either. She had a cleavage that often exposed more than was strictly necessary in a work environment, and a perfectly rounded bottom to balance her. Being close to her excited him.

But he was her boss and she was only a few years older than Ashling and Sean.

He knew he was taking a risk when he suggested this trip and, as he sat there studying her face, he still wasn't sure if he'd do anything untoward. He wanted to. What red-blooded male wouldn't, he reasoned. But he was in control. Lorcan Overend was always in control, wasn't he? That's what he had told himself for so long that he believed it.

They worked long hours with various meetings – breakfast meetings, so beloved by Americans, and dinner meetings that went on late. After their final meeting, the day before they were due to fly back, he decided to be the benevolent boss and show her a good time, in part because she had been such an asset on the trip and had helped make it so successful. There were cocktails in a dimly lit bar, followed by dinner and champagne in an intimate club with some gravelly voiced jazz musicians and a handkerchief-sized dance floor.

That's when he kissed her.

She looked up at him and said nothing, so he kissed her again and she responded with her whole body. This proved to be just the start. In the taxi, he couldn't keep his hands off her. They collected their keys from reception and reached her room first.

As soon as the door had clicked closed, he began undressing her, his hands touching, seeking and satisfying. It was all over in minutes, but the passion didn't die. It had only just been ignited and it took very little to fan it to sizzling hot again a second time. He never gave June a thought as they came together again in the wee small hours. He hadn't even turned off his phone and it beeped to announce a message as they lay entwined together amid the tossed bed covers, bodies glistening with sweat. He ignored it but when it beeped a second time, he jumped out of bed to see who was texting him at five thirty a.m. Irish time. Was there some crisis at home? He hoped not.

March winds do blow and I can't sleep a wink. I miss having you beside me to keep me warm! Dropped Ash's portfolio in today. Fingers crossed. Hope everything is going well your end. Love you. Hurry home. June xox

He felt as though June has just walked in on them. He couldn't get back into bed with Noelle. He gathered his clothes and went into the bathroom to dress. He felt guilty and ashamed. He wondered how Noelle felt. It was going to be damned awkward having to sit beside her on the plane and work with her in the office after this. *What madness possessed me?*

He was surprised that there wasn't any awkward-ness at all when they met for breakfast in the hotel's diner. She had mentioned she wanted to eat there because she couldn't go home without eating a stack of pancakes in a diner – and the week had been full of breakfast meetings in corpo-rate boardrooms.

When they met, the air was laced with the smell of fried food and coffee. Two large, uniformed cops wearing their guns carelessly, like kids playing cowboys, were having a break in the next booth, laughing across some obscenely high stacks of pancakes. At another table, a group of construc-tion workers in their high-visibility jackets were animatedly discussing some game.

'Can I just have some pancakes?'

'They come in stacks of five,' the server said, impatiently holding his pen over his order pad, 'but you don't have to eat them all, lady.'

'OK, I'll go for them.'

'With cream, maple syrup, honey, bacon, the works?'

She looked at Lorcan pleadingly. He laughed. 'Yes please.'

'The lot?'

'No, just maple syrup.'

'What sort of coffee do you want?' He was about

to go through the full list of the numerous coffee options, when Noelle interrupted him and said she'd be fine with a black coffee.

The server then turned his attention to Lorcan, who ordered in seconds.

'God, they do make life difficult,' Noelle said.

'I know.'

But if he were going to blame anyone for complicating his life, it would have to be himself. Yet it seemed the most natural thing in the world to be here with her, seeing New York through fresh young eyes. But he knew he had to stop this. Dead. Now.

Their food arrived, mountains of it, and she laughed. 'These pancakes taste more like crumpets than crepes.'

They talked about nothing in particular as they ate, and he tried to find the right words. 'Last night . . .,' he began. 'Last night . . .'

He paused when a different server came by their table. 'Refill?' she asked, sloshing the steaming liquid into their mugs with bored abandon.

'Last night was magical, wonderful,' Noelle said, reaching her hand across the table to cover his.

He drew his hand away. 'Yes, it was. All of that. But it was a mistake. I love my wife and it shouldn't have happened. It can't ever happen again. You have to understand that.'

Noelle sat opposite him looking straight into his face for what seemed like an eternity. When she spoke, she did so calmly and deliberately.

'Let me get this right. You slept with me, but it was a mistake. You made love to me, but you love your wife. It didn't seem to be that important last night. Is that an excuse to relieve your conscience or to fend me off? You want me to understand – I'd like you to understand and remember – it was you who took me dancing and who kissed me first and who came to my room. I didn't make a move on you.'

Damn her analytical mind; even is this situation she was capable of thinking logically. 'I know that,' he said, 'but it shouldn't have happened – and it can't happen again. I didn't mean to hurt you.'

She put a hand up to stop him. 'Lorcan, you need to stop lying to yourself. You have feelings for me. I know that and I have feelings for you, but I never acted on them. It's obvious to everyone in the office – and, yes, they've been talking, in case you're wondering how I know that. They've never had any cause before this, and now, when we've acknow-ledged these feelings, you tell me it was a mistake?'

'I do like you, very much. You're a beautiful, sexy woman, but it can't go anywhere.'

'It already has,' she said. 'I never gave you any reason to expect anything from me because I knew you were married, happily I thought, until last night. I love you, Lorcan. I have since you first interviewed me. Now, as you are my boss, perhaps you can give me some time on my own. I'd like to do a bit of shopping. I'll meet you back here in time to leave for the airport.'

'Of course, I'll see you then – and Noelle, I'm truly sorry.'

'So am I,' she said, gathering her belongings. He stood up as she left and sat back down again at the table amid the ever-changing sea of diners. He stared at the snaking line of well-dressed business people, grabbing their take-out, tall skinny lattes, their flat whites, their macchiatos and decaf teas, people whose lives seemed normal and uncomplicated to him. The racket going on inside his head out-decibelled the din of life around him.

Would it be possible to go back to the way things had been? To working beside her? He certainly hoped so, but he wasn't deluded enough to think it would. He hadn't meant to cheat on June, ever, and he never had done on Carol either.

But then he hadn't really given it much thought before it happened. It wasn't as though he had planned it, he told himself over and over again – he had to do that, in an effort to make himself believe it was true. Then he realised that he didn't regret it. He'd have to make sure Noelle didn't say anything in the office. Sean was due to start working with him for the summer and if he got a whiff of any of this it would be disastrous. He'd try and get him fixed up elsewhere – with one of his friends – for the experience.

He wandered around in a daze for the rest of the day, spending a ridiculous amount of money on a silky top for June. He wasn't looking forward to the journey home, six hours sitting beside

Noelle. He wasn't looking forward to facing his wife either. Should he tell her and get it out in the open or would it be better to say nothing? Confession is good for the soul; ignorance is bliss; what happens on tour stays on tour – all the old adages played on a loop in his head.

Noelle had already collected her bags from the left luggage room and was waiting for Lorcan in the foyer when he came back with his. She acted as though nothing had happened and he admired her control. She must be furious with him.

They went through the whole airport rigmarole and when they were finally ensconced in their seats she said, 'Lorcan. We have to talk about what happened.'

'I know.'

'I can't stay working for you after this.'

'That's ridiculous. You can't just go. You're invaluable to me and to the company and you've a great career ahead of you. You can't throw all that away because of an indiscretion.'

'So that's what it was – an indiscretion? I'm so glad you clarified that because all day long I felt like you thought it was a turn with a hooker, except that you forgot to leave the dollar bills on the pillow when you made your hasty departure. Yes, indiscretion sounds more classy altogether,' she said calmly.

'You know it wasn't like that,' he said, unintentionally raising his voice. 'Look, this is not the time, nor the place, to be discussing this. Please don't do anything hasty. Think about it over the weekend and we'll talk on Monday.'

'I agree, but I've already done my thinking. Now I'm going to watch a film.' She reached down to adjust her seat and he knew the conversation was over.

Despite knowing with every fibre of his body that he had done something wrong, he found himself reliving what they'd done, what she said, how she smelled and felt, and what her touch had done to him. Her scent hung on the air between their business-class seats, tantalising him. He wanted to reach out and take her hand, tell her that he wished things were different – that he'd like so much more. He was acutely aware of her every movement as she lay there on her recliner and, from her breathing, he knew the instant she fell asleep with her earphones still plugged in. Then he thought of June – trustful, loving, kind-hearted June, and he felt physically sick.

He knew his marriage was not what he'd hoped it to be. He had really wanted Carol back and when he couldn't have her, he wanted what he'd had with her. He had jumped in too quickly, desperate for the kids to have a caring step-mother, and June was certainly that. She couldn't have loved the twins any more if she had given birth to them, and she loved him. But she'd also wanted them to have children of their own and he certainly didn't want to go back to sleepless nights, nappies, puking and all the other inconveniences – not at his age. No, thank you, he'd done his bit for the continuance of the species.

He didn't know how he'd act when he saw her at home. In his car mirror, he looked ashen and drawn. He hadn't expected to find her up and dressed so early on a Saturday morning.

'How did it go?'

'Good . . . tiring, and I didn't sleep a wink on the plane coming back, so I feel completely wiped out. I'm going to hit the sack for a few hours.'

'Can I get you something to eat?'

'No, thanks. I had breakfast on the plane.'

He didn't surface until after three that afternoon.

'You look much better,' June said, when he came down carrying the expensive-looking carrier bag.

'I feel it too,' he said, handing over the present. Would she sense this was a guilt purchase? He hoped not.

'Lorcan, it's absolutely beautiful,' she said, fingering the silky softness of the fabric. 'You really spoil me.'

She went over and kissed him and he had to stop himself from pulling away from her.

CHAPTER 30

Noelle had meant what she'd said. She came into the office the following Monday and handed in her notice. She had typed it out in advance and went straight to Lorcan's office to deliver it in person. All weekend, he had thought about what it would be like not being around her every day and he didn't like the idea. He tried to talk her out of leaving, but she was not going to change her mind.

'I can't do this now. I have a meeting at ten o'clock. Let's have a drink somewhere away from the office after work and see if we can't sort this out,' he said to her in a last-ditch attempt to get her to stay.

She agreed reluctantly. But that rendezvous was acrimonious to start with. She was still angry and hurt. She told him she felt he had used her and she couldn't possibly stay on now that circumstances had changed – especially as he had been the one to change them. The bottom line was that she wanted to continue seeing him, but she couldn't do that if she worked for him.

He felt even worse about the whole situation.

He was ready to admit to himself that he had wanted it to happen all along. It was no accident that he'd taken her to New York or that they had ended up in her bed.

'I love you,' she said.

He took her hand before he spoke. 'There's no future in this for you. I won't ever leave June no matter what my feelings are for you. You need to know that. My children lost their mother when they were young. Then I met June and she was happy to love them like her own. They love her like the mother she is to them and there is nothing and no one in this world that will make me put them through all that pain and heartache again. So there's no future in it for you, Noelle.'

'Why don't you let me decide what's in it for me?'

'If you're willing to see me on those terms, then that's your decision, just so long as you know that they won't change, ever, no matter what.' He spoke as emphatically as he could.

'Well, I do want to keep seeing you – more than ever after the other night – but I won't stay in the office. I couldn't keep up the pretence in front of the others. Would you help me get a new job?'

'Of course I will. You could always work from home for me, though.'

'No. I'd find that too lonely. I enjoy the buzz of a busy office.'

'Then stay until we've found the right place for you to go to.'

She agreed to that. It was after eight and neither had eaten much all day. He suggested a quick bite somewhere. He texted June to tell her he'd be later than he thought, and that was how he ended up driving Noelle home to Rathgar.

That became a pattern over the next few months. She rented a townhouse in a small, gated development in a secluded side road, so his comings and goings were largely unnoticed. In spite of this, he was running out of excuses at home to explain away the recent changes in his routine.

He decided to take action the following Monday. All he had to do was choose his moment. He hadn't seriously tried to find a new job for Noelle – but that would now be his priority. He called her in to his office to discuss it with her when his PA knocked on his door to announce that a client had just arrived for their appointment. 'Great. Please send him in.' He then turned to Noelle. 'We'll talk after work.'

'OK, I'll leave early; you can follow me home and I'll cook.' She dropped some keys on his desk before she left. 'I got those cut for you.'

He had no time to react so he pocketed them just as his client was being ushered in to his office. There was no discussion that evening because they ended up in bed after they had eaten.

'Mrs Fitz is going to think that you've gone off her cooking if you leave another of her dinners untouched,' June said when he arrived home after eleven.

'Those sods from the bank have screwed us enough already. I honestly didn't expect to have to wine and dine them as well,' he lied. 'I'm wrecked from making so much small talk and I'm more than ready for bed.'

'Sounds like a good idea,' she grinned, 'so am I.'

'That's not what I meant,' he said, and pushed past her.

June had put aside the notion of having children after her second miscarriage, and decided to concentrate on the good things she had. She could see the advantages of not being encumbered with a small child, not only for her and Lorcan but for the twins. Put a toddler into their family equation and it changed the dynamics dramatically. But Lorcan's increasing curtness had started the feelings of doubt again. She had tried hard to rekindle the closeness in their marriage since they came back from South Africa but it didn't seem to be working. If anything, the barrier seemed to be becoming more impenetrable and his work more and more important.

That night as she got ready for bed, she thought back over Lorcan's unnecessary bluntness and the distance that had opened between them and she made a decision. She was going to start putting her career first. In fact, she was putting her career before everything else in her life.

Despite her wide knowledge of the wine industry, June realised that it was infinitesimal in the wider world of wine. She decided to go all the way to the top and aim for a Master of Wine qualification. It was ambitious and would take several years, and even then all the study didn't guarantee success. It would be difficult – though she only realised how difficult when she read that, over seven years, only something like eighty-five candidates from various countries achieved the lofty MW status.

There were other avenues she could have taken. She could be happy getting a sommelier classification, but she wanted the best and she knew that the MW qualification was regarded as one of the highest standards of professional knowledge in the wine world. Even if she never got it, she'd have learned an awful lot.

Hennie encouraged her in all his mails and the odd phone call.

'I know we're in the middle of a worldwide recession, but that will pass and there'll always be a demand for experts in the field. Go get those qualifications and you'll be ready to take it on.'

He also tried to persuade her to take a few months out and stay with them, but she held off making a decision about that. The twins had their Leaving Cert coming up and needed stability at home. She also recognised that accepting such an offer would signal the end of the road for Lorcan and herself, and she wasn't about to give up on them. She was no quitter.

She enrolled in various programmes, some online, and for others she attended classes in Dublin. She needed to study for foundation, intermediate and advanced accreditations in Dublin in preparation for the serious business in London and work in between too. Before being accepted there, she had to submit her own tasting notes and an essay. But she was happy to take as much time as was needed and that would probably be a few years. Now, she had to tell her bosses.

'You'll be taking us over one of these days,' JP said, giving her a hug.

'Perhaps,' she smiled, 'although I've a manic time ahead. Do you think I could work part-time? Kelly knows the ropes better than I do now and she can replace me.'

'That shouldn't be a problem. She's good, but we're not letting you go that easily.'

'Don't worry, I've no intentions of disappearing,' she said. 'I'll have to focus, but you know you can always get me if you need me.'

June settled down to the challenge. Lorcan appeared to be thrilled for her, and not to mind the hours she spent studying. He boasted about her at the yacht club, where some enthusiasts had already started their own Wednesday Wine-Wannabe nights, or the WWWs, and she had been a guest twice. At home, he never mentioned her achievements.

Penny gave a dinner party to celebrate June's decision. In reality, she had given her kitchen a very expensive makeover with sleek black and white state-of-the-art German units and appliances and June knew she wanted to show them off. June had actually grown quite fond of Penny as she'd got to know her, and she looked forward to the meal. She figured there was probably a hidden agenda this evening too, and it soon became apparent what it was. There was a recently widowed neighbour, a retired auctioneer in his early sixties, who she had taken under her wing, and it was no surprise to find two of the 'potential wives' she has previously chosen for Lorcan sitting at the table.

'They're still desperately seeking,' Des whispered to him as they sat down.

Lorcan felt sorry for Penny's latest project and wondered if he should warn him off, but he didn't have much chance to, and Penny was in fine form, hinting at the misery of loneliness and of possible future liaisons.

'Irish men tend not to remarry after separation. Widowers do, though, don't they?' she remarked to no one in particular.

'You mean like me?' Lorcan said, challenging his hostess.

'Oh, I didn't mean that,' she said.

'Wasn't it Oscar Wilde who said a second

marriage is the triumph of hope over experience?' the widower, who was called Mark, asked.

Toni, one of the wives-in-waiting said, 'I didn't know him. In fact I don't know anyone called Oscar, I always think it sounds like a makie-up name, don't you?'

There was no way to reply to that, and she continued, 'But in my experience, Irish men prefer to have affairs and there are plenty of women who are happy with that, but I won't go in the back door with any man. If he wants to take me out, he'll do it publicly and not furtively. My grandmother always told my sisters and me, if a relationship has to be a secret, you shouldn't be in it.'

'That's good advice,' the other wife-in-waiting said. 'I have a friend who was someone's mistress for eight years – he was the love of her life and she thought she was his. She believed everything he told her. You know – the wife doesn't understand me, that kind of stuff. He made it all sound believable and sincere, because he always said he wouldn't leave her until their kids left school, and she was prepared to wait. Believing that his commitment to his kids was a virtue – that he just wouldn't walk out on them.'

'That's what I mean,' Toni said. 'Women can be such fools when it comes to married men. Did she not see, or did she not want to see, that he was a cheat and a liar?'

'Maybe they really did love one another and

maybe he thought he was being honourable by not walking out,' Lorcan said, and this got a reaction from everyone around the table. Lorcan felt like he was being ambushed.

'Honourable? He was a scumbag – wanting and getting it all – not caring who he was hurting.'

'Honourable? Is that what you call using two women and using his kids as the justification to keep it going without rocking either boat?' asked one of the wives. 'I guarantee he never had any intentions of leaving.'

'I agree, but don't they say love is blind?' said June.

'Or very stupid. My friend put up with him never being there for her at Christmas or holidays and other special times. Then he died suddenly of a heart attack on the golf course. She found out while she was away in Spain – he was supposed to be joining her for the second week.'

'So she didn't even get to go to his funeral or to say goodbye?' Toni said.

'No, but the guy he was playing golf with, and who called to tell her he was dead, streamed the removal and funeral from his phone and she watched on her laptop as it was happening.'

'How very modern!' said Lorcan. 'The stress of trying to juggle all the subterfuge and deception probably got to him in the end.'

'And very sad,' said Toni. 'She couldn't even grieve for him publicly. If he were serious about her, he would have left everything for her. And now that he's gone, she'll see what he was really like and where she came in his pecking order. That won't ever make her feel very good about herself, will it?'

'Isn't that a bit harsh?' Mark asked.

'It may be, but it's true nonetheless,' said the wife-in-waiting who had told them the story. 'What has she got now of all those years she gave him?'

'Nothing – but a feeling of betrayal,' said Toni. 'That's what I mean, affairs with married men are a disaster. I'd rather stay single than be used like that by some guy.'

'It's not always men who do the dirty,' said Penny. 'Look at Zoe Synnott and that Italian TV chef – I see they announced their engagement recently.'

'You have to give her some credit for leaving her marriage instead of stringing her husband along,' Toni said.

'That sounds like a bit of fuzzy logic,' Mark said.

Penny agreed. 'At least with a widower you know where you stand and—'

'I think we need more wine,' Des said pointedly. 'The glasses are all empty over this side of the table. And speaking of wine, June, tell us about this master's thing you're doing. What's involved?'

'Lots of study, theory, essays, dissertations – not very exciting but more than enough to keep me out of mischief for a while,' she said.

'Will you be doing vertical and horizontal tastings and blind ones too?' asked the widower.

'Of course,' she laughed.

'That all sounds very sleazy – you never told me about those,' Lorcan teased. 'Can we try them out at home?'

He always does that, June thought, *gives everyone the impression that we have a great sex life. If only they knew it was almost non-existent these days.*

June had accepted that her husband didn't really want to have sex with her, and she convinced herself it was to do with their age difference. Maybe all couples were like this, but it wasn't exactly the sort of topic you brought up at dinner parties.

'Behave yourself,' she said, explaining that there was nothing sexual in the concept at all. 'It's quite simple. A vertical tasting involves trying different vintages of the same wine from the same winery, whereas in a horizontal one, they use wines from the same vintage but from different estates.'

'You'd need a lot of bottles to do that, wouldn't you?' Toni said.

'How do you know about those things?' June asked Mark. 'Are you into your wine?'

'Not at all. I just enjoy drinking it. I Googled wine terms when Penny told me you were coming – so I wouldn't appear stupid – and that's when I found out how fantastically ignorant I really am on the subject. My wife was diabetic and never touched the stuff, so there's a large gap in my education that needs filling. But I never knew there was so much to learn. We didn't do too much in the last few years, so I've a bit of catching up to do.'

'You should come along to one of our wine evenings or classes. They're great fun.'

'I'll certainly think about it,' Mark said.

'Good God, they'll all be experts in no time, Penny. We'll not be able to get away with serving up Aldi specials any more,' Des said.

'Well, I'd like to assure you, you'll still get them at our place,' Lorcan said. 'Just don't let the wife know.' Everyone laughed at that.

Engrossed with her studies and her family, June enjoyed working part time. The Macy brothers had given her free rein to buy wines for a new restaurant, which she found very flattering.

To make things better, Danielle had just told her that they were coming back to Ireland to live later in the year. The super drug, which was how it was being referred to, was cleared for general release. It was going to be manufactured close to Dublin for the global market. The pharmaceutical company Froggie worked for already had a sizeable facility there and they were in the throes of a major expansion and they asked him to head up marketing for Europe. This was the prestigious and lucrative promotion he had been hoping for.

'You're so lucky the way life's worked,' June said to Danielle during one of their regular phone calls.

'I know. We've so much to be grateful for,' said Danielle. 'Although, initially, he'll have to do a lot of travelling, but at least it won't be for weeks at a stretch like now when he disappears off to obscure places in South America with unreliable phone coverage, and I'll have my family and friends around me.'

'I can't wait. It'll be fantastic having you back. When is all this happening?'

'We'll be over for most of May and we might do a bit of house-hunting then. I intend getting back into teaching if I can find a suitable placement and with crèches and all that to consider, we need to be sure we're in the right area. If we don't find anything at that stage, we'll rent. We'll have to come back here to pack everything up for shipping though.'

'Why don't you take over Raglan Road until you do? That way you won't have to make any hasty decisions.'

'But what about your tenants?'

'That's not a problem. They're all short-term lets; I'll notify the agency as soon as I get off the phone.'

'Are you still toying with the idea of selling?'

'Not seriously. I flirted with the idea when I got married first, but I know Mum would be very upset if I did. It's not what she'd want me to do. It was intended as my home or as a way to ensure a steady income. Obviously Dad and she discussed this when he was alive, but it would be perfect for you both, and for Alison and Ben while you're finding your feet. They'd have the garden to play in and their Auntie June could take them to feed the ducks in Herbert Park.'

'They'd love that. It sounds like the perfect solution, if you're sure. I can't wait to tell Froggie. He'll be thrilled. And I can't wait to see you. I've been away too long.'

'Far too long.'

CHAPTER 31

'Mommy, Mommy, look at this, there are monster fish in the pond. Monster orange and stripy fish,' Ben shouted in his best New Jersey accent. He ran inside to find Danielle. He'd just discovered the pond in Hill Crest.

'Now, do you see why we had to get out of the States?' Froggie said to Lorcan. 'I don't want my kids talking like that and calling their mother "Mommy"! Is that pond safe for them to be near?' he asked, as Alison toddled unsteadily across the grass to investigate. 'You can't be too careful with little ones.'

'There's a strong grid just below the water – to keep the herons away. The first year we had one that devoured all the fish. They cost a fortune to replace, but I find them fascinating,' Lorcan said.

'We felt a bit awkward bringing the kids over here after the difficulties you and June have had, but she seems great. Her usual happy self.'

'She is,' he answered, 'but it took a lot out of her.'

'It must have, out of the two of you. You've a

great spot here, though, with the view out over the sea. I'd love to get something like this for us. I've had enough of corporate living. The house in the States was great, but having work colleagues and their families knowing every single move you made was stifling. I feel that I'm putting down real roots for the first time since we got married, and I want to get it right.'

'You're buying at a good time, although prices are still dropping. My advice would be to keep renting for a while and take your time looking – it's a buyers' market out there. I know June will be happy to let you have her house until you find what you want.'

'Yes, but she doesn't want to charge us rent,' he said. 'That's fine for this fleeting visit but we can't expect to stay there for a few months when we get back.'

'That's between her and you. I'm not getting involved.'

Froggie scooped his little daughter up before she plunged her hands into the pond and he swung her up to sit on his shoulders. Just then June called them in for lunch.

They'd only been able to get two weeks away in the end but had been able to catch up with most of their relatives and friends. June and Danielle spent as much time together as they could, even though they knew they'd see each other again in a few months. Lorcan was still busy with work, and she had to remind him over and over again to make time to see them, but apart from that day he scarcely did.

The week after they left, the Leaving Cert exams began for Ashling and Sean. As always, these coincided with glorious weather. The twins headed off early to talk to their friends and buoy each other up before facing the first paper. June was picking some heavenly scented sweet peas for the house when her mobile rang.

'It's your mother.' Young Joe sounded anxious. 'She's slipped in the garden and twisted her ankle. I'm not sure if anything is broken, but she can't put weight on it. She was just half lying, half sitting when I arrived ten minutes ago to do the grass. I was going to call the ambulance, but she doesn't want me to. I thought I should ask you first. She'll not be able to make those steps in the house, but I'd be afraid to try carrying her.'

'No, don't even think about that. I'll be right there. I'll phone an ambulance straight away.'

She found her mother in a lot of pain, her lower leg and ankle swollen and tender. Minutes after she arrived, the ambulance pulled up. They put her on a stretcher with blocks to stabilise the leg and June followed in her car as they took her to the nearest A&E. She was triaged and seen to pretty quickly. After she was x-rayed, the verdict was indeed an ankle fracture. To be absolutely sure that surgery or strengthening with pins wasn't necessary, they'd have to wait until the swelling went down and x-ray it again the following week.

They put on a cast and a doctor said, 'If that gets any tighter or you can't move your toes freely come in to us straight away.' He also told her there was no question of her going back to her own house.

'That's no problem, she can come to me,' June said.

They showed her how to use crutches and negotiate stairs. 'Keep the weight off it as much as possible and come back to see us in the fracture clinic – you'll be given an appointment on the way out.'

'I hate to be such a nuisance,' Branch said on the way to Hill Crest, 'but could we call by the house so that I can pick up a few things?'

'Of course. We can go back any time you want.'

'Have you told Lorcan he's going to be saddled with me for a few weeks?'

'I did. I phoned him and he's delighted. He's very fond of you, you know.'

If June expected to hear her say 'and I'm very fond of him too', then she would have been disappointed.

The twins fussed over Branch, making her cups of tea and telling her about their exams. Kelly arrived one afternoon with the latest gossip magazines and Branch was very touched.

'You didn't need to take time off work,' she insisted.

'Yes, I did. You were very good to Cara and her family when they were over. I'll never forget that.

They're always asking about you. And it's because of you we healed life-long rifts and had a chance to talk things out properly. It took a long time, but we now have a proper mother–daughter relationship.'

'You mean you fight all the time,' June said, 'like us.'

'We do not,' said Branch.

'I know that. No, I mean I can be a proper mum and a grandmother, albeit a very young one,' Kelly laughed. 'Did June tell you that we're off to Spain on a fact-finding mission in July?'

'A fact-finding mission?' June laughed. 'That's a euphemism for a wine trip – a festival actually. It should be great fun.'

June enjoyed having her mother about and insisted she have her history group and some of her active retirement friends around for coffee. They even had one of her musical soirees. The kids survived their exams and delighted in her eclectic mix of 'old timers', as they called them, and loved when she had them around. Penny called one afternoon when June and Branch were sitting in the garden. She brought flowers, a cake, and Mark, her widower neighbour, with her. She'd asked him to accompany her to an auction, because she was interested in a particular piece of furniture she'd seen in the online catalogue. She followed June inside when she went in to make tea for them all.

Mark apologised for barging in. 'I feel I am

intruding on your privacy,' he told Branch. I don't know you and have only met your daughter once, but Penny is very forceful when she gets an idea into her head.'

'Oh, don't worry, I know what she's like. She can't bear to see people on their own. She probably has us married already.'

He put his head back and laughed out loud. 'You *do* know her! I'm sorry to embarrass you.'

'You haven't in the slightest. She's so obvious about it, you have to laugh. She means well, but if you're her project, you better hope someone else loses their partner soon so that she'll move on.'

He didn't answer immediately and Branch apologised. 'I'm so sorry. That was really crass of me. I didn't mean it quite like that – or to upset you.'

'You haven't, honestly. It's refreshing to meet someone who speaks frankly. I'm so tired of everyone pussyfooting around me, afraid to mention my wife's name or anything concerning her. When she was ill, everyone spoke in platitudes. We all knew she wasn't going to get better, but no one would acknowledge it, to me anyhow. So I had to pretend too.'

'That must have been hard. My husband died suddenly, so I didn't go through that, but death makes people behave strangely sometimes. I had some friends who avoided me because they didn't know what to say and then others who used phrases like those television mediums use, saying he, "passed over" or "passed away" or just "passed". He didn't pass anything – he died, plain and simple.'

'I hate those phrases too. How long ago did he die?'

'It's nine years now.'

'And were you subjected to this round of introductions by your friends?'

'No, and my friends had more sense than to suggest it,' she laughed.

'Lucky you. Have you ever been tempted to marry again?'

'No, and I never will. I've grown to love my independence. I've lots of good friends – male and female – and lots of interests, and that's the secret of keeping happy. I'm looking on this part as a new stage in my life, and I'm enjoying every bit of it. It gets easier, I promise you, but there's no way to hurry the process, unfortunately.'

'I know, and I suppose I am very lucky to have a caring neighbour like Penny. She was great when my wife was ill. She's very kind, you know.'

'I do know that, even if she can be a bit overpowering.' She stopped talking when she saw Penny coming across the patio carrying a tray.

'You two seem to be getting on well together.'

'Like a house on fire,' they said in unison. They looked at each other and laughed the way conspirators do. They stayed a good while and June showed them around her garden.

'You know your plants and flowers,' she said to Mark.

'Only in the past few years. I never had much interest in the garden before then. My wife did it all. She loved it and when she wasn't able to do it any more, I felt I should make an effort. It's actually very therapeutic,' he said.

Branch waved a crutch at him. 'Not always, it isn't,' she said, and they all laughed at her.

When there was only her and her mother in the house, June would often hear the strains of the piano echoing through the silence, and it brought back memories of her childhood when both her parents played. They preferred to do that than watch television. Her father had favoured Beethoven and Sibelius, while her mother loved the French composers Ravel, Debussy, Fauré and Saint-Saëns. They had passed on their love of music to their daughter and when she had discovered how much Lorcan enjoyed classical music, it had seemed like a good omen. She loved nothing more than to enjoy a concert with him or to sit and listen to music while they read or she studied in the drawing room.

With the exams behind them, the twins were heading off to France for their usual stay with their grandparents. Lorcan had become even more grumpy and snappy and was often late back from the office, eating dinner in front of the television on his own, or refusing it altogether. June worried that he really hadn't wanted Branch around, but he had never shown any hint of animosity.

Before long, Branch was back in her own house and managing perfectly well on her crutches, going out to long lunches with her friends. Nonetheless, his behaviour was very out of character and June wondered if he could be sick. He dismissed the idea of a check-up and, short of dragging him to the doctor, there was nothing else she could do.

When she discussed this with Branch, she said, 'He's a big boy now and he has to make his own decisions. Perhaps he's just overworked. Have you asked him directly? Could he have money worries? Lots of people have lost a lot of money with this recession – maybe he made some bad business decisions or investments and he doesn't want to tell you?'

'I never thought of that.'

When June broached the subject later that day over dinner, he assured her he hadn't. Although she didn't understand all the intricacies of software development, June did understand that when there were problems, they could be very worrying and challenging, not to mention costly and damaging for their users. No matter what the cause, she felt a break from the office, from routine – and from her – might be just the tonic he needed. He loved France and he got on very well with Carol's parents.

*   *   *

June collected her mother and they went to the hospital to have her cast removed. The break had been hairline and they saw no reason why it would give her any trouble in the future.

She was getting out of the car, carrying the now redundant crutches, which the hospital no longer recycled for health and safety issues, when she dropped her bag on the floor and everything fell out. June picked the bits and pieces up and said, 'Now, let's get you inside and settled.'

'I'm not an invalid, you know.'

'I do know, but please take things easy for a bit, just don't go mad doing the garden. Let Young Joe look after it.'

'I will. Stop fussing over me. You're making me feel old and I'm not!'

'I know that. What are you going to do for the rest of the day?'

'I'm going to take your advice, take it easy for a bit and then see if I can get in to any of my smart shoes. I'm going out to dinner tonight,' she paused for effect, 'with that nice Mark I met in your house.' She grinned mischievously at her daughter.

'Penny's Mark? Good God, Mum. That's a surprise.'

'I don't think Penny actually owns him.'

'Where are you going?'

'He wouldn't tell me. It's to be a surprise.'

'I'll be dying to hear all about it.'

'And I might tell you. Thanks again for all you did during this ankle business. You've been great.'

'That's what daughters are for,' she said, kissing her mother. 'Enjoy tonight.'

'I'm sure I will,' Branch said, grinning as she waved her daughter off.

CHAPTER 32

Lorcan and June were in bed together. She had just come back from the wine fair in London and she was exhausted. He kept tossing and turning, but he wasn't asleep.

He was fed up with the deception, the double life he was now leading, but he didn't see any way out of it. He'd had to tell Des because he'd become suspicious. He'd noticed Lorcan taking intimate calls when they were out sailing and had guessed they were not from June. He confronted him and told him he was mad, jeopardising everything good in his life.

Des told him to wise up. 'Get over her,' he almost shouted at him. 'You're not unique panting after a younger woman. It's called a mid-life crisis. We've all been tempted. You've had your fun, Lorcan, now run a mile. It's not worth ruining everyone's lives for, is it? And it's not fair on June or this woman.'

'If I told June—'

'Christ, man, have you no sense at all? That'd be insane. Don't even think about it. If you told

June, do you think she'd say, "Thanks for being honest, now forget about it, I know I will" and everything would be hunky dory? Stop deluding yourself, Lorcan. You're not an idiot. She'd never trust you again and you couldn't blame her for that – could you? And how would you intend explaining it to the kids? Have you thought about that? They'd never forgive you either. They think the world of June.'

'Noelle knows all that.'

'I hope for everyone's sake you're right. You have a marriage and a lifestyle that most men envy. You've great kids too. Wise up and get out of this mess before it implodes on you.'

Now, as Des had predicted, everything was imploding, and he couldn't stop it. He tossed and turned.

Oblivious, June tried to console him and told him he was working too hard. She told him he was turning into a workaholic when he had no need to. His business was a success – it always had been – he didn't need to work for money any more.

'If anything,' she said, 'you should consider cutting back.' She rolled over on to her back and said, 'I have a proposition for you. Why don't you go off with Ashling and Sean for a bit of a break? They'd love to have you on their own and a change would do you good. Who knows where they'll be next summer.'

'They'll probably be off working abroad with their new college friends and have outgrown their grandparents,' he said.

'And us too more than likely.'

June eventually went to sleep. He didn't. The following morning, he surprised himself by answering her proposition. 'I think that's a brilliant idea. I'll go to France with them before they go to the grandparents. Wouldn't you like to come along too?'

'Of course I would, but Kelly and I have already booked to go to that crazy wine festival I told you about in La Rioja at the end of the month.'

He knew she'd had a busy time what with her mother staying, and then with her tenants leaving Raglan Road and getting things ready for Danielle and Froggie's arrival.

'That sounds like a good solution all round,' he said, kissing her automatically on the cheek. He felt he'd been given a reprieve. Hopefully, by the time she came back, he'd have sorted something out. How he was going to do it he had no idea, but something had to give. He couldn't go on like this for much longer.

Mark arrived promptly to collect Branch for their dinner appointment. She managed to fit her recently liberated foot into some fashionable pumps that matched a dress she had bought before her fall but hadn't yet worn.

'I'll be the envy of everyone in the restaurant,' he said. 'I hope you like where we're going – I booked a table in The Pink Pepper Tree. Do you know it?'

Branch hadn't been in the place since Peter and June had split up. She didn't think it was necessary to explain that history to Mark, so instead she smiled and said, 'It's perfect. It's been a while since I was there.'

Peter greeted them warmly, hugging Branch. 'What a nice surprise, I haven't seen you for so long. You picked the right night to come in – my parents and Rosa are over for a holiday. Come and say hello to them.'

They had often been to Branch's house in the past and they invited Branch and Mark to join them. She didn't know what to say. Mark didn't know any of them and she didn't know anything about him, which could make the whole thing awkward. Peter seemed to sense this and suggested, 'That'd be a bit of a squeeze in this corner. Why don't you all join up for some drinks in the conservatory later? I'll put a table by for you.'

'Perfect,' Branch said. 'Enjoy your meal.'

'Are you that well known everywhere you go?' Mark asked when they were seated.

'Definitely not. My daughter and Peter, the owner, used to be an item – well, they were for a good few years. His father is Portuguese. His mother is Irish. They live over there. For a time,

I thought Peter was going to be my son-in-law. I often wish he were, but a mother is not supposed to say those things out loud, is she?'

'So long as she doesn't say them to her daughter or her family I think it's allowed,' he said. 'We can't choose who our children marry and they wouldn't want us to either. I've only met June a couple of times and she seems happy. Lorcan too.'

'I like to think she is, but I've never quite understood Lorcan, and after spending quite a bit of time with them recently over this ankle business, I've come to think he's a bit shifty. I never noticed that before but he strikes me as a man with secrets.'

'Everyone has secrets if you dig deep enough.'

'Well, maybe I'm being paranoid. And you, Mark, have you secrets?'

'Yes – dark ones. I resented my wife's illness. I really did. I resented what it did to her and to our lives. She was an invalid for seven years and that curtailed everything we had enjoyed together. It put the kibosh on travel, on going out – even the cinema was off limits. I felt so trapped. I tried not to show it, but she must have sensed my resentment sometimes.'

'You're being very hard on yourself. I think those are the most natural feelings in the world. I know I'd have felt the same way.'

'Do you know one day when she was in hospital having treatment, I went to the latest James Bond movie and I never told her. I felt like a schoolboy playing truant.'

'That's punishable by hanging – an offence like that.' They laughed.

'I've never told anyone that before. Actually, I don't think I ever really admitted it to myself. It feels good. I've only known you a few hours, and you've already prised open my dark side. Thank you.'

'For what? Being your sorcerer or confessor?'

'Neither. A new and good friend, I hope,' he said, lifting his glass. 'Let's drink to friendship.'

'To friendship,' said Branch.

Later in the conservatory, they joined the Bragas for some port and caught up on all the gossip.

'Rosa's winery is going from strength to strength. She's even broken into the Irish market,' her father said proudly, 'haven't you?'

'It's only a modest order.'

'Well, that's great news,' Branch said. You have to start somewhere. The first wine I ever bought was Mateus rosé. When I was at college it was the height of sophistication to have a candle in one of their bottles and let the wax melt all over it. That was the only Portuguese wine we knew.'

'God, that brings back memories,' Peter's mother said. 'And we used to buy Black Tower or Blue Nun if we were going to anyone's flat for dinner. That was before I met you,' she said to her husband. 'Actually you couldn't really call it dinner, it was usually a one-pot wonder.'

'Wasn't Blue Nun the one they advertised as "wine that could be drunk throughout an entire meal?"' Mark asked. 'It had a nun in full regalia on the label – there was probably a subliminal message in that somewhere to try to make us drink responsibly.'

'And did it work?' asked Rosa.

'Definitely not,' said Mark.

They went on to discuss Peter's wine list, and his mother took the opportunity to talk quietly to Branch. 'It's a pity we've all lost touch. We used to think we'd all be family one day. Instead, he married that gold digger. Did you know she's gone off to live in London with her Italian stallion?'

'Oh, I have missed nights like this,' Branch said.

'You know you're always welcome to come and stay with us.'

'I might take you up on that offer sometime and you'll be sorry you invited me. How is Peter coping since the breakup? I didn't like to ask.'

'He refuses to discuss it. He just says we all make mistakes. I never took to her. She was no June! How is June and that husband of hers? She never misses a Christmas card or a birthday.'

'She's great and he's . . . well, he's not Peter either!'

'What are you two whispering about?' Peter asked, refilling their glasses.

'Men!' they both answered, and laughed.

When Lorcan and the twins left for France, June felt a weight lift. She hadn't realised how tense she had become around him. She often found herself looking at him as though he were a stranger and not her husband, the man with a soft side who had once bought her a teddy bear and with whom she had shared intimacy.

CHAPTER 33

Kelly had tried in vain to get them two rooms for the Battle of the Wine Festival, as everything has been booked up months in advance. If they had imagined there would be more demand on hostels than luxury accommodation, they would have been wrong. Eventually, they got a room in the Parador de Santo Domingo de la Calzada in a neighbouring town to Haro. A warren of Gothic architecture, it had originally been a hospital, dating back to the twelfth century, but there was very little that was institutional about it now.

'It's quite magical,' June exclaimed as they wandered into the courtyard and admired the floodlit building and Santo Domingo's imposing cathedral in the town. They had eaten a hearty dinner, during which the waiter had spent a good five minutes telling them where everything came from – the vegetables, the lamb, the game, the fish, the cheeses, and the wines – the names, which meant nothing to them, tripping off his tongue with pride and ease.

'Do you think it's haunted?' asked Kelly.

'I bet anything it is! Even if it's not, I'm sure they'd say it was. A friendly ghost is always good for business,' June laughed.

They got up very early the next day and dressed in old white t-shirts and trousers, just as the manager had told them. 'Pack a change of clothes and shoes,' he'd said, 'and put them in heavy plastic bags, because you'll be soaked through. I'll send some bags up to your room.'

'Thank you, but we don't intend taking part in the battle,' June said.

'Believe me,' he replied 'there is no such thing as an onlooker or spectator there.'

They set off with their bundles to Haro, where the annual *Batalla de Vino* was taking place. June had recently been concentrating on the Rioja region in her studies. She knew a lot about its robust Tempranillo grapes and how these were often blended with Garnacha, Graciano and Mazuelo to give them balance. She knew some of the characteristic notes included spices like cardamom, cloves and nutmeg with hints of tobacco, leather and berries. Before she completed her essay, she wanted to visit some of the lesser-known producers and do some tastings. When she mentioned it to Kelly, she'd jumped at the chance to come along, and as their free time happened to coincide with the festival, they thought they'd take it in too.

The receptionist at the Parador had made a phone call and as a result they left their bags with the obliging owner of a pastry shop in the square. There they joined the onlookers already lining the streets to watch the procession of young and old, wearing white shirts and red scarves, as they passed on their way through the vineyards to mass at the Hermitage of San Felices. The mayor led the way on horseback and everyone carried receptacles of some sort – buckets, bottles, kiddies' water pistols and jugs, some even had backpack sprayers – all filled with red wine. When mass was over, all hell broke loose and the battle began. Everyone started throwing the wine over each other, some 300,000 litres of it flying about. Everyone was fair game. In no time at all, the crowd had turned into a ruby-coloured mob, tannin stains spreading through their clothing. The roads ran with rivulets of wine and the revellers made their way back to town for noon.

'I thought I'd be too old for this,' Kelly laughed as a young guy with a spray gun doused her gleefully.

'You're never too old to have fun, señora,' he said, kissing her on the cheek, and he was gone.

'You're right there,' June agreed.

In the Plaza de la Paz, the pastry shop owner allowed them change out of their wine-soaked clothes and they found a table in the square and ordered some tapas and wine, served from a glass this time. Bands played and although the battle was over, the revelry continued. In the local bullring, the hardy lads, whose alcohol-fuelled egos made them believe they could be the next El Cordobés, took on some heifers to the delight of the watching crowds.

'I'm not sure that that experience added anything to my education, but I thoroughly enjoyed it,' June said.

'So did I. It's been wonderful,' said Kelly. 'Branch would love this – she's such an adventurous spirit. How is she since her fall?'

'Never better. It's as though it never happened. She's busy organising a trip for her art group to Tuscany.'

'She's amazing.'

'I know. She has the right attitude to life and she never takes herself too seriously.'

'And what about you? What's going on in your life?'

'I have to admit, I'm really enjoying the freedom of being away from the family for a bit. It's been a bit tense at home lately.'

'Really? For any particular reason?'

'You'll think I'm mad, Kelly. Call it a sixth sense, or intuition or whatever you like, but something's not right, and I wish I knew what it was. Isn't that crazy? I feel I'm sitting on a track waiting for a train to hit me.'

'That's not like you.'

'I know. But I can't seem to shake it off.'

CHAPTER 34

It was a year since Lorcan had decided that Noelle should leave his company, that once she was working elsewhere it would be easier to tell her it was all over. But he still hadn't really looked to find her another job. He kept her working on projects that needed her involvement to ensure they were followed through properly, projects that kept her close to him day and night. He didn't want to let her go, but leading this double life was taking its toll. He was uptight all the time, afraid of being discovered, but he was also tired of lying and tired of trying to orchestrate reasons to be absent from home.

It had been going on for over a year, and June deserved better. She had completed their lives when they'd been fractured. He had loved her when they'd married. The kids had grown to love her unconditionally, as a friend rather than a step-mother. He had never factored a Noelle into their lives, but now she was in his life, he couldn't contemplate her not being there.

Instead of rejecting her overtures, he had rejected his wife's – and he'd done it so often that she had stopped making any towards him. His guilt made him act coldly, often even cruelly, towards her.

June had tried to get him to plan a holiday for them both.

'Now that the twins are heading off to the States with their college we should take advantage of the freedom and of being totally without ties, for the first time.'

'You knew they were part of the package when you took me on,' he said. He knew he was being mean.

'I did, and I never looked on it as a chore, as your remark implies. I just thought a break for the two of us might be good. This relationship is not working, Lorcan. You may be able to fool yourself that it is, but it's not.'

In a dash of reality, he knew he couldn't put the kids through losing someone else they loved. In his skewed psychology, he had convinced himself that if he wasn't nice to June she wouldn't be hurt if his duplicitous secret ever came out. He had also managed to convince himself that if he did remove Noelle from the marital equation, then things could go back to the way they were before she happened along and that June would still be part of the family. And that time had come. He had to act now before he was caught out.

The next day, still with a firm resolve and before he had time to make any calls, Noelle asked if she could see him for a few minutes, on a personal matter. This was unusual, as they had agreed only to talk business at work, everything else for after-hours.

'Of course, come in,' he said, closing the door behind her. No one suspected a thing and if they did, they hid it well. 'What can I do for you?'

Without preamble she announced, 'I just wanted to tell you that I'm pregnant.' He felt his world shift. This couldn't be happening. He had lots of acquaintance in business and in the sailing world who'd had affairs – they didn't have babies though.

'Are you sure?'

'Positive. You don't look very happy.'

'I'm in shock. It's the last thing I expected to hear.'

'We can't talk here. What about lunch time?' she asked.

'I can't meet at lunch, I have a client coming in.'

'After work then?'

'Righto. I'll come on out to your place.'

'OK' was all she said, but he knew she could read the alarm and shock on his face. He hoped he'd be more composed by the time he met, but he wasn't. All day, he kept thinking about what he'd say to either of his kids if they came home and told him they were going to be a parent – and they didn't already have a spouse and family to complicate matters.

When he arrived in Rathgar, she had dinner waiting, but before they sat down he blurted out, 'I thought you would have taken precautions—'

'Why didn't you?'

'I assumed you were on the pill. Aren't most women?'

'No, as a matter of fact, they aren't,' she replied. 'It's not like eating chocolate buttons, you know. It doesn't agree with everyone.'

'This doesn't change anything I told you when we first started seeing each other. I'll never leave my marriage. I've made that very clear.'

'You did, Lorcan, perfectly. And I didn't ask you to. But you didn't tell me I couldn't have a baby.'

'You mean you tricked me?'

'No, I just didn't do anything to prevent it happening, and neither did you. So don't try the blame game on me. I am very happy to be pregnant and I had hoped you would be.'

'This doesn't change anything. I'll never leave my wife.'

'I know, you keep reminding me of that. But I am curious – are you sleeping with her too?'

'I refuse to discuss my marriage with you, Noelle. It's none of your concern. Our relationship is, but not hers and mine.'

'So where does that leave me? I assume you'll take responsibility for this child.'

'Of course I will. I love you, Noelle, you know I do, and I'll be as good a father as I can. You'll not want for anything, either of you. I won't run away from my responsibilities, but I can never integrate you into my real family,' he said, and the irony of his statement struck him as he uttered the words.

If he had felt trapped before, he now felt himself imprisoned in a cell of his own making.

'I had expected a happier reaction. Now I see I'm relegated into an unreal family category.'

'That's not what I meant. I'm sorry. I'm still in a bit of a flux. I never expected to be hit with this bombshell. Of course I'm pleased. How long have you known?'

'I suspected it about a week ago. Now I'm certain.' They sat down to eat.

'See, you've had time to get used to the idea. I'll come around. Just give me a few days. I promise. I am delighted, really I am,' he said, and even to his ears it sounded as though he was trying to convince himself that that was the truth.

'You needn't worry. I'll not come knocking on your door, upsetting your life. And you can accept my notice this time – there's no way I can stay on with you now. We'd never be able to keep this quiet. I've been working on my CV and assume you'll give me a good reference.'

'The best,' he said, leaning across the table to kiss her. She responded as she always did with fervour and passion and they eventually made it to the bedroom. He went through the motions of love-making but his heart wasn't in it. He needed time to deal with this new complication. Even if he ended it between them, there would always be a child out there who was his and to whom he had a duty. But hadn't he a duty to his wife and that hadn't stopped him turning his back on her. He didn't like himself very much at that moment and wondered how he had ever managed to get three good women to love him.

If he didn't sort things out with June, he'd lose her. They all would. That night he slept with her for the first time in months.

PART IV

CHAPTER 35

'I think it's time I went out on my own,' June told Lorcan at breakfast one day. 'With the kids finally qualified, I feel I'm ready to take the next step. What do you think?'

'I think you're right. They don't need us anymore. All that studying and hard work you put in – it's time to reap the rewards. Will you be looking for premises? Where would you like to be?'

'I'm not fully sure, but I'm going to talk to the guys about it. I owe them so much for the faith they've shown in me. I don't want to set up in competition to them either, so I think I'll concentrate on consultancy and education first. I love teaching people about wine and there are so few places here where you can get those services at a higher level.'

June's job had been her salvation and she told Danielle it had been the only thing that had stopped her feeling completely lost.

'I know he's tried, but whatever we had is gone. He's reached the point of detaching almost completely. When we talk, it's about banalities and I could quite easily have had more engaging conversations with someone in the supermarket.'

'It just doesn't seem fair. Have you said anything to him about it?'

'Frequently. He tells me I'm imagining it and just stays working longer hours than ever. I sometimes think he says as much to me as he does to Mrs Fitz. He's hardly ever home for dinner or at weekends anymore, and as the business has grown he spends more time flitting around the place.'

'That's the world we live in nowadays.'

'And I understand that better than anyone. I did and do my fair share of it too. Look at all the time I've spent away in the past few years. It's just that when we are together we seem to be so . . . disconnected.'

'Maybe he'll never change, and you have to find your happiness elsewhere.'

'You mean have an affair?'

'No, I didn't, but maybe *he* is.'

'He's too wrapped up in his business to have time for that. Besides. he has no interest any more, so I'm going to find my happiness elsewhere – I'm going to go it alone.'

'You're going to leave Lorcan?'

'No, though if I hadn't had all that going on, I think I'd have bailed long ago. And there were always the kids to consider. Now that they're off doing their own thing, I feel this is where my liberation begins, but first I'm going into business for myself.'

'I'm delighted to hear it, and about time too.'

June told Danielle how the Macy brothers had told her they were thrilled for her and had been expecting it to happen at some stage.

'What took you so long? You've been making quite a name for yourself in the global wine fraternity,' JP had said. 'Not only by getting that elusive Master of Wine accreditation, but as a knowledgeable and affable connoisseur and entertaining speaker.'

'And you're better qualified than either of us. Look at the invitations you get to speak at conferences and seminars, and that network of contacts you have will stand to you wherever you go.'

That was one of the things she loved most about her job, running in to people in different places. She'd been able to catch up with Rosa at the Vinhos e Sabores in the city of Braga in Portugal and they'd gone out to dinner together.

'Look at you, Braga's Pink Pepper Tree Reserva picking up awards. Who would have thought that would happen?'

They fell into the same easy companionship they had always enjoyed before . . . well, before things went wrong, as June liked to think of it.

'Did you hear the latest on that wagon, Zoe?' Rosa had asked. 'Well, the latest is she's left her Italian lover and has moved into a Mayfair apartment – with an Iraqi property developer. She met him one night in Adamo's restaurant. Isn't she some operator?'

'I wonder how long that will last? How is Peter doing? Has he met anyone else since she left?'

'He never says and he never mentions her. He just says, "We all make mistakes," and changes the subject.'

'I agree with him there. Give him my love when you're talking next.'

Her meetings with Hennie were more arranged – they consulted with each other and their diaries and met in California, at Megavino in Brussels, as well as more recently in London. She was a guest speaker at both the Boston and Miami wine fairs, something he joked about when they met in London. 'I suppose you're too important to come and visit us now.'

'I told you when I was there at harvest last year that I'll always have time to do that, Hennie. In fact, I might just head your way later this year again. As you well know, there's been great growth in demand for South African wines here and I need to keep up to speed. You know, the problem with having got that MW is that everyone expects me to know everything now!'

'Hah, and you expect me to be sympathetic? You brought it on yourself.' He laughed and so did she. 'Didn't you know that you have to be careful what you wish for because you might just get it?'

'Always the philosopher, Hennie. Always the philosopher. Now, I need to talk to you because

I want your advice. I've decided to go out on my own and I'd value your counsel.'

'It's lovely having you all here together,' June said to the twins as she served dinner for them and Lorcan. 'It doesn't happen often enough.'

'Yeah, the only time I get a decent feed is when sis here blows into town,' laughed Sean, 'or when Mrs Fitz makes me a casserole to take with me.'

'You could learn to cook, you know,' Ashling teased him. 'I bet the cooker in your flat has never been used.'

'Wrong!'

'I meant apart from heating up plates for take-aways or pizzas.'

'When you next come back from your fancy fashion house in Milan, you can come and christen it yourself. In fact, you could show us how to do it.'

'I hardly have time to dress myself these days with the pressure of the autumn shows looming.'

'Maybe when I sell my first bit of software, I'll steal Mrs Fitz to do it for me.'

'I might get there first if that high-street chain takes another of my pieces.'

'Oh, I do miss the friendly fire,' said June, 'but whatever happens, your dad and I couldn't be more proud of you. Could we, Lorcan?'

'I suppose they turned out OK,' he said, grinning at them proudly.

*   *   *

Danielle often popped in with her two on Saturday mornings for some Auntie June time and to share their news. She was busy trying to maintain a healthy work–life balance. Ben told June he'd decided he didn't like his teacher because she smelled of onions, while everything in Alison's world and crèche were rosy, so long as she had Lalaloopsy by her side. They were engrossed doing a jigsaw puzzle on the floor.

June filled Danielle in on the twins' latest news. 'Well, lady,' Danielle replied. 'I think you can take some of the credit for their achievements. They got lucky with their wicked step-mother.'

'I got lucky with them too. I wonder what your two will do when they grow up.'

'Ben will be an anarchist if early behavioural patterns are any indication. He can be a wilful little devil at times, and as for madam over there, she'll end up as a boardroom diva. No glass ceiling will hold her back, if she can get around other men like she does her father. Now, how are you doing?'

'I'm great. I've made lots of decisions and I think I'll use Raglan Road for my classes and tastings. Wouldn't it be perfect?'

'Absolutely.'

'I'm hoping to take Kelly with me as my assistant. She can look after all the admin stuff too. I'm finishing up completely at the end of the month, and I'm taking a month off to plan things properly before I do anything.'

'We'll all have to go out for a night to celebrate.'

'That sounds great. I wouldn't count on Lorcan dragging himself away from work, though. He's become more obsessed than he ever was. He's never home these days, as you know.'

Although Danielle and she shared all their secrets, June held back on telling her friend everything about her disastrous marriage, out of a misplaced sense of loyalty to Lorcan. And she worried that if she started talking about how she felt, she wouldn't know where it would end. Yet, deep down she knew she had to leave him. What she didn't know was how she'd tell Sean and Ashling.

He refused to discuss their problems, denying there was anyone else. Whenever she challenged him about his long hours, he said things like, 'It takes a lot of time and effort to keep this show on the road and someone has to do it.'

She didn't really understand what the problem was. Money wasn't an issue, it never had been – June knew they weren't short of a euro or two. She just didn't understand why he had to work so much.

June managed to keep everything to herself and not tell anyone how she was really feeling. How could she explain the emptiness to her friends or her mother when she couldn't explain it to herself? Also, Branch was getting older, and was facing a hip replacement, and June didn't want to worry her. To everyone else, she had it all – sitting pretty in her stylish home in Killiney, surrounded by stylish things – but she'd learned that you didn't need to be on your own to feel isolated. You could be surrounded by people and still be drowning in loneliness. Only Danielle and Kelly had any idea of the problems she and Lorcan were having – and then, they only knew some of it.

June and Penny had formed a friendship over the years; when June had got used to Penny, she actually grew to like her a lot. One evening, they were having a meal out in a new Indian restaurant in Dalkey.

'How's Amanda getting on with her travels?' June asked after they'd been seated.

'She's heading for Uluru with her nomadic friends, having the time of her life. For a young one who loved her comforts, I'm amazed she survived the first few weeks, never mind eight months, roughing it in a converted van in Australia. As for Des – he'll never grow up. He never leaves me alone now that we have the house to ourselves. I suppose Lorcan is the same, can't get enough of it, you know?'

'No. No, he's not.'

Whenever June had tackled him about his loss of interest in the physical side of their marriage, he just told her that was natural. 'You can't keep up the level of ardour we had forever.'

She'd begun to believe that he genuinely had

lost his sex drive – maybe it did just happen like that.

'June,' Penny said, reaching her arm across the table, 'is Lorcan playing away from home?'

'What? Of course not. What do you mean, Penny?'

'I mean has he another woman on the side?'

'Why would you think that?' she asked, incensed.

'I don't have any reason, but it's just a feeling. You haven't been away together for a while and he's different somehow.'

'We've both been very busy and with my new business plans and all that . . . What exactly do you mean by different?' she asked. She knew he had changed, but she hadn't realised that it had become obvious to others.

'He's trying too hard to be amusing and interested, as though he was thinking of something or someone else all the time. He never was like that before. You need to keep an eye on him or he'll be poached away from you.'

Although annoyed with Penny's meddling, something about that exchange resonated long after. Did Penny know something she didn't? Did Des?

Had she failed to live up to Carol's image and standards? Lorcan had never made or voiced comparisons, but had he thought them? Had his first spouse been a better lover, a better wife, better company, a better mother? She told herself to give it one last shot. She tried harder. She made herself go sailing with Lorcan, Penny and Des, enjoying a meal in the clubhouse afterwards. These were the times when life resumed a sort of carefree normality that gave her hope that they could rekindle what they had had when they first met.

Once, though, she made the mistake of mentioning to Lorcan what Penny had said, and he exploded.

'The bitch, the stupid interfering bitch. Isn't that typical of Pushy Penny – always meddling. Don't think I don't know that I'm under scrutiny all the time, you watching me, and your mother, clocking my comings and goings. I'm not stupid,' he'd shouted at her, jumping up from the table and knocking his chair over.

Shocked, she'd said, 'You're imagining things, and what do you mean about my mother?'

'Never mind. Just butt out of my life.' He grabbed his car keys and didn't come home until very late that night. June couldn't help wondering what he'd meant about her mother. She had never noticed Branch watching him. Did Branch know something? Was there anything to know – except that she was in a seriously dysfunctional marriage and she needed to get out of it, sooner rather than later? She could always move back to Raglan Road, but she wasn't a quitter and she needed to get to the bottom of Penny's comments,

Lorcan's reaction and his accusation regarding her mother.

They continued to eat away at her so much that once she was even tempted to sit in her car close to his office when he said he was working late. She needed to see whether he was, and, if not, where he was going or with whom, but she stopped herself. How dare Penny put such thoughts into her head. If she stooped that low, what did it say about her and Lorcan's relationship – that the trust was broken or that they didn't love each other anymore? Did they? Did she still love him? Would she care if he were having an affair? After his last outburst, she wasn't sure – she wasn't sure about anything anymore.

That was when she told Danielle everything. 'I thought I was in a worthwhile relationship, but I now realise I'm not. I've been deluding myself.'

'What about booking a romantic weekend away? Or perhaps counselling?'

'A romantic weekend would be impossible – we hardly talk to each other anymore and when we do it's not really talking, it's more like exchanging communiqués. Any time I try to go deeper, he tells me to get a life. His favourite opt out is, "Well, you promised for better or for worse and this is me at my worst. So deal with it." It's very hard to argue with that kind of logic, so I've given up. Do you know what I feel like – a sponge that has been squeezed dry. I'm going to leave him.'

Her voice broke and she realised that that's what she really wanted.

As was often the case in Ireland, September was masquerading as a summer month and had been delivering sunshine and warmth for a few weeks.

'You can't go there, Danni,' Froggie told her as they showed their kids how to plant spring bulbs in their own little garden patch. 'You can't interfere in anyone's marriage.'

'But she's my friend, and I can't do nothing. She's postponed the opening of her business for another month and that's not good.'

'I thought that was because the builders were unhappy at knocking down that interior wall in the basement.'

'Well, there is that too, but Branch told me she saw him in a restaurant with some woman one night and they seemed to be more than just good friends. I mean, Froggie, I can't just pretend everything is normal after that.'

'You have to. If you talk to Lorcan, he might take it out on her. By taking sides, you'll only make matters worse. She's capable of making up her own mind.'

'Do you think he's changed?'

'We didn't really know him before. He always struck me as someone who was great with the grand gestures, but a bit uptight at the same time. I don't think I could ever say I got to know him in the real sense. He never really let me in. Sure,

420

he's a great host, but it's easy to put on a good show for an evening. Maybe he's one of those house devils and street angels.'

'What if he does have someone else on the side?'

'Then maybe he'll get tired of her and come back to June and all they'll both remember is that you interfered in their marriage and you'll forever after be the baddie.'

'It's hard to watch her being so unhappy.'

'I know, love, but that's all you can do. Be there for her. It might be better when her business is up and running.'

'I hope you're right.'

CHAPTER 36

October came in with the morning and evening sea mists that left no one in any doubt that winter was waiting in the wings. The air was tangy with the smell of a neighbour's bonfire as June pulled up into the driveway of Hill Crest and got out of her car. It was mid-afternoon and she'd just come back from a three-day seminar in France. Mrs Fitz was there to greet her as she tossed her bag down in the hall. 'I have the kettle on,' she said.

'And from those gorgeous smells, you've been baking too. Mum's on her way, so can you put out an extra cup.'

'It's nice for you having her around.'

'I know. I'm very lucky. She enjoys staying here with me when Lorcan's away – I never feel quite the same when there's no one here and it gives us a chance for some girly time.'

With that, they heard Branch's car arrive. Mrs Fitz produced one of her calorie-laden chocolate confections and as they made a dent in it Branch asked, 'How many nights am I staying?'

'Only until the cake runs out,' June laughed.

Mrs Fitz sat down at the table with them and said, 'Don't mind her, I'll make one for you to take home with you. It freezes well.'

'With my sweet tooth, it would never last long enough to get to the freezer door.'

'How do you keep so trim, both of you?'

'Good genes – we're like greyhounds – all the women in our family are like that,' said Branch. 'You must be exhausted, June, you've been on the go so much lately.'

'I am a bit flaked. The worst part is hotel pillows – even if they give you a pillow menu – they are never the same as your own.'

'A pillow menu? Is there such a thing?' Mrs Fitz asked.

'There is indeed – you can even make your choice online in some places.'

'I don't think I'd ever get used to living out of a suitcase all the time,' Mrs Fitz said. 'Even in those five-star places you stay in. Though there were times when my hubby was alive that I wished he'd disappear for a night or two, it took me quite a while to get used to the empty house when he died. That's why I was so delighted to get this job.'

'I know what you mean,' said Branch. 'I found that very tough in the beginning after Brendan died, and I joined all sorts of organisations – even the dahlia society – and I don't particularly like dahlias, too many earwigs,' she chuckled. 'We're never happy, are we?'

'I found it hard when the kids moved out at first. When they were at college and even after Sean went into a flat, he was always dropping in and with his friends too. Lorcan has been away a lot recently, so the place does feel unusually empty. We do seem to have been passing each other in the hallway for a while now. He'll be back at the end of the week though.'

'Then can you both stay put for a bit and take it easy?' her mother asked.

'Yes. Apart from organising my inaugural seminar and finalising my tasting lists and supplies, collecting the stationery from the printer's, cleaning up after the builders, and checking that I haven't left anyone important off the guest list, yes, I'll be able to take things easy.'

'Forget it,' said Mrs Fitz. 'That's how she can eat and still look like a greyhound.'

'Where's Lorcan this week?' Branch asked.

'London again – some job or other over there is taking up a lot of his energies.'

'You should try and go away with him next time. Shouldn't she?' Branch said to Mrs Fitz.

'Don't encourage her or I'll be redundant.'

'There's no danger of that – we couldn't manage our nomadic lifestyles without you.'

Later, June and Branch ate a pasta dish with salad and some vinho verde that Rosa had sent, her first foray into white wine. She mentioned in the accompanying note that Peter was finally considering moving back to manage the family estate, much to his father's delight.

'What's happening between you and that nice Mark?' June asked her mother as they settled down to watch a documentary she'd recorded. 'You've been friends for a long time now. Am I going to need a new hat sometime soon?'

'Definitely not. We're very happy the way we are. He's great company and my friends all love him, especially the music crowd. In fact, we're all considering a musical-themed holiday next year.'

June was working her way up to telling her mother that she was going to leave Lorcan and move back into Raglan Road. She had decided she wouldn't leave until after Christmas. She wanted to tell them all together, the twins and Lorcan face to face. But before she could say anything, the buzzer on the front gates sounded.

'Are you expecting anyone?'

June looked at her watch. It was almost ten o'clock.

'Definitely not at this hour.' She went to the intercom. Through the window she could see blue flashing lights at the top of the driveway.

'Mrs Overend?' No one ever called her that. 'Mrs Overend, it's Sergeant Murphy. Could we come in? It's about your husband, Lorcan.'

'Oh, God no. Is he all right?'

'I'd rather discuss this in person if that's OK with you. Are you on your own?'

'No, but come in.' She pressed the button for the gates to open and went to the hall door. A young female officer accompanied the sergeant and they both got out of the patrol car. It was she who spoke next.

'I'm afraid there's been an accident, a hit and run we suspect, and your husband was knocked down. He's alive, but injured and unconscious. He's in St Vincent's.'

'In London?' June asked.

'No, in Dublin.'

'There must be some mistake. Lorcan's in London. He won't be back for a few days – that's why my mother is staying with me.' If she noticed the glance that passed between the two of them, she didn't react.

'I have a photocopy of his driving licence and the registration number of the car he was about to get in to when he was hit,' the sergeant said. He handed both to her. 'We have the car keys too. They were on the road close to where he lay.'

'I'm confused,' she said. 'Where did this happen and when? I just got home from France this afternoon and there's a message from Lorcan on my phone. He's in London. He didn't mention he was coming back early.'

'It was in Rathgar. Some joyriders we think. There have been several reports of a vehicle speeding up and down the side roads in the vicinity around the same time. The driver didn't stop, and we have an alert out for the car, but they'll probably have abandoned it somewhere by now.'

She repeated, 'Why would he be back in Dublin without telling me? And what was he doing in Rathgar?'

'I'm afraid I can't answer those questions for you, Mrs Overend, but I think you should go the hospital right away,' the female officer said. 'Would you like us to take you there?'

'Thank you, but I'd prefer to drive.'

'I'll come with her,' Branch said.

'I'm so sorry to be the bearer of bad news, Mrs Overend,' the sergeant said as they left.

June thanked him for coming to the house to tell her personally. She knew he had known Lorcan for a number of years.

'It's all part of our job, but let's hope he makes a speedy recovery. We'll be in touch.'

They were admitted straight away into a cubicle in the A&E department. June was still convinced there was some kind of mix-up, but that changed when she saw her husband in this foreign environment. Congealed blood made the head wound appear larger than it was and the angry bruising and grazing on his cheek and chin added to her worries for him. Lorcan lay there motionless: his breathing hardly audible. There was a terrible stillness about him that was so unlike the vibrant man he was. Now, he was attached to drips and various machines that beeped a strange semaphore she couldn't understand. She took his lifeless hand.

'Lorcan, it's me, June,' she said, leaning down to kiss his forehead. It was clammy. 'It's going to be all right,' she muttered, not knowing what else to say.

A sharp-suited consultant, who had obviously been called away from some social engagement, flicked the curtain back. A young doctor and a staff nurse followed him.

'We are going to take your husband for a scan to see if we can establish the extent of the damage.'

'How serious is it?' she asked.

'It's impossible to say until we have the scan results. He's been pretty badly injured.' He spoke with an air of quiet authority that made her want to believe him. 'There are signs that he may have damage to his internal organs where the car went over him so we've sent for another specialist to look into those injuries.'

The car went over him? June was shaking and the tears she'd been holding in began to spill as she let out a cry. She tried to talk but the words wouldn't come out.

'Let's stay positive for the moment. We'll do everything we can for him. I assure you he's in good hands. He looks a strong, fit man and he's only . . .'

'Fifty-two,' she answered.

'Fifty-two, that'll all stand to him.'

'His daughter is abroad – should we contact her?' Branch asked. 'And his son?'

'Yes. I think you should,' the staff nurse said as the porters arrived to take Lorcan for the scan. 'You can use your mobile phones outside in the waiting area, and come back in to us when you're finished.'

'Should I come home?' Ashling asked on hearing the news.

'I think it might be best, but honestly I don't know what to tell you. I'll text you when I know more.'

'Is Sean with you?'

'No, Branch is. I'm just going to call him. I wanted to get you first. I'm sorry to ring in the middle of the night like this, love. I'll keep you posted, I promise.'

Sean's reaction was more concise. 'I'm on my way.'

There was only one chair in the cubicle and Branch insisted that June sit on it. From beyond the curtained world, staff were dealing with all sorts of emergencies, trivial and life threatening. Occasionally amid the sounds of creaking trollies and swift footsteps, moans could be heard from the distance and snatches of fragmented conversations intruded into their thoughts.

'You were out having a few beers? Obviously more than a few from the state of you,' someone said good-humouredly. 'We'll put a stitch in that and let you sleep it off for a few hours.'

'That's grand. Sure I was only out enjoyin' meself with the lads,' was the slurred reply.

From the next cubicle another disembodied voice asked, 'Do you remember what happened? Can you tell me your name? How many fingers am I holding up?'

Then a woman said, 'He was painting the ceiling in the hall. He almost had it finished when he knocked the can of paint over. He tried to stop it falling and fell off the ladder. I called the ambulance when he couldn't speak to me.'

'It's probably just a concussion, but we'll check him over to make certain we don't miss anything. We'll keep him in for observation overnight and he'll be back home to finish the job off in no time at all.'

The curtains were pushed open again and Lorcan's trolley wheeled back inside and locked in position. He didn't appear to have moved a muscle in the interim.

June looked up expectantly at the nurse, who seemed to read her thoughts. 'We just have to wait for the consultants to give us the results. They'll be here shortly.'

Shortly dragged on forever.

Sean arrived and said, 'I thought Dad was in London this week.'

June didn't want to get into that with him right then so she simply replied, 'No, no, he had a change of plan.'

And still they waited. It was well after two when the consultants came back to them. The one they had met earlier had shed his tailored jacket some-where along the way. The other looked out of character in a logoed golf sweater over a tieless shirt. If he resented being called out of bed, he didn't show it.

'As you know, your husband has had a severe blow to his head and face. He has a hairline fracture to his cheekbone too. However, there are signs of internal bleeding in his head. It's impossible to say if this has stopped or not. If it hasn't, it will put pressure on his brain that could cause permanent damage. As a precaution, I'd like to get him into theatre straight away to ensure that doesn't happen. In cases like this, prevention is better than cure.'

'He will be OK, won't he?' Sean asked.

'Let's hope so. We won't know for certain if he did sustain any lasting brain damage until he regains consciousness. I know it sounds terrible, but the procedure is a tried and tested one, so let's stay positive.' He smiled a smile of encouragement at them all and turned and introduced his colleague.

'I'm afraid my news is not much better. There's some quite serious internal organ damage and bruising which need urgent attention too, but we'll know more when we operate.'

Minutes later, Lorcan was wheeled away to theatre.

'When did he last eat?' the staff nurse asked June.

'I don't know. He wasn't expected home for dinner last night,' she said, thinking on her feet. 'I don't know if he had eaten before the accident or not. Sometimes he just makes a snack if he's late.'

Sean put his arm around her shoulder.

'Can we wait here?' asked Branch.

'There's no point – he'll be taken to the IC unit when he's out of theatre and that could be in several hours. My advice to you would be to go home and try to get some rest, but I know you wouldn't listen to that,' she said with the air of someone who had seen it all and could take anything in her stride.

'You're right,' Sean agreed with her. 'I'll stay if you like, June, and you two can go. I'll ring you as soon as there's any news. I'm going to give Ashling a bell anyway. I promised her I would.'

'We'll all stay,' said Branch. 'Isn't there a family room where we can sit and wait?'

They were directed to a room in a different part of the building, and sat to continue their vigil. From a vending machine close by, Sean kept them supplied with oversweet hot chocolate and greyish-looking coffee in waxed paper cups. The hours ticked by and the first tentacles of dawn were beginning to clutch at the sky when the original consultant came in, still gowned up.

'We've stopped the bleed and alleviated the pressure it was causing, but we're not out of the woods just yet. Your husband is in a critical

432

state and we're going to keep him in an induced coma for the next twelve to twenty-four hours, possibly longer, then we'll review the situation. The downside of this is we're going to have to wait a bit longer too before we can tell if any permanent damage has been done to his brain. My colleague will fill you in on his other injuries in a while. I'm sorry I can't be more specific at this point, but he's stable and that's good.'

'When will he wake up?' Sean asked, 'and what's involved in this induced coma?' The surgeon explained the procedure and how it worked.

The sun had risen fully on a promising day by the time the second surgeon appeared. 'I'm afraid we had to remove one of the kidneys, but there are thousands of people functioning perfectly well with only one. There is bruising to the other one and if it shows any signs of distress, we may have to put your husband on dialysis for the period of recovery, but it may not come to that,' he told them.

'How are his kidneys damaged if his head took the impact?' asked Sean as he processed this information.

'I understand this was a hit and run, and from the injuries it would seem as though your father was actually run over by one or more of the car's wheels, hence the internal damage. We're going to keep him on a ventilator to assist his breathing for the moment and that will take some of the pressure off for him too. At this point, rest is vital to his recovery. You need to get some too. You have a very worrisome time ahead of you all.'

June thanked him, but she refused to go home. She was determined to be there if there was any change. Branch understood. 'Sean, maybe you'd run me back to Hill Crest. My car's there.' En route, she mentioned how relieved she felt that June had got home from France the previous day.

'What's going on, Branch? I spoke to dad yesterday and he said he was in London for the rest of the week. I know he did.'

'June thought he was there too – that's the only reason I was staying with her. He must have had a change of plan at the last minute. I'm sure there's a perfectly simple explanation – you can ask him when he's well again.'

'If you've your things at Hill Crest, why not stay on. There's no point going home and June will be glad of your support. I'm going to crash there for a few hours and go back in. Ash will be there too whenever her flight arrives.'

'That's a good idea – a kind of HQ until things get back to normal. Mrs Fitz will be delighted to have you all to look after again. She was bemoaning the fact that she didn't have enough to do anymore.'

'She needn't worry – that can be easily rectified,' he said, 'and it looks like Dad will keep her busier than ever when he comes out of hospital.'

'I'll let her know,' Branch said, hoping that he *would* come out, 'she likes feeling wanted.'

The next eight days went by at an anxiety-filled, pedestrian pace, each of the family recalling and relating any change or overheard comment by the medical staff that might prove to be significant.

After twenty-four hours, they stopped the barbiturates they had used to reduce the metabolic rate of the brain tissue and the cerebral blood flow, releasing Lorcan from his induced coma, but he remained deeply unconscious. As his breathing improved, they deemed that no further assistance was needed to regulate that. The remaining kidney showed no signs of distress either. And that was when the real waiting game began – waiting to see if his eyelids would flicker or his expression change or his fingers twitch. Waiting to see if he would respond to their voices, their touch – to anything.

The hit and run had made it into the papers and onto the national radio bulletins as Gardaí appealed for witnesses to contact them. So far no one had. One of Noelle's neighbours, an elderly man who had been out walking his dog, had been the first on the scene. He'd heard the impact as he was making his way down his heavily shrubbed driveway but he hadn't seen it happen. He'd been the one to dial 999 when he saw the man lying on the roadway.

Nothing happened. The days dragged. They

were all exhausted. June was too tired to answer the phone. Kelly, Mark, Neil, JP, Des and Penny were among those who offered to come in and sit with her. So did Danielle and Froggie. Branch and Mrs Fitz were stalwarts, saying and doing all the right things at the right times. Somehow, the days went by, interminable and with a monotonous uncertainty. June tried to work through her business plan checklist, but realised it would have to take second place for another while. She was glad she hadn't posted the invitations to her first seminar. They were written and stamped, just waiting to be mailed.

And then Lorcan woke up.

CHAPTER 37

There seemed to be bright lights shining everywhere. They blinded him as he tried to open his eyes. It was too much of an effort, so he stopped trying. Strange sounds echoed around him. Where was he? Was Noelle here? No, that was definitely June's voice – and Ashling's – was she not in Italy?

'Dad, Dad, it's me. Can you hear me?' Ashling sounded excited.

He couldn't respond.

'He definitely opened his eyes for a second. Honestly, I didn't imagine it.'

'I'll call the nurse,' said June.

He was aware of someone checking his pulse, the tightening and loosening of a blood pressure monitor on his arm and the noise of it exhaling as it deflated, like an emphysemic old smoker.

'He may not remember anything about the accident or immediately before it when he wakes, so don't bombard him with questions or be upset if he's confused initially.'

The accident. What accident? He tried to remember. It was very busy and he wished they'd all go away and stop making noise – just let him rest – but they didn't. He decided to sleep anyway.

When he woke again it was quieter and he could hear someone breathing close to him – a slow, steady rhythm. Who was it? He tried opening his eyes again and after a few attempts he succeeded. His son was fast asleep in a chair by his bed. Lorcan could make out monitors and other pieces of medical equipment. But what was he doing here, in bed, in a hospital and where? It was dark outside and in the distance a siren sounded, another ambulance bringing someone else to hospital?

That was it – he remembered now – the approaching siren as he lay face down on the road near Noelle's house. He had tried to tell the paramedics to go and get her. She'd know what to do. But he couldn't talk and there was a lot of blood. He didn't like its metallic taste and had tried to spit it out. But his head hurt and his chest hurt. He felt as if a huge weight lay on him and it all took too much effort.

Who told Sean about the accident? Did his son know about Noelle? Exhausted, Lorcan fell sleep again.

'No change,' Sean told June on the phone the following morning. 'But I'll stay until you get here.'

It was mid-morning when Lorcan finally came

to. The smiles of relief and love on the faces of his wife and daughter made him wince. Did they now know his secret? Did they know about his other family? They should be here too. He had to contact Noelle as soon as he could.

'Where's my phone?' were his first anxious words, asked as he tried to sit up and look around him.

'Darling, work can wait until you feel better. You've been very ill and need to take things easy.'

'I endorse that advice,' the consultant said, entering the room quietly behind them. 'No stress, no pressure and no worries for a while.'

That's easy for you to say, thought Lorcan. 'When can I go home?'

'We need to make sure you're in full working order first. It'll take a little while before you feel like your old self again, but we'll let you home before that. You've had surgery and you need to get over that too. You may have memory lapses, especially around the accident itself. These are to be expected, so don't let them faze you. And I think your family should leave in about ten minutes and let you get some real rest. They've been very devoted sitting here all week. You're a lucky man in lots of ways.'

'A week? I've been here a whole week?' He began to panic. He had to talk to Noelle. Let her know what happened.

Over the next few days, he remembered it all in graphic detail. He had been at Noelle's since the weekend but everyone thought he was in London. The plan had been that they would fly to Paris for a romantic few days – her sister had already taken their daughter to stay with her – and they were about to go to bed when Lorcan realised that he'd left his passport in the office.

'I'll nip back and get it now, rather than risk anyone seeing me there in the morning.' He had parked his car where he usually left it, in a side road around from her townhouse. He had just pressed the remote to open his car when he heard the screeching of tyres and felt the impact simultaneously, and then he felt a terrible weight go over him. Then nothing. Then voices, excruciating pain, an ambulance siren, then nothing, nothing at all until he came to in the middle of the night with his son sleeping beside his bed in a chair.

'I need my phone.'

'It's with your things, Mr Overend, but I'm afraid you can't use it in here. The signal can interfere with the heart monitors,' a nurse told him.

He had to get it. *Does Noelle even know what happened?*

Progress was slow, but it was progress and, bit by bit, he improved, albeit painfully at times. He still had periods of forgetfulness but he was aware enough to let nothing slip when June and Sean both questioned him about what had brought him back to Dublin that day and more specifically what he was doing in Rathgar. Amnesia was the best excuse – he'd stick with that one – he couldn't have made up that excuse if he'd tried.

He moved to a nursing home in the middle of November, five weeks after the accident. He had a pleasant room overlooking the car park and some manicured grounds. The twins celebrated their twenty-second birthdays a few days early before Ashling went back to Italy. She'd be home again for Christmas. June and Sean went back to work and synchronised their visiting times so that they wouldn't clash. Lorcan argued that he didn't need so many visits anyway, and was quite specific about when he wanted June to visit. She humoured him.

'If I didn't know you any better, I'd swear you didn't want me coming in at all,' she joked, but he didn't reply.

Christmas was very different to previous ones, although they decorated his room and put up a tiny tree for him. At home, June did all the normal things to make the twins feel welcome when they moved home for the holidays. Mrs Fitz baked a plum pudding for Lorcan and they had their turkey and ham with him in the nursing home. Then they all went to Branch's for another dinner and spent St Stephen's Day with Danielle and Froggie. The New Year slipped in almost unnoticed. June even went to bed before midnight. Next year would be better. It had to be, hadn't it? *How can I leave him now, in this state?*

With Froggie and Danielle's encouragement, she

set a date to start her new business – her father's birthday, 1 March. By then, Lorcan should have responded to his physiotherapy regime, but no matter what happened, she was going to go ahead with her plans.

She visited him daily, and one afternoon she arrived at the home earlier than usual. She stood back to let a young woman and a child out of the lift. They smiled at each other and went their separate ways. On the landing, she asked about Lorcan's progress and the cheerful nurse said, 'He's doing really well – he should be home with you in a week or so. I was just going to check his blood pressure.' They walked together to his room and the nurse said, 'Who's a popular fellow today – you've another visitor.'

June walked around the bed to give him a kiss while the nurse continued her ramblings. 'The little one is gorgeous. Is she your grand-daughter?'

His negative monosyllabic reply gave nothing away. June was curious, but knew better than to quiz him while the nurse was still in the room.

'Who was your visitor, then?'

'Just someone from work.'

'I hope she didn't tire you out, bringing a child in with her.'

'She didn't.'

June took off her coat and was folding it when she noticed a bunch of keys on the window ledge. She didn't know what stopped her saying anything about them to Lorcan. Maybe it was knowing that the young woman and little girl she'd met earlier had just been to visit him. *Who were they?*

She looked out the window and saw them standing by a silver car. The woman was going through her pockets and her bag, and then the little one's pockets. It was obvious to anyone watching that she was searching for her car keys. She turned and walked back into the building. But it wasn't she who came to retrieve them from Lorcan's room – it was one of the nurses.

'I'd forget my head if it wasn't attached,' the nurse laughed. 'I left my keys on the window ledge when I was in earlier. Sorry to bother you.'

'No bother at all,' June said. She kept an eye on the window and a few minutes later the young woman emerged and, after settling the child in the back, she drove away. Something didn't add up. June was unsettled by the morning's events and decided to make some investigations of her own. But a phone call later that day put all thoughts of it out of her mind.

'I'm afraid your husband has had a seizure,' the impersonal voice at the end of the line told her.

He'd had another one by the time she arrived back in. At times, he seemed confused; at other times perfectly lucid. June and Sean had a conference with his medical team and they warned them that this could happen again. Such seizures were as a result of his brain injuries.

Over the next few days, he rallied well and

seemed to be making good progress. June was finally feeling more confident about his recovery when she bumped into the young woman and the little girl again in the car park.

She suddenly realised why Lorcan was so fixated and specific about her visiting times. He didn't want them to meet.

The next day, she decided to arrive an hour earlier and parked in sight of his room. She saw her pull up, take the child out of the car seat and go inside. Minutes later, she saw them through Lorcan's window. They stayed about half an hour and when they left, June followed them at a distance. A few miles away, the silver car drove along the road where Lorcan's accident had occurred before indicating and turning into a complex of townhouses. June drove farther along and reversed into a gateway, waiting a few minutes before driving back. She glanced in and saw the pair walking up to a house with a green door.

All the uncertainties and conjectures lifted. Her doubts had been confirmed. Lorcan had not been in London, he'd been in his love nest, with this woman, whoever she was. *He hadn't forgotten what had happened – he was trying to cover his tracks.* Then she was struck by a thought that took her breath away. *Was the child his too?* That was too cruel to contemplate, but she had to find out.

Over the next few days, she stalked the driver of the silver car. She learned where the little one, whom she heard her calling Adelaide, went to crèche and where they shopped. But she said nothing to anyone about her suspicions. She gave Lorcan every opportunity to tell her, but he never did. She didn't know how she would react if he did confess, but at least now she knew she hadn't been imagining his behaviour.

She felt totally trapped. She couldn't just walk out on him, not now, not when he needed her. But as she lay in her bed at night, she argued with herself and wondered why she shouldn't leave. He'd made it quite clear to her that he didn't need or want her. It wasn't her place to tell his children about his lover either or the possibility that they had a half-sister, was it? She had to take some action though.

She'd confront the woman whose name she still didn't know.

CHAPTER 38

Throughout January and February, a series of strokes had left Lorcan with a useless right side and an aversion to physiotherapy and to anyone who tried to help him. June's business plans were put on hold again. He sat propped up against the pillows in the same position for so long that you could have made a cast of his shape from them. With each one of these episodes, a little more of him seemed to disappear. June was watching him give up and gradually shutting down and she felt sad, sad for what they'd had together and for what they might have had.

She knew he was far too young to die, and that he must be resentful and frightened. There was a time he would have been able to admit that to her, but not now, not any more, not even to himself. He had been important in his world, and it had been important to him. But that world had become clouded with secrets and deception and he was having difficulty separating the different elements.

He opened his eyes. 'What are you still doing here? Didn't I tell you to go home?'

'Right. OK. I just thought I'd stay . . . in case
. . .' She reached her hand over his to offer
comfort. He pushed it away.

'In case what? I might disappear? I'm not likely
to escape, am I?'

He closed his eyes again. On the surface, she
seemed to cope with his insensitivity, but deep
down he still had the ability to hurt her.

That night, Lorcan suffered a major stroke. The
medics said he would not have felt a thing. It was
over immediately. June rang his daughter and son
to tell them. Branch came over and Mrs Fitz went
into overdrive. But there was another, more difficult, call to be made. She picked up the phone to
dial and put it down again. No, she decided, this
had to be done in person.

She told them she'd be back in a while and
headed for Rathgar. The silver car was parked
outside the townhouse with the green door. She
rang the bell and Noelle answered, a flicker of
recognition and then the realisation of what this
visit meant, flashed across her face.

'I'm June Overend.'

'I know, and I'm Noelle. No. No. Don't tell me
it's bad news.'

'I'm afraid so. Lorcan died early this morning,
very peacefully.'

'Oh, God . . . no.' The woman walked back into
the house, leaving the door open.

June hesitated but followed her inside. Her eye
was immediately drawn to a framed portrait of

Lorcan on a shelf and several other smaller ones of him with Adelaide and Noelle. She had a flashback to the first time she went to Bayvue and had been confronted with photos of Lorcan with Carol and the twins when they were younger. She remembered feeling like an intruder then. She had the same feeling now, but this time, the woman in the pictures was alive and Lorcan was not.

'I sensed it was coming. My dad died in much the same way, but that doesn't prepare you for when it happens, does it? It's a shock,' Noelle said. She had regained her composure in a way that won June's admiration.

'She's a beautiful little girl. She has his eyes.'

'We think so – or we thought so. I still do. You never had any children?'

'No. I didn't.' Perhaps Lorcan had told her about the babies she had lost, but she couldn't – wouldn't – tell this stranger her most intimate secrets.

'Did he know you knew about us?'

'No, I didn't tell him. I might have if he'd got better, but it never seemed the right time and I think I would have preferred him to be the one telling me,' June said. 'But I wanted to tell you in person that he was gone and not let you read it in the paper or find out when you went to the home.'

'Thank you. This can't be easy for you. I appreciate that.'

'It's not, but I need to talk to you about something else.'

The caterers came promptly at 9.30 and with
respectful efficiency set up a buffet and bar, all
watched over by the eagle eye of Mrs Fitz.

June had seen to the flowers in the rooms,
purple hyacinths and yellow tulips, and despite
the wind outside and the scudding grey clouds,
the sun broke through just as the mourning cars
arrived to take them to the service. A promise
of spring on the first of March, the day she
should have started her own business, and her
father's birthday. Lorcan's brother, his wife
and their two grown children had arrived from
the UK the previous evening. Ashling and
Sean were waiting for June. Sean had written
and gone over his eulogy several times for them,
a loving, sometimes humorous, sometimes
heart-rending tribute from an only son. Ashling
had a favourite poem to read. She was afraid
to try anything longer in case she wouldn't get
through it.

'I've got your coat,' Ashling said, holding it up.

'I don't need that. I'm not going to the funeral,'
June announced, moving aside.

'What?'

'I'm not going to the funeral.'

'You're not going to the funeral?' Ashling echoed
in disbelief. 'You can't not go. What do you
mean?'

'Exactly that. I'm not going.'

'You can't do that,' Ashling repeated.

'I can and I am. Now, you go and say your goodbyes to your father. I'll do mine in my own way. Make sure you tell everyone they are invited back here afterwards.'

Ashling turned to her twin, a pleading look in her eyes. 'Sean, you've got to do something.'

'It's June's decision. I'm sure she's given it a lot of thought.'

'You can't stay here on your own. I know it must be really hard for you, but you're just panicking,' Ashling said. 'We'll be there with you.'

'I'm not going to be on my own, Ashling, Danielle's on her way over. And I promise you I'm not panicking. Sean is right – I have given this a lot of thought. Now, go – everyone will be waiting for the family before things can get under way.' She walked them to the hall door.

'What'll we tell people?'

'Nothing, Ash. This is my choice. I don't want to be there. That's all.'

She waited until they were in the car before going back inside. She walked into the drawing room, her lovely blue and yellow room, and went to the picture window that overlooked the sloping lawn. Over the next few weeks, the fringe of daffodils and narcissi would redefine its wintery profile. It was from this vantage point that she always enjoyed the most glorious views of Dublin Bay. She turned away and thought, *It's over. Isn't life strange? It's not how I would have wanted it to end, but it has. I'm free.*

In no time at all, the first cars arrived back. Froggie, Penny and Des, Mark and Branch, several of the twins' friends, JP and Neil Macy, Kelly and some more of June's work colleagues. Lorcan's brother and his family were next and were followed by lots of their yacht club friends. Carol's parents had flown over from France the previous evening and they came back too. They had refused June's invitation to stay at Hill Crest, saying she had enough to think about without house guests.

'Peter was there,' Branch said. 'He sent his condolences and best regards. He made a point of telling me although he's in Portugal a lot these days, he's always at the end of the phone if you need a friend.'

'It was nice of him to go,' said June.

'He was always very thoughtful,' said Danielle.

No one remarked on the presence of the young woman in black who had been at the funeral home. She'd held a little girl by the hand and they'd sat near the front and placed two long-stemmed white roses on the coffin before it was taken away.

If they had asked, June would have told them they were there at her invitation, representing her. But they didn't.

CHAPTER 39

'There's an awful lot to do when someone dies. I never realised just how much before,' June told Danielle and Froggie. They had agreed to be with her when the solicitor came to go through Lorcan's papers. It transpired that Lorcan had left her an extremely wealthy widow. He'd made generous provision for the twins too, including leaving them the yacht.

'I'm not going to stay in this house.'

'I've heard that you should never make decisions like that immediately after a bereavement. You might change your mind and regret it later,' Froggie counselled.

'I know, but it's not exactly a normal situation, is it? I love the house itself, but I haven't been happy here for a good while, and there are the twins to consider. Don't worry, I won't rush in to anything; for now, I'm going to go back to Raglan Road.'

Lorcan's solicitor arrived at that point. There was no mention of a second family – no paper trail to be discovered – apart from a single receipt for the townhouse in Rathgar. Lorcan must have bought it at some stage, but there was only his name on the deeds. Danielle looked enquiringly at June and she told her she'd explain later.

There was also a sealed letter for Sean. She didn't want Sean and Ashling to learn about their half-sibling through some legal mouthpiece and that was why she'd asked for this meeting first, without them being present. She'd deal with that when the shock of losing their father had finally sunk in, not now.

June instructed that the Rathgar property should be transferred to Noelle in trust for her daughter. They made arrangements to go to the various banks and she asked the solicitor to draw up a fund to cover all education and related expenses for Adelaide.

'June, you don't have to do that,' Danielle said. 'She's not your responsibility.'

'I know I don't, but if she had been ours she would have the best chances possible in life, and I know that's what Lorcan would want for her too.'

In the weeks after the funeral, everyone was very solicitous, calling and phoning to make sure she was coping. She was sad – but her sadness came from her regret that a relationship that had started out so wonderfully and so promisingly had not worked out. Lorcan had never been and would never be the love of her life, but she had loved him – not as intensely as she had loved Peter, but it was real love nonetheless. She had nothing to feel guilty about.

Bartley Bruno still sat on a blanket chest in her bedroom and occasionally she'd take him up and hold him as she remembered. It was in this position that Sean found her when he came to take her to lunch one Sunday, a month after Lorcan's death.

'I never heard you come in. I was miles away,' she laughed. 'I was just looking at those boats out there and reminiscing.'

Her reverie stopped abruptly when he announced, 'I know about Noelle and about Adelaide too.'

'How? When did you find out?'

'Dad told me a few weeks before he died. Just about her, but not about the child. I remembered meeting her once or twice in his office, but I never suspected anything. I admit I kept pushing him to know why he had lied to me about being in London the day of his accident. Maybe I shouldn't have, but I knew something didn't add up. That day I was talking to him at about five o'clock and he told me he wouldn't be back until Friday, then presto, a few hours later he's run over in Rathgar.'

'But I don't understand . . . How did you know I knew?'

'I didn't, until last week. He made me promise if anything ever happened him that I'd contact Noelle. He'd left all the details with his solicitor. That's what was in the sealed envelope. I couldn't face doing it straight away, but I had to do it so

I went to see her yesterday morning and she introduced me to my half-sister. That was quite a shock
and then she said you'd met and that you'd told
her she should go to his funeral instead of you.
That that's what Dad would have wanted. That
took some courage and it must have been hard
on you.'

'Don't worry about me, Sean. I figured you
suspected something that morning. You knew that
was why I didn't go, didn't you?'

He nodded. 'I kind of guessed you suspected
something. I'm sorry. Really I am. You didn't—
you don't deserve this, June.'

'I'm so relieved it's out in the open. I loved your
dad, but not what he had become or what he was
doing. You and Ashling must have known things
were bad between us. It would have been hypo-
critical to have gone and pretended to be the
grieving widow, knowing what I did. I knew he
would have preferred that she was there instead
of me. Can you understand that?'

'Easily, but it's hard. How could he have deceived
us all like that?'

'I don't know. I've had time to get used to the
idea. But now we have to tell your sister. She's
hardly talking to me and she won't return my calls.
She's still not forgiven me for staying away from
his funeral.'

'She will when she knows the reason why. Leave
Ashling to me. You know you've always been
much more than a mother to us both, you're our

mate too, and we don't want that to change, ever. You're very important in our lives, and always will be.'

'Thank you for that, Sean. I really want that too.' They hugged each other, both with tears in their eyes.

'I'll fly over to her for a weekend and tell her face to face.'

CHAPTER 40

June may have been running away when she agreed to a lecture tour with the South African Wine Development Association at the end of July, but she didn't care. In the five months since Lorcan's death, she had been able to concentrate on her freelance consultancy and, when the opportunity came, she jumped at it.

Before she left, she dropped in to Macy Brothers to catch up with everyone. 'I've loved working here and really appreciate your faith in me. I miss you all.'

'We're very proud of you, our own highly successful protégée.'

'You're embarrassing me now, but I hope I can still pop in for a coffee every now and then.'

'Only if you bring the bikkies,' Neil said.

'Make that chocolate-covered Mikado,' said JP, 'and promise not to poach any more of our staff.'

'That's a deal,' she said, and they shook hands on it.

Kelly was relishing her new role and her new office in the basement of Raglan Road. June was trying to settle back in to her old home. When she needed a break, she'd take her coffee out into the garden. The shrubs and climbers were massed with blooms as summer rolled on, and the ceanothus bushes were shedding their powdery flowers in blue pools along the pathways. Mrs Fitz decided it was time to reduce her hours – she'd go to Branch one day a week and to June on another and she's be willing to help out with wine tasting nights too. Remembering Froggie's advice, that it was too soon to make any important decisions, June had let her stay at Hill Crest for a while as caretaker.

Armed with new ideas and enthusiasm, June made her first foray into her new life, taking advantage of an opportunity nudged along, no doubt, by some of Hennie's ever-increasing web of contacts. He was one of the founder members of the South African Wine Development Association and three and a half weeks away in the southern hemisphere with him as company sounded very appealing. She was going to fly on to Australia and New Zealand afterwards, to visit growers, producers and buyers.

She found she didn't miss home at all. There was a certain liberation in being with people who knew nothing of her circumstances. Whenever she remembered everything that had happened over the past year, she put it out of her mind. She was getting good at that.

Back in Dublin she caught up with her friends and with Branch. Then she was off again. This time to some of the wine harvests in Burgundy. In between, she was asked to contribute a regular wine column to one of the Sunday newspapers. She set about this with gusto, trying to write a few weeks in advance so she could relax if she had to travel. She was invited on to the examination panel of the Guild of Sommeliers of Ireland and was appointed as one of the wine advisers for a leading supermarket chain.

Invitations arrived to various food and wine events. And, as the autumn drew in, Macy Brothers invited her and Kelly to join them at the Association of Restaurateurs Awards dinner. Thrilled to be asked, she couldn't wait to catch up with them all.

The venue was glittering, the style impressive, and she met many old and more recent colleagues and acquaintances. It was a relatively small world and she was now well known within it. She had bought a plum-coloured dress for the occasion and some elegant high slingbacks in gold. The dress was simplicity itself, with a soft draped panel across the hipline, which showed off her trim figure. She wore two chunky gold strands around her neck and matching bracelets on one arm.

'You look great,' Kelly told her when they met.

'So do you,' June replied, 'that red is marvellous on you.'

'I do my best,' she laughed. 'How are you feeling?'

'Do you know something? It's the first time I've felt so carefree in a long time.'

'And it shows. You look amazing.'

The meal was a showcase for the best of food and artful presentation, with different guest chefs participating. Its wines were wonderful too. The presentations took forever, with some winners determined to make the most of their few minutes of podium time.

'He thinks he's won an Oscar,' Neil whispered as one droned on and on about his wonderful staff, his grandmother's recipes and his expansion plans. Eventually he was cut off by the erudite master of ceremonies, who knew he still had many more awards to hand out and that he was in danger of losing the audience's attention.

The overall Restaurant of the Year winner was announced while they were chatting. When the clapping had died down, she saw Peter mount the steps to the stage to accept the cut-glass trophy. She looked at Kelly, who just laughed.

'You knew?'

'JP was on the judging panel. He wasn't sure if you'd mind or whether he should invite you to come tonight, so he asked me what I thought and I said of course.'

His words of thanks were witty and succinct and he went back through the tables to his own. June knew she had to go and congratulate him, but every time she looked across, he seemed to be surrounded by well-wishers. She waited, and the crowd eventually thinned out.

'June! How lovely to see you. How are you?' he asked, embracing her. His smell was as familiar as if she'd hugged him only yesterday and she wanted to stay there in the safety of his arms. But he released her. 'I was sorry to hear about Lorcan. Are you doing OK?'

'Yes, thank you. I'm fine. There's no need to ask about you. Congratulations on your award. It'll be a Michelin star next.'

'And congratulations on your new venture too. Branch keeps me informed. She's quite a regular.'

'How do you manage to juggle running the estate and the restaurant?'

'With good staff and lots of air miles.'

'That must be difficult, but obviously you are doing something right to get this accolade.'

'You should come in with Branch and Mark some time and help me celebrate.'

She was aware of people waiting to talk to him so she said, 'That sounds good.'

'Let's say Friday next. OK?'

'I'll see if I can make it. Congratulations again, Peter. Well done.' She turned and went back to Kelly.

'I still can't make my mind up whether to sell or what to do with the house. The twins don't mind what I do. They have no interest in it. Sean says it's far too big for him and he doesn't want to be saddled with the upkeep of the grounds either. He'd rather have a pad in New York.'

'I can understand that,' said Branch, who had phoned her daughter. 'What about Ashling?'

'I can't see her coming back here for the fore-seeable future. Dublin's not exactly at the cutting edge of fashion design and she says she wants to make a name for herself first and that could take years. She says she'd like to have a pad here, but she doesn't want to invest in anything yet until the market improves, or at least stabilises some-what first.'

'And that sounds very sensible too. They're all grown up now and have to be allowed make their own way in life.'

'I suppose you're right. Hill Crest was their home with me – Bayvue was theirs with Carol. I think I'll get on to the letting agents and see if I can get an embassy let for a few years, then they can decide.'

'Now on a different topic altogether – are you going to come out with Mark and me to Peter's place on Friday? He told me he'd asked you.'

'You've got very pally with him, haven't you?' she laughed at her mother.

'No. Peter and I were always very pally, as you put it, and Mark loves The Pink Pepper Tree. So that's a date – keep Friday night free. The table's booked. Have to go now, off to my history group. Bye.'

She rang off before June could think up a plausible

excuse. Branch was nearly seventy and never stopped going. June hoped she'd have that energy at her age.

No sooner had she hung up than the phone rang again. It was Penny. She had tried several times to get June to join her and Des at various functions in the yacht club but June had always refused.

'Now, I know you're probably not up to big occasions yet, but I'm having an intimate dinner party. There's someone I'd like you to meet. He's a widower who loves his wine. It's next Friday night.'

'Oh, that's such a shame, Penny. I already have a date for Friday. He's divorced and knows his wine too,' she said mischievously, waiting for some comment, but for a change Penny was at a loss for words. She knew that titbit would fly around Penny's circle within minutes. Lorcan would have got a laugh at that.

She went upstairs and pulled down the attic ladder. She knew exactly what she was looking for – the platters she had bought in France at a flea market all those years ago with Danielle. Gingerly she took them from their bubble wrap and put them on the kitchen table. With her index finger she traced a line on the oblong one with its colourful lobster pattern; the circular one was embellished with an overall painting of mussels. Then she unwrapped the individual finger bowls that matched them. She washed, dried and wrapped them up again. She could still see Danielle laughing at her when she bought them – wondering how they'd ever get them back to Ireland – but she had never given them to Peter, there had never been the chance.

She remembered Kelly saying that when your past comes calling, you shouldn't answer the phone. How right she was. June had long ago decided that there was no point dwelling on those things any more.

She'd bring the platters and finger bowls to the restaurant when she went along on Friday and close that chapter of her life too.

CHAPTER 41

Peter came to hold the door open when they arrived for dinner. He kissed June and her mother on both cheeks and June handed over the box to him.

'Can you put that somewhere safe for me until later?' she asked.

'Sure, I'll put it in the office.' He took it from her, turned and went upstairs – the same stairs on which she had heard him talking to Zoe. It was her first time seeing the stained glass window that she had done the drawings for. It looked terrific. But she couldn't say anything, or remark on it. Leave it there, where it belonged, in the past. She was saved from any more self-recrimination by Peter's reappearance. He took them to their table. It was set for four. He went off to get menus and she asked, 'Are we expecting someone else?'

'Only Peter,' said Branch. 'I asked him to join us; after all, it's his award we're here to celebrate.'

Before she could comment, he was back and sitting down with them. Branch took it upon herself to start the conversation, while June composed herself. 'I hear you're spending a lot more time in Alentejo these days.'

'Yep. The old man is delighted on two counts, first that I'll end up running the estate and secondly that he was right that I'd end up running the estate. You know how he loves to be right. I'm heading back again next week for a bit. Max is a great manager here, so it's in good hands when I'm not around.'

It was as though the past eight years had never happened. They talked and laughed, reminisced and caught up on each other's gossip, much of which Branch and Mark already seemed to know. The evening flashed by and June realised there had been no awkwardness at all. It seemed perfectly normal to be sitting there in Peter's restaurant with him, her mum and Mark.

It was after one when they left and it was only when she was getting ready for bed that June remembered the box with the platters. She'd forgotten all about them.

It took her a while to get to sleep that night. Nothing had changed and yet everything had.

She still felt the same way about Peter as she did in her twenties, when he was a constant feature in her mind, her dreams and her plans. She wondered briefly if he felt the same. He'd be forty next birthday and she pictured him riding around the estate in Portugal with his father on their Lusitano horses, discussing the olive crops, the yields and probably now inspecting Rosa's vines too. She could see the sprawling pink pepper trees, especially the huge one with the seat underneath, where his grandfather used to go to take refuge from his grandmother and smoke his pipe. She could smell the garlicky aromas that emanated from the kitchen, and remember the long meals they shared outside on the terrace in the evenings.

Eventually she fell asleep.

She woke with her phone ringing beside her bed. It was half ten.

'Hi, Miss Cusack. It's me.' He didn't need to say any more.

'Mr Braga. You're up early.'

'I couldn't sleep. When you left I remembered that you'd left your box in my office. Would you like to call and collect it, or I could bring it out to you, if you'd prefer?'

'It's OK – it's for you. I completely forgot about it.'

'For me? What is it?'

'A gift. Why don't you open it and see?'

'Because I'm still at home. Besides you should never open presents alone. There's no fun in that. Come in and have lunch with me.'

She didn't need to give that invitation a second thought. 'Righto, I will. See you later.'

The box sat on his desk, unopened. They didn't need words, but the silence between them wasn't an awkward one – it was one of complete ease and understanding.

'Well, go on and open it. I've had it a long time.'

'Then another little while won't matter, will it?'

'I suppose not.'

He reached across for her hands and said, 'June, I'm so sorry.'

'So am I.'

'Let's get out of here and go somewhere we can talk.'

She nodded and they headed for Herbert Park. Kids fed the ducks, families pushed buggies, couples walked hand in hand, joggers sweated as they overtook everyone else on the pathways. Two swans sailed majestically by and he asked, 'Do you still believe they mate for life?'

'Do you still think they just imagine they do because they all look the same?'

They laughed together. Could he know how much she missed hearing that in her life?

Their seat, the one they always used to take, was free.

He told her marrying Zoe had been the biggest mistake he'd ever made. 'I knew before we walked down the aisle that it was wrong. You were already with Lorcan. You looked good together when we met that day in the Westbury, at Christmas time. Do you remember?'

She nodded. She remembered that very well.

'So I settled for second best, and it wasn't good enough, for either of us. Zoe was more in love with the idea of being married to my lifestyle than of actually being married to me. She loved the media attention and she saw the restaurant as a way to give her access to celebrities. That seemed to matter to her. I did try my best to make her happy, but I'm not stupid. I knew she was on the lookout for a higher profile – then enter Adamo, and she was gone like a flash, though that didn't last either. I believe she's with some Bohemian prince or something now. But what about you, June, were you happy?'

'Initially yes, but not in the end.' She told Peter how she and Lorcan had met that fateful weekend after her abortion and on her thirtieth birthday. 'I was lost. I'd just seen you and Zoe in the Shelbourne and if I'm totally honest, I settled for second best too. I used to imagine you'd change your mind and want me back, but when I read the articles in the papers that you got engaged, I lost hope of that ever happening. I was happy at first, but I was miserable in the end. I had decided to leave him when he had the accident and I couldn't turn my back on him then.'

She told him about her pregnancies, his affair and his love child. She told him everything, but most of all she told him how she had missed him.

'I always loved you, you know. Second best was never good enough.'

He put his arm along the back of the bench and looked her directly in the eyes. 'I've never stopped loving you either.'

He took her hands in his. 'You promised me something a long time ago.'

'Did I?'

'You did.'

'And what was that?' she asked.

'That you'd say yes the next time I asked you to marry me.'

'I remember that.'

'Well, I'm . . . I'm asking you now.'

'What? To marry you? Tell me, Mr Braga, do you actually have a ring this time? I seem to remember you never had before.'

'I've had it for over eight years,' he said, taking a little box out of his pocket.

'I don't believe it.'

'I had it for your thirtieth birthday, but if you remember, things didn't go exactly according to plan back then, did they?'

'They certainly didn't.' She paused. 'Well then, Mr Braga, I suppose a promise is a promise.'

'Is that a yes, Miss Cusack?'

'Yes. I think so, Mr Braga. It's a yes. A very definite yes.'

'Good, then let me give you this,' he said, and he took the ring with its pink diamond centre from its box, kissed it and slipped it on her finger.

'We've a lot of catching up to do,' he said when they stopped kissing.

'And a public park is no place for that,' she laughed, pushing him away. 'C'mon Mr Braga, let's go back to my place. We can begin there.'

And they did.